The O[...]

The lowliest of the low, Sinbad the Porter is accustomed to being called the *other* Sinbad in deference to the far more famous Sinbad. But now he has been recruited by that Sinbad to undertake a journey by sea, to replenish the Sailor's diminished fortune—and to avoid a very troublesome djinni.

The other Sinbad, who has always longed for adventure, soon finds that one should be careful about what one wishes . . .

Don't Miss These Exciting Adventure Series by Craig Shaw Gardner . . .

The Ebenezum Trilogy
"Readers who enjoy Piers Anthony's XANTH novels will find Gardner's work right up their alley." —*Voya*

"If tongue-in-cheek fantasy is your cup of brew, this trilogy is worth reading." —*SF and Fantasy Forum*

The Ballad of Wuntvor
"Gardner uses giddy humor to good effect."
—*Publishers Weekly*

"Funny books. Buy them. Laugh." —JOHN MORRESSEY

"Delightfully funny, off-the-wall entertainment."
—LIONEL FENN

The Cineverse Cycle
"Absurdist humor at its best." —*SF Chronicle*

"Carries silliness on to greater heights or depths, depending on your view." —*Westwind*

"A laugh riot." —*Starlog*

Ace Books by Craig Shaw Gardner

The Ebenezum Trilogy

A MALADY OF MAGICKS
A MULTITUDE OF MONSTERS
A NIGHT IN THE NETHERHELLS

The Ballad of Wuntvor

A DIFFICULTY WITH DWARVES
AN EXCESS OF ENCHANTMENTS
A DISAGREEMENT WITH DEATH

The Cineverse Cycle

SLAVES OF THE VOLCANO GOD
BRIDE OF THE SLIME MONSTER
REVENGE OF THE FLUFFY BUNNIES

The Sinbad Series

THE OTHER SINBAD

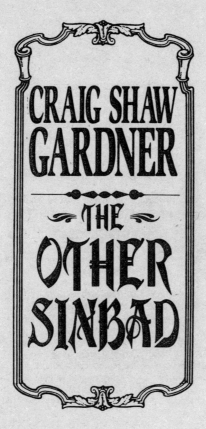

CRAIG SHAW GARDNER

THE OTHER SINBAD

ACE BOOKS, NEW YORK

This book is an Ace original edition,
and has never been previously published.

THE OTHER SINBAD

An Ace Book / published by arrangement with
the author

PRINTING HISTORY
Ace edition / November 1991

ISBN: 0-441-76720-6

Ace Books are published by The Berkley Publishing Group,
200 Madison Avenue, New York, New York 10016.
The name "ACE" and the "A" logo
are trademarks belonging to Charter Communications, Inc.

PRINTED IN THE UNITED STATES OF AMERICA

10 9 8 7 6 5 4 3 2 1

TO FLO—
  Who nursed me back . . .

♦

An Introduction,
in which the true nature of the story is first revealed.

Ah. Let me tell you a story, then, about a time very long ago, or perhaps only yesterday; and a place that never was, but will always be.

It was (and is) a city, but not any city, no glorified village nor swollen township, but the most magnificent of metropolises, so far across that a horse at full gallop would take three whole days to circle its walls. And within those walls stands far more than a collection of mud huts and stone hovels, for a hundred times a hundred multicolored towers reach up to caress the clouds, and the avenues at the city's center are so broad that forty strong men striding shoulder to shoulder might walk down them without impediment.

There, I have mentioned the colors, and what colors! For within the city's walls you will see every hue witnessed by man, from the soft pigments deep beneath the sea to the brilliance of the sky and sand, with all the countless shades in between, from the eternal green of summer grasses to that mysterious brown you might glimpse only in a woman's eyes.

By now, you must surely know the place of which I speak. Let me tell you, then, about Baghdad.

I see by the look on your face that it all becomes clear. Now you know I speak of the city of wonders, where exquisite goods from the far ends of the earth are traded every market day, where perfumed gardens stand but a wall away from the dusty streets, and where magic often waits within the shadows to benefit the fortunate or to destroy the unworthy. Baghdad, a place of wealth beyond the imaginings of all but Allah, but a place that holds more than wealth; indeed, a place where you will find a bit of everything. The great city of Baghdad holds every sort of man and woman, from the richest to the poorest, the holiest to the most

1

profane; a place where wealthy merchants and princes may walk side by side with common laborers and the lowest of slaves.

And what of me? I know the poorer quarters of Baghdad with an embarrassing familiarity, for when my story begins, I am but a poor porter, carrying goods from one quarter of our magnificent city to another for whatever coin or barter might be had. And my name? It is Sinbad. No, not the famous sailor, though he figures prominently in my story as well. No, I am the other Sinbad.

My story begins on this particular day, in this particular quarter of the city. Perhaps you have heard another version of the tale, but know that this is the only true version, and I will spare no detail or marvel, whether that fact brings great glory or causes tremendous humiliation, in recounting the first seven voyages, and why they caused the far more important, and even more dangerous, eighth voyage to occur.

You have not heard of the eighth voyage? Well, perhaps my story will be a new one to you, after all.

I trust you are comfortable. Come, come. No fidgeting, now. Are you quite prepared?

◆

Chapter the First,
in which we attend a feast, and our hero detects a difficulty.

The day, at first, was not unusual. It began for me like many others, and I was contracted to carry an especially weighty burden from one particular quarter of the great city to another. Still, the day was warm, and the way was long, and I found my burden pressing heavy down upon my head as I turned this particular corner, and discovered myself in an area of shade in front of a great gateway.

Truly, I thought, this must be the home of some wealthy and fortunate merchant, for the ground before me was swept and sprinkled with rose water, and there was a small but well-built bench set a bit to one side of the doorway, placed there, no doubt, for the benefit of weary wayfarers. Since, at that very moment, I could think of no man more weary than myself, I availed myself of the merchant's kindness, and sat down as I placed my heavy burden on the bench beside me. And, as I sat there, appreciating the benefits of the cool breezes and the scented air, I heard equally sweet music drifting from the gates, mixed with the fine cries of many exotic birds.

At this time, I must admit, I became curious as to the exact nature of my benefactor's estate, and so rose and pushed my head through a particularly large opening in the wrought-iron gate.

What I saw upon the other side caused my breath to leave me and my spirit to soar. Beyond the gate was a great garden, filled with flowers and plants and fruit-bearing trees, a few familiar to me, but many more that I had truly never seen before, so that I imagined they had been brought here from every region of the earth. And standing amidst the flowers and shrubs was a vast throng of guests, their every need being attended to by servants and slaves, even the lowest of whom was dressed in garments of fine silk. Upon the walls were ornate tapestries, while scattered about the grounds were tables and chairs that shone as if they were

3

made from solid gold, such as I imagined might grace the
apartments of only the greatest of sultans.

Of course, I have not yet mentioned the wondrous odors of
cooked meats and fine wines. In all, it was quite overwhelming,
and set me to thinking upon the differences in station that men see
in their lives, and how, in Allah's wisdom, a garden of great
delight might be viewed by one such as myself, so hot, so tired,
so covered by the grime of the city streets, the lowest of the low.

Thus, in such a reflective mood, I decided to sing myself a song
to speed me on my way. So did I begin to sing in my best falsetto:

> *"I swelter through the heat of day,*
> *For hardly any gain;*
> *A porter's life is full of strife,*
> *But I do not complain!"*

Then, as my father taught me, after a brief chorus of "oody-
oody, shebang shebang," I launched into the second verse:

> *"A package sits upon my head,*
> *My back is bent with pain,*
> *My corns are acting up as well,*
> *But I do not complain!"*

Another brief interlude of oody-oodys, and I was on to the third
verse:

> *"The riches I carry aren't for me*
> *In sunshine and in rain,*
> *And my employers never tip,*
> *But I do not complain!"*

"Oh, don't you?" a high voice piped up from somewhere
around the region of my navel. I looked down, being careful not
to strangle on the ornate wrought-iron workmanship surrounding
my head, and saw a child, but what a child. Even though he was
most likely a servant of some sort, he wore a tunic, leggings, and
turban of almost midnight blue, and had eight rings upon his
fingers, each golden circle set with a semiprecious stone.

"I beg your pardon if I have offended—" I began, rather
shocked by this intrusion upon my placid songsmanship.

"What I think doesn't matter around here," the child replied with admirable frankness. "It's what the master wants that's important, and he wants the singer."

"Me?" I asked, still frankly astonished to think so well dressed a servant would even address a personage as humble as myself.

The child suppressed a yawn. "It was you doing the singing out here, wasn't it? Or did I hear a nightingale strangling?"

Here, the child was comparing me to a nightingale! "And he wants to see me for my poor singing?" I asked humbly.

"There is no accounting for my master's tastes," the child agreed solemnly. "Still, he has bade you enter. Would you deny his request?"

I have learned, through my many years in Baghdad, that such a polite inquiry may often be followed by a more forceful form of request, perhaps accompanied by burly slaves sporting sharpened scimitars. Keeping this in mind, I readily agreed.

"But," I still added cautiously, "my song was not yet finished."

"Yes, yes," the child replied with what appeared to be growing impatience. "You hadn't gotten to the all-important, final, inspirational verse, where you talk about all these other people who might complain, but not someone like you who has such tremendous respect for the Almighty."

The child's perception was astonishing. "How did you know?" I asked with not a little bit of awe.

The child glanced distractedly at his fingernails. "Those songs always end like that." He pulled open the gate, then spun upon his heels and walked back toward the garden. "Come on," he called over his shoulder. "You're the featured entertainment." He waved distractedly at a large fellow of the sort I sometimes expected to be sporting one of those sharpened scimitars. "You can leave your burden with Hassan."

And so it was that I entered the household that would change my life. The well-dressed child led me through the perfumed gardens and into a well-appointed building that seemed to me as large as a palace.

After proceeding down a short corridor, carpeted with fine rugs of the deepest red, the child brought me into an inner courtyard where fully fifty of the guests had gathered. On the far side of this enclosed yard I saw a man who I presumed must be my host, a worthy gentleman of late middle years and substantial girth, whose clothing was of such color and refinement that it made all the garments of his slaves and servants seem like nothing more than mere rags. Truly, I thought, this could not be the home of a mere merchant, but must be the palace of a mighty djinni or even mightier king. What could I do but bow and call my blessings to all those assembled here?

My host bade me to come forward and sit by his side. Before I should sing, however, he instructed me to partake of some of the refreshments that the servants carried forward upon golden trays. And what refreshments! The tenderest of meat, the sweetest of fruit, and the finest of wine all passed between my lips as the gentleman and his audience waited patiently.

When I had finished, my portly host asked my name. I did my best to answer him with sufficient style:

"I am called Sinbad the Porter, and I carry great amounts for small reward."

With that, the portly man laughed. "This truly is the work of Providence! My name is also Sinbad, for I am known as Sinbad the Sailor."

Yes, it was the very same Sinbad so famous in song and story. I was astonished that my fortunes had taken such a turn. This man, Sinbad the Sailor? I could scarce believe that this portly fellow before me was that august personage. For one thing, I would have thought he would be taller and thinner, but no matter. I was here, and it was time to sing my song.

So I sang the same sweet verses that I have mentioned before, to a courtyard full of those high above my humble station. And this time I was not interrupted once by the child, who now stood to one side of the master's seat and glowered in welcome silence.

Let me tell you now, if naught else happened to me in this eventful life, the day I sang that song would be one of those crystalline moments that I should cherish for as long as I might remember. That instant alone when I heard all those respected gentlemen join in on the oody-shebang-shebang chorus was enough to chill even my coarse and overheated blood. And this time, without the child's interference, I managed to complete even the final verse and chorus.

My host clapped his hands together when I was done. "Truly, that is a marvelous song, and the last verse wonderfully inspirational." He glanced distractedly for an instant at the snickering child before he continued. "For your song speaks of Destiny, and I have a tale of Destiny as well."

At the mention of the word Destiny, the crowd shifted before us, and made a collective noise that I might have perceived as a polite murmur had not the group's conversation been spiced by so many groans.

The portly fellow with the same name as my own seemed not to notice. "For know, O porter, that my situation has not always been as comfortable as it now appears, and there was a time when as I was as poor—" He hesitated as he took a moment to examine my ragged garb. "Well, perhaps nowhere near as poor as you, but poor enough not to be *comfortable*."

The crowd of respected gentlemen seemed to understand what he was talking about, if I did not. They called lustily for the servants to bring them food and wine as my host settled into his chair to tell his tale.

"Now I shall tell you of the first of my voyages, and how Destiny showed me the way."

I noticed that the groans were back again, although this time they were muffled by the sounds of heavy eating and even heavier drinking.

Sinbad the Sailor cleared his throat.

Had I known what was to happen next, I would have leapt from my place of honor and run screaming back into the streets.

But I did not, and perhaps it was all for the best.

You will have to be the judge.

♦

Chapter the Second,
in which the true nature of the difficulty is
manifested, and there is a further problem.

"Now," my esteemed host resumed, "if all my guests are comfortable, and have all they desire, I shall begin my most amazing story."

I, for one, was quite enthralled with this turn of events. First, I am plucked from the dusty street, then fed with the finest foodstuffs imaginable, and now I was to learn a lesson concerning the great man's Destiny. However, many of the guests seemed somewhat less interested.

"You there!" a man with a long face and a coarse, brown beard called to one of the servants. "Those artfully arranged delicacies that you carry. Unless I guess incorrectly, those are portions of a pickled Rukh egg."

"The very same," the servant replied with the most gracious of smiles. "Each one captured at great peril, then aged and fermented for a full year. Even sliced wafer-thin, as is the egg upon this plate, every piece is worth a king's ransom."

"Exactly," the thin-faced man agreed. "I'll take half a dozen." He scooped them from the golden platter and stuffed them in his mouth.

"Now," continued Sinbad the Sailor, politely oblivious to the excesses of his guests, "many of you may know that I am the son of a wealthy merchant, and, when that great man passed from this world into the next, he left me a considerable sum of money, not to mention great holdings of land and the occasional village or two. I was quite pleased with my newfound wealth, and set about exploring the wonders of the world and and this magnificent city, sampling the rarest delicacies, the richest of clothing, and studying the art of friendship with individuals too numerous to mention.

"Unfortunately," the wealthy man continued in a voice rich with regret, "while I pursued these worthy endeavors, I had neglected to watch my purse strings, and I discovered that my land had all been sold, my villages seized by creditors, and my chest of gold dwindled down to the last few coins. Truly, I became faced with a dilemma, for I was suddenly poor—" The great man paused to glance apologetically in my direction. "Well, perhaps not as poor as *some*, but I knew I would have to act soon so as not to spend my remaining years in poverty. For has not the wise man said, 'A man with a sack of gold may sail forever, but a man without two coins to rub together is lost in a dry and odiferous riverbed without a proper method of conveyance'?"

"So true!" a man with a dark face and even darker beard called out. "Slave! Bring that golden pitcher over here!"

The slave did as he was bidden.

"Tell me," the dark-faced man asked as the slave approached. "Is this not the nectar procured from the mouth of the silver-winged hummingbird, a creature which dwells only near the mythical source of the Nile?"

"You are very knowledgeable," the slave replied graciously. "The nectar is the sweetest of the sweet, but it sours when exposed to the sun, and so can only be transported at great cost during the darkest hours of night. Each sip is worth a sultan's palace."

"Exactly!" the guest called with great relish. "Fill my cup to the brim!"

"But I must entertain you with my story," the elder Sinbad ventured. "I knew at that moment, I must pursue my Destiny"—he shuddered slightly—"or be poor forever. So it was that I took such meager belongings as I had remaining, and sold them at auction, receiving the sum of three thousand dinars. With these monies in hand, I purchased both unique and exotic goods from the marketplace, and passage on a ship bound for distant ports.

"And so we traveled downriver from Baghdad to Basrah, and from there out to the great green sea, and we stopped at many ports, and I sold and bartered my goods to great advantage."

"A most interesting tale," said a bored-looking gentleman at the edge of the crowd as he grabbed a servant by his golden wrist bracelet. "But do tell me. Are not these the most delicate of dates that grow upon the dwarf palm trees found only in the highest mountains in the realm?"

"How wise of you to notice," the servant replied with impeccable manners. "These are the very dates, brought from that mountainous location where the growing season is so short that they must be picked on one certain day, or the fruit will freeze upon the tree."

"And worth a great fortune, are they not?" the bored gentleman remarked as he scooped a handful of the dainty fruit onto his plate.

"So great," the servant replied affably, "that, when certain of the civilized world's wealthier realms decided that they had become too rich to remain upon the common gold standard, they substituted this very fruit for their currency."

"A remarkable fact!" the bored man exclaimed, no longer appearing quite so bored. "You will excuse me while I take a few more." And with that, he emptied the servant's golden tray.

It was, indeed, a remarkable feast that I saw about me that day; a rich repast in every sense. Although I was but a poor porter and unlearned in the ways of the wealthy, I was astonished that even one as wealthy as the great Sinbad the Sailor could afford a feast of this enormous proportion.

"But allow me to continue with my tale," the merchant Sinbad ventured, and his audience did precisely that, with only the occasional sounds of ingestion, mastication, and the sporadic gaseous eructation to punctuate the story.

"Know ye," Sinbad continued, "that, after many days of travel, our ship anchored near a great island, so that the merchants on board might find fruit and fresh water with which to refresh themselves.

"But, alas, this newfound haven in the ocean's midst was not as it had first appeared. My fellow merchants and I embarked upon the island, and many of the others soon had started fires to roast varied meats from the ship's stores. I decided, however, that my hunger was not so great as my need to exercise my legs. So it was that I had ventured to the far end of the island before the cooking smells reached my nostrils to remind me that perhaps I needed sustenance, after all. But I had barely the chance to turn about before the very earth beneath my feet began to shake, and heave up with a great roar, as if that earth itself had cried in pain."

Sinbad paused, as if to allow his audience the proper time to accept the marvels of which he spoke. He waved at the ground as he resumed his tale, as though he still stood upon that enchanted isle:

"It took me but an instant to realize that what we stood upon was not an island at all, but a living thing. I heard the captain calling out behind me from his position still aboard the ship, for he cried that we must hurry back to the safety of the boat. This was indeed no island that we had come upon, but a great whale, which had rested here for so long that dirt had settled upon its hide, and trees had sprung up along its back. It had rested thus for years, but alas!, the cooking fires my fellow merchants had set upon the behemoth had disturbed the creature's repose, so that this same whale, at last, was about to sink into the sea.

"I was truly astonished by how much information the captain could dispense in such a short time, but I had little opportunity to marvel, for the gigantic whale was indeed diving beneath the waves. Water rushed about my ankles as the living island began to move. The merchants left their foodstuffs and cooking utensils behind them as they rushed for the ship, and some fortunate few reached that safety as the captain rapidly weighed anchor.

"My situation was nowhere near so serendipitous. I stood upon the rearmost portion of the great tree-covered beast, a good five-minute stroll from the ship, and I had further taken that stroll when the surface beneath my feet was not pitching and rolling." The merchant rocked back and forth to give his story a visual aid, and, certainly, the motion of his stomach did help one to appreciate his predicament upon the open sea.

"I further discerned that the great beast," Sinbad continued, "which had risen and sunk twice already so that the ocean's water washed over its back and dampened me first to the ankles and then to the knees, was rising for a third and final time, and would truly dive deep beneath the sea, and any merchant still unfortunate enough to be upon this whale's back at that time would be drawn mercilessly beneath the ocean's surface." The sailor clapped his hands sharply, as if to reproduce the sound of the great whale smashing into the waves.

"What was I to do, then, but to put my life in the hands of Allah (as indeed all our lives are!) and jump away from the whale before the creature completed its dive?

"Still, Destiny smiled upon me that day, for I found a great trough of wood, some two feet across and six feet in length, floating upon the ocean, which the merchants had earlier used to aid in the preparation of food. I clung to that floating expanse of wood, and, kicking with all the might left within me, I survived the great waves that threatened to overwhelm me with the whale's descent, and steered myself toward an isle that I perceived in the distance."

Sinbad the Sailor paused, and his guests, none too quiet during his telling of the tale, redoubled their calls for more rare meats and

wines, all the while stuffing their prodigious mouths when they
were not complaining that the priceless foodstuffs they had
recently dropped had soiled the fine cushions upon which they sat
(slaves would replace these cushions with commendable speed),
and belching with ever greater relish. Although I had little
experience with the customs of the wealthy, still I perceived that
one not so wise as Sinbad might have taken offense at this display,
but the merchant host merely smiled and nodded and continued
with his tale.

"Once I had reached the island, I rested for many days, feeding
myself upon the several varieties of fruit that grew prodigiously in
many shaded groves. Thus did I regain my strength, and resolved
to explore this new place to see what else I might discover. Little
did I suspect, though, the marvels that were to follow, for I walked
until I reached a broad and sandy beach, whose white crystals
shone with a radiance second only to the sun, and there saw some
creature move in the distant haze."

The aged Sinbad frowned at the memory. "At first I was filled
with fear, suspecting the beast to be another monster from the sea.
Still, does not the wise man say, 'No one grows richer who does
not take a closer look'? So it was that I approached the unknown,
and marveled as I realized that this was no monster at all, but a
magnificent mare who was tied to a stake driven deep into the
sand. So wondrous a mount was she, in fact, that I found myself
walking ever closer, until I was halted by a sudden cry.

" 'Who are you?' called the first voice my ears had heard in
many days. 'And how come you here?'

"I turned and saw a man, of cheerful appearance and demeanor,
approach me across the sand. I greeted this stranger, and soon
related the means of my misfortune and my deliverance. The other
man exclaimed at the good fortune of my survival and, taking me
by the hand, led me into a deep cave unlike any I had ever seen,
for the cave was the height of five men, standing shoulder upon
shoulder, and was twice as broad as it was tall. Further, the cave
was furnished not like a hole within the earth, but like some great
hall in a palace, with many fine rugs and cushions, and I was
shown a place of honor and fed until my appetite was sated."

This mention of food seemed to excite the crowd, who called
even more zealously for replenishment of the rapidly disappearing
foodstuffs.

"So it was that I," the noble Sinbad shouted over the din of his
audience, "whose desires to explore the unknown had already

gotten me into enough difficulty for a dozen men, felt compelled to ask a question of my own, concerning our surroundings and the mare upon the shore.

"With that, the other man nodded and replied, 'I am but one of many who serve our great King Mirjan, and watch over his horses. Every month at the new moon, I am charged to take a fine blood-mare from the king's stables, and stake her thusly upon the shore. With the fall of night, her scent will attract a sea stallion, who will emerge from the waves and look to the left and look to the right to see that no human is near.

" 'Thus we hide in this cave while the sea stallion covers the mare, and gets her with foal. Once the stallion has completed his task, he will attempt to lead the mare back to his ocean home, but the rope and the stake will prevent the mare from following. Then will the sea horse send forth a great cry as he strikes the mare with his head and his hooves. When we hear the stallion crying so, we know his work is done, and with great shouts and banging of swords, we drive him back into the sea. But the pregnant mare, when her time is due, gives us a foal worth a king's ransom.'

"And, indeed, even as the stranger finished speaking, I perceived a great whinnying come from beyond the cave. We both rushed toward the noise, and there I saw, in the faint light of the evening stars, not one horse but two.

"And what a horse the newcomer was!" Sinbad clapped his hands with delight. "Perhaps it was only the starlight, but I swear to you that the stallion was the deep green color of a storm-swept sea, its hooves as dark as polished coral, and its matted mane the texture of seaweed floating on the incoming tide.

"A dozen other men appeared around us then, and they sent up a great shout, and beat their swords upon their shields. The great stallion reared upon his hindquarters in fright, and bolted from the shore, galloping into the sea until he was one with the rolling waves.

"With that, the other grooms came to greet me and offered me a fine horse on which to ride. In this way, I was taken into their city, and, after a suitable invitation had been arranged, before their king.

"The gracious monarch asked to hear my story from my own lips, and I related it much as I do so now. And when I had finished, the king exclaimed that any man who had survived such a great and terrible adventure must surely have a long life written for him, and honored me by appointing me as inspector of ports and shipping."

At the mention of this new, and potentially complicated, development in the voyage, the merchant's guests redoubled their shouting and clapping, not for Sinbad's tale, but for his servants to redouble their efforts to replenish the guests' food and drink. Indeed, the story had grown to such a length and complexity that even I found my appetite returning.

"So it was that I fulfilled my duties faithfully for many months, becoming in the same time one of the most favored at court. But in all that time, I never forgot my homeland, and as day passed after day, I longed ever more to see the greatest city of them all, Baghdad."

The merchant's voice warmed as he continued: "Then one day, a great ship arrived in the harbor; a ship which carried many merchants and a great quantity of goods. The sailors unloaded all as I and my assistants dutifully listed each item that entered the port, and, when there appeared to be no more, one of my subordinates asked of the captain, as was his duty, if there was any more aboard that the captain might wish to declare.

" 'Alas,' the captain replied, 'there is still a quantity of goods on board, but they belonged to one of our fellows who drowned through unfortunate circumstances, and so we must carry them with us until we may return them to his family in Baghdad.'

"I was standing but a short distance from this exchange, and could scare believe the words that had entered my ears. 'Captain,' I called to the other man. 'What would the name of this unfortunate be?'

" 'Sinbad the Sailor,' was the captain's reply.

" 'But I am that Sinbad!' was my answer."

The boy, Achmed, leaned down to whisper in my ear: "My master has always had a certain difficulty remembering faces." I blinked, shocked for an instant from my enthrallment at the tale. That, I surmised, would explain why the sailor did not instantly recall the captain's face or voice or, indeed, the exact name of the ship that the sailor had so recently ventured upon.

"So did the captain examine me," the wealthy Sinbad continued, as if no such explanation were necessary, "and I the captain, until each recognized the other from our long travels together. And, since he had so long thought me dead, I further reminded the captain of certain details and events upon the voyage that only one present could have recalled. With that, the captain was amazed, and said that surely, I had been given a second life.

"Indeed, I could scarcely believe my own good fortune, and caused the captain to have my goods removed from the ship and taken to the marketplace, where I sold them to great advantage, all save for a few of the richest and finest items, which I put aside as a gift for the king.

"When the benevolent King Mirjan heard of my fortune, he gave gifts to me in turn, and further gave me leave to return to my homeland." The now beaming merchant spread wide his arms, as if he might hold all of the city in his grasp. "So it was that I returned to Baghdad a wealthy man, and have retained the great king's gifts to this very day."

"A most excellent story," the fellow with the long face and coarse beard remarked without much enthusiasm. "Now I must refresh myself with more pickled Rukh egg."

"Indeed," the dark-bearded man added, pausing only to yawn prodigiously, "it was an inspirational tale. Now, where has that slave gotten to with that nectar?"

More of the guests might have joined in on this somewhat less than wholehearted appreciation of their host, save that about half the number in the great hall were so sated by rich food and drink that they had fallen into a deep slumber.

"It is certainly an excellent story," Sinbad the Sailor most heartily agreed. "And one that puts me in a generous mood.

"Jafar!" he called as he clapped his hands. "Where is that head of the household when I need him?"

"Here I am, O munificent one!" a cracked voice called out from amidst the sleeping throng.

I turned in the direction of the voice in order to get a better view of the man who ran the merchant's affairs, and saw a person hobbling in our direction, leaning heavily upon a polished rosewood cane; a man who was so thin and bent that he looked aged enough to be the grandfather of my grandfather.

"Most excellent Jafar!" my host exclaimed as he waved one of his hands in my direction in such a way that the jewels on his many rings shone brilliantly in the afternoon sun. "You see before you a poor unfortunate."

Jafar stopped his hobbling progress and stared at me for a long moment. "Indeed I do, O generous one."

"Very good!" He waved his hand above my head again. "Give this poor unfortunate a hundred dinars."

Jafar seemed to sigh. "I would expect no less, my cornucopian master."

I was quite overwhelmed by my sudden good fortune. A hundred dinars for me? Because of my station and the irregular nature of my employment, I have always had to be careful with the occasional dinar that might come my way. The manner in which this man dispensed his wealth was not only surprising but a little alarming, for, until now, I had not known there was such great wealth in even a sultan's palace. A hundred pieces of gold; I did not believe I had ever held half that much, not simply at one time, but in my entire lifetime!

Perhaps, however, it was only my perspective that was in error, and what the merchant had said about me was true, and I was indeed poorer than poor. Perhaps people exchanged a hundred dinars and more a hundred times a day within the perfumed gardens of these inner courtyards. It was a sobering thought, and an exchange that I might hope to observe more often.

"And invite him back on the morrow," the merchant continued, "when I tell the tale of my second voyage, which I assure you is even more grand and wonder-filled than the first."

The elderly gentleman nodded his head distractedly. "There is but one minor difficulty with your request, O your excessiveness. I am afraid we might not have a hundred spare dinars about the household."

No dinars? I thought as a hole formed to drain the hope from my heart. Perhaps it was my destiny to be poorer than poor.

"No dinars?" the merchant responded with the first trace of anger I had seen in all that long day. "What sort of a household are you running here? Next, you will tell me that we are running low on our rare foods and fine wines!"

"I thought, O most opulent of the opulent, that I should wait for the guests to leave before I mentioned—" Jafar began haltingly.

"Well, you shall find the dinars before our guests leave!" the merchant said forcefully.

Jafar mumbled in that way the aged comment on events to themselves, and turned to hobble away.

Sinbad studied the deep blue sky above the courtyard. "Still, the afternoon is but half spent." The merchant smiled once again upon his visitors. "And while Jafar fulfills my bidding, I will further entertain my guests with the beginnings of my second voyage."

I found it remarkable that I could still hear a chorus of groans over the prodigious snoring that surrounded us.

"Now, know that at first I was happy with the peaceful life of Baghdad—" the merchant began. But I and those guests not yet lost to sleep had no ears for his words, for the moment he had begun to speak a great cloud of violet smoke exploded some ten feet over his head.

It was to his credit that even the merchant noticed this interruption.

"Eh?" he remarked with some distraction.

It was then that the violet cloud looked down at those assembled in the inner courtyard. Yes, the cloud had a pair of eyes, each eye as wide across as the heads of a dozen men. And after the eyes, there formed a great nose and ears the color of aged bronze, and a mouth that smiled from that deep green expanse with surpassing cruelty, and I realized this was not a cloud at all, but the magical head of an evil djinni.

"Sinbad!" the djinni demanded, his voice the sound of swords clashing at war.

At that instant, I found myself compelled, as if by evil magic.

"That is my name!" I called at the same instant and with the same words as the man who was my host.

"What?" the djinni replied in a voice that indicated he was even less pleased than he might have been before. "I have come to seek Sinbad. There will be retribution!"

"That is my name!" both the merchant and I cried again, the words torn from our lips before this horrible apparition.

"You have callously destroyed—" the djinni began, then hesitated. "On your reckless voyages, you have thoughtlessly upset—" He paused again. "I was sent to rend and tear—" He hesitated once more. "It is no use. I have been sent to utterly obliterate Sinbad—"

To my horror, I found myself again shouting, "That is my name!" along with my fellow.

"—but which one?" the djinni concluded with a note of despair. "I could kill you both—but no. A working djinni never kills anyone—for free." He rumbled softly to himself for an instant, the sound of thunder before a flood. "I will have to retire to review my commission. But know this, piteous mortals, it does you no good to fool the djinni. When my punishment comes, it will be swift and terrible!"

There was a second explosion, and the djinni was gone.

What should I do? What had actually happened? I did not know if I wanted to laugh in relief or shiver in fear. I turned to my host, seeking answers.

But there was no answer there. My host had collapsed upon his great chair, eyes closed, head lolling, as oblivious as his sleeping guests.

The great Sinbad the Sailor had fainted.

◆

Chapter the Third,
in which the problem is considered,
and a solution is most eagerly sought.

Most of the guests, many of whom had been roused by the rather loud djinni, gave their thanks to the host and took their leave in a remarkably short time; so short, in fact, that the merchant had not yet had the opportunity to regain consciousness.

"This sort of thing happens all the time," a child's voice said by my side. I turned to regard the perpetually smiling Achmed.

"You have constant visits from evil djinn?" I asked with some astonishment.

"Well, perhaps not that specific occurrence," Achmed replied after a moment's consideration, "but it is always very lively within these walls."

At this point, it might not have been unwise to request an explanation, save that I was somewhat fearful of what the boy's exact definition of "lively" might be. Perhaps, I considered, there were some advantages to being poorer than poor.

"But the other guests have fled," Achmed remarked pointedly. "What causes you to stay?"

Now it was my turn to pause and consider. I had just been confronted by an evil djinni who had threatened me, and forced words to come unbidden to my lips. Surely, a prudent man would have fled, screaming, into the late afternoon. Yet, as this all-too-clever lad had pointed out, I still remained. But for what reason?

Upon reflection, I realized there was more than one possibility. Some might say I would not leave until I had exhausted any chance of receiving my hundred dinars, but I believe there was a far greater truth. I had certainly been fascinated by the wonders of his first voyage, and I believe that I had indeed developed a certain affection and respect for this elderly and very generous merchant.

Not, of course, that one could lightly dismiss the possibility of a hundred dinars.

"You can forget about the hundred dinars," Achmed remarked with remarkable prescience. Such remarkable prescience, in fact, that I stared at the lad in incomprehension.

"At this time, I doubt that Sinbad the Sailor has two dinars to clink one upon the other," Achmed continued with that same cheerful demeanor that might become annoying if one were exposed to it over a great expanse of time. "Think upon it, O lowest of the lowborn." The child waved at the leftover foods and dirty goblets scattered about by the recently departed guests. "Do you have any idea how much this sort of party costs?"

This servant seemed to be implying a certain lack of planning on the part of our gracious host. "You are saying that the most gracious and generous Sinbad is without funds?" I objected with what I considered good reason. "Wouldn't a merchant of your master's stature know of such things?"

Achmed dismissed my objection with a wave of his palm. "The merchant would never concern himself with such trivial matters." He patted his silk-covered chest. "After all, what are servants for?"

I paused to consider the implications of all this.

"Pardon?" I asked after a moment.

"It is quite simple, really," Achmed replied smoothly. "Sinbad is of too high a station to consider how his money is spent, and so depends upon his servants and slaves to do so. Unfortunately, the servants, while quite capable of spending that money, are unable to halt that very spending without a direct order from their master. And the master would never give such an order, since he is, of course, high above such things." Achmed's grin grew wider with the surpassing simpleness of it all.

I frowned. Perhaps there was some logic somewhere within his presentation. One thing became increasingly obvious: Being among the poorest of the poor did not prepare me for the complexities of this household.

Still, I could but try to aid my limited comprehension. "Forgive my lack of knowledge," I attempted once again, "but if there is no limit on how rapidly his money is spent, how does Sinbad remain a wealthy merchant?"

"Think upon it further, O miserable porter," Achmed said in turn. "Did you not ever wonder why Sinbad was forever going upon perilous voyages?"

Achmed's point was well taken. Even I—a deficient, unknowledgeable porter, as the child had reminded me—even I had wondered, with what rigors I had heard of in the recounting of the first voyage alone, why any sensible man might ever venture from Baghdad again once, let alone six times. "So Sinbad must travel to foreign lands in order to regain his wealth?"

"Ah, great is the answer when even a common porter may reflect upon the truth of it!" Achmed cried in triumph. "The exalted Sinbad may be terrible at holding on to a dinar, but there is no one that is his equal at buying and selling."

"Oh, woe, woe!" my host's voice echoed from within his palatial estate. "It has gotten as bad as that?"

Another, more muffled voice replied, the tones too low for me to discern their import.

"Worse?" Sinbad's voice rose even higher than before. "What of—" The other voice replied in the same indecipherable tones. "But does that not mean—" Sinbad rejoined before the other voice muttered on. "Even my beloved—" Sinbad interjected, his voice by now choked with extreme emotion. "That can't include—" The merchant once again let his voice be heard after another moment's murmuring. "No, no, not the *camels*!"

"The camels?" The invariable smile upon Achmed's ever-cheerful lips seemed to waver. "It is worse than even I had thought."

It was then that my host reentered the courtyard, his appearance so altered that I might not have recognized him, save that he was trailed closely by his faithful Jafar, who continued to murmur what I now took to be apologies. Great tears stained the merchant's generous face, and he had rent and torn his fine clothes in numerous places, so that they were now little more than silken rags. His servant appeared almost as distraught, his words rising and falling as he wrung his age-spotted hands.

"So sorry—" I caught before Jafar's words once again faded beyond the understandable, but then, "know the sort of money it takes," and a bit later, "truly a sultan's ransom," and further, "no one could have foreseen the sudden rise of Rukh egg prices, especially considering the economic fluctuations—"

Sinbad the Sailor halted suddenly as his eyes once again fell upon me. "Oh, that my namesake should see me so!" He waved distractedly at the elegant rags that had once been his clothing. "Know now that all my wealth has fled, so that I am as poor—" The merchant hesitated to regard me for yet another instant.

"Well, perhaps, not as poor as *some*. Still, my fortunes have vanished from their coffers"—he waved his outstretched hands—"so that I must part with even the rings upon my fingers to pay my creditors."

Sinbad looked up to the sky, as if he might seek some answer within that bright blue vastness. "All my servants know what this means."

Indeed, I was about to ask if my host might inform me about this meaning as well, when the child by my side placed a cautionary hand upon my unwashed sleeve.

"Wait," Achmed cautioned me, "and all shall become clear."

The merchant sighed prodigiously. "I must go upon another voyage."

Jafar stopped his muttering, his apologies replaced by a look of horror the equal of any I had ever seen. At my side, Achmed nodded with a smugness that was indeed becoming increasingly irksome with every passing incident.

"Now, now, good Jafar," the merchant said in a soothing tone. "Perhaps this time we shall not encounter the troubles that plagued me on those earlier voyages. Perhaps upon this occasion those legions of untamed monsters and unspeakable horrors I have encountered before will trouble other travelers. Perhaps a life of adventures upon the oceans of the world has even given me enough foreknowledge to avoid further travails."

"And perhaps camels will fly," Achmed added in a low tone meant only for me.

Sinbad took a deep breath before he continued, sucking in his prodigious girth so that it looked, well, slightly less prodigious. "Still," he said in the level voice of a man used to command, "whatever will come is in the hands of Destiny. So must we take what pitiful amount remains and venture forth without—"

"Without awaiting the terrible vengeance that surely shall befall you?" an overly loud voice grated overhead. There, above us, was the head of the evil djinni, having appeared this time without even the beneficial warning of violet smoke.

To his credit, this time the merchant prevented himself from leaving the world of the conscious. "Vengeance?" he remarked instead in a voice now as soft and uncertain as the djinni's voice was loud and overpowering.

The evil apparition smiled, truly one of the most unpleasant expressions I have ever seen.

"Sinbad," he said.

"That is my name!" both the merchant and I once again said before we might even think.

"You will not escape me so easily this time," the djinni continued in an even tone. "The great and terrible Ozzie has returned."

"Ozzie?" I cried, almost as involuntarily as the words that had just passed my lips.

"A caution, porter." To my surprise, it was the smiling Achmed who warned me. "The naming of djinn is not the same as our own."

The lad had a definite argument in his favor. I should be the last of those to comment on the giving of names. Many in the poorer section of our magnificent city had often made disparaging comments upon my being the namesake of mighty Sinbad the traveler. And further, has not the wise man said, "People who live in habitations made of nothing save windows should not make a habit of tossing about large rocks"?

But still, Ozzie?

"You will not fool me this time with your human tricks," the gloating djinni further remarked. "I have learned certain information from he who employs me which will assure that I shall discover the Sinbad I seek."

"That is my name!" both me and the merchant screamed.

The deep green Ozzie continued as if we had not even spoken. "And when I do discover the subject of my search, my vengeance shall be beyond human imagining!"

"Djinn always talk like that," Achmed confided again in the quiet tones that perhaps were meant, against all reason, to reassure me. "It makes them feel important."

Importance? If that was the djinni's intention, I felt he was succeeding with an admirable skill. My knees were wobbling in such a fashion that I imagined they were submerged in the ocean and being sucked away by the outgoing tide.

"Now I will learn the truth," Ozzie stated with a certainty that gave me an even greater chill, the equal of any fever I had ever suffered. I glanced over at my host, and discovered an ashen quality to his face, as if he had seen his own death.

"Both of you are named Sinbad," the djinni began, ignoring our chorused response, "but only one of you is wealthy beyond imagining." His smile broadened to show great teeth, each half the size of a full-grown man. "Who is that Sinbad?"

This time, both the porter and the merchant were silent. The smile vanished from the apparition's countenance.

"Another human trick!" the djinni roared. "You seek to avoid me by the use of language. But Ozzie is no mere monstrous supernatural apparition. No, Ozzie is a master of the human tongue." He paused, as if savoring his mastery. "If you will not talk about riches, then who among you is not wealthy?"

Both the sailor and I rejoined in our involuntary chorus: "That is my fate!"

The djinni roared above us with the volume of a hundred storms. Both Sinbads took some steps away, awaiting the demon's terrible anger.

Instead, the great and terrible Ozzie sighed.

"No, no, no. I do not believe this," he rumbled. "What has gotten in the way of my terrifically violent retribution?" The djinni's great eyeballs rolled back and forth in his gigantic face, looking first at the sailor, then at me. "Perhaps, you might tell me, my information was incorrect. Perhaps there are even more Sinbads lurking about in this vile-smelling human habitation." His voice rose in exasperation. "Why, then, can't I simply kill *all* of you?"

The apparition allowed himself a second sigh. "Yes, I know as well as you that I cannot. There are rules about this sort of thing, after all. Oh, I hate it when I have days like this!"

The djinni spent a long moment muttering to himself before he again turned his attention to the mortals beneath him. There seemed to be a red glow forming in the back of his eyes, as if his anger were fueling great fires within him; fires that might explode violently outward at any instant. He looked, hard and long, first at the mighty sailor, then at my own pitiable self. He opened his mouth to speak.

"Drat!" was all he said.

He took a deep breath, causing the wind to shift and dust devils to form about the courtyard. His eyes swiveled outward, so that one regarded my famous namesake while the other studied me. "Know this, O Sinbads. I will fulfill my most dreaded task. And, once I learn the truth, neither of you shall escape your fate. To force a djinni to return a third time is to invite certain doom!" He paused again, and once more allowed the slightest of smiles. "I just thought I should mention that."

With that, the great green horror was gone, his disappearance accompanied by a crash so loud that one might imagine the sky itself had been rent asunder.

Achmed poked a sharp elbow into my rib cage. "What did I tell you about this happening all the time?"

I did not at first respond to the youth. In point of fact, I felt too numb to respond to anything. A porter's life had never been so filled with excitement. The high point of many a day before this current one might consist of such excitement as obtaining an extra overripe pomegranate or half-stale loaf of bread. How appealing that rotting fruit and moldy bread seemed at this juncture. After all, what did a mere hundred dinars mean when your life was in peril?

"Well," my formerly wealthy namesake said with a sigh of his own. "It appears, as the wise man says, that our corpulence has taken residence among the flames. There is nothing for us to do but to begin voyaging immediately."

Us?

The great and mighty Sinbad had said that word as if it included all who currently stood within this room, even a certain poor and inconsequential porter who simply happened to be passing by the gate at an inopportune moment. Us? It was indeed true that this same merchant had fed me a far richer meal than I had ever experienced; and had told me a story filled with such dangers and marvels that I had sat enthralled; and further had offered me riches beyond any of my expectations.

Us?

However, it was also true that this same benefactor also gave me my first opportunity for conversation with a hideous monstrosity that, until this recent incident, I had only heard about in stories; and further, this self-same adventurer was proposing that we all go on another one of those marvel-and-danger-filled voyages.

Us?

I could still hear the djinni's storm-filled voice calling my name; a name that now seemed to be both my fortune and my misfortune. Because of that very name, that Sinbad, there was no way I could be uninvolved.

"A voyage!" Sinbad the Sailor cried, and I could hear the love of travel in his voice.

"A voyage!" Jafar echoed, but from his mouth the word was transformed into a great, overburdening task.

"A voyage!" Achmed chortled, as if he had never heard of so great an adventure in his short life.

The elder Sinbad clapped his hands, and Jafar began to shuffle off with grim purpose, followed closely by a whistling Achmed. The merchant fell in behind his servants, and motioned for me to join the procession.

What could I do? There was no way to escape.

I was going on a voyage.

Chapter the Fourth,
in which hasty preparations are made,
and we are confronted by certain
more welcome surprises.

The household was in an uproar, and with every step that we took, the chaos seemed to double.

Jafar had led our procession first to a room filled with weighty tomes, each the height and breadth of a grown man's arm. After picking one particular volume, and flipping the parchment therein until he reached a particular page, he let out a gasp not unlike the death rattle of a sickly goat.

Carefully avoiding the gaze of the other members of our procession, he moved quickly into the next room, which was filled from top to bottom with scrolls and scraps of paper, each one covered with finely formed numbers in great profusion. The three of us followed in respectful silence.

After a moment's consideration, Jafar moved to the furthest corner of the room, and carefully pulled forth a crumpled bit of parchment from the bottom of a precariously piled heap. It only took him a moment's examination before he let out another sound not unlike a corpulent man choking to death on a chicken bone.

The Jafar was off again, at a speed that would have been astonishing for even one of Achmed's tender years. The rest of us were hard-pressed to pursue, but pursue we did, through three successive doorways, ever deeper into the palatial home, then into torchlit darkness as we descended a long, winding staircase into a subterranean chamber far beneath the house.

The panicked Jafar was there before us, staring at a massive wooden door crisscrossed with an ornate metal latticework that must have added an extra quarter inch to the face of the door. Reaching deep within his robes, the merchant's head of staff pulled forth a great key that was mottled green with age, and inserted said key into a padlock of equal antiquity.

With shaking hands, the elder turned the key, and the padlock groaned with a sound the equal of Jafar's most recent exclamations. The lock parted, and the elder removed it. The ancient hinges screamed like lost souls as he opened the door leading to the room beyond.

I craned my neck to see what lay beyond that door. What, I wondered, could be so important as to cause the elder's panicked flight?

Jafar picked up a sputtering torch from its brass fixture upon the wall, and thrust it forward, into the newly opened room. I squinted, trying to discern some recognizable shapes among the torchlight's shifting shadows, but, aside from a broken piece of pottery, saw nothing but bare floor and wall. As far as I could discern, that room contained nothing at all.

Jafar made a sound like a dozen eunuchs falling from a great height upon sharpened stakes, and fell at the feet of the merchant Sinbad.

"Beat me, master!" the faithful servant wailed. "Whip me! Throw me in chains!"

"Pardon?" the merchant started, as if he had been pulled away from his own deep thoughts. He smiled as he recognized his servant. "Oh—Jafar, most certainly. Now, what was it that you wished to tell me?"

"I must be punished!" Jafar pleaded, quite beside himself. "I do not deserve to exist!"

"Ah, good Jafar," Sinbad counseled wisely. "That destiny is not yours to decide. But what is it that truly troubles you?"

Jafar waved frantically at the opened room. "Look beyond you! That is our treasury! But where there should be gold, there is nothing but cobwebs."

Sinbad squinted past the servant's gesticulations. "*This* is our treasury?" He glanced once again at our surroundings. "Oh, perhaps it is." He wrinkled his nose to the profusion of dust. "It certainly could use a good cleaning."

Achmed whistled softly at my side. "I do not see how the treasury could be any cleaner."

"Oh, woe is me!" Jafar beat his head upon the paving stones. "Woe are all of us! How could the money have vanished so quickly?"

"Beg pardon," I asked, striving to understand the exact nature of the catastrophe, "but are you saying that the funds have disappeared with more than usual speed?"

The servant nodded with such rapidity that I feared his aged head would fall from his withered neck. "I knew our accounts were low, but *this* low? I have made some mistake in my addition. I have grown too old. I am no longer a useful member of the household staff." He tugged at his master's robe. "Beat me as an example! Lop off my head and display it for all to see!"

But the merchant once again shook his head. "Then who would figure my accounts? No, good Jafar, your head is much better placed where it now resides."

These reassurances were all very well from the good-natured merchant, but I was once concerned about the disposition of the funds. Perhaps I was overly worried concerning the fate of so many dinars since I had seen so few. So it was that I felt it prudent to ask a question:

"But would you say, good Jafar, that the disappearance of the gold was entirely natural?"

This query hit the elder with such force that he forgot to wail. "No, now that I think of it, our remaining funds disappeared with such rapidity that I was totally unprepared—but what could it mean?"

It was exactly as I had suspected. I further remarked, "Did it ever occur to those gathered here that, if recent events are not precisely natural, then they might be unnatural?"

My once-wealthy namesake frowned at this suggestion. "Wait, good porter, are you saying that my current total lack of wealth might be due to supernatural forces?"

I could see that the wily merchant had caught my meaning. "Say a certain djinni," I continued, "who, when thwarted by the merchant's sudden lack of funds, might cause whatever funds that might remain to disappear as well?"

"And would such a creature alert my master's creditors," Achmed piped up, "so that they might arrive suddenly at our front gate and demand immediate payment of all our debts, so that the great Sinbad might have to sell this palatial home simply to satisfy their demands?"

"My palatial home?" Sinbad replied in a whisper that bore the weight of awful revelation. "Surely, child, your question is entirely hypothetical in nature."

"Only so hypothetical," Achmed replied, "in that it was related to me by your gatekeeper, Hassan, immediately before we began this trek around your house in search of gold."

"But this is inhuman!" Jafar exclaimed with even more vehemence than before. "What manner of—"

Whatever Jafar was next to say was lost beneath a deep

rumbling sound, like a summer thunderstorm, or the laughter of a large head the color of aged bronze. And all of us in that subterranean vault knew that the sound of thunder would never reach this far beneath the earth.

"Perhaps, then"—the mighty Sinbad's voice fell to a whisper— "there will be no voyage, after all." Still, there was a faint look of hope in his eyes. "Unless we avoid my creditors and sell these rings upon my—" His voice died in his throat as he raised his hand. Where once four golden rings with ostentatious stones graced his hand, now there was nothing but bare fingers.

I thought I heard the thunder again.

"Then there is naught left for us!" Jafar's eyes flew about, as if seeking some symbol of the severity of their plight. "We are, all of us, to fall from wealth and luxury and grovel with the common man, doomed to be no more than"—his eyes fell upon me— "porters!"

"Porters?" With that, even the great Sinbad the Sailor seemed on the verge of wailing. Still, he gathered up his substantial resolve, and even smiled at me as he spoke. "But no, there is no need for despair. We have an actual porter in our midst, who can tell us of the brighter moments among the poorer classes." His smile became the slightest bit uncertain. "Truly, there must be happy events in every man's life."

The brighter moments among the poorer classes? I concentrated, doing my best to succinctly describe my life. "There are, of course, the long hours—"

"Yes?" the merchant prompted eagerly.

"Then," I added, "there is the incredibly low pay—"

"Oh." Disappointment seemed to creep into the elder Sinbad's voice. "Long hours and low pay? Is there naught else?"

"Well," I further considered, "you can look forward to the occasional whipping—"

The elder Sinbad did wail at that, and he was soon joined by Jafar and Achmed.

I frowned. This would never do. Even though I was but a poor porter, I was not given to despair. The worst of whippings will have an ending. I held up a hand for silence.

The three others, shocked that a miserable man of the streets could so demand their attention, immediately quieted.

"Porters may be miserable," I stated with some emotion, "forced to eke out a half-starved existence surrounded by the squalor of the streets."

I shook my head as the merchant made a small sound in the back of his throat that might have grown to a renewed wailing. When I again had silence, I continued. "But porters are nothing if not resourceful, despite whatever trials—natural or not—we might face. We learn in our trade that there is wealth all about you. You only have to look."

So saying, I entered the empty treasury, hoping it was not quite so empty as it seemed. In my years as a porter, watching the stones beneath my ever-moving feet, it has always amazed me what pieces of gold and other objects of value might lodge themselves in the cracks and corners of the streets of Baghdad. A fortunate discovery here and there over the course of my young years has led me to keep open eyes in every situation. I trusted those same eyes would help me here.

I moved to the far side of the room and picked up the cracked piece of pottery.

"Aha!" I exclaimed.

There was indeed a piece of gold beneath. I picked up the first of what I hoped might be many treasures. But where else in this all-too-empty room might the wealth be hiding?

I found a space gnawed through the brick in the room's darkest corner. No doubt it was a passageway for rats. In the entranceway to the passage, I found three more golden coins. I held them up for the others to see.

"Then we are not bankrupt?" Jafar called feverishly.

"We are far from rich," Achmed cautioned.

"Still," I said with that same confident smile reserved for potential portage customers, "there may be more wealth hiding in the many cracks here about. Forgive my impertinence, O great merchant, but you once had such enormous wealth that perhaps that fraction that remains will be enough to do us some good."

Sinbad did not seem to even notice my overfamiliarity. Instead, he smiled.

"If we can book passage on a ship—any sort of ship at all!" he exclaimed with that same tone of wonder with which he had described his first miraculous voyage. "Even a hundred dinars will be enough!"

A hundred dinars? I grimaced at the task. It would be difficult, but in a world of vengeful djinn and marvel-filled voyages, perhaps it was not impossible. So it was that I continued on my ever-more-intimate examination of the room. The floor of the vault was covered by crumbling bricks. I therefore turned my attention to the multitude of cracks in that lower masonry. By methodically traveling from one corner of the room to the other, I uncovered seven more bits of gold, as well as a small ruby. But I had almost exhausted all the hiding places in this tiny room. We would fall far short of our goal.

But still the merchant urged me on. "Even less than a hundred dinars may seal our fortune!" He chortled as he thought of it. "Who is to say we cannot purchase passage on a less-than-perfect craft, one with a hole to two? We can sleep upon the deck! Repairs can be made! Are we not able-bodied men?"

If my namesake would not admit defeat, then neither would I. I instructed Achmed to climb upon my shoulders and examine the uneven brick walls above my head. The first thing he located was a moldy piece of cheese. But two walls later, he found a woman's ring with a stone of deepest green.

We examined the remaining wall, and even the ceiling, for further hiding places, but no more were to be found. But, I considered, if there were no more gold hidden within things, what of the gold hidden upon people?

I removed the child from my shoulders and asked the others if they carried any dinars upon their persons.

Only Jafar nodded as he pulled forth a pouch both far too small and far too light. He opened the bag and spread its contents upon his opposite palm. There had been six dinars within.

"Perhaps," Sinbad the Sailor tried to cheer us with a voice that was much too quiet, "we can consider a ship with more than a hole or two."

I counted our collected fortune. Having had little money in my life, it has always given me pleasure to count and recount what I own, but there was small pleasure here. In all, there were seventeen dinars, a small gemstone, and a woman's ring of unknown value.

"Seventeen dinars?" Jafar bemoaned.

"Well," the sailor continued, "perhaps seven or eight holes."

"A handyman's special," Achmed confided in me. "For this money, our conveyance shall be more hole than boat."

"Now, Achmed," the sailor replied with the most subtle of laughs, "we do not know what the marketplace may bring. We need not secure an entire ship for ourselves, but merely book passage on a ship traveling in the proper direction, wherever that may be." He paused, the slightest of smiles forming behind his well-groomed mustaches. "And, most importantly, you have not considered my knack for salesmanship."

And so saying, Sinbad led our small band up from the vault and completely out of his palatial home. When we reached the entryway, I looked for the parcel that I had brought here in the first place, but could see no sign of it.

"One of the servants has delivered the goods for you," Achmed explained. "My master thinks of everything—save money."

Jafar opened the front gate for his master. I scampered to follow.

And so we left the home of the once-wealthy Sinbad, and ventured out onto the street. The street, which was my true home, and had offered me a freedom I had never realized until I stepped inside that house of marvel tales, exotic foods, and djinni curses. My host had asked what advantages a porter might have, and I realized now that there truly was one advantage to my former life—when the time living upon the streets of Baghdad was all my own, and I was free to work or free to starve. Not a great advantage, perhaps, but one that I might sorely miss.

I will admit now that there was a moment, when we first stepped out of the gate and onto the common cobblestones, that this freedom seemed very dear indeed. Perhaps, I thought, I should just turn away from the others and walk briskly along, as if in the middle of my own business, which, whatever it might be, had absolutely nothing to do with sailors named Sinbad or djinn named Ozzie.

But my feet followed the others.

Perhaps it was that I knew there was no escape from supernatural monsters who chuckled like thunder, and were I to attempt escape, there was a strong possibility that I would be thrown into perpetual torment instead.

But perhaps there was another reason. As I have previously mentioned, in the short time I had known him, I had become rather fond of the generous but somewhat strange man who also bore my name. Or perhaps it was simply the current level of activity that I found about me. This tumult was also something new to me. A porter's life is arduous, but it is very rarely exciting. Then, of course, there was the issue of the hundred dinars which the merchant assured me would be coming to me—someday.

Or perhaps it was simply that my feet knew better than I that there was no escaping Destiny. Whatever the reason, from that moment forward, I felt my fate was sealed with those of the sailor and his noble band.

That worry out of the way, I followed the others down to the docks, those same docks on which you may board a ship downriver for Basrah and thence out to the sea.

It was then I looked out at the dozen upon dozen of sailing craft about the harbor, half the vessels still and silent, as if at rest before their next adventure, the rest festooned with bright sails to catch both the evening tide and the fading crimson rays of the sun. So many ships, and so many stories beyond the walls of Baghdad, and I was to be one of them. I, who had never stepped outside the city walls, who had never been in the river above my waist, who had spent his entire life surrounded by a thousand men and camels; I was going out to sea. I, who knew what every day of a porter's life would bring, was going out to face the unknown.

Actually, it was rather exciting.

"Now," Sinbad announced to his following, "let us see what my bartering skills can bring." He waved at a gentleman, with a neatly trimmed beard and dark blue robes of obvious quality, who stood at the bottom of a gangplank. "You, sir!"

The other gentleman nodded in greeting. Even in his somewhat shredded silk garments, the merchant Sinbad still appeared to be a man of some means. Perhaps we would be able to strike some sort of bargain, after all, no matter how modest our means.

"Sinbad!" the other man called. "I have just returned from your most excellent feast!"

"Oh, my—most certainly—you did?" the merchant replied in modest confusion.

"Is this not the famed sea captain Hutan?" Achmed mentioned helpfully. I remembered again the child's comment on Sinbad's memory for faces.

"Hutan? Most certainly!" The merchant's face became animated with friendship, as if that recent passing doubt were no more than a momentary gastric distress. "And did you appreciate the pickled Rukh eggs?"

"Not one tenth so much as the fermented nectar carried by those hummingbirds," Hutan remarked with great amiability. "But why does a man of your rich tastes call upon a humble sea captain?"

Sinbad the Sailor stepped forward, clapping a comradely hand upon the captain's shoulder. "Ah, my most learned and understanding Hutan, that is indeed a question of great perception and insight. For you know that I have a reputation as a traveler, from which I have gained great fame. What fame, too, might come to the captain of the vessel with which I will sail on my eighth and greatest voyage? There could be no monetary amount put on that amount of fame!"

Sinbad's words were impressive indeed, even though I had no exact idea of their precise meaning. Apparently, the sea captain had a similar reaction, for, after he frowned and spat into the fetid water of the harbor, he asked the following question:

"As the wise men say, 'Fame can be greater than riches, as a blessing or a curse.' " He squinted at the elder Sinbad, as if it might help him see deeper into the merchant's meaning. "But what is it that you want from me—exactly?"

"Ah, good Hutan," the merchant continued as if that were the very response he had anticipated, "you do strike at the heart of the matter. The answer is simple in the extreme, and of no great burden to you. Your ship is surely traveling past Basrah and thence out into the southern ocean. What great hardship should it be, then, if you were to take on four extra passengers?"

"Ah!" the captain remarked after taking the time for another precipitate expectoration into the odiferous fluid at our feet. "So you wish passage." He regarded us with a parsimonious eye. "For your entire entourage?"

"Entourage?" The merchant laughed as if Hutan had told the funniest story Sinbad had ever heard. "You do us too great an honor, O noble captain. There are but four of us. Almost too few to notice on a busy ocean voyage."

Another wad of spittle sailed harborward. "So you do not wish to spend much money?"

Sinbad the Sailor spread wide his arms in mute submission, bowing to the ship captain's superior intellect. "Alas, due to circumstances beyond our control, and much too complicated to be of interest to a man with your hectic schedule, we find ourselves forced to economize. We can, however, make ourselves useful in other ways."

"Could you perhaps state the figure that you were planning to spend?" the captain asked.

"Jafar can do your facts and figures," Sinbad answered. "He has performed that function in my household for years."

"Exactly what can you afford?" the captain insisted.

"Achmed is very able," Sinbad replied. "The energy of the young is truly amazing."

"A price or no dice," the captain said with finality. Then he exhaled. Then he appeared to hold his breath. At last, he said, "Seventeen dinars."

"Seventeen dinars?" The minuscule size of the sum caused the captain to swallow rather than spit. "Truly, you are the king of jesters. And you have not even mentioned this other fellow." He indicated me with some disdain. "The very poorly dressed one in need of a bath?"

"Ah," the merchant said as he smiled upon me with generosity, "this man is also named Sinbad."

"Truly?" Hutan had the expression of someone who had just eaten a bad fig. "How unfortunate for you."

"No, no," Sinbad insisted with that same mercifulness of tone, "he has already brought me great luck, and I am sure that he will bring me great fortune. Besides, he is a porter!"

"A porter?" The captain at last appeared interested. "A life full of ship's drudgery will be a respite for a porter. Perhaps we can strike a bargain, after all. No more quibbling, now. What, good merchant, do you truly have to offer as passage?"

The merchant shuffled for a moment from foot to foot. "We have our good health and cheery spirits to help speed the voyage. We also have seventeen dinars," Sinbad stated with finality.

The captain sighed heavily. "That sounds like no bargain to me. My ship is in need of repairs, and I was hoping you might be able to provide the funds to speed the process. Without the money, alas, it might be a month or more before we are able to set sail."

A month or more? I thought again of the vengeful djinni. What damage could the great and terrible Ozzie do to us in the space of a month or more? I hastily pulled my namesake aside.

"O great Sinbad," I sputtered in my quiet but frightened manner. "A month? A curse? Horrible retribution? Ozzie?"

"Alas, good porter," the merchant confessed in equally low tones. "I was surprised to do this well in the bargaining. Passage for four for a mere seventeen dinars? I suspect Hutan's brain is still slightly addled by that nectar, and had hoped to strike a bargain before he sobered. As bad as our negotiating situation is here, we will probably fare far worse in any other attempt."

Far worse? For the first time, I felt like joining Jafar in a hearty wail.

"Ho! You upon the docks!"

Both the merchant and myself turned at the sound of the hail. We spied two burly men who carried a great load between them. As they approached at a brisk trot, I could see their burden was a large and elaborate palanquin painted with golden highlights that caught the evening sun in such a manner that the whole convey-ance seemed to shine.

The two men halted smartly but a few feet before us. Though their load was of enormous size and most certainly heavy, no doubt with an occupant inside, there barely appeared to be a drop of perspiration upon their large and incredibly well developed muscles, and they breathed as if they were upon an evening stroll. The man in the front, who had tattooed his face with an elaborate design, perhaps to detract from the fact that he had few teeth, spoke directly to the merchant.

"Are you, then, Sinbad?"

It took me an effort of will not to join in as the merchant said, "That is my name!"

The tattooed man's mouth twisted into a grimace that might have passed for a smile had there been more teeth present. "Ah. We have been seeking you. We have a proposal that might be of some interest."

"Get to ta point!" his equally large colleague shouted from the rear of the palanquin. "We got business!"

"Yes, of course," the tattooed man continued, as polite as his companion was rude. "We understand you are about to go on another voyage."

Sinbad nodded pleasantly, as if he expected his every action to be common knowledge. "That is indeed the case. At least, we are as soon as we complete our negotiations."

"A voyage?" shouted the colleague, who sported a livid scar that ran from beneath his left eye to the right side of his chin, so that it formed an "X" with his overly active mouth. "On dis garbage barge?"

"Yes, the ship does appear to be in some need of repair," the polite fellow agreed affably. "But that can be easily corrected." He turned his attention back to the merchant. "You are, sir, that same Sinbad who survived seven incredible voyages, returning from each wealthier than you had been before?"

"I am the same."

"Good. We want no mistakes. Any fellow on the street could be named Sinbad."

Any fellow on the street? I felt suddenly uncomfortable, perhaps because of the polite man's tone. Or could it be that I felt his rude companion was staring straight at me?

From the merchant's next question, I surmised I shared some

of my unease. "May I be so rude as to ask why you have such an interest in my affairs?"

"As perilous as your voyages are, you have an amazing knack for survival," the tattooed man replied. "We must travel a perilous ocean trip ourselves, out to the southern islands. Considering your reputation, we would be foolish not to throw our lot in with you. But my friend voiced some concern over the condition of the sailing craft. And I must admit, as we approached, we overheard the captain's complaints." He threw a large and heavy bag that clanked as it hit the dock at the captain's feet. "Will this be sufficient to tidy up your ship?"

The captain agreed and called out to his crew to go in search of the necessary supplies. I was amazed. In a matter of moments, we had actually managed to secure passage and repairs for our sailing craft.

"This sort of thing happens all the time," Achmed assured me once again.

I was beginning to think, with a life as eventful as the merchant's, all sorts of things happened to him all the time.

"But we are to be sailing companions!" Sinbad continued with great joviality. "At the very least, we should introduce ourselves before we begin our voyage. These are my servants, Jafar and Achmed. And this man is my traveling companion, also known as Sinbad."

"Another Sinbad?" the polite man said with some astonishment.

"Dat's one too many," the man with the scar growled. When he glanced at me, he seemed to shiver. "Mebbe two too many," he added.

"Ah, my friend does not—" The man with the tattoo hesitated before he continued. "Well, in all actuality, he does mean it. But rest assured he only acts upon it when he is provoked." He smiled again at the merchant. "And as to introductions, well, I have gone by many names. But for purposes of this voyage, you may refer to me by the name of my favorite tool." He reached into his sash and pulled forth a short, sharp blade. "You may call me Dirk."

"He's particular good at disemboweling," his friend added.

"As to my traveling companion, he goes by many names as well, although none so polite as mine. Some have called him 'The Fear That Comes in the Night,' others 'Your Worst Nightmare Made Flesh.' Of course, no one calls him any of those things for long."

"Interesting," Sinbad replied, as if he met men called "The Fear That Comes in the Night" every Thursday. "But how might we address him?"

"It is indeed," Dirk agreed, "*all* in how you address him."

The man with the scar nodded eagerly. "If ya pleads wit me, I mights lets ya live."

"But as pleasant as it is to become acquainted, we have things we must do before we set sail." Dirk nodded to his fearsome companion. They once again grabbed the palanquin.

"But wait!" Sinbad spoke as if there had not been a single veiled threat. "Is there not a third member of your entourage?"

Dirk shook his head. "We carry nothing out of the ordinary."

But at that moment I saw something that belied his words. On the side of the conveyance that the two men lifted there was a screen, and through the holes in that screen I spied three of the most delicate fingers imaginable. They were the fingers of a woman, but no ordinary woman, for they were long and delicate and golden-skinned, with perfectly formed nails.

Dirk followed my gaze to the side of the palanquin. "Fatima!" he called sharply. "You are not to leave your hands for the outside world to see!"

The hand was withdrawn with the most delightful of high-pitched laughs.

"You did not see that hand," Dirk said to me.

Alas, but I had.

Dirk scowled. "Begging your pardon, but Fatima, if you were to address her—which you will not." He glanced back at his surly companion. The companion shivered for a second time, and both men gazed upon all of us in turn. "Act as if she were not there, but we are, as are our dirks, scimitars, and well-muscled arms capable of breaking bone with a minimum of effort."

The man with the scar smiled at the very suggestion.

"We wish you a pleasant preparation for the voyage," Dirk remarked. And with that, he and the Scar carried their palanquin up the gangplank and onto the waiting ship.

"So we will escape Baghdad, and perhaps discover the reasons for the djinni's great anger," Achmed said to break the silence. "Destiny is again on our side."

Destiny? At that moment, I did not care for Destiny. At that moment, I could only think of a hand, and a laugh.

At that moment, I feared I had fallen in love.

♦

Chapter the Fifth,
in which the voyage begins
and almost ends simultaneously.

What, then, is love?

We have all read the poets, who speak of fragrant fields and crimson sunsets, but I suspected, even in that reading, that there was more. For one thing, there was this nauseous feeling in the pit of my stomach. Then there was this total feeling of unreality, as if I might lose my sense of balance at any minute and go tumbling not just from the side of the ship, but from the very face of the earth.

And all this from the glimpse of a hand and the sound of a laugh? Ah, but what perfect fingers those had been, so slim and nearly as golden as the metal grille they rested against. How wonderful they would look, adorned with golden yellow rings against that golden skin, rings with great jewels that might only begin to hint at the true worth of those fingers. And that laugh, like the ringing of bells caught in a breeze in the heat of summer, the sort of sound that betokened the great relief of a cool wind from the sea. I had seen more than a hand, and heard more than a laugh. I had found a new way to look at the world.

But this woman of mystery came with two guardians. I could see no way to share my newfound ecstasy with her; indeed, I could discern no way of standing within a dozen paces of her palanquin. These two large, overmuscled, and very angry men seemed to discourage even the merest glance over to their side of the deck.

Yet I did not despair. A day before, I had known nothing of love. A day before, I could think of nothing but a life of carrying things upon my head. Who knew what the next day, even the next hour, might bring?

And so we prepared for our voyage. The generous contribution of Dirk and the Scar allowed for the captain to proceed quickly with repairs as well as to lay in a substantial store of provisions for our journey. Still, it would take a matter of days to complete these preparations, and in that time Sinbad resolved to go through his personal belongings and find certain merchandise that we could take with us for purposes of barter.

The captain gave our other passengers two small cabins within the vessel. The merchant Sinbad, Jafar, Achmed, and myself, due to the nature of our contributions, would have to sleep upon the deck. I helped Sinbad with a dozen errands, to both fill my time and attempt to redirect my thoughts from certain fingers and certain laughs. I paused often to sigh.

And, once every day, immediately after the noontime prayer, the two burly guards would bring the palanquin with its hidden occupant up from the hold. They would then proceed to march the conveyance around to afford the unseen Fatima some air and sun.

She was so close at these times that I might have run across the deck to touch her! But, with the guards' attitude, they could as well have marched her palanquin a hundred leagues away. A single step in their direction would result in baleful glares. A second step would bring drawn scimitars and strangulation cords. I never attempted a third step, deciding it was better to resume my stationary but decidedly nonviolent sighing. And every time their circuit of the deck was complete, the guards and palanquin would disappear belowdecks, and I would return to work, overjoyed to have been so close, and frustrated to still be so far away.

So went my existence, until we were at last prepared for our journey. On the night before we were to set sail, as I helped Achmed to ferry the merchant's goods on board, I became aware of an additional duty which I must perform before our travels commenced; that one last thing, a much less urgent task in my former life, but, with thoughts of Fatima ever in my mind, now so necessary.

I decided it was time for a bath.

I told Achmed of my concerns and he agreed, indeed, that bathing might be a positive activity, especially considering that he had noticed a certain tendency for the captain, crew members, and even Jafar and the other Sinbad to congregate upon the far side of the deck whenever I was upon the near. Achmed was, in fact, so enthusiastic about my idea that he further found me some cast-off clothing from the merchant's slaves, worn silks and cottons a hundred times finer than the rags I was used to. Achmed then went on to state that, in the interests of mercy to all concerned, my current clothing would be burned.

We finished with our tasks at last, and I received my new

clothing from Achmed well after midnight. So it was that I descended the gangplank to take my bath in that quietest of hours, just before dawn.

Never in all my life had I heard the world so still. I could not detect a single voice or footfall or clattering wagon wheel. Even the barking dogs and warbling nightbirds seemed to have found their rest.

I was, perhaps, the only one wakeful in all the great city of Baghdad. And I was truly thankful for that peace and privacy. As I have mentioned before, water and I are not on the most familiar of terms, and I was happy there would be no one to witness my discomfort.

I thus lowered myself from the side of the dock, placing one foot, then another, ever so cautiously into the river. To my immense surprise, the water was pleasantly warm—much the same temperature as the nighttime air—and the rocks that I eventually found beneath my feet had been worn smooth by the action of the tides. It was altogether a relaxing experience, and I resolved, once Fatima and I were truly joined together, to pursue this sort of thing more often.

I lowered myself further still, so that the water covered me to my shoulders, and exhaled deeply, listening to that total lack of sound that covered all of Baghdad. What a perfect time, I thought, to compose a new song to my beloved. The first rhyme appeared within my mind:

> *Ah, my thoughts do often linger*
> *On the perfection of a finger—*

But in that predawn stillness, when even the wind is afraid to whisper, I imagined that I heard a woman laugh.

My first thought was that it might be the laughter of my Fatima. I could feel my heart beat a rapid rhythm within my chest. New words sprang to fit my song:

> *Sweet mystery of life you seema*
> *To be a woman named Fatima—*

But then the laughter came again, as if mocking my earlier perception. Wish fulfillment aside, I had to admit that this laugh, while delightfully feminine, was unlike any sound I had ever heard made by human voice. It was, indeed, unlike any sound I had ever heard before, seeming somehow more like the result of some agitation of the waves about my chest than a noise carried upon the early morning air.

My heart went from a rapid beat to an almost total collapse. If that sound did not come from a human voice, where could it originate? I had already had far too close an encounter with a djinni. Were other spirits preparing to toy with me as well?

I thought then that I heard the laugh for a third time. The water parted before me, not as if a person or thing had broken through the surface, but rather by the total separation of waves, as if someone had pulled apart a pair of liquid curtains to reveal a doorway beyond. And from that empty space in the midst of the water, an apparition rose before me in the river.

It was a woman, but a woman whose skin shone in the moonlight with the green of the sea, and whose hair was the deep brown of the plants that grow beneath the waves. As she rose from the depths, as some human woman might ascend a flight of stairs, I realized she wore no veil over her face or other clothing to cover her almost human form. Yet she stared boldly at me as she revealed her torso, and smiled at me with deep green lips, as if that nakedness were her natural state.

"You are a man," were her first words to me. "I have never seen a man."

Her voice was not a proper voice at all, but rather all the sounds of the river around me, and of the river's mother, the sea. In every word she spoke I could hear the waves lapping against the sand, and the sound of fishes leaping in the sun, and that laughing trickle of water as it rushes over stones, and the bright noise of gulls swirling far overhead to call out their warnings.

"But I have been searching for you, ever so long," her water words continued. "I have wanted my first man to be very special. Might your name be Sinbad?"

"That is my name," I said once again, but this time with far more wonder than fear. Why would such a vision be seeking such a man as I?

Her smile broadened at that, and I could see that her teeth were as white as pearls. "I have heard much about you. Still, from the tales of your adventures, I thought you would be an older man."

Perhaps, I realized, I was not so fortunate as I thought. So enraptured was I by this vision from the deep that I had forgotten all about my position in the world. Why, after all, would such a magical creature be seeking a poor porter?

I explained to this enchanting being, in my halting tones, and I must admit I was better able to construct sentences when I was not looking directly at her, that there was not one but two Sinbads, and she no doubt sought the one who had garnered fame for his many voyages.

"Perhaps I was," she replied, "but I do so no more."

"Ah," I replied, finding my gaze drawn toward her upper torso like iron to a magnet. "Then you have come all this way for nothing." I did not yet perceive her true meaning. I turned away again in a futile attempt to gather my thoughts.

"No, Sinbad," she answered, and when she said my name, I felt not water but fire deep within, "I have come all this way to be with you."

"Pardon?" I asked, finding my gaze locked upon her one more time.

Her smile grew even broader than before. It seemed to shine faintly, like the cool glow of the moon. "I have never seen a man before you, my Sinbad, but, now that we have found each other, I have no desire to seek any further."

What was this creature professing? "B-but I am but a porter—" I sputtered.

"Porter? I am not familiar with the word," the vision before me continued, "but I am sure it must be a position of great importance if someone like you has been chosen to fulfill it. How fortunate that I have found you." She drew deeply of the early morning air. "I admire the way that you smell of the earth." She took a step toward me as I looked down at my own naked form and realized, among other things, that I had not proceeded with my bath. "Don't you think that mixes well with the smell of the sea?"

I did not know what to say. I did not know what to do. The sea nymph took another stride toward me, and I realized that I knew nothing at all.

A cock crowed on shore. The sun's edge crept over the horizon to turn the sea nymph's shoulders from green to gold. Dawn had arrived.

"Oh, dear," said the nymph before me as the smile vanished from her face. "I have overstayed my time. But you have not seen the last of me."

I could not think of a proper response. How could my throat be this dry when I was surrounded by water? "We will speak again, then?" I asked before she could flee.

"Ah, my mighty Sinbad, we shall do more than talk." Her

smile was back for an instant as she lowered herself beneath the waves, and the ocean closed about her like curtains covering a hidden room. I found myself staring at those first pink rays of dawn as they were reflected off the dancing water.

"Look at where our porter has found himself!" someone shouted above me.

"In the water?" another voice called back. "Providence is indeed kind!"

"But we must set sail with first light to traverse the river's twists and turns," I was reminded by Achmed's ever-cheerful tones. "Quickly, Sinbad, get back on board. It would be a shame to leave such a sweet-smelling porter behind."

The crew of the ship roared as I managed to pull myself back upon the dock and quickly donned the clothes Achmed had provided me. I even more rapidly climbed the gangplank as the sailors released the ropes from their moorings. I had barely regained the deck when the two dozen strong-backed oarsmen began to push the craft downriver. But, as the wise man says, better is the man who arrives at the last possible moment than the one who misses the opportunity altogether. I was on board, and we were headed for adventures beyond a porter's meager conception.

I saw the extremely ugly and tattooed head of Dirk towering above the collected crew members, and was struck by a thought as startling as a ray of sunlight in the midst of a thunderstorm. I was back upon the ship, that same ship that contained a golden palanquin, within which dwelled a woman named Fatima.

Fatima. It was a name that promised wonders. I thought of her golden fingers and that warm, human laugh.

Then I thought of green skin, and a smile that glowed like the moonlight. This situation, I had to admit, was confounding.

Before, I was in love.

Now I was confused.

It did nothing but increase my consternation to realize that Dirk and the Scar had once again brought their palanquin up upon the deck, no doubt to allow the conveyance's charming occupant to witness the beginning of our voyage. There was Fatima, so close yet ever beyond my grasp. My thoughts wandered, much as my gaze had not so long ago, to that mysterious woman of green who seemed about to grasp me as dawn had arrived.

What could any man, even a poor porter such as myself, do but smile? I had not even left the harbor, and already I had been faced with wonders undreamed-of in my former life. What could possibly happen next?

At that moment, a cloud covered the sun.

"And what is this?" a thunderous voice boomed overhead. Before I had even looked above, I knew the nature of this newly arrived cloud; that it would be composed entirely of purple smoke surrounding an emerald visage. Ozzie had once again graced us with his presence.

The djinni's arrival was followed by a long moment of silence upon the ship around me. Sinbad the merchant, flanked by Jafar and Achmed, glanced at me with a certain resignation that I most certainly shared. And no member of the crew replied, either, most of them occupied in active cowering and quiet bemoaning at the arrival of the apparition.

Ozzie waited no longer for an answer. "Sinbad," he intoned instead.

"That is my name!" both I and my elder counterpart responded loudly.

"Oh, I do enjoy it when you shout like that," the djinni replied warmly. "We of the supernatural persuasion receive so few rewards, we must take our pleasures where we may."

But then Ozzie's evil grimace turned into a sinister glower. "But what is this movement I detect upon this craft? I trust that you did not consider leaving Baghdad before I have had my vengeance." The purple cloud behind Ozzie's head flashed with lightning. "I warn you, those who attempt to escape the terrible wrath of Ozzie only invite an anger even more terrible still!"

At this, the crew graduated to active shrieking and hand-wringing.

"Perhaps," the djinni rumbled, "you need a small lesson. Say a ten-foot hole in the bottom of your craft, causing it and all its contents to sink rapidly to the river bottom. A few dead crew members, horribly mangled by the swift currents that flow out toward the sea, should indicate the seriousness of my cause."

With that, Ozzie smiled again, a horrifying sight. "But my two dear Sinbads have nothing to fear. Oh, my, for the man I seek, death by drowning is far too merciful." The djinni chuckled. The crew wailed and beat miscellaneous body parts upon the deck.

"Quickly!" a man shouted on the deck behind me.

Out of the cowering crowd came Dirk and the Scar at a brisk trot as they carried their elaborate burden between them. They were attempting to escape with their palanquin, like rats before the ship went down.

"What is the meaning—" Ozzie exploded, but paused, almost as soon as he had begun. "Oh," he added after a moment's observation.

I was amazed at the audacity of Dirk and the Scar in the face of the supernatural. But the two men's cowardice seemed to have certain benefits. Indeed, their rapid movement appeared to disconcert the djinni, whose grin of triumph turned to a frown of confusion.

"So many considerations," he muttered darkly. "The djinn's code of honor, the unnecessary expense of magic, those hidden variables that only become apparent at the last instant."

The apparition seemed to be talking more to himself than to any of those potential victims on the ship below. And others seemed aware of the change as well. I noticed that the crewmen around me were cowering somewhat less than before.

The djinni sighed, causing the immediate shipboard temperature to drop considerably. "Oh, spoiled dates! I wish they would better prepare me for this sort of thing." He shook his head. "The bureaucracy around here is amazing."

Yes, I was quite certain now that there was not a single crew member still wringing his hands. And even the cries of terror that had once surrounded me had decreased in volume and frequency.

I believe that even Ozzie realized that his moment was passing.

"Do not think," he rapidly added in his best thunder voice, "that this minor setback means that my vengeance will be any less horrendous." Somehow, though, the conviction was no longer in the apparition's rumbling tone. Still, he pursued his dramatic recitation.

"It will be more dreadful than dread itself, more terrifying than the very nature of terror," he continued, more, it seemed, to convince himself than any of us standing below. "Most of all, yes, most of all, it will be, yes, it will be—extremely unpleasant!"

But the tension was gone. The djinni's gaze flew from the merchant to myself to the palanquin and back to the merchant; a gaze that but a moment ago seemed to contain fire. Somebody in the crowd yawned audibly.

"Pitiful mortals!" Ozzie shrieked with a volume the equal of a storm at sea. "I will take your ship as a child takes a toy—I shall call the elements to rend and tear your craft like parchment—I will summon up the spirits of the doomed to torment—" He paused like some gaping idiot who had no words inside him. The djinni shook his massive head and forced out the syllables: "I'll—I'll—well, I'll certainly do *something*!"

And then the djinni was gone.

There was no silence this time. "Back to your stations!" the captain shouted. "Man those oars! By evening we shall see the sea!"

And so, astonishingly enough, we were off, abandoned by a suddenly uncertain djinni. Perhaps it proved the truth of Dirk's assertion that, wherever Sinbad traveled, luck was sure to follow. I trusted then that luck would remain with us still out upon the great ocean, where we might face horrendous obstacles, terrible monsters, the unchecked forces of nature, and further things undreamed-of and perhaps inconceivable to the human brain.

Would that it had been as simple as that!

♦

Chapter the Sixth,
in which alliances are formed,
or so we think.

I was soon to learn that, with Sinbad the merchant, nothing was ever simple.

The crew, so silent before, grew very noisy very quickly.

"They have brought a djinni down upon us!" the angry voice screamed.

Other equally irate voices joined in.

"They are accursed!"

"A pox upon the name of Sinbad!"

"Throw them over the side!"

"Remove them before they doom us all!"

The vociferous crowd surged around me, sweeping me from my feet. I saw that Sinbad, Jafar, and Achmed were in similar circumstances and that, indeed, we were all being carried toward the ship's rail.

"Hold where you are!" a voice shouted above the panicked crowd. The crowd took no particular notice. I saw the bright blue river beyond the puny railing with an amazing clarity. I was about to gain a familiarity with that river that I had never dreamed of. I considered it a pity that I had never learned to swim.

"Wait a moment," the rough voice commanded, "if you do not all wish to join these four in traveling over the side!"

The crowd hesitated a bit at that, but were reassured by the superiority of their numbers, and returned to their surging.

A crew member screamed as he flew from the deck to the river. The crowd sputtered to a halt, and I saw that Dirk stood between them and the rail.

He held his short knife in his hand. "If you take one more step forward"—knife and hand jabbed toward the sky—"you shall learn how I gained my name."

The crowd grumbled, but seemed incapable of making a decisive move.

"And if you do not put those men down," Dirk further stated, "my compatriot will be glad to give a number of you your very own trip over the side."

The other large man appeared next to his friend, a crew member dangling from each of the Scar's coconut-sized fists.

"I likes tossing people," the Scar added with a grin. "I makes a game of it"—he paused to shiver violently—"and sees how many times dey skips before dey sinks."

Both Dirk and Scar thought that was hilarious. The crowd took a step away from their laughter.

"Think for a moment, crewmen," Dirk said with his golden tongue. "You are all experienced sailors. You know that ships often face great troubles when they leave the charmed city of Baghdad. But all of you are also well aware, through the tales of his seven perilous voyages, that no one has faced more trouble—and survived—than Sinbad. Look at this merchant!" He waved his hands at my portly namesake. "Does he appear to be the sort of man used to physical hardship?" He laughed far too harshly. "And still this aging, overweight, self-important man not only continues to live, but he continues to triumph! Truly, this Sinbad is a charm against calamity!"

The crowd was speechless.

"You!" the captain called from the far side of the deck. "Crewmen! Back to work! We have a cargo to trade before it spoils!"

That appeared to be the very excuse the crowd needed. The crew put us down with utmost care, and returned to the work at hand as if all that had transpired had been but a jest. Dirk and the Scar both looked at our recently rescued group and made twin expressions that might pass for grins upon the faces of almost any other mortals. I wondered if, indeed, they wished to be our friends. However, they turned and walked away before I could inquire as to their true motives.

"That was an unfortunate altercation," our captain remarked as he sauntered in our direction, "but all of us must take responsibility for those things that we bring on board."

"I was surely thoughtless." Sinbad the merchant bowed before Captain Hutan in total humility. "It was remiss of me not to mention our little difficulty with the djinni."

"I should say so." The captain nodded solemnly. "At the very least, I would most certainly have raised the price of your passage." He narrowed his eyes as he gazed at the merchant. "But Sinbad the Sailor knows that."

Captain and merchant laughed together. Achmed smiled. Even Jafar tittered. Only I was too shaken by recent events to attempt to join in the social mirth.

"What of the man who went over the side?" I asked.

The captain shrugged. "We have extra crew members."

"On a voyage like this," Achmed added cheerfully, "they always need a great many extra crew members."

The captain turned away and went upon his business. Apparently, crew members were worth a copper piece for an entire crop. A porter's life is cheap, but these fellows seemed worth nothing at all.

I sighed. "That is small reassurance," I said to Achmed's questioning gaze. These days, I reflected, I found very little to reassure me.

Achmed reached up to clap me on the shoulder. "You are too sensitive, porter. Any self-respecting crew member should be able to swim, especially in something as simple as a river. Save your pity for those that we lose in the storm-tossed sea." He paused, and glanced again beyond the ship's railing. "But speaking of the river, I could have sworn that you were talking to someone during your sojourn down there."

So my meeting in the river was not so private as I had thought. Now, here was a question to ponder. Should I tell the lad about the sea maiden, or would any mention of it bring as much laughter among the crew as Achmed's jibes about my bathing?

But I had other questions as well. What exactly had happened between me and that sea creature? Now that I was back on the solid deck of the ship, the words and images of our encounter seemed to have happened in some distant place, as if when I entered the river, I had entered a dream as well.

"Ah," I said, still trying to put my thoughts in place. "The river." Achmed looked expectantly in my direction, as if my musings should continue.

"You!" another voice thankfully interrupted my none-too-speedy reverie. Or at least I was thankful until I identified the owner of that voice.

"Ragman!" The Scar beckoned me with a hand that might crush a bird or strangle a man without apparent effort. "Come here dis minute!"

Was the Scar referring to me? "Ragman" was not at all how I

pictured myself. Actually, the rags I wore now were quite elegant, at least in comparison to my usual garb. Still, I supposed I couldn't depend on someone with the demeanor of the Scar to list a discreet politeness among his many attributes. I nodded, and quickly approached the frowning man.

"Dere is someding you must do!" he barked as I stopped just out of reach of his massive arms.

"I?" I said rashly and without proper foresight of the potential consequences.

"Dis instant!" His countenance twisted into an even more hateful grimace than any I had seen before. "If you value your life!"

I thought fleetingly of our recent rescue by Dirk and the Scar, and of this man's attempted smile; that perhaps something else, even some element of kindness or warmth, might lurk within that murderous exterior. But there was no altruism here now.

Instead, the man's face seemed alive with anger; his scar, in fact, appeared to pulsate with it, as if unadorned rage emanated from that livid crimson line; and his breath fell sour upon me, as if his mouth were filled with the remnants of a diet of raw meat. I would have perspired if every pore in my body had not gone suddenly dry. Now that I was at this close a quarter with the villain, I suspected that there was indeed nothing beyond that murderous exterior than perhaps an equally homicidal interior.

He grabbed me by my worn silk shirt. Apparently, his arms were longer than I had surmised.

"Now!"

I could do naught but nod.

He nodded back and handed me a knife.

A knife? What could be the meaning of a knife? Did he wish me to kill someone else? Or was I being invited to commit suicide?

He grabbed my knife hand, and, with his own free fingers, pointed at a site upon his back. "Scratch dis spot right here—with da hilt!" he added with a certain degree of menace.

I did as I was bade, using all my strength to rub the flesh beneath the cloth on the Scar's shoulder with the knife handle. He, in turn, brought forth a noise like a great beast purring after he has made a kill.

"Enough!" he cried when my fist had nearly become numb to the wrist from the intensity of the rubbing. He held out his hand. "Return da knife!"

I gave him back the blade, handle first.

"One favor deserves anudder." His mouth twisted into a position that might again pass for a smile. "When it comes your time to die, I'll does you a favor, too"—he shivered more violently than he ever had before—"and kills you quick."

He turned away and left me feeling as if I had just glimpsed a warrant for my own death.

"Pleasant fellow," Achmed said at my elbow. "You must get together and do this more often."

But the majority of the day passed without further incident, as we rowed downriver toward the sea. The regular beating of the drum and shifting of the oars had a calming effect upon me, and I soon found myself gazing peacefully toward the shore, almost as if I were in a trance. I thought again about the water maiden I had met on the night before, and how perhaps everything upon this river might seem something like a dream.

The elder Sinbad and Jafar actually took the opportunity to rest, falling asleep on two of the great bales that rested upon the cargo area at the rear of the vessel.

Achmed remarked that, once the merchant awoke, it might be prudent to ask him about some of his other voyages, since they certainly seemed to be affecting our current journey. I plied the youth with questions after this remark, but, aside from a few veiled references to giant birds, ogres, cannibals, being buried alive, and sailing ships filled with apes, Achmed stated that it was best to leave things for his master to explain.

Not five minutes had passed, however, before the youth made an unfortunate sound with the back of his throat, followed by the statement: "Perhaps I shall wake my master, after all."

"Why?" I called back. "What is amiss?"

In answer, Achmed pointed ahead, to a point where the now broad river passed between two hills. I could see nothing unusual about the river, which here looked flat and still, and nothing upon the hills save a few scraggly palm trees. It was then I realized that the boy pointed at neither water nor land, but at a tiny speck in the sky.

"You can see something that far away?" I asked in wonder.

"I have good eyes," he replied. "Children always do."

Apparently, it was up to me to ask the next question. "And what do you see?"

"It is a bird," he replied quietly, but with a certain fatal tone in his voice. "A very large bird. And not just any bird. It is a Rukh."

"A Rukh?" a crew member shouted. Even though Achmed

spoke in quiet tones, the crew seemed to have remarkably good ears.

"Oh, woe!" a second crewman wailed.

"We are doomed!" a third joined in.

This time, however, the captain was prepared for the disturbance.

"Remain at your stations!" he shouted forcefully to the crew. "This Rukh—if Rukh it be—is far from home, and may have lost its way. We are still upon a calm stretch of the river. Even if the boat were to somehow capsize, all of us could easily make it to shore." He waved at the land not a hundred feet away. "We do not even know if this bird is headed in our direction, nor if it will even notice our tiny ship."

"And the seeds of dates are always diamonds," Achmed commented. I wondered how he could be so certain that the captain was incorrect.

Still, the crew seemed to have some belief in the captain's words, and more or less returned to the regularity of their rowing.

I looked aloft again. Now I could truly tell there was a bird flying toward us through the sky, though in size it looked no larger than a sparrow.

"It may indeed be time to wake the master." Achmed turned quickly and headed for the bale that served as the elder Sinbad's bed.

I turned my attention back to the sky. The bird was now the size of an eagle, and growing larger with every beat of its wings. The crew had also taken note of the ever-expanding winged creature, for the rowing at first became more erratic, and then ceased altogether. The bird was the size of a horse, then of a dozen horses.

"Rawn," the bird called out in the still sky.

"Hmm?" Sinbad the merchant called out from somewhere behind me. "Is something amiss?"

"Look to the sky," Achmed replied.

If indeed the merchant could see the sky. With every passing moment, there seemed to be far less blue and far more bird, with ever larger dark gray wings and a bright yellow beak that might snap up a man as a sparrow takes a worm.

"Rawn," the bird called. "Rawn." And yet, to me, it sounded like something else.

From the commotion on deck behind me, I surmised that Dirk and the Scar had joined us as well.

"Rukh?" the less polished of the two screamed. "We gots no protection against Rukhs!"

"A Rukh?" Sinbad the merchant repeated as he walked up next to me. "A giant Rukh?"

"No," Achmed answered with remarkable curtness as he, too, reached my side. "Not simply a giant Rukh. I believe this is a specific giant Rukh."

"Oh, dear." The merchant smiled at me as if he might apologize. "Perhaps it is the time to tell my namesake another explanatory story."

"It may be the proper moment," Achmed once again corrected, "but from the direction and speed of that great bird, I don't believe any of us have any time at all."

"Rawn," the bird called. Even though the bird was still hundreds of feet away, I looked up to see very little sky and a great deal of Rukh. And, yes, the great bird appeared to be looking straight at us; or, more specifically, the creature was gazing with a certain fixed purpose at the merchant Sinbad, as if it recognized the man, and wanted to renew its acquaintance in a particularly painful and final manner.

"Oh, dear," my elder remarked with remarkable brevity. "This does not appear to be for the best."

"Rawn," the bird called again. "Rawn."

Now I knew what the Rukh's cry sounded like to me. It was a word that men used.

It sounded like "ruin."

Chapter the Seventh,
in which birds
are not the largest problem.

How does one describe a bird as large as the Rukh?

One might mention that its feathers were the length of three grown men placed end to end. Or that one clawed foot might enclose a two-story dwelling within its talons. Or that every time it beat its great wings, it set up such a disturbance upon the waves that the boat tossed with the ferocity of the worst of storms.

But none of the above facts would begin to describe the awestruck terror I felt at the approach of this creature. I was certain that any instant I should be torn apart, or swallowed whole, or perhaps merely crushed by the great talon of a bird that cried "ruin." It bore down upon us, so long that all the river beneath was in shadow, so large across that it might have covered half of Baghdad.

"Rawn!" the bird screamed. "Rawn!"

And it flew on by.

Jafar hobbled forward to stand with the rest of us. "Are we spared?"

"More likely that the great bird is playing with us," Achmed replied with far too much reason. "We are such tiny morsels, it would be a shame to eat us all at once."

"Wait a moment." I looked at the others in my party with some astonishment. Perhaps it happened that I was but a common porter, and so could not imagine the fate Achmed had envisaged for us. Perhaps because I had spent my life moving my feet with great weights upon my head and shoulders, I could not comprehend this danger from the sky. Certainly this bird was large, and certainly he was flying overhead; but my companions were forgetting the most central fact of all: Who could truly tell what a bird was thinking?

I mentioned this to the others as the bird circled overhead.

The merchant shook his head at my remark, his expression an

odd mix of bemusement and fright. "That might very well be true, good porter," he allowed with gracious good manners, "save for certain involvements I experienced upon my past voyages."

"Unfortunately," Achmed answered in his usual helpful fashion, "my master has led such a rich and rewarding life that he is involved in almost everything."

Jafar nodded sagely. "There is a negative side to being wealthy beyond belief, especially when that wealth disappears." He looked to his master with a renewed hope. "Are you sure you wouldn't like to beat me, O overlord—just a little?"

"Not now, Jafar," his master remarked not unkindly. "I must tell my namesake of my prior experiences with the Rukh. For you see, I first met these great birds upon my second voyage."

"Yes, I suppose there's no avoiding it," Achmed agreed without due enthusiasm.

"So it was that there came a time that I tired of my riches and began to look fondly upon once again taking a journey out upon the open sea," Sinbad began, as if he were repeating a story he had told often before.

"Not to mention that most of your money had been spent," Achmed added with his usual cooperative air.

"Well," his master admitted, "there was that, too. Still, this was before Jafar was a regular part of my household—"

The majordomo wailed at the mention of his name. "Are you sure, O your autocraticness, that you couldn't hit me just a few times for the sake of form?" he added with the slightest tinge of longing in his voice.

"Not now, Jafar," the merchant replied in his usual companionable tone. "As I had begun, I once again sought adventure upon the open sea. So it was that I sold what belongings I had remaining to buy goods that I might trade to advantage upon the ocean routes, and further secured a sturdy ship filled with other merchants of like mind."

A shadow once again fell upon us all. Achmed frowned as he gazed overhead. "I think, O venerable master, that perhaps you should leave out some of the finer details."

"Perhaps the child is correct," the merchant replied with obvious regret. "I do hate to edit my tales, but still—" He, too, glanced overhead as the far-too-large shadow was replaced again by the shining sun, and, after a moment's pause to shiver, quickly resumed his story. "Our ship made good time, I made the usual advantageous trades, and all was fine until we reached a certain island. So glad was I to once again be on land that, as the others gathered food and water to replenish our supplies, I settled down in a shady grove and had soon fallen fast asleep."

The shadow fell over us once more as I once again heard the great bird's angry cries.

"Beg pardon, master," Achmed urged, "but perhaps you should leave out even a few of the middling details."

"My young charge is no doubt again correct," the merchant Sinbad allowed. "When I awoke, I discovered I was alone. My shipmates had left, unaware that they had abandoned me to fate. So it was that I wandered the island—"

"Rawn!" the great bird screamed as it once again drew close.

"—until, on top of this high hill, I spotted a massive white dome. Yet I could see no door or other means of entrance—"

I noticed at this juncture that the crew was beginning to scream and moan again.

"—and so contented myself with counting the steps it took me to circle this object that shone so blindingly in the sun, one hundred and fifty paces in all—"

"Rawn!" The bird swooped so low that its mighty claws almost skimmed the surface of the river, and its great wings spanned the whole width of water from bank to bank. Mayhaps, I thought, it intended to rend the ship in half.

"The greatest of pardons, O mighty Sinbad," Achmed once again interrupted, "but perhaps it would be prudent if you left out all but the point of your story?"

Sinbad indeed spoke with greater speed than ever before: "I used the Rukh to escape from my plight by unrolling my turban, and tying one end to my waist and the other to the great bird's legs. Thus was I transported to a valley of diamonds—" But the merchant's voice deserted him as the bird swooped upon us.

"Rawn!" The Rukh flew upward at the last possible instant, but the ship shuddered and shook as the great bird's claws flicked against its tipmost mast. I staggered three steps across the deck as Sinbad and Jafar both clutched at the railing. Achmed danced nimbly out of our way.

Again, the bird flew on.

"—thanks to which, with the help of the birds, and some men as well, I became even richer than before and came home," Sinbad finished abruptly, so that he could await his fate in silence with the rest of us.

I frowned. It seemed to me that Sinbad's story lacked a logical conclusion. Surely, it was the fact that we were due to die at any second that accounted for the boldness of my next question: "Certainly you used the bird for transportation, but is that any reason for it to come seeking you?"

"Well," the merchant confessed with a touch of shame, "in the valley of the diamonds, where the men rode upon the birds, they also happened to beat them so that the Rukhs would drop the precious stones."

The bird rose further in the air as it continued to travel downriver. A forlorn hope caused me to wish that the creature was done with us, that it had given us its intended warning, or perhaps merely satisfied its curiosity about our ship, and would now fly back to wherever it truly belonged. Whatever passed through the brain of that bird, I still could not see the logic of the elder Sinbad's argument.

"Still," I ventured boldly, "would even a beaten bird follow you to the ends of the earth?"

Sinbad frowned at the suggestion. "For revenge? Well, perhaps it does sound a little foolish when you phrase it so. But if this bird is bent upon vengeance, what might be its motive?"

Jafar paused in his wallowing obeisance to cough. "Forgive me, master, but there was that other matter——"

The answer came to me with the certainty of the sun rising at dawn. "It wouldn't have anything to do with serving pickled Rukh eggs at your banquet, would it?"

"The banquet? All is my fault!" Jafar once again bemoaned. "I must be punished. Kick me! Whip me when I am down!"

It was with a certain inevitability that I looked up to see the great Rukh spread its wings and turn about.

"Perhaps the venerable Jafar would care to stand at the top of the mast for the bird's next pass?" the child Achmed suggested gently.

The merchant shook his head. "We are not ourselves. The Rukh has undone us every one."

I could not agree. Now that I had somehow passed beyond my fear of the great bird, I was not going back. Porters must, by the very nature of their occupation, be a stubborn breed. I had not spent my life eking out my miserable existence to have that life snuffed out by an overgrown eagle. The djinni had been turned away from our destruction before, although I did not yet know the exact circumstances of its rebuff. Perhaps the Rukh could be rejected as well.

It was not that I did not see the reasons behind the merchant's fear. The great and terrible bird had already passed close above the ship twice, the first time disturbing the craft with its wings, the second time brushing the ship with its claws. And it came now for the third pass.

What is it about threes? There seems to be some sort of rule about them. It is a powerful number, since, as we are all aware even though no man truly knows the reason, many things, from wishes to curses, come in threes. And what descended upon us now seemed as much a curse as I had seen in my short and limited life.

"Rawn!" the bird screamed as it swept down again, flying so low over the water that it might almost swim rather than fly. Its head seemed the size of a house, and as it rushed forward I imagined I could see us all reflected in the great bird's eyes: the ship, and all of us upon it, so tiny that we appeared to be no more than insects floating upon some child's plaything. It was a plaything, I realized, that soon might reside in the belly of the Rukh.

The bird screamed as its claws rose to meet our prow, a scream so wild and high it sounded as if it held the echo of every man and woman that the Rukh had brought to death. Ruin indeed.

I had begun my final prayers when the bird lifted its head and flapped its wings, barely missing the ship as it rose rapidly in the air, causing a wind so great that two of the ship's sails were torn, and the boat almost capsized. But the boat righted itself, and the captain quickly called for the damaged sails to be pulled down, and replacements hoisted in their place, as the Rukh traveled higher, ever higher, until he was no more than a speck in the sky.

But why this sudden turn of events? It was almost as if some invisible hand were turning the monster away.

Whatever caused the change, the crew was jubilant.

"It is a sign!" one called.

"It is an omen!" another added.

"It is a portent!" a third rejoined.

I could not tell if the three were agreeing or arguing. Were not sign, omen, and portent essentially the same? Perhaps, in my limited life as a porter, I had missed the finer points of soothsaying.

"Yes," replied the crew member who had shouted first. "But a sign of what?"

The second crew member became more thoughtful as well. "Is the omen good or bad?"

"This sort of thing could portend almost anything!" the third crewman agreed after a fashion.

All three speakers turned to regard the four men in my tiny party.

"Perhaps," one of the crewmen suggested, "it would be best to throw them over the side, after all."

" 'Twould be best to return to your oars, and put your backs into it!" the captain remarked by way of countersuggestion. "All three of you will go over the side if we do not make the open sea by nightfall!"

The crew quickly returned to their stations, and we made rapid progress down the broad waterway. Still, I held some questions as to the nature of signs, omens, and portents.

"When you spend a great deal of time with my master," Achmed suggested in a whisper, "it appears that *everything* portends something else."

I could sense Achmed's meaning; this was certainly more complicated than anything I had ever imagined in my former life. But that had been another life, back in Baghdad, and I would have to alter my whole way of thinking if I was going to survive in my new world, on this broad river which led us to the sea.

"But both Rukh and djinni seemed tied in to Sinbad's venerable past," I mentioned with a deferential nod to my elder namesake. "Might I assume that there were other incidents in your history that might also affect us?"

"Indeed so," the elder replied with a world-weary smile. "Why, I remember how the third voyage began—"

"Begging your pardon, O most eloquent master," Achmed interjected once again, "but, with the speed with which events have occurred upon this ship, should we allow you to proceed with the tales, we shall be dead three times over before we reach the fifth voyage." This statement was once again accompanied by the child's dazzling and ingratiating smile, a device by which, I realized at last, the child kept his listeners from summarily killing him.

This time, even Jafar added his voice. "Beat me, your imperiousness, but the child is correct. As much as you have honed each story into a magnificent auditory experience, we must get to the heart of each tale if we are to determine what forces work against us here. Beyond which, there is this other matter which I wished to mention—"

"Very well!" his master interrupted. To my surprise, the great Sinbad did not seem in the least offended by his servant's impudence. "Honed each story!" he mused. "Magnificent auditory experience? Very well. I can restrain my art for a single day. Let us consider who the players were in the other tales."

"Oh, that," Jafar noted. "There was, of course, the ship commandeered by apes. And this other—"

"Then there was that giant with the taste for human flesh," Achmed related with some relish, "not to mention the cannibal tribe with the enchanted food that turned men into cattle ready for slaughter."

"Whence I escaped," Sinbad explained as he warmed again to the telling, "only to come to a kingdom that, though as prosperous and happy a place as I have ever seen, harbored a horrible secret"—the merchant paused to shiver—"that whenever a husband or wife should die, the other marriage partner was shut up in the burial crypt while still alive."

"Or the wizened creature who appeared to be a helpless old man who could not cross a shallow river, until he sat upon your shoulders and revealed himself as a demon who could not be dislodged," Achmed further remarked with some glee.

"And, of course, that other matter," Jafar insisted, "the unfortunate incident of the Rukh's egg." The majordomo paused to shiver. The others regarded him at that, and even Achmed was solemn. "In which you killed the bird child, and the Rukhs sought vengeance."

"Could this be one of the same birds?" Achmed asked, for once not supplied with all the answers.

"Only the Almighty may fathom the thoughts of birds and beasts," Sinbad agreed. "But still, why here? And why now?"

Their discourse gave me much to ponder, although I thought I should know more of the specifics of the individual tales before I reached any definite conclusions.

But all pondering was gone for the time, at least, when the crew rowed the craft beyond a great outcropping of rock, and we saw the sea.

The men cheered to reach the first of their goals, but I thought I heard a touch of awe in those cheers as well. Perhaps I was attributing my own insecurities to the crew. The ocean stretched out before me, a flat blue-green expanse below the brighter blue of the sky; and both sea and sky went on forever. I was a man used to alleyways and hovels: close, dark spaces where you could always reach a wall. It had been difficult for me to board a ship, but at least here there was a railing to hang on to, and, if the worst occurred while on the river, my beloved land was never more than a few feet away; feet that I might somehow traverse despite my lack of swimming. Or so I could reason with myself.

But the ocean? No one could reason with anything as large as the ocean.

The captain pointed out Basrah on the banks where river and ocean met. It was a fair-sized town, but nothing compared to Baghdad. I could see no more than half a dozen palaces with the naked eye!

We were so well supplied that we did not need to stop, but instead could head directly down the channel and out to sea. Surprisingly, even though the breeze in afternoon will often blow from sea to shore, the wind today was doing quite the opposite, and the captain made hasty instructions for full deployment of the sails to take advantage of this circumstance.

The wind caught the sails like a man greets his lover, and we were soon propelled out of sight of land.

"Captain!" a man called down from a lookout point high atop the mast. "Storm clouds on the horizon!"

Captain Hutan smiled grimly at the news. "I should have known there was something odd, with the wind shifted so. Well, my ship has weathered a storm or two before." His grin broadened as he looked at the four of us. "Those of you new to this kind of travel will have your sea legs ere long."

There were chuckles from those crew members close enough to hear the captain's words. The captain continued, in a much less humorous tone, to issue commands that might save the ship. And the clouds rushed toward us with all the speed that the Rukh had shown before.

The sea was all around us now, and great waves broke over the bow. I wondered how wet I would get before I gained my sea legs. Still, at least this trial was of natural origins; the sort of thing captain and crew were familiar with. Or so I thought at the time.

"Sinbad!"

Both the merchant and I turned at Achmed's cry.

"We have more trouble!" the boy shouted hoarsely to be heard over the rising wind. He pointed back in the direction where we had last seen the land. "Look to the horizon!"

There, barely large enough to make out the crooks of its wings, was the Rukh, headed for us once more. Perhaps, I thought, Rukhs have never heard of the rule of threes. Perhaps something had prevented it from destroying us before, something the great bird had had to kill before it returned to do the same to us.

For its intent was clear as it rapidly descended upon us, even though I could no longer hear the bird's eerie cries over the great noise of the wind.

It was scant consolation.

◆

Chapter the Eighth,
in which an unkind sky
is a greater friend than the sea.

"Aye," the captain called over the wind as I pointed out the large bird. "I see him, too. Come on, you drudges!" he called back to the crew. "Man those oars. We have a bird to escape!"

"But how do you escape a bird of that size?" I called back.

"By rowing into the storm!" the captain replied succinctly, as if that were all the explanation that was needed. He himself traveled quickly to the bow and picked up the two great batons and began to beat a rapid rhythm upon the drum. The oarsmen pulled with the beat, and we were soon progressing rapidly through the ever-increasing waves. The boat pounded and shook every time we hit a new wall of water, as if we crashed through something of a much more solid consistency.

It was an action that made my stomach lurch as well, and an action that made me wish that I had either eaten a much heartier meal while still on the calm river, or, conversely, that I had never ever thought of the very idea of food in my far-too-miserable life. The captain had mentioned gaining sea legs. I wondered if he had been attempting to show mercy when he omitted any mention of sea stomach.

Still, we rowed, and still the Rukh pursued us. But I noticed that the great bird did not seem to gain on us so quickly as before. I turned back to face the captain, and was hit full in the face by a great gust of wind and sea spray.

It was then that the captain's plan hit me as well. We were traveling to meet the storm, directly into the wind. That meant the great bird had also to fly against the wind, and while we in the ship were lashed by waves, the bird must fight the even-more-treacherous air currents of the storm above, and spend its strength by beating its wings against the gale.

The wind seemed to rise now with every pull of the oar. What had started as a shrill whistle had transformed itself into the howl

of a hundred women, wailing for the dead. I no longer heard the
sound of the oars, and the drumbeat from the bow became nothing
but a dull, intermittent thud, percussion for the wail of the wind,
as if the beats counted the passing souls of the damned.

I turned back to the stern, and saw that the great Rukh had
hardly drawn any closer. In fact, it appeared to hang suspended in
the air, its huge wings working furiously to keep it from being
pushed away by the gathering storm.

"Keep at the oars, men!" The captain's voice barely carried
over the shrill gale. "The Rukh is being left behind!"

So we might be free of the vengeful bird, at least in the face of
the storm. But at what a cost?

I turned back to the bow, and saw a wave before us that reached
twice the height of the ship.

"Steady on, men!" I heard the captain cry. But the rest of his
words were lost in wind and water. I saw the others in my party
grabbing hold of the rail. I decided that I had best do likewise as
the ship began a slow climb up toward the crest of the wave, far,
far, far too slow, rather like an overladen cart pulled by a single ox
up a steep hill that somehow became ever steeper.

For the wave grew before us, rising faster than we could rise
upon it. It towered above us to the height of the greatest minarets
in Baghdad, and then it stretched upward to twice that height. And
when I thought that nothing on earth or sea could rise higher still,
it redoubled in size, and then doubled again, so there was nothing
before us or to either side but water. Then did I look up as far as
I could see, and noticed that the great wave had a crest of foam the
width and height of my beloved city, and that crest curled over us,
so that the wave even hid the sky.

And the great curl of the wave descended upon us. The ship
shot forward as the wave crashed around us with such force that
I half thought my arms would be ripped from my shoulders, and
my body tossed into the deep while my hands still grabbed the rail.

Then the water was gone, and we once again rode a boat atop
the sea. I looked about, and saw that somehow all three of my
immediate company were still with me. Some others were not so
lucky, for I saw empty space where half a dozen oarsmen had sat
but a moment before.

Somehow, the captain had reached our side. "I have never seen
waves of this size or strength before!" he called, his voice barely
carrying, though there were but a few feet between us. "This
storm is not of natural origin!"

Achmed said something that was lost to the gale. The ship tossed forward on waves that, while great, were still within human imagining, but ahead, I could see that the ocean once again rose toward the clouds. I turned, and indeed could no longer see our pursuer. The Rukh had vanished from the sky; a wise bird to flee such an assault. If the captain was correct about the nature of the storm, it appeared we had escaped one curse to fall into another.

I glanced back at my compatriots, and saw the captain regarding me. "The bird seems to have flown above the clouds," he called, confirming my own thoughts. "Would that we could do the same."

Then came the rain: a hard, drenching rain, making the sea and sky almost one. I turned my face down so that my mouth would not fill with water. And the ship was once again moving, this time downward, like a man unable to stop from falling down a hill of sand. And when we reached that deep trough, how high would be the next wave that greeted us?

As we descended, the wind's screams diminished, muffled by the great mountains of water that surrounded us, so that we fell down into something that seemed almost like silence, as if the great rain about us were drowning sound before it began its true task of drowning men.

It was in this almost silence that I heard the two screams.

The first was the scream of a bird, carried somehow down to us on a great wash of water. And the answering scream was that of the men around us, for they realized that the Rukh had not disappeared, but was somehow above us, as if it had risen over the clouds only to escape the wind, so that it could again fly above us to fall from the sky, and nothing so simple as the fury of a storm could curb its vengeance.

Out of the dark cloud and water overhead came an even darker shape, plummeting toward all those tiny souls on that insignificant craft below.

And then our tiny ship began to climb the next insurmountable wave.

I tried to shield my eyes from the rain as I looked aloft again, and felt the storm diminish as the great shape descended. I realized that, before it destroyed us, the Rukh's tremendous form was shielding us from a portion of the gale. It grew swiftly overhead, although, even now, as we rode upward on the wave, the great bird seemed to be falling back toward our stern.

The captain's hand was on my shoulder. "Come with me and grab a vacant oar. We'll outdistance that hellspawn yet!"

I rushed forward as quickly as I dared across the slippery deck, and sat on a bench next to the captain.

"Pull, men," the brave Hutan called to the others, "if you don't wish to end up as birdseed. Pull for your lives!"

And so I pulled, and felt the rain fresh on my face again. I risked a look over my shoulder between pulls on the oar, and saw a great claw reach for the ship's topmost mast; reach but not touch. Then did we climb even higher upon the never-ending wave, and the wind hit us again so that the topmost mast was split in two, and the lookout still aloft fell screaming into the sea.

But, as terrible as the wind was to our craft, it was far worse for the great bulk of the Rukh. The bird screamed its frustration as it was pushed away from our ship, and, as the gale redoubled, it fell tumbling end over end back toward the distant land from which we had come, as helpless as the tiniest sparrow in the face of the great storm. A moment passed, and the Rukh, so close to crushing our craft in its massive claw, was no more than a small spot upon the horizon, and then was completely gone from sight.

The crew cheered as one, happy, at least, to be free of one danger. And the next great wave broke over our bow.

I was lifted bodily from the bench on which I sat. In that foolish moment of elation, I had ignored the storm about me, and not looked for something to secure me.

I realized, as the water carried me aloft, that I was headed over the side.

Once again, I was surrounded by the sea. Except, this time, I feared it would be forever. What little light the storm had afforded left me, and I descended into a lightless and airless world. I thought of moving my arms and legs, to somehow struggle back to the surface, but, besides the fact that I had never learned to swim, I knew the storm above me would offer me no relief. Perhaps I had no choice but to prepare to die.

It was then that I heard the woman's voice.

"You return to me so soon."

Only when I opened my eyes did I realize they had been closed. I saw a bright, white light, surrounded by a figure of green. It was the sea nymph, and the light was her smile.

Her strong fingers touched my neck just below each cheek. "You may breathe now."

All my fear fled at her touch. I did as I was bade, and the water that entered my lungs tasted as sweet as spring air.

After a moment, the nymph spoke again. "It is good that you have come to me." Her fingers lightly brushed across the lids of my eyes.

I blinked, and my eyes seemed to become accustomed to this great ocean depth in much the same manner as my lungs. I could see the maiden clearly now, every inch of her bare green flesh waiting, as if for me to take her in my arms.

I felt that I should speak to her in turn. I opened my mouth to try my voice.

"I fear that I have not come voluntarily," I admitted as my own somewhat muffled voice came to my ears. "There is a great storm above, and I fell over the side."

The nymph still smiled, though there seemed to be a touch of sadness to it now. "I know of the storm," she said. "It must be, then, that I have come to you again. So be it. I am happy I was here to save your life. You are meant for better things than a sudden death. You are meant for me."

I stared at this creature, not human, perhaps, but all too human in other ways. I stared not from fear or amazement, but because there was no way I could take my eyes off her beauty. Her hand touched my elbow, and my skin there tingled with the warmth of a desert fire in the coldest night.

"I have come to seek companionship. I have been drawn to you, much as you lure stallions from the sea to mate with your earthbound mares." Her arms were suddenly about me. "Our races are more than compatible."

Even here, in this strange new world, I could sense that compatibility. I could especially sense it when I looked at the woman's large, dark lips, then let my gaze wander to her buoyant breasts, her tight stomach, her flaring hips. If not for Fatima—

But what did I know of Fatima? A hand and a laugh, nothing more. Oh, certainly, they were a very special hand and laugh, the sort of hand and laugh that one could expect to witness perhaps only once in an entire lifetime. But who knew if I would ever witness more than those elegant fingers and that voice fit to grace the palaces of heaven? And who knew what the remainder of Fatima even looked like, although, now that I thought on it, I was quite certain she must be magnificent!

Here, now, I had a woman before me that presented her whole form to me, the very opposite of the unknown Fatima! Although, now that I thought on it, I knew the curves and crevices of this creature's body, but I wasn't too sure as to her exact species. And I had a question or two as to the exact nature of my present location, not to mention how I managed to still be alive. Still, here was this fantastic creature, who by her actions invited me to couple with her here, and live with her forever within the ocean depths.

It occurred to me then that a stay forever within the ocean depths might be perceived by certain individuals as one definition of drowning.

"I can see you are not quite prepared to make your decision," the sea maiden stated with remarkable prescience. "I shall return you to the world of the surface. But first I have a final task."

She drew closer still to me then, and placed her lips full upon mine.

"Now you will again be able to breathe air," she said as she released me. At that instant, I doubted I should ever breathe again. "Once you return to the surface, all will be as it was." She reached out a single finger, and ran it down the length of my nose. "Ah, but we will meet again. And the third time shall be something special."

With that, she seemed to sink beneath me. At first, I thought she was swimming away, but then I realized she did not move at all, and it was I, instead, who was rising. I blinked again, and all below me turned to darkness, but above me I could see the light of the surface world.

I could also see something floating upon that surface; something that I hoped might be my salvation. It appeared from below to be an odd collection of logs, roughly tied together with rope. Still, it looked solid enough. Perhaps the sea nymph had truly saved me.

I grabbed for the edge of the raft as I broke through the surface and took a great gasp of the rain-laden air. The storm was still all about me, but the waves seemed to have abated somewhat, and I was able to clamber aboard.

I stared straight into the face of another man.

I calmed myself after a moment of fright. This raft was large enough for two. And the other occupant looked to be an older man, somewhat disoriented by this turn of events. I thought it best to offer him my most humble greetings.

He looked at me as if I had not spoken at all. I wondered if he was blind or deaf or both. Now I felt as disconcerted as I had imagined him to be.

"Do you speak?" I asked far too bluntly.

At that, he smiled broadly. "Greetings! This is the first time I have ever had a visitor upon my flimsy craft!"

So he had chosen to speak to me at last. "Yes," I answered quickly, eager to strike a positive note. "I must apologize for my abrupt arrival."

The other man suddenly frowned. "Of course I speak. Are you deaf? Did you not hear my greetings?"

"Well, most certainly!" I blubbered. "I did not wish to offend—" My voice died in my throat. Why did I feel this conversation had grown out of control?

The other man's anger seemed to soften, if only a trifle. "Well, you should apologize, but for your rudeness, rather than your arrival."

I decided to follow the other man's lead. "Well, I will certainly apologize if—"

"You certainly have offended me!" the man screamed suddenly. "I warn you, I am a great magician. Who do you think quieted the great fury of this storm?"

But, even if I could make sense of this conversation, I had no answer to his question, for I saw a great shape loom out of the rain behind the other man, a shape that looked much like a sailing ship.

"A ship!" I called. "Bound straight for us! If you are truly a magician, you must do something!"

The older man chuckled as if he had not heard me. "Well, perhaps I am hasty, and should accept your apology, after all. It is amazing how compliant people become when they realize you are a magician!"

I recognized the carved figure upon the bow of the craft before us, and realized I would never learn the answer to the riddle of the magician's conversation, for we were to be sunk by the very ship that carried the rest of my company!

For the sake of form, I screamed.

Chapter the Ninth,
in which what happened before becomes clearer than what happens now.

"Ah," the elderly man across from me spoke as if it were every day that you were about to be smashed to bits by an onrushing ship. "Why didn't you tell me?"

"But I did—"

"It does no good to scream," the other fellow replied with a frown. "No time for emotion, no, no, no. A spell is what is called for here."

I was shocked into silence. Had I screamed?

Well, I had, a moment before. Odd that the magician should bring it up now. Perhaps, I decided, my most prudent course of action would be the continuation of utter silence. My companion on the raft seemed well pleased with my decision as he snapped his fingers three times and made three mystic passes while muttering three words of great complexity, none of which I had ever before heard.

The ship, which had been headed straight for our tiny raft, appeared to be veering to our left. Strangely enough, it also appeared to be sinking. Would the magician scuttle the other craft in order to save our lives? This would never do! Somehow, I had to put a stop to it.

"A thousand pardons, O great magician!" I spoke rapidly yet politely, doing my best not to offend the respectable and—as I now saw—no doubt enormously powerful gentleman again. "But must we doom these others to save ourselves?"

"What was that you said?" the mage asked with some confusion. "But you did *what*? The youth today! How do you expect to have a respectable conversation if you do not finish sentences!"

I felt once more like a dinner guest who arrives to discover his invitation was for an entirely different season of the year. I stared at the magician. It was as if the man were having this conversation in another place and time entirely. I glanced back at the sinking ship. Perhaps, I thought once more, I should not attempt to speak to this man at all, but should communicate exclusively through some other means, such as grunts, sign language, or elaborate and detailed written notes.

However, all was once again not as it had first seemed. As we turned back toward the craft which I had once called home, I had an abrupt realization. That ship was not actually in the process of sinking at all. Instead, the raft, and both of us who sat upon it, had risen into the air above the waves to the height of one grown man standing upon the shoulders of another, and we were flying to the right-hand side of the still water-bound craft.

"Oh," I said, more an exhalation of surprise than an attempt at further conversation.

"Oh, this is really too much!" the magician cried in exasperation. "Who exactly am I dooming, and how? I'll have you know I only use the very most positive magics, and am offended that you should imply anything else." He waved a tattered sleeve over the side. "I want you off this raft, young man, at once!"

Dooming? I thought. I hadn't said anything about doom. Well, actually I had in that last speech I made some moments before. It was rather like his delayed reaction to the scream. Perhaps, I thought, this older man had difficulty hearing and recognizing the finer points of conversation. On answering him this time, I therefore spoke slowly and carefully, so there could be no error.

"I apologize, good sir."

The magician flew into a positive rage. "Oh? Is that all you can say is 'oh'?"

Oh, indeed. I blinked. I frowned. I blinked again. It was as if, whenever I made an utterance, he would only then hear that thing which I had spoken before. Would such a circumstance be possible? I realized now that I was dealing not only with a magician here, but with actual magic in practice, a subject about which, despite recent encounters with a sea nymph and djinni, I was still woefully underinformed.

But I was not without hope. Should this oddity of delayed hearing indeed be true, my conversation with the magician, although naturally confusing, might still be possible. If, however, as I now assumed, my audience experienced this postponement in hearing, then the mage had yet to listen to my apology. It was therefore up to me to speak again.

"I believe I can see the problem," I said, perhaps being more bold than I should when addressing so great, albeit confused, a personage.

"Apologize?" the other man barked. "Only now do you apologize?"

Yes, it appeared that I was very much tagging along with the correct caravan. I was further encouraged to remark: "We are having some difficulty communicating."

"Problem?" the still furious magician retorted. "My only problem is removing you from this raft."

I decided then that the direct approach was best. "You are not hearing what I am saying."

"A difficulty that will shortly be resolved," the magician reassured me brusquely. "If you do not wish to go voluntarily, there are ways to make you go. I shall turn you into a gnat or a guppy or something else equally insignificant!"

Gnat or guppy, my resolve could not waver. I swallowed, and continued. "My lips! Look at my lips! Do they match my words?"

"Communication?" the magician raged, apparently quite beyond reason. "I'll show you how I communicate, young man—" His hands once again flashed at his sides. "With magic!"

This had better work quickly. I could already imagine the gnat wings sprouting upon my back as I shrank to insignificance. If only I could get him to understand! But how could he understand something that he hadn't heard? And—again I realized—he would not be able to listen to my last speech unless I made another.

"There is magic afoot here!" I insisted.

"Lips? Words?" The man frowned as he squinted at me. Then, as if I had performed some magic of my own, all the anger instantly went out of him. "Oh, dear," he continued, now the voice of concern rather than rage, "this is a problem. Are you ensorceled?"

Me? Under the power of sorcery? Did not this great magician even realize the nature of his own affliction? Still, I should proceed with caution. It would do no good to once again anger this powerful gentleman.

"Beg pardon, sir," I therefore said, "but I believe that it is you who are under a spell."

"Magic indeed." The mage nodded his head sagely. "And powerful, too, to change the very nature of speech."

I brashly continued, knowing that he should hear my words eventually. "You do not hear the thing that is said to you, but instead hear what has been said before."

"Me?" the mage replied skeptically to whatever I had said a moment before. This talking to someone out of step with you was a tricky business. "You obviously know nothing about the nature of magic!"

Ah, dear. I could feel the anger once again brewing behind his brow. "That is most certainly true," I continued with great earnestness, "but I believe that both of us are endowed with certain powers of observation."

But the mage's face grew red and puffy. "I'll have you know I hear perfectly well! Simply because I'm old does not mean that I am deaf!"

"I did not mean—" I began and ended immediately, once again totally undone by the conversation.

But the magician was anything but undone. "Certain powers of observation!" he raged. "Are you saying that you observe that I'm deaf? Whether you are already cursed or not, young vagabond, I once again can see a gnat spell in your future!"

He seemed to be growing angrier by the minute. Perhaps I was trying to communicate with him on too complex a level. If we were going to talk across this supernatural barrier, I should begin by presenting simple concepts. I realized I must start again, and quickly, if I did not wish to experience gnathood.

"I do not wish to anger you," was the simplest, and truest, thing that I could say.

"There you are, not finishing your sentences again!" he fumed. This speech delay seemed to become more difficult by the moment. But might there not be a way to defeat this clever sorcery?

What, I considered, if I said the same thing twice? Would he not hear it properly the second time? It was certainly worth the effort.

"I do not wish to anger you," I said again.

He looked at me blankly. "Now what? Speak up! I can't hear a word you are saying!"

I had not imagined he would stop hearing me altogether. Perhaps, I considered, that idea was not so clever as I had thought. "Oh, dear," I remarked.

The magician grunted with some satisfaction. "And well it is that you should not anger one of my power and encyclopedic knowledge of gnat spells." Still, he seemed somewhat calmer than before. At last I had said the right thing.

"But what do we do now?" I said, more thinking aloud than continuing the conversation.

The mage's frown deepened. "No need to repeat yourself. I know you don't wish to anger me. I heard you the first time!"

Oh, no. Now he was no longer responding to the last thing I had said, but instead the statement I had made before that! I realized then that my idea had not been clever in the least.

I must admit, at that moment, that I felt a rare moment of total frustration, and lost my usual porter's resolve. "This conversation is getting us nowhere!" I screamed in anxiety.

"Oh, dear, indeed," the magician agreed with something I had said far too long ago.

I waved in perplexity at the air about us. Should this raft fly on forever, with us eternally unable to communicate? "Should we not land?" I further shrieked.

The mage nodded, as if he might have even heard my question. "I, too, have considered what we should do next. This flying spell is taxing in the extreme. But say—why do we not land upon that nearby sailing vessel?"

So saying, he again snapped his fingers, waved his arms, and said three completely different words than the ones he had used before, although I found these new words no more familiar. The raft halted abruptly, then began a gentle descent toward the ship, which had now somehow positioned itself directly beneath us. At least, I thought as we settled upon the deck, if the magician and I could not communicate, we were thinking in the same general direction.

The magician smiled upon me with a benign tolerance for my ignorance. "So I have rescued us both, still in perfect health. My magic is as potent as the day I first donned these robes!" He waved at the surrounding crew members as the raft settled upon the deck with the slightest of bumps. "To think someone might accurse a magician as powerful as myself!" He had a good laugh over that one.

I looked up from where I now sat at the exact center of the ship. The crew had gathered around us to ring the raft. And I recognized all too well the angry tone of their collective voices.

"I do not think we are welcome guests," I remarked grimly.

"Conversation?" the magician blissfully replied. "Well, yes, we can certainly talk later, after we have made our greeting to our new hosts!"

The crew's grumbling grew louder. I heard the usual low mumbling about signs, omens, and portents, but added to that were further remarks about curses, banes, and scourges.

"You may have to be prepared for a less-than-friendly reception," I cautioned the mage.

He looked at me with consternation. "Land? But we have landed. Sometimes, my boy, I think your mind has been pressed too hard from the weight of the goods you have carried above your head." He smiled upon me in a fatherly fashion. "You are a porter, are you not?"

How could he possibly know that? In my surprise, I did not speak this time, but simply nodded.

"Ah." The mage grinned the grin of the truly knowledgeable, an expression I had become far too familiar with from seeing it repeatedly upon the face of Achmed. "I have a knack for guessing occupations. Part of being a wizard, I suppose."

He was also a wizard who appeared to take no notice of his immediate surroundings, for I could swear that the restive crew that made up those surroundings seemed about to surge forward and take our lives. From somewhere beyond their amassed and angry might, I could hear the captain calling for them to stand aside or face dire consequences.

But still, the magician across from me seemed blissfully unaware of the bent of the mob that surrounded us. Perhaps, I feared, he could only hear the first threat after the third threat had been uttered. Or mayhaps his curse was such that he heard the crew's background mumblings not at all. Whatever his problem, he stood and greeted the crowd in a most respectful fashion.

"My name is Malabala," he spoke to all those gathered around us, "seventeenth in the noble line of Malabalas, all great wizards and greater princes, and all from a far-distant land which—" He paused, his smiling countenance momentarily creased by a frown. "Oh, dear. It is a far-distant land that I seem somehow to have misplaced." He shook his head, and replaced his frown again with a smile. "But I assure you, sirs, that is a setback which is only temporary. I shall tell you all about my homeland when next it comes within my inner view." He chuckled humbly. "When one is a wizard, one has so much on one's mind."

The crowd, perhaps disconcerted by the abstract and uncertain nature of the magician's speech, parted before us, and the captain strode through, followed closely by my merchant namesake and his two attending servants.

"Greetings, O noble magician!" the captain called. "For you strike me as a man who uses magic for naught but good."

"A good magician?" a crew member wondered loudly.

"The only good magician is a dead—" A second crewman left his sentence unfinished after a look from the captain.

"My magic is of the purest sort!" Malabala reassured the crew. "I have no truck with demons and the like, except to send them back to the dark hells from which they came!" He turned to me and said in a lower voice, "I see what you mean about our reception. But I have handled worse crowds than this."

Sinbad the merchant stepped forward to ask the next question. "Then was it your intervention that calmed the storm?"

"Then he is against demons?" one of the crew members shouted in a somewhat more positive fashion.

"Perhaps he can banish our evil djinni!" another crewman agreed.

"Yes, it was certainly I who calmed the storm," Malabala remarked with the sort of humility only practiced by men of great power. The crew cheered at that, and I realized that people were now speaking so rapidly that it might also appear the mage Malabala was holding a rational conversation.

"Truly he is a great magician!" someone shouted.

"Now our voyage will be genuinely blessed!" added another.

Malabala frowned. "Did someone mention a djinni?"

"He stopped the storm!" a third crew member rejoiced. "And banished the Rukh!"

"Without doubt, nothing can happen to a ship with so great a guardian," a fourth continued.

"Well," the captain added in the loud voice of command, "perhaps we should make our guardian comfortable so that the rest of us may return to our work?" The crew returned quickly to their stations as the captain turned to walk among them.

"Rukh?" Malabala frowned. "I saw no Rukh!"

I looked down to see Achmed tugging upon my sleeve. "I fear that the magician will soon have to change his statement," the lad remarked. And this time, even Achmed wasn't smiling as he pointed toward the bow of the ship.

There, indeed, was a far-too-familiar black dot upon the horizon. Perhaps the crew did have good reason, after all, to be cross with their four passengers.

"It is the Rukh!" someone screamed, his voice instilled with the proper degree of terror.

Again? I sighed. All this peril was becoming rather tiresome.

The great bird grew rapidly nearer, as if its quest for vengeance would never tire.

◆

Chapter the Tenth,
in which there is some cause for rejoicing
and some further cause for other things.

"Rukhs?" the great magician Malabala said with an expression that one might assume when one had recently eaten an especially rancid date. "Ugh."

Most of the crew seemed to no longer be listening, having once again resumed what appeared to be their favorite pastime, that of running aimlessly about on the deck and screaming for salvation. The captain in their midst was again shouting for order or some such. His words were again lost in the general din.

"Their huge bloated forms blot out the sun." said Malabala with continued distaste. "The wind from their wings can ruin a perfectly good dinner party." He paused to wrinkle his nose even further. "Have you ever been caught beneath them when they have recently finished eating? Filthy creatures!"

"Rawn." The Rukh was close enough so that I could again hear its high and fearsome cry. "Rawn."

But could our enchanted magician hear that cry as well? And might he stop his complaints long enough to do something about it?

"Oh, enough of my reminiscence!" cried the mage, and this time he appeared angry with himself. "If I had been paying less attention to distracting that Rukh before, and more to the weather, I perhaps could have even stilled the storm!" He made three more mystic passes with three more mystic words.

The cry of the Rukh was gone, and in its place was naught but the sounds of sea and wind. I looked back beyond the bow, but saw nothing but rolling waves and almost cloudless sky.

The crew noticed the Rukh's sudden absence as well, and stopped its participatory panic to rally about the magician.

"What has happened to the Rukh?" I called over their collective clamor.

"Three cheers for Malabala!"

"Truly he is a prince among magicians!"

"I sent him home," answered the still calm magician. "I may be powerful, but I am also compassionate."

"Do I hear correctly?" another voice called out from the midst of the crowd. "Have we found a liberator to rescue us from dire misfortune?"

The crowd, which seemed to have become very proficient of late at parting and re-forming, once again drew aside to reveal Dirk and the Scar, who carried their ornate palanquin between them. They trotted quickly across the deck, as if the heavy box they carted weighed no more than the fresh sea air through which they passed.

"You do not have to cheer me so," the mage said humbly. "All of us are assigned a task in this life, and I do no more than perform mine as best I can."

Dirk and the Scar stopped directly before Malabala.

"And may I ask the name of our liberator?" Dirk inquired in a tone that was more demand than question. He nodded curtly, and both he and his even more ominous companion allowed the palanquin to rest gently upon the ground.

"Ah"—the magician beckoned to the palanquin with his peaceful smile—"that is a most impressive gift that you carry between you. A present for a sultan, is it not?"

Malabala's question seemed to greatly upset both of the heavily muscled and no doubt extremely dangerous pair. The Scar growled and took a heavy step toward the magician. But he halted his assault when Dirk held up a cautionary hand. So the Scar waited, like some great beast who is only considering the most propitious moment to charge, while Dirk spoke in a most unreasonable tone:

"You do not ask questions about this weight we carry. You have not even seen this cargo that we share. And you have not answered my first question, which I urge you to do with all speed."

"Yes, a gift, most assuredly," Malabala continued as if he had not heard Dirk's threats, which, in truth, he hadn't. "I am good at guessing this sort of thing. Something about me being a magician no doubt. And to answer that crewman there, I am both a prince and a magician. The two occupations are quite complementary—" He paused and looked aloft, as if seeking an answer from the bright blue sky. "—in that place from which I come," he concluded a moment thereafter. "Most assuredly I shall remember my country of origin at any moment."

The Scar resumed his lumbering attack. "I cuts his ears open so he hears better!" he suggested pleasantly.

The smile on the mage's face suddenly fell. "I am Malabala, which you certainly would have already heard if you had been listening but a moment ago. And I am uncertain if I like your tone."

"You are Malabala?" Dirk laughed at that. "I suppose if the same name may be shared by a merchant and a porter, likewise might it be for a great magician and an inept conjurer!" He waved to the Scar to lumber even closer. "We can find far more than our tone to displease you. My friend is very creative."

"I did most certainly answer you!" Malabala stated with an anger equal to that he had shown me upon the raft. "And I shall ask whatever questions I wish, for I am also quite certain that what you carry is a gift for a sultan!"

Dirk only continued to smile. "It is most unfortunate, but you are no longer a fit traveling companion. Please hold still while my partner dispatches you."

The magician raised but a single hand in response, as if motioning the two ruffians to stop before this went any further.

With that, the Scar laughed in the most vile manner imaginable, and made to attack the magician. But, though the villian's legs moved, and the short but deadly blade he had pulled from his sash slashed through the air, he came no closer to Malabala. Indeed, the Scar had no reward for his troubles but a slow rising into the air, where his feet and knife flailed about to no good purpose.

"And I recommend that your partner take some elocution lessons," Malabala further suggested. "I assure you he will have a great deal of time for study in his present position."

"I kills him!" the Scar screamed from his new point of prominence. "I kills him!"

But Dirk did not appear to be so stubborn. Instead, he bowed deeply. "Perhaps we were the slightest bit hasty, O great magician. It occurs to me that you may indeed bear some resemblance to a certain Malabala."

Malabala's whole frame grew rigid with anger. "Is that another threat I hear? I warn you, villains, your very lives are in peril!"

And before Dirk could speak again, he added: "More threats? Very well. I hope you shall enjoy the rest of your lives once I turn you into gnats."

Dirk fell to his knees. "But there was nothing threatening in what I said, good sir. The more I think on it, you must be the great

and powerful magician that I have heard of! Truly, you do mistake
my meaning!"

But Malabala's fury was not so easily calmed; especially
because he had not yet heard either of Dirk's last two remarks.
"You in the air!" he demanded instead. "What was that you said?
If you have any last words before you are transformed into the
most insignificant of insects, you should most assuredly speak
up!"

So Malabala had failed to ascertain the last remark the Scar had
made? It was a remark, I now realized, that the Scar had repeated.

I recalled with a touch of dread what happened the last time the
magician could not hear. But my fear was as nothing to what Dirk
now appeared to be feeling. His smile wavered on his once
far-too-smug face as his knees shook below.

"O greatest of magicians," his once-confident voice now
wailed, "we are but poor travelers, and are to be pitied for our
ignorance!"

But Malabala was still lost in a much earlier part of the
conversation. "Now he threatens to kill me? Being turned into
insects is too good for vermin like you!"

"He is like a child! He angers easily, but it means nothing!"
Dirk fell upon all fours and began to grovel in a most dedicated
fashion.

The magician's next words were said in a far softer tone, but if
his earlier anger was the tip of a raging fire, this new tone was the
white heart of the flame.

"And he threatens me again?" was his question of simple but
deadly intent.

"But why do you react so now?" Dirk paused for but an instant
in his cowering. "He threatened you some time ago and
mmmbbb—no, that is not exactly whffmmmm meant to say. You
will forgive me, O wise and most benevolmmmbbb of magicians,
if I am not at my best in the presnnnn situation!" It was becoming
difficult to distinguish many of the ruffian's words, since Dirk had
now begun to crawl upon the deck like a snake across the sand.

"Only now do you attempt to apologize?" Malabala laughed; a
sound totally devoid of mirth. "You must think me a doddering
old fool to imagine I might change my mind after you have
offended me so."

"Mfffmmm glbbbbb snssrrrrzzz!" Dirk wailed into the deck. Or
something that sounded much like that.

The magician shook his head with finality. "It is too late. Your entreaties fall upon deaf ears." I considered how much irony there was in the magician's words as he began his gestures and words of power.

Dirk looked up in the midst of his groveling.

"Bzzzz bzzzzzz," he remarked. He slapped both hands over his mouth in abject horror.

Malabala paused in the middle of his conjuring. "Still you plead with me? I do not understand. The spell should have begun by now. Words should already be beyond your diminishing abilities."

"Bzzzzz bzzz," the Scar further replied. His mouth opened in astonishment as his knife fell from his slack fingers.

"You yet continue to speak? This is most distressing," the magician fretted. "I shall have to make the spell even stronger, to make you as small to a gnat as a gnat is to man!"

Dirk and the Scar became even more agitated at this, flailing their arms about in what I soon realized might be seen as their first attempts at insect flight. Perhaps I should have been more concerned as to their plight, for could not a similar fate befall any man? Indeed, had not the same gnatty fortune almost befallen me?

But still I could hear their many threats, not so much to the magician as those earlier to my traveling companions and myself. At that moment, I could only imagine that a higher justice was being served, and that these two ruffians might be facing that which my merchant namesake so often referred to as Destiny.

But I would be remiss if I did not mention my second thought, for I also experienced the further realization that, once these two were gone, someone would be needed to tend to the mysterious Fatima. Who better for such a task, ministering to her every delicate whim and fulfilling her every special desire, than an experienced porter?

"And now the spell," Malabala stated with finality. "Say goodbye to your manhood, you insects of moral judgment!"

But before further mystic words could be uttered or mystic gestures passed, there was another of those all-too-common explosions overhead, a noise that sent Dirk and the Scar into a fit of renewed buzzing.

Ozzie had appeared so often by now that I did not even need to look aloft. But for the first time, there was a hope stirring in my heart, a hope apparently shared by those about me, for even the crew remained relatively quiet. We might again be confronted by a djinni, but now our number included a magician!

"Something told me it was time to revisit my beloved Sinbads," the voice of Ozzie boomed above us. Still, he did not inspire the fear that had once been his. Had not Malabala dispensed with the Rukh as one might swat a fly? The magician would make equally quick work of such as Ozzie, once, of course, we could get the magician's attention concerning the matter.

"But I never expected to see Malabala!" Ozzie continued. "One would almost imagine there were forces at work here greater than the djinn!" His sardonic laugh assaulted us with the force of thunder.

The djinni and mage had met before? Perhaps my hope was premature. Reluctantly, I directed my gaze aloft. I certainly did not care for the djinni's unctuous smile.

"Malabala was once very powerful, before he met me," Ozzie said in a tone that, were he not a djinni, might be mistaken for kindness. "Were you not, you pitiful, aged excuse for a magician?"

"What?" Malabala still spoke to Dirk and the Scar, completely oblivious to the peril from above. "You only begin to buzz now? What is it about my spell? Have I not properly accounted for the sea air?"

"Ah," the djinni added with a chuckle. "Malabala cannot hear me yet. Apparently, he cannot hear anything that has been presented to him in quite some time."

Ozzie seemed to speak of this supernatural situation with a disturbing familiarity. Could this djinni be responsible for the magician's curse? I felt my hopes going the way of the rains at the end of spring. It did my crumbling peace of mind no good whatsoever to hear the crew behind me become equally restive.

Malabala frowned at the Scar. "And now you buzz as well? Perhaps the shifting of the deck beneath my feet has altered my mystic passes."

"Come now, magician!" Ozzie's pleasant expression was replaced by a frown. "How long will it be before you can answer? Even I find this too annoying."

Malabala paused again, his expression, if possible, even more bewildered than before. "Eh? Is someone else here?"

"I am a victim of my own spell!" the djinni cried with frustration. "Very well. It shall all be undone for the nonce." Two hands appeared beneath the giant head above, and abruptly clapped. "I hereby cancel all magics!"

"I can talk again!" Dirk cried before he fell into fit of coughing. "That buzzing wreaks a terrible havoc upon the throat!"

"What?" Malabala looked skyward, only now aware of our demonic visitor. "Ozzie? Have I not banished you yet?"

The djinni chuckled. "This would be amusing if it were not so pitiful. And would all of you in the background stop screaming and running about for a moment? I do find it distracting, and assure you that, should you continue, I will do something quite horrible to the lot of you."

Then Ozzie's gaze shifted, so that he appeared to look directly at me, and his next words convinced me that if I were not soon dead, it would be because luck was no longer with me.

"First, however, I must dispose of a minor annoyance," he said with that same damnably pleasant tone. "It is time to rid this drama of the false Sinbad."

◆

Chapter the Eleventh,
in which the very nature of power becomes an issue
of some concern.

So I was going to die. Again.

How does one react when one faces peril with such regularity that it has become the commonplace? Certainly, I did not panic in the way I had the first half a dozen times my life was threatened, and indeed, could barely even tell if the crew behind me was involved in their usual collective hysteria. Instead, I appeared to be approaching each new threat with a gathering dispassion, and, as I examined this latest fulmination, I considered the following thoughts in the same way that I used to treasure small coins in my days of employment as a common laborer:

Actually, being called an annoyance might be a promotion from the rank of porter.

Further, this djinni liked to hear himself talk so much that perhaps I could engage him in conversation to postpone my anticipated doom.

Possibly even more pertinent, the last time we were visited by this gigantic head, he had been forced to leave under somewhat mysterious circumstances. It also appeared to me that this djinni, while being gargantuan and virtually all-powerful, possessed one area where he did not appear extraordinarily gifted, that being in the realm of intelligence.

Therefore, perhaps I could, through conversation, discover the nature of the djinni's mysterious problem, or, failing that, at least confuse the being to such an extent that I should find some other means of survival. In order to accomplish all of this, I should have to gain the djinni's complete attention. But that should be like the games of children to a man who, in order to obtain regular employment, had to shout above a chorus of others in the marketplace.

"O most magnificent Ozzie, who could crush me as a man might kill the most annoying of fleas," I began.

"Yes, that is the least that can be said about me," the djinni agreed generously.

"O most glorious Ozzie, whose head fills the sky like a second sun," I further illuminated.

"Well, I wouldn't go too far," the djinni replied with a chuckle. "But then again, when you are talking about something as wonderful as a djinni, going too far is hardly possible."

"O most breathtaking Ozzie," I continued, certain now that at least the first part of my plan would succeed, "whose voice carries like thunder, but whose true power is so great that it cannot be compared to anything as commonplace as the sun or storms."

"You are very learned for a porter, aren't you?" said Ozzie, positively beaming.

"I hate to interrupt," Malabala interrupted, "but if you're done complimenting this spawn of evil, I'd like to get back to banishing him."

"Oh, be a good magician and go clean your robes or something!" Ozzie retorted. "Remember, I can always reverse my magic removal spell!"

"Magic removal spell!" Malabala snorted derisively. "What a silly idea. Do you take me for a novice?" He paused to look down at his sleeves. "But is my robe that dirty?"

Ozzie spoke again to me. "Are you surprised that I know that now? The bit about the porter, that is. Well, I did have to return to my employer to straighten out a thing or two." He chortled. "And my employer does have a way of discovering the true nature of things."

"There appears to be a tear here and there as well." Malabala shook his ragged robes self-consciously. "Personal hygiene is sometimes difficult when one is lost at sea on a raft."

"But my employer has given me very specific instructions," the djinni continued gleefully.

"What?" Dirk demanded, interrupting the djinni's bubbling effusion. The thug seemed to have finally shaken off all effects of Malabala's spell, and, from his stance and the tone of his voice, was once again his bullying self. "Are you here again?"

"Oh, yes, I am," the djinni replied, his voice a mixture of superiority and surprise. "And apparently so are you. You'll excuse me if I didn't recognize you. At first I had mistaken you for a very large gnat."

Dirk flinched at that, but regained his brutish composure almost instantly. "Do I have to get rough with you?"

With that, it was Ozzie's time to lose his composure. "Rough with me? So soon?" The djinni paused, great furrows forming in the upper region of his hairless cranium. "But I had it under good authority that you were under an enchantment."

"Wait a moment!" the magician exclaimed with great enthusiasm. "I remember my past! Do you believe I didn't even realize I had forgotten it?"

"Oh," Ozzie said with the great slowness of one who only now begins to understand, "you *were* under an enchantment before, weren't you?" He bit a lip the size of a riverbank with a tooth as large as your average mosque. "It was that thing I did to get rid of the magic, wasn't it? That whole Malabala thing." Ozzie made a tsking sound with a tongue slightly larger than our ship. "Me and my impatience."

"Well?" was Dirk's only reply.

"Well, toodles!" Ozzie attempted to grin again without success. "Sooner or later, you know, Sinbad will be mine."

Dirk only glanced at the head.

"Well, perhaps much later." And with that, the djinni again disappeared, and I found myself staring up into a cloudless sky.

"Yes!" Malabala called to no one in particular. "Yes! And my brother, too! How could I have been such a fool?"

"Well, I'm glad we were able to make some things clear around here," Dirk declared. "And now, magician, let us talk plainly here"—he flapped his arms around for emphasis.—"without threats as to who wields the true power in this bzzzz bzzzz bzzzzzz!" Then again, perhaps he flapped his arms in a renewed attempt to fly.

The wizard's words of reply affirmed only what I already feared.

"Pardon me?" Malabala replied. "I can see your lips move, but I can hear no words." He frowned. "Could you possibly be enchanted? That sort of thing seems to be going around." He paused again. "Now, what was I saying? Oh, yes, I knew where I came from." Yet another, even longer pause ensued. "Well, I did know where I came from," he added at last, "a few moments ago."

So not only was the djinni gone, but with him had gone all his works, both good and bad. I felt a tugging upon my sleeve. I looked down, and once again saw the smiling face of Achmed.

"It is good to see that you did not become a permanent visitor among the fishes," the youth remarked pleasantly.

To my initial surprise, I found even this expression of sentiment touching. In the great city of Baghdad, one porter is much the same as any other; now that I had embarked upon an adventure, though, I had a certain importance in the regards of my fellows. To be of honest consequence was quite a new experience.

In actuality, as I had time to reflect upon it, I found it all more than touching; I was beginning to feel a bit unnerved. Not only did my eyes grow moist, but I could feel my knees begin to shake. The way the boat rocked beneath me, I was sure I was going to collapse into a quivering heap at any second. I reflected that perhaps I reacted to more than my newfound importance, and was not so used to facing danger as I had thought.

"Bzzzz bzzz bzzzzz," Dirk and the Scar chorused as they flitted about the deck.

"Now, where was I?" Malabala mused. "Oh, yes. Somewhere in the midst of turning a pair of ne'er-do-wells into insects!" He reached out both of his hands, right hand above left, in what appeared to be a prime conjuring position. He frowned, and moved his left hand above his right.

I took a deep breath in an attempt to calm myself. "I seem to lead an eventful life," was all that I could think to say.

"Life around my merchant master is always eventful," Achmed replied. "But still you seem to survive these events relatively unscathed, much in the same way as my master. Perhaps the very name Sinbad leads its bearer to a charmed existence."

I considered the youth's statement. There were many words I might use for my recent experience. "Charmed" was not among them.

"Now let me examine my handiwork," Malabala mused as he closed his left fist and opened his right hand so that his palm pointed toward the sky. "I must know how far my subjects have come before I determine how much further they have to go."

So the mage was about to complete his insect spell upon Dirk and the Scar. But didn't he realize what the consequences of that culmination might be? Even in my somewhat weakened and perhaps permanently bewildered state, I realized there was a subtle balance of power at work here. As I could see by their current buzzing and running about the deck, Dirk and the Scar could easily be kept in check by Malabala. But, even though he did not realize it, the magician was in turn controlled in some way by the evil Ozzie. And the only thing that appeared to keep the djinni in check was some secret power held by Dirk and the Scar.

If Malabala succeeded, and Dirk and the Scar were indeed changed into insects, it would disrupt this triangle permanently, and perhaps doom Malabala and the rest of us to the worst of fates that the djinni might devise. As unpleasant as those two ruffians were, I therefore could not allow the spell to reach completion.

"Wait!" I called to the magician.

"Ah," Malabala replied to the last statement made within his hearing. "I notice that the recipients of my spell are now doing nothing but buzzing. Such an advanced state will require some minor adjustment." He closed his right hand and extended the fingers of his left, palm toward the deck of the ship.

"You must not do this!" I added.

"Are you talking to me?" Malabala said as he turned toward me, his hands still extended. I fervently hoped that his spells and gestures were not purely directional in nature. "Why should I wait, especially for a porter?"

"There is more here than is immediately apparent, O wise magician," I hastily added, doing my best to add a polite deference to my feeling of panicked trepidation.

"I must not call you a porter?" Malabala demanded. "Such effrontery! I warn you, I have not completely forgiven our last encounter!"

"Bzzzz bzzzz bzzzzz!" the Scar remarked as he flitted by.

"Then why does it take you so long to say so?" Malabala replied to my last comment with a frown. "I do wish you would speak more directly. These days, it sometimes seems like my conversations take forever."

I felt the same way. Still, I had to persevere, for the sake of us all. "I feel there are great magics at work here."

"Now, *you* are buzzing?" Malabala looked to the ends of his ragged sleeves. "Oh, dear. I should be more careful where I point these hands."

"Bzzzz bzzzzz bzzzzz," Dirk remarked on his circuit of the deck.

"I should certainly say there are great magics at work here," Malabala retorted. "Am I not a great magician?" He paused to frown at the semitransformed ruffian. "But why do you speak intelligibly again? And why is your voice that of the porter?"

This conversation was once again not proceeding in the most advantageous of directions. How could I broach the answer without again offending the magician? I could but try: "I fear that you yourself are under a spell, O greatest of conjurers."

"Oh, dear, porter." Malabala made an unfortunate gurgle in the back of his throat. "There you go, buzzing again. I must remember, especially when I am angry, that I need to contain my magic." He opened both his hands and wriggled his fingers. "Howsoever, I am sure I can devise a quick corrective spell."

I took a wary step backward. What would happen if he tried to turn me back into a man when I hadn't already been turned into anything else? This magic was a tricky business. But how could I get him to realize things were not exactly as he perceived? Last time I attempted to alter the spell, I had only made matters worse.

Still, a porter is nothing if he is not persistent. Malabala was hearing the right things at incorrect times. I decided, therefore, to make the wrong things sound correct.

"Bzzzz, bzzzzz bzzzz," I ventured.

"The gall!" Malabala cried as he turned again to Dirk. "A magician of my stature under a spell? If I was not already in the midst of turning you into a gnat, that remark alone would be sufficient cause!" He began to wave both hands, fingers extended, in Dirk's general direction, but paused as quickly as he had begun. "Still, I wish I knew how you were doing that trick with the porter's voice."

I swallowed, my throat no doubt dry from its long exposure to sea air. Perhaps this misunderstanding was working to my advantage at the moment, after all. "While this lowlife is certainly totally unwarranted in his questions," I said, beginning where I believed Malabala perceived himself, "even I, though I have a far more limited knowledge of magic than a learned man like you, fear there might be more at work here than is readily apparent."

"Bzzzz bzzzz bzzzzzz," the Scar remarked as he swooped about.

This time, the magician nodded thoughtfully. "There you go, porter, buzzing again. However, what this scarred fellow says has some merit. My spell seems to be bouncing among you. Perhaps that crafty djinni has left some residual spells about that are still affecting some of our company. For one thing, why is everybody always talking with the porter's voice?"

So Malabala would listen to reason, at least after a fashion. I did my best not to become too excited until I had managed to get him to fully understand the situation.

"Pardon my impertinence," I said, "but I fear there is more at work here than even the djinni's spells."

"Bzz bzz bzzzz bzzzzz!" Dirk remarked, flapping his arms

even more quickly as he leapt over ever greater expanses of the deck.

Malabala's face was creased with a frown. "Even as great a magician as myself could be incorrect. Unlikely, but not impossible. There is obviously something wrong with the speech patterns here."

He closed both conjuring hands into fists. "I should forgive the impertinence of some of your suggestions. After all, you are not yourselves. It is my firm belief that the evil Ozzie has enchanted all of you. This sort of thing is a subtle business. Only a great magician like myself would be immune to such an assault!"

But Malabala had turned everything completely about! He must be too close to the spell, and the reality before us all was still beyond the mage's grasp. How could he be immune, hearing everything as it actually occurred, while all the rest of us were cursed to say things before we realized we were saying them? How unlikely.

But, I realized, it was not impossible.

Could this whole ship be cursed? Was I truly buzzing as Malabala believed, and so completely enchanted that I did not realize it? Who could say no? And besides, what was that humming in my ears?

I shook my head to clear it of errant thoughts and noises. I had had enough of idle conjecture. It mattered not who was truly enchanted, so long as the wizard's recent course of action went no further.

"Then you will not proceed with your insect spell?" I asked.

"You are correct," the wizard replied after the Scar had buzzed on by. "There are excessive enchantments here already at work. Perhaps it would be unwise to increase the magic hereabouts. Things can happen when there is too much bewitchment that even a conjurer of my gifts might have trouble coping with."

Malabala turned back to me with what seemed a look of genuine compassion. "The one thing I am sorry about is that you will be cursed with that buzzing for the time being. It will wear off eventually"—he glanced askance at the still sprinting ruffians—"as will these other side effects, so long as I do not complete the spell." He flexed his fingers as he placed his arms back at his sides. "I suppose I would be more seriously concerned if you were more than a porter."

At that, the magician exhaled, and seemed to waver upon the deck, as if a great exhaustion had overcome him. "Still, I am not at my best," he admitted as he again managed to balance himself against the pitch and roll of the ship. "Might someone know where I might obtain some new robes?"

Sinbad the merchant stepped forward at that. "Achmed, if you would take him down to our stores in the hold? After the service he has performed for us, the least we can do is refurbish his outfit."

The lad took the magician by the hand, and led him across the deck to the hold as the merchant turned to regard me.

"Good porter," my elder namesake said, "you have done us a great service here, in a crisis in which I was not enough in evidence."

Now that I thought upon it, what the merchant said was quite true. I wondered if the vicissitudes of a long and largely pampered life had changed this once-great adventurer into the cowering specimen I had witnessed during our recent troubles. Jafar stepped up by the merchant's side and cleared his throat noisily.

"If it is in my power," the other Sinbad quickly added, "I shall see that you get not only your hundred dinars but an appointment upon my household staff."

New events had been appearing with such frequency that I had almost (but not quite) forgotten about the hundred dinars. And now I was offered an appointment to the merchant's household staff. It would be rather nice, all in all, to give up my portering for an accommodating job in a large and stately home. Jafar saw fit to clear his throat a second time.

"Certainly," Sinbad further remarked after a quick glance at his aged majordomo, "my mind has been greatly occupied by things that I have discussed with Jafar."

"The Rukh is not a good sign," Jafar agreed.

The elder Sinbad shook his head rapidly and again launched into conversation before there could be any more throat-clearing upon his servant's part. "For some reason, Jafar believes that we may be due to visit some of the locations and events of my past voyages. I am not sure of his precise reasoning—"

"You have not heard the tales as many times as I," Jafar interrupted his master.

"But I have been the one telling them!" the great and revered Sinbad objected.

"Still, you have not had to hear them," Jafar insisted. "There is a difference. Having listened, at the very least, repeatedly to your adventures, I have had cause to notice certain patterns of events.

I fear I can discern these same patterns about to repeat themselves within our present circumstance."

"Simply because a Rukh pursues us?" Sinbad demanded.

"The storms," was Jafar's simple reply.

"There are always storms at sea," was Sinbad's initial reply. But then he added, "Well, perhaps not so much at this time of year. And there did seem to be something not particularly natural about those storms, didn't there?"

The elderly servant did naught but nod.

"However, for your conjecture to be true," the noble merchant replied, "we should then encounter those whom I met upon my third voyage." He paused, and into his eyes came that dreamy look that men always get when recounting their greatest achievements or relating their deepest desires.

"It was on the third voyage," he began, "when my ship was driven inexorably toward the Isle of the Apes. But the apes were not what we were to fear the most."

His story was interrupted by a cry from the lookout far overhead. We all looked aloft as that crewman announced he had spotted a ship upon the horizon.

"But the apes were what we had to deal with first," the famous Sinbad added when it became apparent that no further information would immediately follow from above. "For they swarmed over the ship with a fearsome screaming and baring of teeth, so that all the crew and passengers fled to the nearby island, only to see the apes sailing our ship away as if they were men!" Sinbad shuddered. "No one knows what happened to that ship full of apes."

"Until now," Jafar added.

I was about to ask the aged servant what he meant when the lookout called down to us again.

"Captain!" he yelled. "On the other ship! There is something amiss with the crew!"

And, after a moment's pause:

"They do not appear to be human!"

◆

Chapter the Twelfth,
in which what has happened on other voyages
is considered in unfortunate perspective.

"This is precisely what I feared," Jafar said with remarkable poise.

The wise Sinbad took a moment to begin speaking again. "I am afraid that the most analytical of all my servants is again correct. It is indeed as if my life is happening all over again." The merchant mopped his brow with the back of an equally moist hand. "You heard, O porter, of my first voyage back when I still had a roof over my head. My second voyage, including my first encounter with a Rukh and my unfortunate decision to eat its egg, I managed to summarize between recent moments of terror. Jafar has impressed upon me now that I should tell certain facts concerning the rest of my voyages."

"All of it, O greatest of tale tellers," Jafar said with a surprisingly severe tone.

"Even those bits I have been known to omit in the past," the honorable Sinbad admitted with a certain shamefaced humility.

"Including the two-headed cyclops," Jafar warned, "O most gifted of truth benders."

"Even that?" The once-wealthy Sinbad stared moodily at the deck. He sighed, and spoke again. "I suppose my adventures have not always been as noble as they seem. But would you want to stage huge dinner parties, with your guests consuming a sultan's ransom in delicacies that you have obtained from about the globe, and then be forced to tell them how you were less than adequately prepared at some time for the danger that was to come? Perhaps, in the interest of a good story, I have stretched the truth ever so slightly."

"Tell all, O master of fabrication," Jafar insisted.

"Not that I have made them more fabulous for my greater glory," the scrupulous Sinbad continued, his face the very mask of misery. "In plain fact, in many cases, I have made them less fantastic, to cut out, shall we say, certain ambiguities."

"The cyclops," Jafar prompted.

"After the apes, of course, there was the ogre." The illustrious Sinbad sighed as if he felt the great weight of the truth. "When the apes took our vessel, we found ourselves trapped upon this tiny island, which held but one great house, and in this house lived a creature who liked to make his meals of men. He began by eating the most corpulent among us." The substantial Sinbad hugged his ample frame. "At the time, I was quite gaunt."

Jafar was once again prompted to make a noise in the back of his throat.

"Yes, the cyclops," Sinbad added with all speed. "When I have spoken of the ogre, I have generally omitted the fact that he had two heads. Things in life are not always so clear-cut as they are in stories. One head was very persuasive, but the other was nothing but a beast. You would agree totally with the first head as the other one ate you. Each head had one eye—a pair of cyclops, you might say—so that, between the heads, the creature had the usual complement of two. Howsoever, he also had two mouths, and one of them needed constantly to be fed."

"Such is the dichotomy of life," Jafar replied wisely.

"The rest of the story is much as I have told it before." He barley glanced at Jafar before he continued. "Well, not precisely. I did devise a plan to kill the giant and escape upon a large raft that I built with my fellows. But when the day came for action, the ogre, who somehow divined our intentions, was so wild and bestial that we but managed to knock him over both of his heads with great lengths of wood, rendering him unconscious." He waved away any objections that his majordomo might have. "Yes, yes, I know I used to say that we blinded him. It somehow sounded much more poetic than clopping him over the head. The truth was that once the giant had fallen, we were all quite afraid to do anything further in case we might wake the creature all over again.

"That being the case, the remaining crew ran quickly for that spot where we had hidden our great raft, and we immediately pushed ourselves out to sea. But before we were twenty feet from shore, the cyclops returned."

The increasingly fastidious Jafar began to clear his throat.

"Certainly," the ever-more-discomfited Sinbad added instantaneously, "I used to speak of a female ogre, more horrible in appearance than the one we had blinded, who led her mate to shore and added to our destruction. It was another plot device, which, like others of its kind, alas, leads to certain holes in the plot. My guests, fortunately, have always been too busy stuffing themselves and imbibing freely to ask me where this female was all the while her partner was wolfing us down one by one; as well as ignoring such pertinent facts as: If I saw the ogre eat us one after another, then what, perchance, did the female eat?

"But that is not the point." The miserable Sinbad pushed back his turban, which had begun to creep forward upon his dampened brow. "In reality there was naught but the male, and he took one great stone after another, and threw them at our retreating raft. Three of those stones hit, and knocked all but three of us from the raft, but those of us who remained managed to row to such a distance that even the giant cyclops's missiles could no longer reach us."

Sinbad paused at last and allowed himself to smile, as if telling the truth had finally released a great weight from his soul.

"And?" Jafar prompted.

The merchant started a bit at the sharpness of that single word. "Well, the part about the giant snake was more or less exactly as I had reported it," Sinbad said.

"Then report it again," Jafar pressed, "O most honored delineator of prevarication, for our young companion should know of the truth before it again repeats itself."

"Very well," the newly unostentatious Sinbad replied. "At last, we three remaining survivors rejoiced, for what we thought were favorable currents had led us to another island, which seemed from our vantage point offshore to be a place of great tranquillity, laden with great copses of trees full of many fruits and coconuts. And we discovered this island just at the proper time, for our raft, which had been made quickly and out of what meager materials were available upon the Isle of the Apes, was falling apart from a combination of the grinding force of waves and the briny, soaking effect of the seawater upon our makeshift ropes, so that by the time we reached the island, our conveyance had become little more than a collection of loosely connected logs."

Sinbad sighed, a certain sign he was warming to the tale. "Once we landed upon the island, we realized, however, that this place was not the salvation that we had wished, for at dusk we spotted a giant snake the length of ten tall men. It was the color of blood, and slithered across the sand toward us with astonishing speed.

We ran to a nearby grove of trees and began to climb, but the great snake was faster, and caught the last of the three of us, and swallowed him in but one extremely noisy gulp."

The loquacious Sinbad continued with the ease of one at last well familiar with his tale. "We noticed the following morning that the snake was no longer in evidence, and surmised that it preferred to sleep while the sun was high in the sky. So we did our best to explore the small island while we were relatively safe. The two of us considered building a new raft, but realized that, with so many members of our crew now dead, and we that remained greatly weakened by days at sea, it would take us far too long to complete it. Still, we took what knives and other utensils we had managed to save between us, and, before the sun could fall too far in the west, felled some good-sized branches to begin our task.

"But the sun did fall, as do indeed all men and other creatures in their time, so we thought to take the precaution of climbing a particularly tall tree, and, nestled in the upper branches, be out of the reach of the fearsome serpent.

"But the great snake did sneak upon us, the sound of its slithering movements lost beneath the rustling of palm leaves in the wind from the sea. It was only through the great good fortune that I had sat slightly higher in the upper branches than my fellow that I escaped and he was swallowed in two great gulps, giving him only enough time to scream horribly before he was de-voured."

Jafar cleared his throat yet again.

"Yes, well," the merchant amended, "I was also able to climb faster than my fellow. I was very spry in my youth. In addition, I have always been well motivated by fear." He looked askance for the first time at his elder servant. "This total honesty tends to disturb the rhythm of my tales, don't you think?"

"It is only through this honesty that we defeat what is yet to come," Jafar said with a reason befitting his years.

At that, the recalcitrant Sinbad once again submitted to his servant's wisdom. "So must every man accept the sum of his years," he said in that kind of singsong that one always hears associated with pontification, but then the cheer returned to his voice as he further said: "But I have not yet finished my story."

"You should do it quickly," a child's voice piped up, and I realized that Achmed once again stood behind me. "The apes are almost upon us."

I looked away from the merchant then—for I had become

enthralled by his tale, honesty or no—and noticed that a subtle change had taken place upon the deck before us. While Dirk and the Scar had slowed down to merely walking about the forecastle and buzzing ever so occasionally, some other crew members seemed to be getting back into the habit of running about and making noises of their own.

"I have left Malabala safely belowdecks," the young servant explained when he realized his master had ceased to speak. "He seemed too tired to even examine a new set of robes, preferring instead to crawl upon the top of one of the bundles and immediately fall asleep."

"Fast asleep?" Sinbad the merchant asked with a frown.

Achmed nodded. "I tried gently to wake him, but he steadfastly refused."

"It is best not to toy with magicians," Sinbad agreed.

"We still have to worry about the apes, O most malingering of speakers," Jafar reminded his master.

Ah, yes, the apes. It occurred to me that we had first heard of their approaching ship some time ago. "They do seem to be taking their own time to get here, do they not?" I asked.

"Who can fathom the thought processes of beasts like that?" the other Sinbad sagely counseled.

"It is no doubt also our great good fortune that apes are not well known for their navigational skills," Achmed added with his usual good cheer.

"But they will arrive eventually. Continue your story quickly, O master." Jafar paused and frowned, obviously concerned that he had spoken such an impossibility. "Well, at least so quickly as you are able."

"Very well," Sinbad rejoined, once again well pleased to be telling his tale. "During the daylight hours, I looked about the island for a hiding place or some other way to escape the snake, but there seemed to be none. I stared out to sea, but could see no ships upon the horizon. I could do nothing but return to building my raft, and hope that I could assemble enough of it before nightfall.

"My hopes vanished as I looked to the position of the sun to the west. Alas, I had taken so long exploring the island and seeking a nonexistent ship to rescue me that all but an hour or two of daylight had fled. There would not be enough time to build any sort of a raft."

"The apes are taking more time than necessary to get here,"

Achmed remarked as the merchant paused to take a breath. And yet I thought I could hear the faint cries of beasts carried by the strong sea winds.

"Quickly, now, O master of verbosity," Jafar urged.

"But, looking upon the branches we had felled so recently"— Sinbad spoke more rapidly, although he did not seem to be decreasing his total number of words—"an idea came to me, and I strapped those pieces of wood about my body using the ropes I had managed to devise—" Jafar cleared his throat again. "Oh," Sinbad added, "I suppose the manner of devising is not important. But I did manage to pad my person with a great amount of wood as nightfall approached. And, as the sun sank below the horizon, the snake came for its evening meal. But, as wide as the snake's mouth was, my wood-laden body was wider, and the snake could not fit its mouth around me."

"Most excellent," Jafar interrupted. "I believe that is all our young friend needs to know."

"But I am only now reaching the best part of the story!" the merchant protested. "Where I am rescued, and—"

"And the captain of the ship," Jafar summarized for his master, "hearing your pitiful story, said he would give you the goods of a merchant who had been lost upon a previous voyage. And he said, these are the goods of Sinbad the Sailor, which astonished you, for you did not recognize the captain—"

"My master never does," Achmed interjected. "He is terrible with faces."

"—but you took these goods and traded them to great advantage," Jafar continued, "returning to Baghdad an even richer man than you had been before."

"Well, yes," Sinbad protested, "that is the essence of it, but what about the rhythm, the majesty of my telling—"

The merchant was interrupted by a great scream upon the part of the crew.

"Apparently the apes have arrived," Achmed remarked as he darted quickly toward the rail. "And it appears," he called back, "that they wish to board us!"

Jafar was not at all surprised.

"It begins again," he said with finality.

Chapter the Thirteenth,
in which there occur some unflattering comparisons concerning apes and men.

I pushed my way through the ever-more-panicked crew until I could see what was happening beyond the railing. There was a vessel much the same size as ours, with fully fifty creatures milling about upon the deck. But the crew of this other ship, though they wore the same robes and leggings as the crew about me, showed by their bent, shuffling gait, and their hirsute faces and heads, that they were not human in the least. Though dressed as men, this was a crew of wild apes, and, from the proximity of their ship and the shouted command of the well-dressed ape who must serve as their captain, it did indeed appear they were about to board us.

"We are doomed!" a crew member shouted close by my ear.

"Ook, oook ook!" an ape called from the other craft.

The situation certainly did seem to be severe. Still, there was something about this other craft that appeared somehow disturbingly familiar. Whatever it might be, it kept hope alive within me.

"Perhaps," I stated, "there is some way we might reason with these creatures."

"You have never met wild apes before," was the elder Sinbad's miserable reply.

"That may be an advantage," Achmed added cheerily.

The boy's remark surprised me. Did the youth also notice something about this other craft?

"All is lost!" another crewman yelled from farther up the deck.

"Scree scree hoo!" one of the distant apes seemed to call in return.

"We might as well throw ourselves overboard," a particularly vociferous crewman wailed, "and subject ourselves to the mercies of the open sea!"

"Hoo scree gibber ook ook ook scree scree scree hoo hoo ook!" wafted over from the other craft.

I realized then that, while I had been looking for some small similarity between what occurred on these two vessels, the resemblance was instead very great indeed. I took one more look at the crewmen running and screaming around me, then returned and studied the frenzied movements and shrieks of the nearby apes. Despite the fact that one ship was filled with humanity and the other with beasts, both crews appeared to be acting in an almost identical fashion.

I thought about those stories I had heard concerning the race of apes, and how, in their movements, they sometimes mimicked the race of men. But the actions of these beasts seemed to go beyond mere imitation. In point of fact, one particular collective action seemed almost to entirely rule out the possibility of imitation, for exactly as our crewmen did everything in their power not to look at the approaching ship, so did the vast mass of the apes only look over upon our vessel in the most furtive of fashions. Perhaps the apes were more than mere ravaging beasts. Perchance, as this new evidence showed, they were every bit as frightened as was our own crew.

The ships grew ever closer. Our crew screamed. Theirs ooked and gibbered. Perhaps, I thought, these other creatures were not quite as frightened as those immediately about me. Certainly, enough of the apes seemed to be obeying their captain's orders so that they would eventually run their ship against ours and then board us. Our captain, in the meantime, was screaming his own orders in an attempt to repel those boarders, but absolutely no one on this ship save myself appeared to be listening.

A voice even more used to command than the captain's roared above the hollering throng:

"What exactly is going on up here? How can you expect me to get any rest at all with such a commotion! And to whosoever is the perpetrator of this cacophony, I warn you, too, that it is extremely unwise to disturb a sleeping magician."

The crew about me quieted somewhat at the threat. I turned to see Malabala once more among us. He did appear much more the professional magician in the deep amber robes that Achmed had provided him. He also appeared even more perturbed than I had seen him before.

"We are about to be boarded by a crew of wild apes!" I called to him over the reduced caterwauling.

Malabala frowned. "Eh? Speak up. I cannot hear you over all this noise!"

His sleep, then, had not affected the curse he was under.

Unless, I considered, the magician was correct, and it was all the rest of us who labored under the djinni's spell. Whatever the truth was mattered not, though, unless I could somehow inform the wizard as to the severity of our predicament!

The crew screamed with renewed vigor as our craft shook. The other ship must have collided with our own.

The first of the apes vaulted onto the deck before me.

"You must devise a spell to save us!" I called to the magician as I turned to face this first boarder.

"Apes?" the magician called back to me. "Yes, I can see they are apes. I may be old, but I am far from being blind!"

Malabala had, of course, not heard my most recent statement. But if the wizard spoke further, I did not hear him in turn. All my attention was focused on this thing before me.

The creature was a full head shorter than I, but compensated by being twice as broad in the shoulder as myself. Its powerful arms hung so far below the sleeves of its robes that its knuckles almost scraped the rough boards of the deck. It regarded me with two small, deep black eyes, set far apart in its face, a face that actually seemed to hold a remarkable intelligence, at least until that moment when the creature opened its mouth to show two sets of razor-sharp teeth.

So I should have to fight for my life. I realized then that I held no weapon or other means of protecting myself save for my wits.

The ape lifted its great arms to either side of its massive shoulders. "Scree!" it demanded. "Scree scree!"

How was I to reply? Perhaps, I thought, there had indeed been intelligence within those bestial eyes. Perhaps this creature would respond to reason, after all.

"I most humbly beg your pardon," I began quickly, "but we have not been formally introdu—"

"Scree!" The ape beat upon its chest. "Ook ook scree!"

I realized then that the ape and I were quite possibly having a fundamental difference in communication. At the very least, beating upon one's chest did not seem to me to be an automatic sign of friendship and understanding.

"Stand aside, porter!" Malabala called from behind me. "I shall devise a spell to neutralize these beasts!"

From my position near the rail, I could see another dozen pairs of hirsute arms climbing the side of the ship with alarming ease. "Please do so quickly, O great magician," I shouted over my shoulder, "for there are dozens more of the creatures clambering up the sides."

"A spell?" the magician shouted back. "Why do you call back what I have only barely said? Has the appearance of these apes addled your brain?"

The first ape advanced upon me, and I decided that an addled brain was the least of my worries. But I feared that my further communication problems with the wizard might result in that sort of delay by which my brain might cease to function forever.

A pair of hairy hands reached for my neck. The creature was so close that I could smell its fetid breath.

"Ook!" it demanded. "Ook ook!"

What could I do? The creature did not appear to be prepared to listen to human speech. And yet, in its repetitions of sounds, it did express, in its own strange way, a desire to communicate.

A porter is always very adaptable to the needs of his employers, for their small payments mean the difference between a full belly and starvation. Perhaps, I thought, I needed to be as adaptable to the present circumstance.

"Ook," I replied.

The ape's powerful hands paused but inches from my throat. "Scree?" it inquired.

So I was still alive. In some way, then, I had indeed begun to communicate with this beast. Realizing I had little to lose but the threat of imminent strangulation, I tried again.

"Scree," I said with authority.

"Scree?" it replied, then turned to the others of its kind who even now were climbing over the railing. "Scree!" the first ape announced. "Scree ook!"

"I seem to have established some sort of rapport with these creatures," I said to those around me.

"We can plainly see that there are other apes on board!" Malabala replied. "One of you others should get this poor demented porter out of the way before he harms himself."

But I would not so easily be pushed from the center of this drama. I thought about the way in which the apes had acted on board their own ship, and how they had seemed almost as frightened as the men about me. I suspected now that perhaps the apes meant us no harm, but had instead been thrown in our direction by that very Destiny that my elder namesake was so often prone to mention. Perhaps we might even devise some way in which ape and man could work together to solve Sinbad's riddle.

But how could I speak with them so that they might understand? I had heard this ape before me utter two distinctly different sounds, each of which seemed to have a separate meaning. Perhaps, I thought, things would become clearer if I said the two of them together.

"Ook scree," I remarked to the ape.

"Ook scree?" the ape replied in astonishment. He turned to his fellows in a greatly agitated state. "Ook scree!"

"Ook scree!" they all chorused with equal excitement. "Ook scree!" All the apes on board turned back to me in great anticipation.

This most recent event caused me to pause. I realized now that the real problem was how I might speak with them so that I would be the one to gain understanding. Perhaps, I thought, I could achieve even more positive results if I turned the two sounds around.

"Scree ook," I further spoke.

"Scree ook?" the first ape cried, the excitement in its voice replaced by a great anguish.

"Scree ook?" the other apes added in a collective wail. "Scree ook?"

Whatever I had said, the apes seemed no longer content to merely watch me, but instead approached me with their clawed hands outstretched and a murderous intent in their eyes.

What had I said to upset them so? There was no way for me to know. More importantly, however, was what I might say next. From the angry looks upon the apes' faces, I realized I must say it hurriedly:

"Scree ook ook scree ook ook!"

The apes all paused and regarded me with open mouths.

"Ook?" the lead ape said to its fellows in great astonishment. "Scree ook ook scree ook ook! Hoo hoo ook gibber?"

At that, the apes made a sound that sounded disturbingly like laughter.

As puzzling as this last reaction was, I decided it was better than being pummeled into oblivion by a large collection of hairy arms. I decided to try again:

"Gibber. Hoo hoo ook ook. Scree scree."

The apes were screaming with laughter now, and slapping their hands against each other. The more complex the group of sounds I made, the more the apes appeared to enjoy it.

"Perhaps I underestimated your abilities," Malabala said at my side.

"Thank you, O great magician," I said most humbly.

"Ah," the mage replied with an understanding smile. "Speechless at the approval of as great a man as myself? Believe me, porter, you are not the first. Still, you do not need to address me in the tongue of the apes, although I assure you that I understand that language well enough."

He knew the language of the apes? The hope that I had thought extinguished within my breast once again showed the faintest of sparks. What could I do but beg for an explanation:

"Oh, tell me of this language, O great magician!"

"It was simplicity itself," said Malabala with that tone of humility only employed by those who believe themselves anything but humble. "I replaced the banishment spell that I had been preparing with one that would facilitate my understanding of their speech."

I supposed that this self-congratulation was only what one should expect from someone of Malabala's exalted station. However, it was not bringing me any closer to a true understanding of my predicament, especially considering that the so-recently-entertained apes now again appeared to be turning restive. There was naught for me to do, then, but to proceed in my dialogue with the wizard from simple begging to outright pleading.

"Please, O greatest of wizards!" I cried with perhaps not the calmest of voices. "Could you but give me some examples of the exact meanings of some of the exchanges I have had with the apes?"

"But I have already begun to tell you of the language!" Malabala cried in exasperation. "I swear, O porter, you seem to communicate with the apes in a far better manner than you do with me." He sighed, and continued in a much calmer tone. "Still, as the wise man says, you moved forward upon the proper extremity with your very first statement, complimenting them upon their fine, shiny coats."

I had done that? How clever of me. I was winning a game I did not even understand.

"I am unsure of some of the things you have said, however," the wizard further related. "Especially that next bit. Apes do not appreciate falsehoods. They have very strong arms and sharp teeth, which they do not hesitate to use at the slightest provocation."

Upon further reflection, I decided that perhaps the game I played was too dangerous. I waited in fearsome anticipation of the wizard informing me as to exactly what error I had committed.

"Still, I admired your courage," the wizard reflected, "when you declared a blood duel against their finest warrior."

Oh, dear. A simple ook and scree could convey a blood duel? This didn't sound like a game at all.

"Of course," Malabala discoursed agreeably, "all duels were forgotten with what you said next. What a bold and daring way to save the rest of the passengers and crew! And may I be the first to congratulate you on your impending marriage to their queen."

Marriage to their queen? Cursed be the moment I first attempted an ook with my teeth and tongue! The apes began to advance upon me once again, not, I discerned now, to tear me limb from limb, but to join me in eternal bondage to one of their own.

There seemed to be a great variety of information conveyed by this simplest of languages, threatening a blood duel at one moment and proposing matrimony at another. Could these various ooks and gibbers have an assortment of meanings? I considered those other human languages I had heard during my service as a porter in the great city of Baghdad, and how inflection and tone could change the very definition of the words used. Perhaps intonation had something to do with meaning among the apes as well. Perhaps it was the pleasant tone I had been using that had gotten me into this marriage trouble.

I therefore attempted to scream my next statement in as angry a voice as I could manage. "Ook gibber gibber scree ook ook ook!"

The apes thought the statement was even more hilarious than my last.

"An interesting ploy, porter," Malabala remarked with admiration. "It was a noble attempt, but doomed to failure. Anything you say now will be treated as no more than a joke. Their queen has been seeking a new mate for a very long time. I doubt anyway that apes care that greatly who cleans their sanitary facilities."

One ape used his elbow to poke another in the rib cage. "Ook gibber ook scree," he said shyly.

"Scree scree scree!" the other replied with great enjoyment.

"Ook scree gibber gibber!" a third chimed in merrily.

This exchange before me brought a night chill to my heart. Their actions reminded me of nothing so much as a group of bored porters exchanging ribald jokes upon a slow evening. And I felt in this case the witticisms must be at my expense.

"The apes are having a conversation of some merit." Malabala turned away from me as he addressed the rest of the human crew. "The porter, of course, has already perceived a general sense of their discourse. For the rest of you, however, I will give a rough translation. Of course, it has do to with the wedding." He paused for a moment as the apes continued, the magician no doubt silently rephrasing the ape vernacular into terms humans could comprehend. "Something about a beheading if the porter is unable to perform. Apparently there is quite a ritual involved." He smiled warmly at me. "But with your understanding of the ape tongue, I am sure you will be able to handle any difficulty."

When I considered it at a later time, I believed it was that mention of beheading that caused my resolve to snap. I had trusted my luck far beyond the ability of my wits. And didn't Malabala realize that he was the one who failed to comprehend?

"I don't understand anything at all!" I screamed in the magician's ear.

Malabala regarded me with a mixture of pity and continued noncomprehension. "Why do you gibber at me? It's a shame that your human speech has none of the subtlety of your dialogue with the apes."

But my endless quest for understanding was momentarily forgotten when, at that intent, the apes seemed to break into what I could only describe as a simian version of poetic song, delivered in a choral style:

"*Ook ook gibber scree,*
Gibber scree gibber scree,
Hoo hoo ook, ook hoo,
Gibber scree gibber scree!"

"Ook!" the first ape called to me when he and his fellows were done. "Ook scree!"

With that, the magician's face took on a look of great astonishment. "Now they are singing? How talented are these creatures! It is a little ditty about the wedding night, laced as these ditties are with the usual hyperbole. That is, if apes are capable of hyperbole." He paused to shake his head in amazement. "I would think that that particular act would be impossible. Perhaps if you had a tail." And then another pause. "Well, perchance apes have more stamina than humans. I tell you, porter, with every passing moment, I have more respect for your courage."

I could think of nothing else to say, at least to the magician. Whatever I tried to communicate, he would only hear that last thing I had said some time ago, whatever that was. Unless he heard my words coming from the tongues of apes and their words pouring forth from mine. How could I overcome a curse that I didn't even understand?

Obviously, Malabala was to be of no help at all. I would have to utilize whatever wits I still had about me to extricate myself from this predicament. There was but one comfort to this situation; I could imagine no way that it could get any worse.

I decided to continue talking ape:

"Ook! Ook ook ook ook!"

"The apes believe that suggestion is hilarious as well," Malabala translated through the simian laughter, "although they do admit your recommendation for the use of bananas in human sacrifice has some merit."

Well, that hadn't made the situation any more palatable; although, as I thought on it, I realized Malabala was probably translating something I had actually said earlier. This whole process made my head hurt.

Whatever the solution, I realized it couldn't be accomplished on ooks alone. I needed to mix my sounds more judiciously.

"Scree," I began in a level tone. "Ook scree gibber hoo."

Malabala translated one of the ape's responses, either to what I had just said or to something from earlier in this conversation. "No, the apes cannot take the entire crew to witness the wedding. However, they feel it was very thoughtful of you to ask."

I suppose there was some consolation in knowing that, while I was to be sacrificed to inhuman lust, at least I had spared all my traveling mates from any sort of similar bestial fate. Howsoever, before I could take solace in my martyrdom, the lead ape ambled up to my traveling companions and pointed to Achmed, Jafar, and the merchant Sinbad with a remarkably human gesture.

"Ook?" the ape inquired.

"Ook," I replied, since further words failed me.

Malabala further interpreted. "The apes have answered that, seeing such graciousness in a lowly human, can they do otherwise than return the politeness? Therefore, they will allow you to choose a few others to accompany the wedding party."

Then that was the answer I had just given the ape. I wondered what that answer was.

The first ape turned to examine the wizard. "Scree?" the ape queried.

"Scree," I answered, since something of the sort was expected of me.

"Yes," Malabala continued, "your three companions may accompany you."

I felt terrible. Through my thoughtless remark, I had doomed Achmed, Jafar, and the other Sinbad to share my fate. If not for them, I wouldn't—well, now that I thought upon it, if I had never met them, I wouldn't be here at this moment. Still, while it may have been fully justifiable, I did not consider it charitable to force anyone into my situation.

Achmed looked at me and shrugged. "It is thusly that the macaroon falls apart."

But the first ape had moved onward, and now stood before Dirk, the Scar, and the palanquin that hid the mysterious Fatima. And now, presumably, the ape would ask me whether or not I would like to bring these three along as well. Fatima! My heart ached to think that not only would I be married to a gorilla but that I should never see my Fatima again. Not, of course, that I had seen the entirety of her thus far, but I cherished the possibilities inherent in that hand and that laugh. Still, there was no way I could subject anyone as fair and delicate as the woman in that box to the horrors of a ship full of apes. And, to be truly telling the truth, I would not miss the lost companionship of Dirk and the Scar.

So this time I would have to answer the ape in the negative. I waited for his word; what was it to be, an ook or a scree? Nonetheless, I wished I were better informed pertaining to what answer I had given concerning the magician.

The ape pointed at the two men and the litter.

"Gibber?" he requested.

Gibber? What should I say to that? I knew that two ooks equaled yes, and had no information yet on the result of two screes. It did not help that both Dirk and the Scar glared ominously in my direction as I attempted to make my decision. Nevertheless, two of anything might mean yes in the ape tongue. I therefore decided I should venture something entirely different.

"Hoo hoo," I replied.

"Now the ape and the porter have decided to bring along the silly old fellow in the bright robe." Malabala paused. "Is that ape referring to me?"

I experienced great relief. Apparently, two of anything did indicate the affirmative. I may have doomed Achmed, Jafar, the merchant Sinbad, and Malabala, but at least my beloved Fatima would be safe. The ape waved at the captain and the rest of the crew.

"Ook?" the creature asked again.

Thus we had returned to the first question, one to which I knew the answer. It occurred to me that, knowing what I was saying for the first time since the apes had arrived, perhaps I could undo all that I had done. For if I were to answer even this sweeping question in the affirmative, mayhaps the apes would decide I had again asked for too much, and would thus leave everybody save me behind.

"Ook!" I responded with great force.

"They have decided to bring the two big men and the lady in the box as well," Malabala commented in the driest of tones.

"Ook ook!" the first ape commanded, and, at his order, another two dozen apes swarmed on board the craft.

"Ook?" I replied, more from total bewilderment than any desire to communicate.

"Some of us are indeed fortunate that the porter decided to leave the captain and crew behind," were Malabala's final words before he was borne aloft by a brace of apes.

I had? But I said ook. I decided that there was no doubt about it. Language was indeed a tricky thing.

I had no time for further thoughts, for I was picked up in turn and carried upon the shoulders of half a dozen apes.

I had a premonition that I was about to attend a wedding.

♦

Chapter the Fourteenth,
in which our porter's troubles cease to add,
but begin to multiply.

I had also reached another of what were becoming all-too-frequent revelations.

This situation with Malabala and the apes was, to say the very least, unique in my experience. Howsoever, it had taught me an important lesson. Before I met the merchant Sinbad—could that only be a day ago?—I had thought that the worst that might happen to a man was to be helpless before the forces of chaos; to be lost to the overwhelming might of nature, or the supernatural, so that one's fate was totally beyond one's control.

Only now did I recognize how wrong I had been. There was indeed something worse, far worse, than having no conception of what was to happen next. And that was to have that same conception of what would happen next, but only after it actually happened.

This was the very nature of Malabala's translations, which seemed, in keeping with his curse, interpretations of not the most recent thing spoken, but the thing before that. And that curse the wizard suffered appeared sophisticated in the extreme, for it seemed to delay both ape and human speech so that the mage could keep them completely separate, and so confuse me to an even greater extent. Before, I had feared the djinni's magic. Now, I admitted grudgingly, I admired it as well.

So were my thoughts as I was carried bodily by the apes away from my sailing vessel and onto the simians' craft. There were no doubts for my future. I had no future worth considering so long as the anthropoids' plans for me continued on their present course; and, as I took a final glimpse at the ship we had so recently vacated, I saw the captain and crew quickly man the oars and row away from us as rapidly as they could, so I could expect no help from that quarter, either. Beyond that, I was in the hands of that Destiny that my elder namesake was so fond of.

It was the hands of the apes, however, that lowered me down upon the deck of the second ship. The others quickly followed, so that I was soon joined by my three original traveling companions, as well as the magician, and the two ruffians and their palanquin. From the cries I had heard behind me when I was first hoisted aloft, I imagine Dirk and the Scar at first attempted some resistance. They were soon overwhelmed like the rest of us, however, for there seemed to be a never-ending supply of apes that overran the deck. So did the two join us now; disheveled, disgruntled, but essentially unharmed.

"Ook," the first ape addressed the hairy fellow dressed in a captain's garb. "Gibber ook!"

"Ook?" the simian captain asked as he regarded me with some amusement. "Gibber gibber scree!"

The anthropoid crew found this all highly amusing. But the captain quickly cut short their mirth, barking a series of what could only be commands.

"Even the captain, it appears, greatly admires our porter's courage," Malabala once again interpreted. "The queen of the apes is well known for her formidable nature."

So I was to be married not only to an ape but to a formidable ape. The wise men have often spoken of the peace that descends upon he who is about to die. I have already mentioned that so much had threatened my welfare in these past few hours that I, through either an increased familiarity with danger or being in a perpetual state of total shock, no longer immediately fell into an attitude of total fear.

The more I thought on this marriage, however, the more I realized it was far more than mere death. The queen of the apes might be able to keep me alive for days, weeks, even months. And to what ends?

I again became afraid.

"Help me, O wizard," I called to Malabala.

"Scree! Scree gibber!" the captain shouted to his crew.

"Why do you scream?" Malabala asked me with a tone of genuine curiosity. I had screamed? Perhaps I had, in the recent past, say, when I was overwhelmed by apes. Screaming was the sort of thing that was becoming a commonplace in my existence.

Jafar stepped forward and bowed. "My master wishes you to know that you have our condolences."

The merchant pushed the majordomo aside. "In these matters, I must speak for myself." His large hands grabbed at his stomach, so that he wrung large quantities of fat as he spoke. "I am afraid I can do little for you in this circumstance, even upon those promises which I have already made. It is certainly a shame about those hundred dinars. Rest assured that, once I do obtain the money, it will be used to construct a suitably tasteful monument to your sacrifice."

I was greatly affected by this admission. "I would like to thank all of you," I said slowly, careful not to become overwhelmed by my emotion. "In these few short hours, my life has been changed and enriched." On a certain level, I genuinely meant these words. Still, it was a shame about those hundred dinars.

"Help?" Malabala interrupted. "How do you need help?"

At last, the magician had managed to hear my words. I decided to answer him swiftly, before I had any further distractions. "What gift I had for understanding these apes seems to have fled me."

"Wedding nerves, no doubt," Achmed commented.

"You need help to be thanked?" Malabala asked in some confusion.

"No!" I shook my head with a substantial energy. "I need you to translate!"

"Why has your ability fled?" Malabala asked at last. "Of course, I am constantly amazed that someone as simple as you, who imagines that as great a magician as I could possibly be under a spell, should have such an ability at all. Still, I have heard stories of simpletons with huge memories or a great facility for numbers. This is no doubt the case here. At least the fates will be served, for in marrying an ape you shall seek your own level."

"O great wizard, take heed!" was my response, for I was far beyond taking offense at such a powerful yet confused mage. "We need your aid if we are to survive."

"Translate?" Malabala's eyebrows rose in comprehension. "Most certainly. Why did you not say so?"

The wizard finally understood, and barely in time, for the captain of the apes strode between us again.

"Ook! Gree ook!"

"They will give you a few moments to prepare yourself for the queen," Malabala interpreted.

The door to the space belowdecks swung open and slammed against the deck.

"Scree scree ook!" the captain commanded.

"Are you prepared to meet your bride?" was Malabala's delayed explanation.

But I had turned upon hearing the loud noise, and saw a sight I would not be prepared for were I to live to be a hundred times a hundred. Thought after thought raced through my head, most of them futile visions of escape. But my more rational mind told me the following:

Among the race of men, the male tends to be larger than the female. This does not hold true, though, of all of the species, and, if the queen was at all typical, it seemed to be anything but the case among this variety of ape.

She strode across the deck, surrounded by an honor guard of ten male apes, all of whom appeared to be far smaller than she. But as to her true size I could do naught but conjecture; and that conjecture was not of the most positive nature.

Perchance it was the many white veils that covered the majority of her form and cloaked her face; the manner in which they blew in the sea wind made the creature beneath seem more the size of a tent than a single being. Or perhaps it was the occasional glimpse I received of arm or leg as her tent flaps—rather, her dress—blew away from her body. If the captain and the other apes about me had biceps twice the size of those of men, the appendages that I saw under that gown resembled biceps not at all, but rather begged comparison to tree trunks covered with hair.

"Yes," Malabala said as he placed a reassuring hand upon my shoulder. "I shall do what I can for you." He spoke as if he had actually heard the last thing I said to him. Perhaps, I realized, I had screamed again.

"Ook scree ook!" the captain remarked.

"Presenting the queen," said Malabala.

I felt heavy ape arms upon my shoulders, forcing me to my knees.

"Ook scree ook gree greech hoo hoo ook!"

"Kneel!" was Malabala's somewhat redundant translation.

"Ook gibber," the captain continued. He functioned, apparently, as the official spokesman, or—more properly—spokesape, for the group.

"You will not be married immediately." The ape was speaking rapidly enough that I could make some sense of the proceedings even with Malabala's delay. "There are rituals that must be observed."

I did not like the sound of that word—rituals. But we were not to be married at once? I was uncertain whether to be relieved or filled with fear. At one point, I believe I had been looking for a quick end at the very least, not to mention something with a minimum of pain. Now my future was far less explicit.

"Gibber ook gibber," the captain further explained.

"First, there will be the courtship."

Courtship? That did not sound at all quick, and it had the potential to be anything but painless.

"Ook gibber ook," the captain stated more forcefully.

"Most suitors die during the courtship. It saves immensely on wedding expenses."

Well, maybe the end would be more speedy than I had thought. Why didn't that make me any happier? I glanced at the immense queen. I obviously had a certain ambivalence toward this whole event.

"Gibber gibber ook ook."

"If they do not meet her standards"—Malabala's voice echoed the force of the captain's past remark—"she kills them quickly."

Did she now? Perchance I had been premature in my acquiescence, and there were some choices open to me in this matter. Perhaps it would be better to die as a man than to live as an ape suitor.

I looked up from where I knelt, and saw that the great queen had stopped but a few paces before me. At this distance, I could see that the veils on her face were somewhat translucent, and, if I looked closely, I could see the outlines of her fangs, fully as long as the fingers on the hands of the tallest man. My eyes wandered down to where her two great hands peeked out from beneath the sleeves of her gown. Her fists were easily the equal of my head. One of her ape servants held aloft a silver tray for her approval. I could see that, atop that polished metal, there crawled more than a dozen fat, white grubs. She nodded politely to her servant as she swept the grubs from the tray with but a single movement of her tremendous paw and popped the lot of them into her mouth. She quickly swallowed and, after a moment of picking grub bits from between her teeth with a mud-encrusted thumbnail, belched with great satisfaction.

Yes, I decided, it would be far better to die as a man than live as an ape suitor.

"Ook ook gibber scree," the ape captain announced.

"You may look up and regard your bride-to-be."

I was taken aback by the wizard's most recent translation. I had already looked up in the face of this monster queen without waiting to be told, at least by a human tongue. Could there be some truth to Malabala's contention that I did understand the ape language? Perhaps, though, it was more likely that I merely understood the severity of my present situation.

It was in that instant that the queen's gaze locked with mine, and I felt a jolt upon that contact unlike anything I had ever experienced. With my insufficient command of language, I might only describe it as an unreasoning terror leavened by moments of screaming, mindless apprehension and stark, naked fear, but such a paltry depiction would do little to indicate the depth of my feeling.

The queen's fangs twisted behind her veil into what might have been a smile.

"Ook," she remarked.

"Allow the queen to judge you," Malabala remarked to something said some time ago.

"Ook greech sree hoo," the captain further elucidated.

"She likes the spirit of this puny man-thing." Was Malabala actually translating for the queen? "For now he may live."

So she spared me because I had looked her in the eye. I was taken aback in that instant by the power of fate. If I had not looked up a moment before, might I already have been removed from this life of misery? How ironic is the hand of Destiny! Unless I was being held for some higher purpose, and was not meant to die until that purpose had been fulfilled. Perhaps it was not my destiny to be torn apart by those lustful ape claws, or crushed by tons of gorilla flesh.

Hope rose within me at this thought. Over and over again, I had been shown that I had met the merchant and his party to be a part of a greater adventure. How could I come to doubt it again? Well, when one looks into the eyes of a giant gorilla who is about to become one's bride, one can surely doubt a great many things. But I had to look beyond the immediate dangers.

A life as a porter had given me certain gifts, and I should look positively upon them. The streets of Baghdad had made me cunning, the porting of goods had made me strong, the long periods between meals had made me wiry. Surely, one of those attributes would help me to prevail.

"Ook gibber gibber," the captain persevered.

"First there is the exchange of song," the wizard explained.

A song, then? I had been good at songs, which I had invented constantly to relieve my days of endless labor. Perhaps I had been too good. I remembered when I had paused to rest outside Sinbad the merchant's palatial home, and had been moved to sing. There was no escaping it; it was a song that had gotten me into this mess in the first place.

And now I had to sing to this giant female.

Even for one as poetic as myself, this would be a challenge. Perhaps if I catalogued her best attributes. However, looking into that bestial face, such values as best and worst didn't seem to apply. I decided to sing about everything; everything, that is, that I might see poking through her yards and yards of veil.

The captain gave me a swift nudge with his very sharp elbow. Apparently, the suitor was the one who was supposed to begin.

I had but a single resolve in this matter: Speaking in the language of the apes had given me enough trouble. I would not go so far as to attempt a song in the simian tongue.

So it was that I began, in a voice perhaps not so strong as I have sometimes found within my capability:

> "Oh, your hair is brown,
> And your—uh—pelt is brown,
> But it certainly is shiny.
> And your hands are brown,
> And your eyes are black,
> And your fingernails are very grubby."

It was perhaps not among the best of my songs, but I was under an undue amount of pressure.

"Scree," the captain remarked authoritatively. Apparently, I had passed that test.

"You begin," Malabala explained.

So it was that I felt a rough hand grab my chin, and felt my head jerked roughly so that I was gazing directly into the eyes of my betrothed, a position from which I instinctively understood I would not stray if I valued my continued existence. So it was that I listened to my bride's vocal contribution, a song that went on for quite some time, although all the verses sounded more or less like this:

> "Okk okk gree gree ook
> Gree ook scree ook gree
> Ook okk gree okk ook
> Hoo hoo scree scree scree!"

"Now our beloved queen shall grace us with her vision," was the first thing Malabala said, no doubt the words of the captain rather than the queen. But the song went on at such great length and with such a prodigious number of verses that even the wizard's curse could not contain them all, and so he translated while she still sang:

"She says she'll stay with this puny human despite the fact that he has less hair than an ape child," the wizard related. "Then she goes on in great detail to describe his pallid skin. The rhyme scheme and allusions to his coloring are quite complex, but I can summarize by citing her numerous unflattering comparisons between the porter and night slugs."

At last, she seemed to have completed her recitation. With that, the apes about us shouted in unison, a sound that managed to be both frightening in the extreme and somehow exhilarating at the same moment, a heartfelt reaction by the entire crew to the superiority of the queen's verse. Even without a true understanding of their language, even I could appreciate that she was an obvious master of the form.

"Ook ook gibber ook!" the captain again spoke.

"That last verse has some quite effective metaphors," Malabala continued, at last examining the end of the queen's song. "You may be pallid, but so are bananas."

Bananas? I felt as though my heart wished to stop beating in my breast. I knew what I was reminded of when I thought of bananas. Still, perhaps the wizard was wrong in his choice of fruit, or I was wrong in my choice of metaphor, and the queen was only discussing food.

"Gibber gibber ook!" the captain further announced.

"The pallid male has passed the first test!" Malabala translated with authority.

At that, Sinbad and his servants crowded about me.

"We never had any doubt," the merchant assured me with great cheer.

"I am sure we will triumph and my master will be saved," Achmed remarked. "Only the particulars are left up to you."

"That is," Jafar added dourly, "if we ever get away from these apes."

But both Achmed and the merchant recoiled as another ape stepped between us, this one carrying another silver platter. This new plate was piled high with a mass of wriggling white slugs too numerous to count, if one actually could contain the contents of one's stomach long enough to attempt such an exercise. It became even more difficult to contain my own stomach as this platter was thrust beneath my nose. I could not help what happened next, for human thought gave way to brute reaction on my part. I retched as quietly as possible and pushed the plate away.

The platter ended up beneath the queen's nose. She tilted it upward with but one of her great fingers. The massive pile of slugs went rolling into her open maw.

"Ook gibber ook!" the captain declared.

"The second test begins!" Malabala informed me after the event.

"Scree scree okk ook!" the captain further announced.

"The pallid human has passed the second test!" Malabala added cheerfully.

I noticed then that the queen of the apes was once again regarding me, but in a different way from before. In truth, she looked at me with what, in a human female, I might almost take for a gaze of tenderness.

I found this latest development more disquieting than anything that had gone before.

"Ook," she said.

"Ook?" I replied, afraid of what this might mean.

"Prepare yourself for the third and final test!" Malabala interpreted the last thing the captain had said.

"Greech okk hoo hoo," the captain commanded.

"The queen states that if the puny human should show her his banana," Malabala further interpreted, "she will be glad to display her casaba melons."

"You again have our condolences," Achmed conveyed to me in a low tone.

The sound that came out of me then was far less scream and more low, misery-filled moan. Whatever might have been its true nature, it led to a further statement from the magician.

"Our brave porter has replied," Malabala translated for the others in our party, "that he will be proud to display his banana whenever necessary."

I had? I resolved never, ever to say ook again.

"Ook gibber ook!" the captain demanded.

"The third test takes place in the queen's bedchamber," was the wizard's interpretation.

I believe my true scream came immediately thereafter.

"Gibber scree scree!"

"The suitor must ask the queen properly for her dalliance."

So not only would I have to perform this act which I could imagine in far too much clarity, but I had to ask for it as well?

I turned to look at the other humans. Whatever would happen to these others if I refused to go any further? I lost no admiration for Dirk or the Scar; if they were to fall to the apes I would not be the sorrier. The loyal Jafar, and even the merchant Sinbad, had both led long and full lives, and would soon be reaching the end of their days, anyway. Achmed, well, the lad was young, but he was clever, and, if any of us were to survive, it would surely be he. The magician, I was sure, could take care of himself, and might be able to save us all if there were any way to truly communicate with him.

That left only one of us completely at the ape's mercy, but that one was the most important to me of all: the beauteous Fatima. What trepidations she must be suffering within her enclosure, so close to the constant, bestial threat of these creatures!

I should have to go through with this third trial, then, for the sake of my beloved. I wondered if she would ever realize the true depth of my sacrifice.

The apes about me seemed to grow increasingly restless. There was no way I could further delay my decision. I therefore asked: "Could you deliver the message for me, O magician?"

"There is no need to scream at me," Malabala chided. "I am championing your cause in this matter, at least when it comes to dealing with apes."

"I should like to ask the queen for the pleasure of her—company," I said in anticipation of the wizard's eventual translation.

"Ook ook ook!" the captain demanded.

"The queen wishes to know details," was Malabala's interpretation.

This was very difficult for me to pursue. How could I give the queen details that I did not even wish to consider?

At last I panicked. Perhaps there was some way I actually could convince Malabala to save us all. Truly, I had failed before, but perchance I had not tried my persuasions with enough vigor. Yes, that was it. More vigor. Outright pleading and groveling was the only answer.

I fell to my knees before the mage. "Please, Malabala, is there no way you can save us?"

"Very well, I will be glad to translate your request for some time with the queen," Malabala said graciously.

"Ook," the queen remarked coquettishly.

"Ook ook scree ook," Malabala replied.

"Her royal audience expects to be royally entertained," he translated immediately thereafter.

"No!" The word sprang from my lips before I could apprehend it.

The wizard frowned then, as if he had just heard my panicked request. "I suppose I might be able to devise some means of escape, if I were not already so fatigued from controlling the storm, and now constantly involved in this translation magic. Language spells are far more draining than people realize." He paused to smile benignly in my direction. "Thus it is that I am doubly grateful that you have chosen to make this sacrifice. The death of but a porter may allow me to sufficiently regain my strength to save all these people of consequence. Would you have me waste that future certainty for a present spell that quite possibly would not work?"

That was it, then. The mage would not listen, and I was doomed to a short but very energetic life with the queen of the apes.

"Uh," was my only response, since my brain had ceased its proper function.

"There!" Malabala said with great satisfaction. "I knew you would agree with my point once you thought about it rationally." He patted me heartily upon the back. "In the meantime, your queen requires an answer."

"Ook," the queen repeated suggestively.

"Fanciful description is a part of the ritual," Malabala explained. "It is expected of you now, as other things will be expected of you shortly. So what shall you do?"

It appeared that I was indeed ooked, one way or another.

♦

Chapter the Fifteenth,
in which salvation may come from the sky if it comes at all.

So I would truly sacrifice myself for the others. At least, if I were to pay this extreme a price, I would be assured of a place in heaven—that is, unless they had rules up there about overfamiliarity with apes. It was time to get on with this. But to do that, I had to make some reply to their request. I spoke the words with some difficulty.

"I shall—certainly—do my best—perhaps—to attempt it— once," I managed at last.

The wizard said he was not familiar with the word "Uh," and could not translate more than two languages at one time. I replied that I would do my best. Malabala then translated something from me for the benefit of the apes, but whether I was answering the current question or one presented long ago had become far too confusing. I just hoped my existent answer suited the present situation. In the meantime, both queen and captain continued their ape demands.

"The queen wishes to skin your peel," Malabala mentioned presently. Then, somewhat later, he answered: "Once is never enough."

"Well, perhaps we could postpone—" I caught myself before I could complete my true desire. "No, Malabala, tell them rather that I—er—will do my best—taking of course into account my physical limitations—to—um—do something twice, then."

Malabala and the apes had a lively conversation.

"The queen does not appreciate false modesty," Malabala said in the midst of it all. "All apes know of the prodigious gifts of human males."

"Ook greech ook scree!" was presently shouted above the melee.

"The third test will commence!" the wizard interpreted eventually. But by that point I saw the apes coming for me.

It would please me to relate that I went to my fate with quiet dignity. However, I would be remiss if I did not mention that there was a certain level of kicking and shrieking involved.

In a matter of no time whatsoever, I found myself thrown roughly down on a pile of bedding belowdecks. My flailing arms caused me to get caught within the bedclothes, and, by the time I had freed myself, all but one ape had left, and that last, veiled creature proceeded to bar the door.

Somehow still, in this worst of situations, hope refused to vanish completely from my breast. I stared up at the great gorilla approaching me. I decided to talk to her again in her own tongue, this time being very careful to avoid the ook word. I could not reason with her in a language I did not understand, but mayhaps I could confuse, or even better, enrage her. Perchance, hope whispered to my soul, there might yet be some way I could dissuade her amorous intentions, and simply cause her to murder me outright.

"Scree," I ventured. "Gibber gibber hoo."

She paused. Had I succeeded in stopping her so soon? She regarded me beneath half-closed eyelids.

"Ook," she whispered in a husky tone.

Apparently, my first attempt at angering her had been somewhat less than successful. If only I could remember the words I had used before to declare a blood duel. But actually, I could remember the words very well; there were only five or six of them in the whole ape language, after all. But those words could mean many things. It was all in the tone, I reminded myself.

"Scree!" I yelled at the top of my voice. "Gibber hoo gibber!"

"Scree?" She ripped aside her veil, her voice filled with passion. "Ook! Ook! Ook!" she said between two sets of sharp, yellowed fangs. She trotted toward me across the room.

Apparently, I wasn't capable of setting the tone properly, either. With the rate the queen was currently approaching, I had to do something else quickly. But my ignorance of the ape's tongue was simply too great for me to zealously continue to speak it. Perhaps, I thought, if I used some sort of universal sign language, along with a few phrases of ape, it would convey that my words were something other than love-torn endearments.

She grabbed the back of my robe and began to pull it over my head.

"Scree!" I yelled as I slapped her hands away, and pulled my tunic back over my head. "Greech hoo hoo!"

But I felt my sandals pulled from my feet at the exact same

moment. How was this possible? I saw that her hands still were not touching me, and I panicked totally.

My worst fears were realized. She was also undressing me with her feet. I should have realized that there was no way I could reject the amorous advances of a quadrumane.

"Ook!" she breathed in and out with a regularity born of deepest lust. "Ook! Ook! Ook!"

But, oddly enough, I found my upper body totally unmolested for the moment. Even though her feet still pawed through the air in an effort to caress me, the queen's hands had temporarily become involved in undoing the complicated clasps and ties that seem to be a prerequisite of all women's clothing.

This, I realized, was my only hope of salvation; and my panic must be served. While her attention was thus distracted, I jumped up and ran.

"Ook!" she screamed as I passed her. My last glimpse saw her trying to free her hands from her many veils. "Scree scree scree!"

If anything, I ran even faster. From the tone of those screes, I had the impression that, should the queen catch me now, she would be even more direct in her demands.

I reached the door and threw the bolt aside with an economy of movement that surprised even myself. I soon had the door open in my amazingly efficient panic and was swiftly climbing the ladder that led above.

"Ook!" came the first of a series of cries behind me. "Ook scree ook!" Unfortunately, these cries were not diminishing with distance. The queen had recovered sufficiently to pursue me.

I pushed open the trapdoor to the deck and burst above. With that speed with which I had arrived upon the scene, all those above, both ape and human, seemed frozen in mid-motion. But I saw them all in that first instant: the ape captain; his surly crew, so little different from the human sailors I had so recently left; the merchant Sinbad, flanked by his two servants; the wise but rather confused Malabala; and Dirk and the Scar, guarding Fatima's box. Ah, sweet Fatima! If only I could somehow apologize for my impetuous actions! But how could you apologize to someone when you have not even been introduced?

I heard heavy breathing on the ladder behind me, punctuated by the occasional ook.

And the ooks seemed to awaken every ape in the crew. I heard a great roar about me as every bestial sailor rushed in my direction.

So there would be no apologies, and no standing still, either, if I wanted to be free of gorilla love. Instead, I ran swiftly across the deck and half stumbled, half launched myself over the side. Perhaps by this time I was traveling a bit too fast. Still, I decided, anything was better than the amorous attentions of the queen of the apes. Even an uncertain fate among the waves below.

In actuality, due to my total inability in the area of swimming, my fate below was probably much more certain. And I seemed to have the opportunity to consider that fate, for time had so slowed for me in my flight that I appeared to hang in the air, there off the starboard bow, for an almost never-ending instant.

Suspended thus, I thought of my earlier meetings with the sea nymph, and how she had said that, on my third visit below the sea, I might stay forever. There were worse kismets, I decided, than spending eternity beneath the waves in the company of a nymph. But I imagined that the sailors, both ape and human, might have another definition for a man spending an eternity beneath the waves, and that definition might be drowning.

Perhaps, then, I was given this suspended time especially, since this would be my final moment in this life, and I should say one last prayer before I was swept beneath the waves.

But, oddly enough, I did not even seem to be approaching the water. Instead, I seemed to be rising away from the waves, as if something had gotten hold of my belt and was lifting me aloft.

At first, I thought I might be the beneficiary of one of Malabala's spells, but when I looked at the ship of apes, which was now positioned beneath me, the wizard appeared to be the only one, either ape or human, not staring and pointing aloft at my position, but instead seemed to be continually translating to an audience which was no longer listening.

My second thought was that the giant Rukh had again returned and was spiriting me away. But would a bird so large, with a single claw as long as I am tall, be capable of so delicate a maneuver as the grasping of my belt? There was nothing else for it, then. I would have to twist myself about to see exactly what was occurring above me. I craned my back and neck about as best I could.

There was no doubt about it. Something had indeed gotten hold of my belt and was lifting me aloft. But the true nature of that thing made my breath pause in my chest.

The creature above me was in one way unmistakably a bird, for she clutched me with a golden claw where her foot should be, and she was covered, head to foot, with bright yellow plumage. Further, her two arms, although each of them ended with a hand of surpassing delicacy, also sported long stiff feathers along their entire length, which she used as wings, riding the wind high over the ocean below. But while she was in part a bird, her form and stature were in all other ways human, so that she had a trim, feminine figure not that different in shape or size from the nymph I had met below the sea.

"So, human!" the bird woman called to me over the whistling wind. Her voice was like a melody, each syllable its own clear note. "You may thank me when we reach my nest!"

So it was that my rescuer turned her head away from me and put a redoubled effort into the action of her wings. I looked before us, and saw that we were headed for an island, and on the center of that island was a tall, dark peak, whose promontory was so high it was lost in the clouds. And, as we rose ever higher, I realized that it was toward those clouds that my rescuer was taking me.

So I hung, suspended in air, far higher than even if I had climbed the tallest tower in all of Baghdad. An odd sort of peace descended upon me, here so far above the world. I heard none of the sounds of the sea where I now flew, nor the discordant arguments of apes and men. There was only the clean, cool air, and the sound of wind punctuated by the steady rhythm of the bird woman's wings.

I looked down below me again, and saw the shipload of apes dwindling in the distance. Of the ship on which I had originally booked passage, there was no sign. Once we had been confronted by the apes, the human captain and crew must have agreed for once and fled the vicinity as rapidly as possible.

My view was obscured as the world turned white. We had entered the clouds. The air had turned chill as well, and I could feel the cool moisture against my robes.

A great dark shape loomed before us. It was the mountain peak. The bird woman gave out with a high piercing cry, as if she sent her greetings to the rocks of her home, and a moment later, her cry echoed back, as if the rocks greeted her in return.

We seemed to be descending, although, in this cloud, it was difficult to judge distances and angles with precision. I twisted about again to stare at my guide. In the muted light, her plumage seemed to glow a dull orange, like a torch shining through the fog. And, as I turned to look at her, her claw released my belt, and

I fell. I heard her laughter, a sound somewhere between the quarrel of a sparrow and the sweet night song of a nightingale.

I fell onto something soft. I looked about me, and saw a collection of cloth and straw, strips of fabric jumbled haphazardly through the long grass.

The bird woman alighted by my side. "Welcome to my nest," she said.

So this was the bird woman's home? I looked about, and saw that, while the space I now occupied was as large as the inner courtyard of Sinbad's palace, it was made mostly of straw, and did indeed have walls of that same material that sloped upward at the perimeter to entirely ring the center. It was indeed a bird's nest, a hundred times larger than any nest I had ever seen.

"Thank you most humbly for my rescue," I said to the bird woman as I bowed my head in respect. "If you had not taken my belt, it would be very likely that I would have drowned."

At that, I looked up, for I once again heard the woman's singular laughter, and noticed that, this close, the woman had a face of surpassing beauty, her nearly human features covered with a fine down of the purest gold.

"I could not let my cousin have you all to herself," the bird woman said. "You were about to go down into the ocean depths for the third and the last time, were you not, my young Sinbad?"

I was astonished at her reply. Was this bird woman implying that she was related to the nymph I had met at ocean's bottom? She certainly knew my name, and more than a little about my history.

"I thought you should know that life held certain other choices," she continued when I made no immediate reply.

What did I know of choices? It seemed in a way that I had made but one, to join the elder Sinbad on his quest, but that choice had led to a never-ending barrage of wondrous and terrifying occurrences. As I thought of it, I realized that all those occurrences had led to other, smaller choices: a great chain of decisions that would last until we completed our adventures, or those adventures overwhelmed us.

It was a sobering discovery for a porter, who now had to choose what to say next to this strange but magnificent creature. I decided, since I still did seem to cling to life, to discover exactly what that life next had in store.

"Why have you brought me here?" I asked of the bird woman.

"Commendably direct," the bird woman replied. "Every creature lives by certain rules. My cousin's and mine are quite similar.

She seeks a man of the earth who has touched the sea. I look for a man with feet upon the ground, but whose eyes search the sky."

So this woman suggested that she might wish to share my favors, too? While not so sensual as the nymph she claimed as kin, there was something sleek and beautiful about this creature, and there was a part of me who wished to feel the softness of her feathers. But I had witnessed too many wonders now to immediately fall under this woman's charms.

"I might fit that description," I replied instead. "But so might many men."

"Laudably humble," was the bird woman's comment. "But know this, Sinbad. Certain men are pursued by Destiny. They are surrounded by it, as a nimbus might surround the moon. The elder Sinbad was such a man, but it slips from him with age. But you, porter, have barely reached manhood, and have embarked upon a new life. And I think that Destiny will smile upon you more with every passing day."

So someone else besides the merchant spoke of Destiny. I was not sure it was entirely to my liking. The freedom of choice was too new to me to have it taken away by some Greater Plan.

"Then the direction of my life is preordained?" I asked the feathered female with more than a trace of distress.

"Nothing is without choice." She smiled. It was an odd sight, for her mouth seemed to have the hardness of a beak. "There are many destinies, but you most likely will figure in a few." She waved her golden wings at our surroundings. "But how do you like my beautiful nest?"

"It is a fine thing," I agreed with her. "Did you build the whole great structure by yourself?"

"I was driven to it," she admitted. "One is nothing unless one has a home."

I took a moment to look about this bird woman's home, and noticed there was more than strips of cloth and bits of straw. In one corner was a pile of parchment, each piece filled with writing. In another was a pile of delicate garments, finer by far than the clothing of the queen of the apes, and a small mirror which a lady might use to admire herself. In yet another part of the nest was a small mound of golden coins, and fine jewels that glittered in even this subdued light.

I looked from the piles of possessions back to the woman's downy face, and she answered me before I had a chance to speak.

"You wonder about my treasures," she said. "I have the human

in me, and am drawn to human things. As I am drawn to you."
She reached out and touched my face with her delicate hand,
which was human in all respects save that it, too, was covered
with the golden down. The tiny feathers felt warm and soft against
my cheek, and I found myself wanting to reach out my own hands
and grasp this woman by her slender waist, and feel all her golden
plumage against my skin.

"Stay with me, young Sinbad," she said, her voice a low trill
of desire. "I will show you things denied to all other mortals. You
shall fly high above the world, and see the entirety of humankind,
and those places far beyond, that no man has ever seen. You will
have no wants, for I can snatch anything you covet from the world
below, and display all those things and more for your pleasure."

Her words filled me like wine, and I felt a light-headed
happiness at the prospect of a life here, high above human care.
But then I looked again at her fine, feathered fingers, and thought
of another hand as perfectly formed that belonged to mortal
woman. This bird woman was asking me to live a life away from
others of my kind. Away from my Fatima.

This nest, and the clouds about me, and the beautiful bird
before me, were all like parts of some wondrous dream. But even
the best of dreams would lose its charm if the sleeper could not
awake. This was the bird woman's place in the world, but it was
not mine, and just as this was her home, so I had my Baghdad. In
my innermost heart, I knew I could not find true happiness with
either of these fantastic women, whether deep beneath the sea or
high among the clouds, for by making either choice I would never
be able to see my homeland again.

"I am sorry," I said to the woman before me, "but I cannot
remain."

The bird woman drew her wings about her, like a pigeon who
protects itself against the rages of a storm.

"So you say now," was her reply. "We shall speak again,
Sinbad."

With that, she spread her wings wide once more, and let out a
cry so high and piercing that it chilled me deep within. Then she
was aloft with a great beating of wings, and I found my belt once
again clasped by her nimble claws.

We flew over the edge of the nest and swiftly down through the
clouds. I saw great outcroppings of rock loom perilously close.
The clouds thinned, and I could see the stones in all their jagged
detail, sure to break and maim any human form that would have

the misfortune to be dropped upon them. The wind screamed in my ears, a high, wild sound that seemed to mock the last cry I had heard from the bird woman.

Then I felt the pressure leave my belt. The bird woman had released her grip, and I was falling free.

"You have made your choice." I heard her bird voice fading in the wind. "Happy landings."

And my body rushed to meet the trees below.

♦

Chapter the Sixteenth,
in which our hero returns rather more to earth,
even though other events do not.

First, I was aware of the crash of breaking branches, hundreds and more than hundreds of tiny bits of wood and leaves splintering beneath me. But I did not seem to be falling quite so fast, so far, or so fully, and was instead smashing from one group of dense vegetation to the next.

It occurred dimly to me that the bird woman must have planned this descent, that I indeed would not die (a thought which did come as something of a surprise), but would survive so that the bird woman and I could meet again as she had promised.

It was all rather a shock. I had gone from a cool place of peace and stillness to crash repeatedly into the forest's outer growth. And the trees were not the only things producing noise, for I also cried out repeatedly. Furthermore, even though none of those things that I descended upon were substantial enough to kill or seriously maim me, they still carried enough substance to produce a not inconsiderable pain, and I imagined my limbs and body would be sore for some days to come.

The crashing ceased, and I realized that my fall had ended. I looked about me, and noticed that the branches I had come to rest upon were those of a bush close to the ground. I had survived, although I was unsure if I would ever wish to move again. I was, however, capable of summoning sufficient energy to groan.

"Who is it?" a cracked and familiar voice called. "I warn you, I am an accomplished wizard!"

It was surely the voice of Malabala.

"It is I," I managed, and my ribs already hurt, even when I talked. "Sinbad."

"Another Sinbad?" Achmed's voice piped out of the forest. "The world these days seems to be crawling with them."

But I heard the telltale sound of snapping branches and rustling leaves, a sure sign that a party of men was approaching me through the woods.

I groaned again to give my rescuers a better sense of my precise location. The snapping and rustling grew gratifyingly closer.

"Look!" Achmed's voice called again. "This is not simply any Sinbad. It is our porter, dropped from heaven!"

I turned in the direction of the voice, and was surprised to see quite a collection of individuals looking back at me; in all there was a total of five men, one boy, and a palanquin.

"What?" The merchant Sinbad frowned at me. "Oh, my. I suppose it is. You'll have to forgive me, my son. I was never too good at remembering faces."

What was the merchant saying? We had left each other scant hours before, and already he had forgotten me? I recalled what the bird woman had remarked concerning Sinbad's aging. What if my patron became too infirm to continue our journey? Even worse, what if he became so confused with age that he forgot all about me, or his promise of a hundred dinars?

"Come," Jafar instructed those around him. "We must free him from those branches!"

"What?" Malabala interjected as he caught up with the conversation. "Miracle of miracles! It is indeed the porter!"

Dirk and the Scar ran forward before anyone else had a chance to move. They drew their curved knives in unison.

"Awfully good to see you again," Dirk said smoothly as they approached. "Certain individuals of our acquaintance would be terribly upset if we were to lose you now."

"Youse don't wanna worry us," the Scar added with an almost toothless grin. "We upsets too easy."

Each man lifted his knife to eye level.

"It is fortunate that you give us something to practice upon," added Dirk with a smile that showed too many teeth rather than too few. "We wouldn't want our blades to dull."

So the two men set to work, and cut apart the bush with silent efficiency, so that the branches about me were reduced to no more than so much kindling. I rolled free and hit the ground with a painful thud.

"Now we'se even," the Scar informed me with a crooked leer. "A favor for a favor." He admired his blade for a long instant before he replaced it in his sash. "So maybe now I kills you slower."

Oh, dear, thought I. Had I but known about that particular

legacy of my rescue, I might have chosen the option of remaining trapped in the bush. Still, with all that had been happening to me as of late, I imagined I should die in a much more spectacular fashion than simple knife wounds. I therefore struggled to stand while ignoring those thousand screaming muscles and bruised bones that announced their presence within me.

Their knife work done, Dirk and the Scar had turned their backs on me and were ambling back toward their palanquin. Achmed, however, had quickly reached my side, and was using what small leverage his light body contained to keep me from falling again.

"We are glad to see you among us again, O porter!" the other Sinbad called to me. "You must tell us of your marvelous travels!"

Jafar cleared his throat.

"Oh, can't he tell it now?" Sinbad asked, and I noticed the slightest of whines in the elder man's voice. "I so want to incorporate these events into my tale of the eighth voyage!"

Jafar's throat cleared once again. The merchant Sinbad sighed and bit his lip.

"Remember your other priorities, O pontificator of prognostication," the aged majordomo remarked.

"My master Sinbad believes this island is somehow familiar," Achmed explained to me. "But he cannot yet quite place his surroundings."

This was certainly a problem to ponder. If this merchant could not remember faces, how could he recognize islands? And yet, from what I had heard of his early tales, I conjectured that his adventures on many of his island visits could be considered less than pleasant. I asked the merchant if that was actually the case.

"Indeed," Sinbad agreed, "virtually every island I have spent time on has been the scene of some danger, has it not? It gives one pause when one considers travel." His voice rose wistfully. "If we had had a choice—"

"Which we did not, O most egregious of spendthrifts," Jafar interjected, quick to put an end to his master's musings. "Since you cannot remember the specifics of this island, we must be prepared for all perils equally. Which brings me back to my earlier request. You must finally tell the porter the whole truth about the voyages."

"The whole truth?" The merchant again sighed heavily. "Yes, I suppose I must."

The more polite of the two ruffians appeared before us again.

"I beg your pardon, but I must request that we cease all conversation for the time being," Dirk said in a tone that spoke more of demand than entreaty. "It grows dark, and it behooves us to return to camp."

He turned from us with an attitude that said there was no choice but for us to follow. Sinbad, who appeared not to relish the truth-telling that Jafar demanded in his future, was the first to fall in step behind the villain. Dirk paused but an instant to reclaim his half of the palanquin, and then he and the Scar were off at a brisk trot. Supported on either side by Achmed and Jafar, I did my best to follow, as Malabala asked no one in particular if it would not be prudent to leave these woods before dark fell completely.

"I confess," I said slowly, for I discovered I needed most of my breath to aid in the simple act of walking, "that I am nearly as surprised to see you here as you are to find me."

"Ah," Jafar replied. "That we are no longer among the apes? The explanation is simple in the extreme. Once you were gone, they had no more use for us, and discharged us from the ship at their first opportunity."

"Actually, they asked Dirk and the Scar if they wished to stay and become part of the crew," Achmed added. "It seems the apes recognize a certain brotherhood with particular humans."

"Or so Malabala translated for us," Jafar amended. "But Dirk and the Scar said they were upon an important mission, and those of us to be left behind were a part of that task." Jafar cleared his throat, as though he were chiding himself this time for wandering so far from his proper topic. "So it was the apes put us off at the first island we came to, along with sufficient provisions for a week or more."

"For a group of apes," Achmed added, "they seem quite humane."

"So it was that we walked up from the beach," the majordomo further explained, "and found a protected bit of ground surrounded by stones on the edge of this wood. It was there that we made our camp, and we were about to settle down for the evening when we heard the great commotion among the trees. We quickly went to investigate, expecting the worst."

"And, of course, found you," Achmed added with one of his most ingratiating smiles.

So it was that we came to their encampment, a small clearing surrounded by boulders on three sides and the forest upon the other. It did indeed appear to be an ideally located site, guarded by

the rocks so that there was only one entryway to guard for those
ogres, giant beasts, or whatever other horrors planned to visit in
the night.

Achmed and Jafar lowered me down upon a grassy knoll so that
my back could rest as comfortably as possible against one of the
flatter of the boulders, and Achmed turned to light a fairly
substantial cooking fire that he must have built before my
tumultuous arrival. Jafar and Achmed then proceeded to roast a
pair of meaty, plucked fowls over the fire.

"Master?" Jafar called.

"What is it now?" The merchant Sinbad had been frowning
back into the forest, pondering, no doubt, whether this was the
island that held the two-headed cyclops, or that place which was
home to the gigantic, man-eating snake, or perhaps some other,
even-more-horrendous location that he had yet to elucidate.

"Now would be an ideal occasion to speak with the porter, O
prince of reverie," Jafar reminded him softly but firmly.

"Um? Oh, yes, I suppose it would be," Sinbad agreed. He
pulled thoughtfully upon his beard. "But where did I leave off in
the telling of my tale?"

"You had survived the snake," I helpfully reminded him, for
the smell of the roasting birds had done much to revive me.

"Ah, yes," the merchant responded warmly, "and then the very
next day I was fortunate enough to be rescued by a passing
vessel."

"Wait for the next part," Achmed called to me.

"When I boarded the vessel," Sinbad went on with the next
part, "the captain of the noble ship took me aside, and confessed
that he was most happy that they had spotted me upon the island,
for he felt he had a debt that he must repay. Indeed, upon an earlier
journey, he had been forced to leave a merchant behind under
less-than-ideal circumstances and he feared that merchant had
been lost forever. So overcome with guilt was the captain, in fact,
that he had not disposed of this merchant's goods, but still carried
them within the hold of his ship."

"And what was this man's name?" Achmed called.

"You can imagine my astonishment," the merchant continued,
"when I found out that merchant's name was Sinbad!"

"You can imagine our astonishment as well," Achmed said
drily as he repositioned his roasting bird.

The merchant went on for a bit about neither he nor the captain
having recognized the other. They never did, I realized. In

Sinbad's tales, and perhaps in Sinbad's life, no one ever seemed to recognize anybody.

"The traditional story forms are always the best," Achmed commented before I could say a word.

"But, of course, I was able to sell these goods to great advantage, and return to Baghdad a wealthy—"

"What if you were to get on to the next tale, O worthiest of word users?" Jafar prompted.

"If you pardon the intrusion"—Dirk appeared among us with a suddenness that spoke of anything but pardon—"my partner and myself, not to mention our charge, have been aware of those cooking smells for some time now, and were wondering when the birds would be sufficiently prepared." He patted his stomach appreciatively. "My partner is not the most pleasant of men when he is hungered."

I never considered the Scar the most pleasant of men under any circumstances. But his mate's speech about their charge was what had given me pause. I was so sore and tired that I had barely spared a thought for Fatima. Fatima! My heart tried to soar within my chest, but was given pause by some very bruised ribs. Still, when I had spoken with the bird woman in her nest, she had said that I had a Destiny, and here I was, back in the presence of my beautiful mystery woman. Could there be any doubt that Destiny would involve her as well? Fatima! Her name alone gave me strength, at least to eat, and perhaps much more!

Jafar stared critically at the bird which he had been cooking at the end of a sharpened pole. "A moment or two more," was his judgment. "That is all."

"Good," Dirk replied. "That will appease my partner. Then we will settle in for the evening. It grows dark about us. The two of us have decided we will take turns keeping watch. There are certain things we are at pains to protect."

At first, I thought the burly man was referring to the fair flower of femininity which they guarded, and mayhap some of the contents of the ornate but perpetually closed palanquin. But then I reconsidered what Jafar and Achmed had told me of on our journey to this camp, and how the two brigands had refused a safe berth among the apes to reembark with the other humans. It certainly appeared they were concerned with far more than Fatima.

I had yet another thought. Could these two also be caught up in this Destiny? Perhaps that was the reason they accompanied both of the Sinbads. Or maybe, villains that they were, they were out to halt the workings of that Destiny. Whatever their goal, I decided this Destiny was certainly not something to be treated casually.

But then the wise Jafar pronounced our dinner properly done, and it was no longer time for Destiny, but time for dinner.

But Destiny would not let us go that easily. After Jafar gave the larger of the two birds to Dirk and the Scar, he took a knife of his own to carve up the remaining bird and distribute it. But as he did this very thing—indeed, just as he was preparing to hand me my fair share—there came a sound from the direction of the beach that under less extreme circumstances might have been enough to completely cause a loss of appetite.

The noise that disturbed us was a roar, both great and strange, for, rather than a sound of anger or warning as you would expect of such a bellow, it sounded like a roar of joy.

"It appears the true nature of the island will soon become evident," Achmed said between bites of bird.

"Oh, yes," Sinbad said, his eyes bright with the reflection of the cooking fire. "This must be *that* island."

◆

Chapter the Seventeenth,
in which two heads
are not necessarily better than one.

I was so hungry that I took a bite or two before I posed the question that weighed so heavily upon all of us.

"Which island?" I asked.

"Pardon?" Sinbad asked after he had swallowed. "Forgive me, porter, but no man is easy to understand when his mouth is full."

I swallowed in turn. I had indeed forgotten my manners. "My pardon, O wise merchant, but which specific island is the one of which you speak?"

Having said my piece, I took another bite of bird.

"Oh," the merchant replied as he lifted another hunk of meat to his lips. "This island."

I allowed myself a moment to swallow and again collect my thoughts, even though I had begun to feel much the same sense of progress as when attempting a discussion with Malabala.

"Yes," I attempted further, "O greatest of merchants, but is this island among those that you have made famous in your tales?"

"How perceptive of you to notice," the merchant agreed. "Indeed it is."

To my immense surprise, both Achmed and Jafar joined in unison upon my next question: "But which island is it?"

"Ah," Sinbad said with a surprised smile. "You need to know which of the many islands I have illuminated in my tales that we now stand upon. That would certainly help in our future plans, wouldn't it?"

Achmed placed a restraining hand upon my shoulder. How did the youth know I had been about to scream? I took a moment and unballed my fists.

"My master will give us the answer in a moment," he whispered in my ear, "but we must wait for it."

Wait for it? I once again had the feeling that the danger might have claimed us by the time the merchant got around to explaining exactly what that danger might be.

"Yes, this is an island from one of my earliest voyages. Hearing that call, I am reminded of occurrences whereby I lost a lamentable number of my traveling companions."

Out of my frustration, I found myself looking for clues to our whereabouts in every one of the many words the loquacious merchant spoke. There was no help there. He seemed to lose a lamentable number of companions no matter where he traveled.

"So we are retracing your earlier voyages!" Jafar called with no little tone of triumph. "I knew that there was a pattern here!"

"The head of my household was ever prompt at discerning these patterns." The merchant nodded his head sadly. "And I do agree that there seems to be another force at work here."

Another force, leading us from island to island? Still, I felt I might know the answer to this one. "Destiny?"

But Sinbad shook his head at that. "Destiny is never so direct. Well, perhaps it is occasionally as I relate it in my stories, but, as I have previously admitted, that is because I have omitted certain embarrassments and loose ends." He glanced at his servant Jafar, rapidly continuing before there could commence any further clearing of throats. "Such as that terrible incident in the fourth voyage concerning the valley of talking figs."

"And on the fifth voyage?" Jafar prompted, now that his master had finally returned to this most prominent subject.

"Yes, I omitted the vile and loathsome creature that even the Rukh fears. I am a man of compassion, and my audience at these times would generally be eating, after all." The merchant smiled after a moment's pause. "About the sixth, I believe I was more or less honest."

"But the seventh?" Jafar prompted.

"You know I cannot talk about that!" the merchant cried, his face a mask of total fright.

"That will be a problem," Jafar agreed solemnly, as if he understood that which the elder Sinbad seemed afraid to explain. "How can one face a danger one cannot even discuss?"

"When one is a servant of my master," Achmed added in his usual helpful tone, "one comes to expect this sort of problem."

I might have found this whole discussion of more interest if it did not interfere with certain more important issues facing us presently. "But concerning our present voyage?" I prompted.

"Ah, yes," Sinbad agreed. "I believe we are visiting the first unfortunate island of my third tale."

That was the most recent that the merchant had related. "The one with the snake?"

"Alas!" the merchant cried. "Would that we had only a giant serpent to face!"

I supposed that was all the answer I was going to get. I thought back to Sinbad's earlier story. What had happened before the island of the snake?

"The cyclops?" I recalled.

"The two-headed cyclops," the merchant agreed, his voice awash with misery. "We are about to be talked into our deaths."

"No one is dying around here," Dirk said from close by my head. I looked up and saw him standing atop the boulder above me. Had he been there for our entire conversation?

"At least," Dirk amended, "no one dies without our express permission. Now, get some rest."

I was too exhausted to do otherwise. I should fall asleep like the proverbial child, and that was if I could keep my eyes open that long. Besides, I thought, in the manner of one looking to reassure oneself, this situation was far different from the merchant's earlier voyage. Firstly, we had a certain foreknowledge of the peril to those who took the earlier journey. That very knowledge would allow us to better prepare for whatever dangers lurked ahead. And further, we had an additional advantage, for we listed among our number an accomplished magician who had stilled a raging storm at sea, and who should be more than a match for any common monster.

"Beg pardon?" said Malabala, who had been remarkably silent through the course of the meal. "A cyclops?"

Perhaps, I considered, my sleep might not be quite so comfortable as it could be.

And, certainly, though I drifted off soon thereafter, I woke up abruptly more than once during the course of the night, and swore that I heard sounds. But the noises that entered my half-asleep ears were no longer joyous roars. No, these times they seemed softer, but closer, and more a series of deep-throated chuckles.

I awoke to Jafar's full-throated wails.

"Oh, woe!" he called to all assembled. "We are surely doomed!"

This was followed by another bellow, and this time it was not the equal of the joyous noise of the night before, but a sound full of anger and frustration emanating from the Scar.

"Dey sneaks around in the night!" the Scar further commented in his overwrought manner. "I kills dem!"

"Before you can do that, little man," a voice even deeper than the Scar's commented wryly, "you'll have to get out."

This situation sounded, at the very least, extremely unpleasant. Still, there was no helping it. I opened my eyes.

I saw the crisscross of bars overhead. I rolled over, the fear overcoming the complaints of my abused muscles, and pushed myself to my knees. I saw the same intersecting bars immediately beyond the rocks on three sides of us, and blocking our escape to the forest on the fourth. The clearing had become the inside of a cage. And it was a very substantial cage, for the bars were all made of rough-hewn logs that must have once been tree trunks, tied together with hemp twice the thickness of a strong man's arm.

I imagined it would take a dozen men a week to construct so large a prison as this. But I further imagined that we were dealing with not a dozen men, but with a single creature of immense size and strength. After all, our captor would have to be quite sizable if he chose to refer to the Scar as "little man."

"Now," the deep voice rumbled from somewhere behind the rocks, "let's get a better look at my dinner."

"I was correct!" cried the elder Sinbad as he stood and pointed with a great and perhaps somewhat misplaced excitement.

"A cyclops?" Malabala added from where he, too, had just arisen. "But I see two of them."

Indeed, as I stood, I gazed in the direction the merchant indicated, and I also saw two of them beyond the boulders and the bars; two heads, that is. And what incredible heads they were! Each of the faces was the unfortunate equal in ugliness to Dirk and the Scar, although the actual head size was perhaps five times as great here as on those of their human counterparts. In addition, the fact that each head sported but a single eye placed immediately above the nose added greatly to the overall effect.

"And I see all of you," the leftmost head of the cyclops said with a grin. Unlike the Scar, this head seemed to have most of its teeth, all of which had an unfortunate tendency to end at a razor point.

"My," the head continued in the most cheerful of tones, "what a pleasant assortment! Muscled ones and fat ones, old ones and an oh-so-tender youngster! And, to top it all off, it looks like I get a surprise in a box! Oh, I can make dinner plans for days!"

With that, the two heads passed by the last of the boulders, and the body beneath strolled out into the full view of the cage's forest side. And it was as Sinbad had said, for we could all now see that it was a single giant being with two great heads, one above each shoulder, with his great body covered by a collection of rags so filthy that they would put the beggars of Baghdad to shame.

The other head frowned and blinked, as if it were just now awaking. "Eat now?"

"Oh, no, no, no, dear brother," the left head chided gently. "We always wait until the sun goes down, so that we may have a proper dinner. And what a choice of dinners we possess." He chuckled with great relish. "I've been savoring this moment ever since I smelled your cooking fires last night!"

The Scar, if anything, appeared even more angry than before. "You can't keeps us here." He pulled his knife from his belt. "We gets out! We kills you!"

"My, my," the cyclops marveled, "such a lot of energy." He raised his left hand to wave a finger at the Scar. "What good will it do you, little man, if you get out of the cage? You'll still be on my island. I'll simply pluck you off your tiny feet, and put your pitifully squirming form back in here. That is, if I don't decide to end your squirming by eating you raw. Raw human!" He made a smacking sound with his lips. "It's quite a delicacy, but you have to eat them fresh!"

He smiled down at the Scar's weapon as one might regard a child's toy. "And do you think I fear your tiny weapons?" He answered his own question with a rich laugh. "No, you little fellows will be much better off just sitting there and fattening yourself up on the food that remains. That's the way I like you, nice and round!"

All of us in the cage were silent for a moment. The giant's suggestion was not the most appetizing of prospects.

But, while the rest of us were temporarily stilled, the merchant stepped forward.

"This is a very attractive cage you have here, O cyclops," he said in the most gracious of tones.

"Why, thank you," the left head replied. "I'm glad you appreciate it. I had it built for this very location. It is such an attractive campsite, don't you think? Nice, level ground, protected on three sides, the promise of an easy escape into the forest, and only a few dozen feet away from that beach that simply everyone washes up upon! You'd be amazed how many shipwrecked sailors have picked this exact spot to spend their first night on the island, not to mention the rest of their very short—but very tasty—lives."

"Most clever," Sinbad agreed. "We were totally fooled into your trap."

"You little humans always are," the cyclops replied in the most irritatingly self-congratulatory of tones. "Say," he asked of my elder namesake, "don't I know you from somewhere? Your very manner of speech reminds me of someone." He frowned as he recalled the incident. "It was a merchant who sold me these rags I wear today."

His left hand moved as if to touch the filthy cloth, but stopped short of actually committing the act. "Said the clothes would last forever," the head continued with obvious distaste. "I humored him, and paid for the goods with some of my best jewels. It was my little joke. Figured I'd get them back when I ate the merchant. Wish I could get my hands on the man today. Not to mention my stomach. I always regret it when I miss a meal."

"Oh, as sad as that story is," the merchant said with the innocence of the newborn, "surely you must be confusing me with somebody else."

The head considered this for a moment. "Yes, now that I think of it, he was a much younger man. Those were the only ones who ever escaped me!" He rubbed his stomach. "My appetite still yearns for them! It is fortunate that you are here to take their place."

"Eat now?" the right head remarked.

The left head ignored his brother, as did the elder Sinbad.

"But it seems to me that you do not make the best use of us," the merchant said instead. "Why keep us here when we can be so useful about the island?"

"Useful?" the left head replied with a frown. "How would you be useful?"

"Oh, we could certainly perform tiresome tasks," Sinbad commented in the most offhanded manner possible. "Say, if we were to gather firewood?"

"Now I recall it!" the left head called out as his brow creased with the pain of the memory. "Those other fellows gathered firewood, too. Turned it into a raft and escaped! Not until after I drowned a few of them, of course." He smiled ever so slightly at the last thought.

"Mere coincidence, I'm sure," the merchant assured him. "We would never think of doing such a thing."

"So you say," the head snapped, as if the mention of that earlier incident had put the thing into a foul temper. "As enjoyable as this meeting has been, I must attend to other needs. I shall be back over the course of the day to visit." So saying, the cyclops turned upon his heels and ambled back behind the rocks.

"Eat now?" the right head rumbled.

"Go back to sleep," the left head rumbled back as both halves disappeared from sight.

"Oh, woe!" Jafar began again.

"Oh, hush," his master chided him. "What we need here is less woe and more work. There must be a way out of this."

"Give my master a challenge," Achmed remarked, "and he is like a man of twenty. Of course, it helps if he can later incorporate the challenge into one of his stories."

I could see the admirable change as well. Sinbad the Sailor, who had seemed totally helpless before the Rukh, the apes, and the power of the storm, was once again in the midst of events.

"At last!" the merchant chortled. "Many of our adventures thus far have been beyond me. And that spell with the djinni still has me totally befuddled. But give me a foe who speaks my language, especially a self-important cyclops, any day!" He looked about the clearing with an evident sense of glee. "You don't think there's anything about here that I could sell him?"

"You can laugh at your verbal prowess," Dirk called from his position close to the bars, "but the two of us prefer to work with our swords!"

"We cuts our way out!" the Scar agreed as he applied his dagger to the thick rope.

For once, I found myself agreeing with the two ruffians. Whatever our eventual plans, we would have far greater options if those plans included freedom of movement.

I walked toward the rapidly sawing pair, using as few of my own muscles as possible.

"Come," I called. "Why don't we lend you a hand, and we'll be out of here that much quicker!"

Dirk and the Scar paused and looked to each other.

"I feel you have shown us but one small portion of your arsenal," I insisted. "Surely you have extra blades that we might use!"

Dirk and the Scar turned to look directly at me. It was not a pleasant experience.

"No one pulls knife on Scar!" was the ugly man's only remark.

With that, they returned to their work. I supposed, if that was their attitude, they would have to do the work alone.

"The cyclops," Malabala said again, as if he were only now joining us in the world of the conscious. "You all will have to forgive me, but this spell the djinni has placed upon all of you makes it somewhat difficult for us to communicate effectively. The strength of that spell is enormous." The magician chuckled in amazement. "Even the apes and this cyclops seem affected! And that nice little touch where your speech comes out a full statement before you actually say it—that is his masterstroke! To play with the very fabric of time itself; my respect for that Ozzie creature grows with every passing moment."

The magician shook his head in an envious manner. "But that is not what I wish to speak about. Instead, I believe we should prepare to eat!"

"That is your plan?" Jafar asked with more than a bit of hysteria. "We should fatten ourselves up to please the cyclops?"

"I haven't pulled a knife on anyone!" Malabala began indignantly, but quickly calmed himself. "How quickly I forget the spell! You are not responsible for your speeches, or, at the very least, your answers are not precisely suited to my questions, or, vice versa, for our conversations are proceeding at different speeds."

So, even though the wizard still absolutely could not believe that he was under the influence of magic, his deductive powers had led him to much the same conclusions that I had made. And it mattered little in reality whether he or I was correct, for both led to the same communication problem. But, once we had addressed the problem, could a solution be far behind?

I, for one, was becoming excited. First, the elder Sinbad, and now Malabala, were showing depths of understanding that were nowhere in evidence during the recent chaos among the apes. With these sorts of resources at our command, how could we help but succeed?

"So how do we escape?" I urged.

Malabala laughed heartily at that. "Oh, no, dear fellow. We eat not to fatten ourselves up, but to give us energy for all that we have to do."

"It is a worthy idea," the merchant Sinbad agreed. "I hereby instruct my servants to prepare us a hearty meal."

"As to our escape," Malabala finally replied to my question, "you will have to trust me, but I am sure a combination of my magic and our mutual skills will soon allow us to escape without a single one of us eaten!"

Even Jafar seemed to brighten at that, and he and Achmed went about gathering foodstuffs to prepare a midday meal. There was some small debate, due to the giant's earlier comments, about starting cooking fires, but the servants soon decided that Malabala could protect us from any cyclopean hunger attacks.

"Food good," the Scar commented. "Cutting's hard."

"I couldn't agree with my companion any more," said Dirk from where he sawed at the other man's side. "There is something you can do for us, after all. The elder Sinbad is revered as a great storyteller. Why not help us while away our work with one of your famous tales?"

"I think it should be the fourth voyage," instructed Jafar, once again in control of his emotions, "in case we should survive this one."

Startled, Sinbad looked from his majordomo to the men with knives. "Yes, a story. I suppose I might tell one. I need to keep in practice, after all." He smiled at that, a bit overwhelmed, I would guess, that he should be asked to pursue his favorite pastime even in these dire circumstances. "Very well, the fourth voyage." He glanced again at Jafar. "And I shall hurry the beginning a bit, so that I will be finished before lunch."

Since that seemed to meet with the servant's approval, the merchant felt free to begin his tale. "Once again, I had returned to Baghdad, with the good fortune to be even wealthier than I had been before. But I thought ever more fondly of my spectacular voyages, of which, this time, the bad parts no longer seemed quite so bad, and the good parts seemed absolutely magnificent. So it was that I decided to set out—"

Jafar interrupted with the usual clearing of the throat.

"Ah, yes," Sinbad amended. "I had gotten into the habit of holding lavish dinner parties by then, hadn't I?"

"You developed the habit after your first voyage," Jafar commented.

"But I do enjoy them so!" Sinbad sighed. "I am cursed with servants who have very long memories."

"From many long years of service, O greatest of fabricators," was Jafar's humble reply.

"Very well," Sinbad resumed with not a little humility in his own voice. "Let it be said that there were also some financial reasons that behooved me to take once again to sea. Whatever the reasons, we had once more taken the familiar route from Baghdad to Basrah and thence down the channel to the open waters. And again, the voyage began well, and we traveled from island to island and land to land, and I traded my goods to great profits, so that I congratulated myself heartily upon my decision to travel once again.

"But there soon occurred an event that caused me to rue my decision, for, one day, when we were in the middle of the sea, far from the sight of any land, I heard my captain call, 'We are lost beyond all hope!,' much in the manner of my servant Jafar's frequent exclamations. And indeed, I looked from the craft, and saw great waves the equal of any in that more recent storm where we found Malabala. On that voyage, we were not so fortunate as to include a magician among our ranks, and so our ship was destroyed by the great waves and torrential rain, and those of us on board were flung out to the mercies of the open sea."

As the merchant spoke, I noticed a change come upon his demeanor, a change I had seen before but only now possessed the knowledge to appreciate. There got to be a different look about his eyes, and soon the whole appearance of his face changed as well, so that he seemed much more the brave survivor of his tales and less the older, rather overweight man who had problems with money.

"But the ship had broken into pieces," the storyteller continued with authority, "and myself, along with certain of the other merchants, was fortunate enough to grab hold of those large planks that were all that was left of our craft. Thus, holding on with both hands and feet, we rode out the fury of the storm, and eventually were washed up upon another of those seemingly endless islands that dot the sea. It was upon that beach that we slept in total exhaustion throughout the night, but upon the following morning we awoke and decided to explore the isle's interior, and it was not long before we spotted a structure that, while being made out of the twigs, branches, and mud usually associated with common huts, was of such a size and architectural complexity that it more resembled a palace.

"Almost as soon as we spotted this extraordinary building, we were surrounded by a large group of men, who were short of stature and generally swarthy in appearance, and these men, who also had a language and manners foreign to us, led my group of merchants to the great building, where we were brought before their king.

"The other merchants thought this a great stroke of good fortune, and, when it became apparent that we were about to be served a banquet, congratulated themselves upon their good fortune. I, however, was not so quick to celebrate, for I thought of all my goods lost to the storm, and all these new potential customers before me, to whom I would now be unable to sell. This realization caused a malaise to settle upon my very soul, so that when the foodstuffs arrived, I found that I had little appetite.

"Soon, though, my fellow merchants and I were presented with huge plates of steaming victuals, the likes of which I had never seen before, being particularly bright in color and sticky in consistency. Nevertheless, my fellows fell upon these foods with enthusiasm, for they had not eaten since before they had been subjected to the rigors of the storm. In my state of mind at the time, however, I could not bring myself to touch a single bite, and instead shuffled the colorful yet gummy concoction about on my plate with the end of my knife." He hugged his stomach for emphasis, a gesture that perhaps, due to the merchant's present corpulent condition, did not carry the dramatic weight that it once might.

Still did Sinbad continue his tale: "For the first few bites, the other merchants kept up an enthusiastic, if intermittent, conversation. But, as they continued to eat, their talking became ever less frequent and their consummation ever more frenzied, until they ceased making any noise whatsoever beyond the sound of ferocious mastication punctuated by the occasional snuffling grunt."

"My master always tells such appetizing stories," Achmed commented as he placed a great kettle of water above the fire to boil.

"Only as these things truly happened to me." The merchant interrupted his story long enough to place his hand over his heart. "But the situation soon became far worse."

"Was there ever any doubt?" Achmed remarked as he turned to fetch more food.

But the elder Sinbad was so carried away that he no longer heard the comments of his servants. "While my fellow merchants continued to guzzle their meals," he continued with great drama, "acting more like beasts than men, our swarthy hosts brought forth great urns filled with a certain ointment. The swarthy men proceeded to anoint the bodies of my guzzling fellows, and that application seemed to make these merchants even more hungry than before, so that they gobbled down plate after plate of this foodstuff, until not only their bellies but their entire bodies expanded in all directions, until they looked more like overfilled water bags than men."

"It was my great good fortune that I had not partaken of the food, nor indeed allowed myself to be anointed with that mysterious ointment, for I soon discovered that these people were cannibals, and that their king enjoyed a roasted man for dinner every night, although his subjects preferred to eat their humans raw!"

Sinbad was about to be eaten again? Perhaps it was only that this very fate was about to happen to us, but it seemed to be a very common subject of the great merchant's tales. Was every island upon the great green sea awash with cannibals?

"The traditional story forms are the best," Jafar assured me as he continued to cut a pile of tuber-like vegetables to place into a stew.

"So did my fear for myself and my friends grow," were the merchant's next words, "especially as I noticed the more they ate, the less intelligent they seemed to be, so that, after they had at last seemed to sate themselves, the swarthy men herded them from the room as one might herd cattle, and, indeed, from that day forward, they were sent out every day to the meadow to feed.

"Still did I refuse to eat, so that in a matter of days I was little more than a shadow with the flesh dry upon my bones, and the swarthy men took little notice of me, since I would no longer make a fit meal for even the most common among them. But this ignorance worked to my advantage, for the cannibals took little notice of me as I crept from their palace the following morning, and made my way out into the fields. There did I see my former companions, but any attempt at conversation on my part was met by nothing but moos. So it was that I left the bloated merchants behind and set off overland, so fearful that I wished no sleep, and eating nothing but those herbs I could find that were familiar to me."

"How is the food preparation progressing?" called Dirk, who

appeared not to be among the most sensitive of listeners. "All this talk of cattle is whetting my appetite."

"Soon," Jafar replied. "We must allow the water to boil, and the taste of meats and vegetables to intermingle."

"It will be unlike anything you have ever seen before," Achmed further reassured the ruffian.

Dirk frowned, but returned to his work. Through great application, both he and the Scar had sawed through about half of two pieces of the great rope.

"Hold!" Malabala called with great urgency, such urgency, in fact, that all of us froze where we were, save that the knives disappeared deep within the clothing of Dirk and the Scar. And it was in this way that the cyclops found us all again.

"You cannot hide your true actions from me!" the left head called with great good cheer. So did this monster already know of our plans? Perhaps he heard so well with those four ears that he was privy to everything we had said!

"And may I tell you," he further remarked, regarding us each as a glutton might regard a plate of sweetmeats, "this does nothing but increase my appetite!"

"Eat now?" said the other head, which appeared to be much more awake than before.

The left head glanced to its right. "When my other half is truly ready for dinner," he said in the sunniest manner possible, "he is absolutely insatiable."

Chapter the Eighteenth,
in which we discover certain facts
concerning the cyclops's eating habits
that we would perhaps rather not have known.

"I know everything," the head continued, confirming the worst of my fears. We were doomed before. If what the cyclops said was true, how much worse could that doom become?

What would be the monster's vengeance for our blatant attempt to escape? More to the point: When you were planning to eat someone, how much more severe could you get? Perhaps, I thought with the slightest of shudders, he now planned to marinate us all while we were still alive. Then again, depending upon the sauce, that might actually be a pleasure.

"Indeed, I know all," the cyclops reiterated, "and my stomach responds accordingly. I could smell the cooking odors all over the island." He pointed an accusatory finger. "You cannot deny it!" Yet the monster did not point at Dirk and the Scar, but at Achmed and Jafar. "You are about to eat lunch!"

"Can we hide nothing from you?" Sinbad the merchant wailed in apparent dismay. "Would you care for a bite?" he added with a smile.

"My mother always did tell me I needed to vary my diet," the cyclops replied with a certain doubt. "Human after human after human; it does get a little boring after a while, let me tell you. Sometimes, of course, I eat them with the clothing still attached. It can be quite unpleasant, you know"—the left head belched for emphasis—"if a cyclops does not receive the proper roughage."

After a moment's pause, he added, "So what are you having?"

The merchant looked disdainfully back at the large cooking pot. "Alas, nothing but a mere stew. We are, of course, limited to what few provisions we managed to bring with us to the island. It is of some small compensation that my manservant, Jafar, is among the finest chefs in all of Baghdad, and the wonders he can perform with even the few spices he now has at his command will as often as not result in a concoction fit for a sultan."

152

"Stew, did you say?" the cyclops mused. "Can he do those same wonders when humans are the meat?"

"Please!" the merchant reprimanded. "You know how chefs are. You might offend his delicate sensibilities."

"Oh, dear, that will never do," the cyclops remarked. "Still, a stew, you say?" His left head grinned appreciatively, but his right-hand head appeared to be drooling.

I could do nothing but admire my elder namesake. He had the cyclops totally enthralled with the idea of stew; and, even better, it was a stew that would contain none of those present as a primary ingredient.

The cyclops seemed more than ready to sample the stew. But, it occurred to me, if we could feed our preparations to this monster, why not further prepare those preparations? After all, we had a talented magician in our midst, and did not magicians have a thorough knowledge of herbs, poultices, and suchlike that could cause all sorts of things to occur, death included? Malabala seemed to have some plan of his own concerning the cyclops. But what if we could simply poison the monster, and then leave the island at our leisure? It was certainly worth consideration. Now, if only I could share my plan with the magician.

I sidled over to the wizard, who was watching the events around him with great interest. "Malabala," I said softly, "if I might have a private word with you?"

"What's that?" he replied brightly. "We're having stew?"

"Say," the cyclops interrupted, "might I try a bit of that before you sit down to eat?"

"Why, most certainly," the merchant allowed generously. He nodded to Dirk and the Scar. "If our two most muscular compatriots might come over here and lift up the pot?"

The two ruffians hesitated, obviously unused to taking orders from any man. But even one as thick of muscle and slow of wit as the Scar must have assumed that my master had a plan, and it was best if they participated. So it was that, after wrapping scarves about their hands to protect themselves from the kettle's heat, they each hoisted a handle and carried the stew to that part of the cage closest to the monster.

But what could the merchant's plan be? There had been no time to add anything to the stew, as had been my thought. Perhaps it had something to do with bringing Dirk and the Scar in close proximity to the monster, so that they could somehow overcome it.

The two blackguards placed the large pot down so that it almost rested against the bars.

"Alas!" Sinbad said with regret. "The pot is too large to pass through the bars. Perhaps you cannot sample it, after all!"

Now I could see the merchant's design! He would have the cyclops bend or break the bars of his own prison, thus affording us an easier escape.

But the monster's left half simply said, "Nonsense," as the right-hand head, quite fully alert, grinned and said, "Eat now?"

With that, the cyclops poked his two hands inside the cage, flicking both Dirk and the Scar out of the way as a normal man might flick a fly. Then did he lift the pot, being not at all mindful of the heat of the thing, and hefted it up to the uppermost reaches of the cage. He pressed his great, right-hand head to a position slightly below that against the bars, tilting it so that his chin jutted well within the cage, and, after a final exclamation of "Eat now!," extended his tongue, which was fully the length of a normal man's arm. Then did he angle the pot in such a way that a great torrent of stew burst forth to splash against the bars and enter his mouth.

All of us within the cage were speechless at this display. It was an awesome sight, especially for someone who unfortunately expected to witness that mouth and tongue at much closer proximity.

The cyclops withdrew his tongue and smacked both sets of his lips. The pot rang like a bell as it fell to the ground.

"Quite tasty," the cyclops remarked with his left-handed lips. But the right-hand head seemed to be having trouble keeping its eye open. "You should enjoy your meal. And eating that helps me stay true to my resolve. I was weakening, you know, and considered munching one of you for a snack."

"We are most happy that you did not have to change your plans," the merchant Sinbad reassured him.

"I do indeed have certain plans for you," the cyclops acknowledged with a yawn. "And if anything, they have grown complex. When we next meet, you must tell me, what does Jafar know of marinades?"

With that, the cyclops ambled out of view. However, he had not traveled very far when we heard a great crashing, as if something of considerable size had fallen to the ground, and, immediately thereafter, a pair of odd, grating noises, like the scraping of rocks, or perhaps two giant heads snoring simultaneously.

"The cyclops generally falls asleep after a meal," the merchant marveled, "but not usually that quickly."

"Now, what did you wish to discuss with me?" the wizard Malabala inquired of me.

"I was wondering if you might—" I paused. Had the wizard already placed a spell upon the cyclops?

"Ah, yes, I must plead guilty to the facilitation of that task," the wizard responded with a chuckle. "When confronted with a supernatural creature which you are unfamiliar with, it is best to test its strength and stamina, if possible in such a way that the creature does not know it is being tested."

"Then, once we sever these ropes," Dirk called back to the wizard, "we can quit this place for good?"

"Did you indeed wonder?" the wizard replied approvingly. "I must admit, you are more clever than you first appear."

Once again, it was becoming unclear who the wizard was talking to. Soon, no doubt, it would become confusing as to what he was talking about. I turned back to the merchant instead, and congratulated him on foiling the monster. What, exactly, I further asked, had been his immediate plan?

The merchant laughed at that. "This was my only immediate plan: It matters not what the cyclops ate, as long as that something was not us. Beyond that, I had no design beyond keeping the cyclops's attention occupied, so that I might look for some means of escape."

"It would be unwise to do so!" Malabala said abruptly. "For I fear my sleep spell will only work for a short time on a creature of his size and constitution. We will have a better idea of the possibilities of escape once we see how long it takes for this creature to revive." The wizard allowed himself a small smile. "Besides, there is another small spell I wish to use on this cyclops."

"I suppose it could have been far worse," Jafar commented with as close to a note of hope as I had ever heard in his voice.

"How?" Achmed demanded. "If we had been forced to eat your stew?"

"Achmed is correct!" Jafar made the woeful realization. "The monster has devoured our entire repast!"

"We still have these vegetables," I commented, waving at the pile of foodstuffs near the cooking fire. "After all, it is better to eat almost anything than to be eaten."

"I could not have said it better myself," Achmed agreed. "We'll make an old wise man of you yet, porter."

Only Sinbad the merchant did not join in our jovial exchange. "It is going to become far worse. Tonight he will bring his *entertainment*."

With the inflection that the merchant put upon the last word, we could tell that the prospect was anything but pleasant.

It was at that very moment that the snoring stopped.

♦

Chapter the Nineteenth,
in which we learn that, sometimes, magic does indeed grow on trees.

The snoring was replaced, oddly enough, by a song. Something about "Do you know the way to Baghdad Bay?," which was foolish, since Baghdad was on a river and didn't even have a bay within a hundred miles. But the tune itself was quite sprightly, and the cyclops was gifted with a surprisingly fair singing voice.

I turned to my merchant namesake. "Is that a sample of the *entertainment*?" I asked in a hushed voice.

"Would that it were," the elder Sinbad answered with some trepidation. "When he comes to *entertain* you, you will never forget it. That is, of course, if you live to remember it in the first place."

But the song faded as the cyclops walked away from us, until it was lost beneath the constant moan of the island wind.

With the monster gone, the Scar returned feverishly to work. He jerked his head toward the pile of vegetables. "Porter! Bring me those! I eats as I works!"

"So will I," Dirk agreed. "I have decided that, no matter what happens, I do not want to come close to that tongue."

So we had, at last, found something that we might agree upon without reservation. As I gathered an armload of greens and tubers to take to the two musclemen, I sensed that, in our shared adversity, we had even begun to develop a certain very odd camaraderie.

"But come, merchant!" Dirk called as he continued to saw on his chosen rope. "You were only half done with your magnificent voyage when the cyclops arrived. Finish your tale while we finish our work."

The merchant smiled, apparently rejuvenated by Dirk's very suggestion. Even the threat of *entertainment* seemed to fade from Sinbad's mind when he was given the opportunity to continue his story.

But Jafar's throat-clearing stopped him before he could even begin.

"O greatest of equivocators," the majordomo said, "you were about to tell us how you survived in this new, strange land for eight days, eating nothing but occasional herbs and such. And while it is a pretty story, it is time that the others knew the truth."

"The valley of the figs?" Sinbad said rather more miserably. "Must I disclose that now? Few things are worse to discuss when other items are being ingested!"

"Come, now," Dirk called jovially. "Nothing can be worse than the sight of a cyclops tongue!"

"Well you may say that, you who have never been inundated by fruit!" He looked pleadingly at his manservant, but Jafar did nothing but utter a single, discreet cough. "Very well. What must be done should be done efficaciously. I shall continue, then, with the true story, and if any of you decide never to eat a fig again in your life, let not the blame fall upon me!"

Achmed dutifully began to pass out vegetables to the others as the merchant resumed his tale:

"It happened in this way," he began, the story he told now nowhere near as polished as his more practiced tales. "Let me see. I had been traveling all night, eager to get as far away from the cannibals as I might, and was becoming increasingly light-headed, for I had had nothing to eat for days besides those few herbs that Jafar mentioned.

"I should note that I had further crossed a range of rugged hills, and was quite exhausted when I came into the valley beyond. You could imagine, then, that not only was I astonished, but I also doubted fully that I was still awake, when I began to hear all those—voices."

He paused at this point, obviously struggling to continue. It seemed to me that he could do with some prompting.

"The voices?" I therefore asked.

"Yes," Sinbad continued with a shudder. "The voices, that seemed to come from nowhere and everywhere. For, while I could see no other human soul in this moonlit valley, but only row after row of fruit-bearing trees, I heard first one, then a dozen, then even more than a hundred of these voices. And what they said to me!" He shuddered then, and looked at the ground, again unable to continue.

I could see now that I was to play an active part in this present drama. "And what did they say to you?" I therefore prompted.

"They said—" Sinbad took a deep breath before he was able to continue. "They said, 'Mister, do you want a fig?' "

He paused again, as if to give us time to accept the weight of his admission.

Someone had to say it, and, from the direction our present discourse was taking, I felt it was required of me.

"A thousand pardons, O great and noble merchant," I therefore began, "but I feel that I am unenlightened concerning our present discussion. What, pray tell, is the horrible consequence of someone offering you a fig?"

"What is the consequence?" the elder Sinbad cried in disbelief. *"What is the consequence?* Well, actually," he continued, calming himself somewhat, "the consequences of eating but a single fig are not that dire, I suppose. But we are not talking about a single fig here. No, we are talking about figs upon figs, fruit upon fruit, thousand upon untold thousand!"

Jafar cleared his throat delicately. "Pardon me, O most talented of prevaricators, but if you might return to a recounting of the actual events?"

"Yes, yes, certainly," Sinbad replied with a renewed resolve. "But you must understand that the very mention of figs—" He paused to take another ragged breath. "Very well. I will reach beyond my apprehension to complete the tale.

"For there were no humans in that valley," he continued, his voice growing stronger as the story unfolded, "nor indeed were there any of the common natural or supernatural sources from which one might experience the sound of voices. And yet the voices persevered.

" 'Figs are among the sweetest of fruits,' they said to me, and 'Figs contain all the essential building blocks of life.' Then 'Three figs a day keep the undertaker away,' and 'A day without figs is like a day without breezes!' Oh, those voices were diabolically clever!

"But night was near an end, and I could see the first ribbon of dawn light up the hills beyond the valley. I reasoned that, if I but kept these voices talking, the ever-increasing light would at last reveal to me where the owners of these sounds were hiding.

" 'Figs are fruits you can depend on!' the next voice said close by my ear. I spun quickly to catch the bearer of that voice, but saw naught but the fruit tree by my side. And, indeed, in the growing illumination of morning, I saw that it was indeed a fig tree.

"But the presence of trees did nothing to solve my riddle; or so

I thought at the time. How, I wondered, could these speakers be so elusive?

"It was then that I realized I had not spoken back to these voices, nor had I made any other noise since I had entered this valley. Indeed, I further considered, if I now began a conversation, perhaps that would at last be reason for them to reveal themselves.

"So it was that I said, 'Why are all these figs so wondrous?' "

The merchant clapped his hands for emphasis. "With certainty, I knew I had fallen upon the answer, for I was answered immediately by many voices:

" 'We are plump!' said the first.

" 'We are tasty!' said the second.

" 'We are ready to be plucked!' said the third.

" 'We desire to be devoured!' added a fourth.

" 'Do not leave us to rot upon the tree branch!' implored a fifth.

"So I had at last made the contact that I had imagined I desired. For, as the voices spoke, I saw the branches of the nearest fig tree shake violently"—the merchant waved his arms in pantomime—"even though there was no wind whatsoever in the early dawn stillness.

"It was therefore that I decided to look even closer upon the fruit of the tree. 'We?' I cried in some amazement. 'Is it the figs themselves who speak?'

" 'What a clever man!' said a voice.

" 'And what an attractive mouth!' added a second.

" 'It would be an honor to be popped into a mouth such as that!' a third continued.

" 'And to be chewed by those magnificent teeth?' asked a fourth. 'Oh, it is a consumption devoutly to be wished!'

"And may I tell you, my amazement grew, for, in the ever-growing light, I saw that, indeed, there were wrinkles and spots upon these figs, as there often are upon wild-grown fruit; but that these wrinkles and spots moved in time with the speeches, as if each fig possessed a tiny mouth, and all these many mouths were producing the very voices that I heard."

The merchant surveyed his audience a moment before continuing. "So it was that I came to the valley of the talking figs. I did not yet, of course, realize the true danger of this place.

"Instead, I decided to determine my exact place in this new scheme of things. So it was that I asked, 'You are indeed figs?' And the fruit of the tree answered me. 'Yes, we are extraordinary figs, but figs nonetheless.' And I further asked, 'And you truly desire to be eaten?' At which point the fruit made a noise that seemed half like branches being blown by the wind and half like laughter. The smaller figs then were silent, and another fig, higher up and closer to the tree, and perhaps twice the size of any of the fruit that surrounded it, began to speak. And this is what the great fig said:

" 'You look to be a well-traveled personage, and so know much of the world. And in your many travels, you have discovered that there is a master plan for all living things. Thus it is that certain men are created to till the fields, and certain men are born to sit upon golden thrones and receive the results of these other men's labors. So it is also that certain animals struggle through their lives as beasts of burden under the heavy yoke of civilization, while other creatures are destined to roam free throughout the wild, unexplored vastnesses beyond the realm of man. So as it is with man and beast, it goes with fruits and vegetables; and we, as figs, must comply as well with our assigned task in this great plan of Destiny. Or, if I were to summarize: Fish have to swim, birds have to fly, and figs have to be eaten.'

" 'So if I were to eat you, I would only be fulfilling the hand of Destiny?' I then asked.

" 'Precisely so,' the great fig replied. 'Indeed, if you were not to partake of us, you could be said to be rejecting the natural order of things.' And, with that, all the branches of the great tree shook as one, as if all the figs were bouncing their agreement."

The merchant sighed as he called up these memories, a long, painful sigh, as if he were approaching the most unpleasant part of his tale.

"Well," he continued with a new weight to his voice, "I was never one to be confrontational with the hand of Destiny. Further, I had eaten nothing but herbs since my companions and I had been washed up on this foreign shore three days before, and the thought of a fat, juicy fig caused my mouth to water profusely.

" 'Very well,' I therefore said. 'If I must do this for Destiny.' "

The merchant reached forward and closed his right hand into a fist. "So it was that I picked a small but perfectly formed fig from the branch closest to my hand, and I swear to this very moment that that fruit squealed with delight as I picked it from the vine. I paused for an instant to examine this fruit I had chosen, and it indeed looked well rounded, and it further shone an especially appetizing yellow-green in the golden glow of the early morning light.

"'Eat me!' the fig in my hand implored. 'Oh, eat me! Why do you make me wait?'

"And, indeed, I did not wish this tiny fig to suffer, so I immediately popped the fruit into my mouth. And as my teeth descended upon the fig, I could have sworn that the fruit that I masticated expired with the most contented of sighs.

"But that was not the last of my surprises, for I discovered that not only could these figs conduct an intelligent discourse but they were also extremely sweet and pleasant to the taste, having the precise components of juice and pulp to make their ingestion a truly joyous experience." The merchant closed his eyes and smiled, as if he were savoring that experience once again. But his eyes snapped open and his smile vanished as he continued the tale:

"'Well?' the great fig next demanded. 'What do you think of the first taste of our tree?'

"'Excellent,' I admitted. 'Never have I tasted so fine a fruit!'

"And with that, all the figs upon the tree gave out with a great cheer.

"'To hear you speak so warms us to our very seed,' the great fig replied with pride. 'For, without someone to eat us, we are forced to do naught but hang about on our branches until we rot.'

"'A depressing prospect,' I agreed, for I perceived that, were I to experience their lack of freedom, I should surely go mad. 'I am greatly cheered that I was able to help one of your number fulfill its destiny.'

"'Oh, do not stop there!' the figs about me shouted. And all around me on the tree there began a great argument among the fruit concerning who had the best coloring and flavor, and who deserved to be eaten first.

"All of this attention had given me a feeling of heady importance that caused me to act rather more rashly than was prudent. I was helping to fulfill the figs' destiny, after all. So it was that I said, 'I may help to settle this argument!' and picked those six figs that were among the most vociferous of the hagglers, and wolfed down their sweet fruit one immediately after the other.

"The remaining figs cheered and begged me to go further, but I had eaten seven of their brethren in rapid succession upon an empty stomach, and thus discovered that I was in some distress." The merchant paused to hold his great stomach in remembrance.

"Well, you shall be in distress no more," a gruff voice came from the rocks behind us, "for now it is time for me to perform!"

Thus did the cyclops reappear before our prison, his announced arrival giving Dirk and the Scar scant seconds to once again hide their knives.

"Now it is time for the real entertainment," the monster said with the widest of grins.

Now did the merchant sincerely appear to be in distress. "But really, we are not worthy!" Sinbad cried, unable to hide the desperation in his voice. "You do not truly wish to *entertain* us?"

The cyclops scoffed at the very thought. "Why should I want to entertain you? You'll be in my stomach in but a day or two. No, this will all be done, in all its glorious detail, to entertain *me*! After all this time deprived of human flesh, I wish to savor the experience."

"Entertainment?" Malabala muttered from where he sat close by my side. "There are many different ways to entertain." Did this mean that the magician was finally going to put his plan into effect? At that moment, I fervently wished that the wizard had told us more of his plans; although the efficacy of that action, of course, would have depended upon our actually understanding his explanation.

"It is time to begin." The cyclops sat down upon a large rock beyond our prison. "I understand that one among you has been telling the rest a story. But, believe me, that story is as nothing compared to the tale that I am about to tell."

"Oh, no!" Sinbad wailed. "Not one of the *stories*!"

The cyclops continued as if the merchant had not spoken at all. "This is the story of the witch, Captain Howdja, and the Pasha of Pardon. Now listen carefully, for if you answer correctly, I shall grant you your freedom."

"Freedom?" the Scar called. "We gets our freedom."

"No," the right head corrected, "only the man who answers correctly shall be freed. That is why you must pay the most careful attention." At that, the left head giggled.

"So it begins again," the merchant murmured with finality.

"What does?" I asked, even though I was afraid what the answer might be.

"The cyclops lures his victims in," Sinbad the elder replied, "and then he leads them to their doom. There is no longer any hope."

"How could you say that?" I asked. "You, who have surmounted incredible odds seven times over, and each time returning from your adventures more wealthy than you were before?"

"You will feel the same," was the merchant's only reply, "once you have been *entertained*."

I could do nothing, then, but face the cyclops and learn the horrible truth.

◆

Chapter the Twentieth,
in which we see that while hunger may be deadly, comedy can be worse.

So we were to be faced, then, with one of those events which even Sinbad the merchant felt was too horrible to tell. Still, the cyclops had offered us our freedom, if we could but answer some riddle or other that he would put to us. Was it not at least worth the effort to listen to the cyclops's tale before we gave up hope entirely? So it was that I turned my attention to the two-headed monster as he began his tale.

"Know you, then," the left head began, "that in a kingdom far from here there lived a vengeful witch, who had been thwarted in her evil desires by that noblest of sultans, the Pasha of Pardon. There she dwelled at the edge of the pasha's domain, in a cave deep beneath the earth, and still did the witch curse the Pasha of Pardon. So great was her anger, in point of fact, that she decided she would send the three greatest demons that she could conjure to destroy the noble man."

"Listen to him!" the merchant whispered to me with disdain. "Not only does he doom us all, but the creature has no flair for storytelling!"

"Professional jealousy," was Achmed's even softer comment as he and Jafar moved closer to the bars and the storytelling cyclops. A moment later, as the magician caught up with the conversation, Malabala strode forward to join them, so that only I, my namesake, and the palanquin that contained Fatima were left behind.

"Thus did the witch call upon all the dark powers at her command," the cyclops proceeded, "and she summoned the three demons by name.

" 'Hoo!' she called, and a twelve-foot-high creature with horns equal again to the size of his great body appeared before her."

So it was that all but the merchant and myself stood in rapt attention, pressed against the bars and listening to the cyclops's every word. The elder Sinbad, conversely, showed a decided preference for fretting by my side, but I must admit there was a certain part of me that wished he would move forward as well.

It was not that I blamed him for his consternation, for, in my experience as a porter I have often felt the cruel hand of competition. I was even willing to ignore his guttural mumbles, which, though they formed no recognizable string of words nor were for the most part even fathomable as intelligent speech, still seemed to regularly interrupt my appreciation of the cyclops's tale.

But I must admit I had other matters upon my mind—well, even that was not the precise truth—for I really had but one thought upon my mind, and that thought rested within that brightly painted conveyance that remained in the rear of the cage while most all of my fellows had been diverted forward. And there it was, the thought that revealed my passion: Oh, if only the merchant could be encouraged to join the others, I should be alone with the palanquin!

The cyclops continued with his tale:

" 'Watzz!' she further intoned, and the second demon, a squat thing that seemed to be nothing more than teeth and claws, appeared before her."

The palanquin! My thoughts raced ahead of me, as if I had already opened the gold-encrusted door and set my eyes upon my mysterious beauty. I realized then that I must prepare myself for that eventuality, or I might freeze at that moment in a terror far greater than any of those monsters had inspired within me, for I would be in the grip of the terror of love.

Very well. I would plan my actions to the finest nuance. I would, of course, have to introduce myself to Fatima in a manner both quiet, to avoid detection by her guardians, and gracious, so that she might have a good first impression of me. That is, if she would consent to speak to a porter at all! Perhaps, I considered, it would be better not to present myself to her, after all, and be content with my dreams. But how hollow are dreams when there is no chance of reality beyond!

Yet did the cyclops proceed with his tale:

" 'Wair!' the witch then pronounced, and another demon arrived in their midst, although this latest one moved with such deadly speed that it was nearly impossible to guess its exact shape and size."

Still, I told myself, all the others were listening to the cyclops for a reason, the greatest reason of all, the promise of freedom. Perhaps I should forget my infatuation and join them, so that we might have a better chance of being saved. Still, however, the jeweled box, with its ever-so-alluring contents, beckoned to me, as if it were nothing but a giant magnet and my heart made of solid iron.

Freedom or Fatima? After the slightest consideration, I realized it was no choice at all, for without Fatima, I would never truly be free!

I stared more longingly at the palanquin than was perhaps prudent as the cyclops persisted with his tale:

"So did this horrendous witch further enchant the three demons, so that they were instantaneously transported to the palace of the pasha. But the Pasha of Pardon was not without his resources as well, for the noble and clever Howdja was the captain of his palace guard."

Even as distracted as I was, I could tell that this was truly a complicated tale. It was so complex, in fact, that even the merchant seemed drawn in, for, though he still muttered to himself on occasion, he also had begun to drift toward those same bars where all the others stood, thus leaving me alone in the back of the cage.

But I was not alone. I was anything but alone!

I stepped closer to the palanquin, and my heart stepped quicker as well. Still did the cyclops continue with his tale, so important to the others, yet so secondary to my fondest desire.

"Now here comes the first question of my tale. It is the entry to the palace, and the demons wish to sneak by the guard. But the captain waits as the sole defense against this evil! You must now think as the captain did to save his noble pasha! My right head will nod if your answers are worthy. Should your answers be false, of course, my right head will be more than happy to devour you.

"So answer truly, for the sake of your life!" He pointed to Achmed. "What would you say if three strangers appeared whom you expected to be demons?"

The child, as always, was ready with a comment. "Um—Who goes there?"

The right head nodded as the left head continued the tale:

"Exactly! Then 'How'd you know?' said one demon.

" 'That is my name!' the captain replied before asking the next question." The cyclops pointed to Dirk.

"The next thing to be said?" Dirk asked, his voice not so

smooth as when he was the one holding the knife. "It would surely be 'What's your name?' "

The right head nodded again.

" 'We have been given away!' said the second demon," was the cyclops's reply as it pointed to the Scar. "And next from the captain?"

"Um—er—um—er," the Scar replied, looking wildly about, either for an answer or perhaps a large stone or other weapon to throw at the cyclops. "Um—er—um—er."

Dirk nudged his companion and made a wiggling motion with two of his fingers, as if to show a man walking.

"Walks—no—leaves?" The furrows rose on the scarred man's brow as he said, "I gots it! Captain says, 'Where's you going?' "

" 'Have we no secrets from this human?' cried the third demon," the cyclops continued the tale. The left head beamed at his audience, sure that they had reached a level of true communication. The audience, for its part, looked about at each other with fully opened mouths.

But even I had paused, caught up in the puzzle of how the demons and the captain had known each other's names. But I shook myself at this pause in the tale, for I had other priorities. Now that I was so close to the palanquin, I knew that I must get even closer. The others were totally enthralled, not to mention thoroughly confused, by the monster's tale. I had to act before my moment had passed, for I might never get this moment again.

As I stepped to the palanquin, I listened to the cyclops continue the tale, almost despite myself.

"But the witch was not to be undone, not even by so clever a captain. Thus had she instructed her demons for even this eventuality, so that the three of them cried out together with such a fearsome roar that the captain was driven back by the very sound!"

It must be now, I told myself again, as I stepped as close to this mysterious box as I dared. I reached out my fingers to brush against the painted side, and pulled them back almost as quickly. The wood was cool beneath my fingertips, and yet to touch that palanquin felt almost as if I were putting my hand through fire. And yet I was far too close, and my mind was far too full of Fatima, for me to back away. I looked at the door before me, and saw, to my dismay, that it was closed by no simple handle but by a complicated clasp composed of a series of three bolts.

I tempestuously grabbed the topmost of the three bolts. It

clanked heavily as it moved aside, but the cyclops's audience were all too enthralled to be distracted.

"The situation was truly dire," the monster continued. "The demons were skilled in their evil, and they quickly had the captain surrounded, and were about to draw out his very life essence! But, at the last possible moment—"

The cyclops appeared to pause at the exact same instant I had decided to draw back the second bolt. I thought the clank this time loud enough to bring all the true believers in Baghdad back to prayer, but only the right head of the monster turned to regard me.

The left head continued with the tale: "—a great tapestry fell down upon the three evil creatures, and smothered them upon the very spot!"

My hand, which had been reaching for the third bolt, hesitated as I anticipated another pause. But the cyclops continued without a discernible break:

"Now, if you value your freedom, tell me the name of the one truly responsible." And with that the cyclops pointed at the members of our party, one after the other.

"What?" the Scar asked, totally befuddled.

"Who?" Dirk corrected his partner.

"Where was—" Achmed attempted to ask.

"Now you are all very wrong! It would certainly not be the demons!" The left head laughed as the right head licked its lips.

"What?" the Scar repeated.

"Who?" Dirk echoed.

"Certainly!" the cyclops exclaimed as if everybody knew what they were talking about. "Watzz, Hoo, and Wair!"

"But how'd you—" Jafar began.

"No," the monster interrupted, "he is the captain."

"The captain?" replied Jafar, now also beyond confusion.

"The captain," the cyclops replied, as if it were the most obvious thing in the world. "Howdja. Quickly now, before I eat you all!"

I expeditiously pulled my hand back to my side as I realized that the cyclops was pointing at me. But how could I deduce the answer without knowing where each of the major characters in this riddle had positioned himself? Therefore, I began with a question of my own:

"Which—" I began.

"Most certainly not!" the cyclops cackled. "She is still stuck back in her cave!" The creature pointed to Malabala as the right-hand head began to drool. "One final chance, or you are all on the menu!"

"Pardon?" the magician replied uncertainly. "I cannot quite under—"

"Correct!" the cyclops screamed, truly beside himself with excitement. "It had to be the Pasha of Pardon himself!" The left head seemed greatly impressed. "Your acumen astonishes me. Perhaps if you answer the rest of the tale correctly, I actually will let you go free. For, you see, there was this shortstop—oh, pardon me, wrong story—that is, there was this majordomo within the palace that went by the single name Eye—"

"What?" Malabala asked.

"No, no, that's one of the demons," Achmed corrected.

"Oh, I see!" the merchant Sinbad said in sudden comprehension of the tale's true nature.

"No," the cyclops contradicted, "that was the palace eunuch!"

But all eyes were again focused upon the monster and his tale. Perhaps what I did next was foolish in the extreme, but sometimes a man must act upon his desires, no matter how wild or how base they may be. With thoughts of beauty beyond imagination dancing through my head, I drew back the last of the bolts.

The door fell open rather more loudly than I would have liked, making the clank of the bolts seems as soft as wind chimes. And from deep within the recesses of the palanquin, there came a very distinct and echoing scream.

I slammed the door shut, and backed three paces quickly away. "Now, how could that have happened?" I began.

"This has gone quite far enough," was the answer I received before I could debase myself any further. But, to my surprise, it was neither Dirk nor the Scar who had spoken, and furthermore, neither one of them had drawn any of their long, sharp instruments of death. Instead, it was the right head of the cyclops whose voice had filled the void, and who further added: "Enough of this foolish entertainment. It is time to eat!"

"I have done what I could," the left head replied with resignation. "But if my audience does not appreciate my efforts—" He let his voice trail off to leave the consequences of his actions unspoken.

"Very well," the right head remarked jovially. "I'm still fairly full from lunch. No need to overdo." He pointed to Achmed. "I think this little morsel will suffice."

The cyclops reached out with both of his great hands and lifted the entire end of the cage from the ground. All those who had gathered to hear the monster's tale backed quickly away, with Jafar wailing, the ruffians calling curses, and even the magician yelling out one of his indecipherable bits of business. All retreated, that is, save the child, who stepped forward as if he were in a dream, and walked quietly forward to serve as the cyclops's meal.

◆

Chapter the Twenty-first,
in which Sinbad must determine
who, exactly, gives a fig.

The cyclops reached forward, scooped up the child, and the right head swallowed him without even chewing.

"You may have to pardon me," the left head remarked. "I seem to have a burp coming on." A moment later, both heads did precisely that. "Still, he wasn't much of a meal, was he? Tomorrow night, I will have to eat someone more substantial."

And with that, the cyclops allowed the cage to crash back down into place. He turned and again ambled out of view, singing another song whose chorus contained the words "I left my heart in Mesopotamia."

Jafar's wail broke the silence that hung about those of us who remained. "Achmed is gone! And he was but a boy—a troublesome lad, sometimes, but his cleverness more than made up for any of his remarks; that is, when his remarks were not in themselves causing trouble. And there was also that perpetual, annoying smile—" The elderly servant wailed again, perhaps to bring himself back to the purity of straightforward grieving without all those outside qualifications. "Still, he was too young to end like this!"

"Your concern for me is quite touching," Achmed replied as he stepped from the middle of the crowd, his smile, as usual, firmly in place. "I will have to remember it next time the servants are due for a raise."

"Achmed?" Sinbad the merchant cried in a voice rich with wonder. "But how have you been saved?"

"There is no need to thank me," Malabala broke into the conversation. "For I am sure you will wish to do so shortly, if you have not already, when you discover the true fate of the boy." The wizard's sigh was heavy with vexation. "This cursed conversation spell has me guessing now what you will say next; it is truly a diabolical thing! But one thing I had no need to guess at was the cyclops's next action, so I devised a quick spell to make him believe he had eaten one of our number when he had in actuality swallowed only air!"

"So you have totally fooled the cyclops!" the elder Sinbad exclaimed.

"We are no longer in any danger of being eaten?" Jafar inquired, the quaver in his voice going from a note of despair to a tone of hope.

"What and who are demons?" the Scar asked no one in particular.

"Quite," Malabala replied to one of the many questions that had been addressed to him. "I felt that, should we be able to deceive the cyclops for a sufficient amount of time, we should then be able to devise a plan by which all of us may escape unharmed."

"Brilliant!" the merchant called to the magician. "Your stratagem should inspire us all!"

"I feel inspired to cut some rope," Dirk remarked with a great deal more ease than that with which he had addressed the cyclops but a moment before. "What say you, Scar?"

"But witch still back in her cave." The other villain shook his head to rid it of errant thoughts, indeed, perhaps of any thoughts. "Scar cuts!" he said next, his voice now also more decisive.

"Ah, and speaking of cutting," Dirk politely segued, "there is a small bit of business I must attend to before I apply knife to rope once more." I noticed, however, that though he professed he would not yet use his blade upon the hemp, he had already drawn his knife. I further noticed that he was walking directly toward me.

He smiled as he approached, an expression that somehow made me more trepidatious than might a look of anger, as if the villain would not cut out my heart because he was enraged, but because he quite simply enjoyed doing that sort of thing.

He stopped but inches away from me, so close that I could count the hairs growing out of the lower portion of his tattoo.

"My dear porter," he addressed me, "you were involved in a small impropriety while we were confronted by the cyclops. Now, I realize that, when a man imagines he may soon die, he might be driven to certain extremes that he might later regret."

Then, I perceived, there was a possibility that this man was not going to kill me? I debated whether or not it would be safe for me to begin breathing again.

"I also believe it would be unwise to kill you, at least at the present moment," Dirk further remarked. I actually took a breath. "I think it would be unwise to kill any of you," Dirk continued, "until after we have escaped from this unfortunate situation." He lifted his left hand close to my eyes, and, with infinite slowness, allowed the sharpened edge of his knife to caress the back of his hand. It drew the slightest bit of blood.

"And afterward?" he remarked casually, as if the blood welling upon the back of his hand were an everyday occurrence. "Well, I might not kill you still, for I may have further use for you. But that might not prevent me from cutting you"—Dirk made a short, slashing motion in my direction with his blade—"in interesting places."

I could not help myself from repeating that word. "Interesting?" I asked.

That only caused the ruffian's grin to widen. "Interesting to me. It will be quite a different experience for you. The places that I refer to are most likely certain areas that you would, shall I say, rather not think about?"

I found myself thinking about those very areas, and what their loss might do to me. It did no good to realize that this reaction on my part had been Dirk's intent, and his speech and actions had been designed to do nothing but intimidate me. It took whatever I had left of my willpower not to cover any of those suggested body parts with my open hands.

"But I must get back to work," Dirk concluded as he turned away from me. "I must keep my knife hand active, and my muscles properly toned." The blade twitched in his hand. "We wouldn't want the knife to slip, would we?"

He turned before I could vehemently shake my head, but I shook my head nonetheless. Dirk had made my choices clear: I either stayed away from the palanquin or experienced the knife. It appeared that the beautiful Fatima was lost to me one way or the other.

All hope in me should have died at that instant. Instead, I promised myself that, next time I approached her, I would address Fatima with somewhat more discretion, or at least in some manner that would not cause her to scream. Do not ask me how I knew this opportunity would occur. Perhaps I was finally beginning to believe in the merchant's idea of Destiny.

"But we must get out of here as soon as possible," Dirk called to the others as he had once again applied his knife to the rope.

"These recent events have done nothing but strengthen my resolve."

From the grunts of assent among the others, it appeared that, upon this point at the least, we were in full agreement.

"So, merchant, continue with your tale, and make it lively now." He pointed with the tip of his knife at the sky, which grew dark with evening. "For I fear if any of us fall asleep before we escape, we may wake up in a monster's stomach!"

"Oh, very well," the merchant remarked, surprised, it appeared, to be thrust again into the limelight. "Now, where was I?"

"You had eaten a fig," Jafar interjected helpfully yet abruptly. "Actually, you had eaten seven figs."

"Ah, yes," Sinbad the storyteller resumed. "And the most succulent of fruits they were. But even the smallest of actions may have great consequences. So it was that eating seven of those fine fruits after allowing myself no true substance for days, I felt the slightest queasiness of the stomach, and then somewhat more than the slightest queasiness, so that I perceived that the figs would not spend a long time within my belly, but would instead be merely passing through before they were returned once again to the soil."

The murmur of assent that came from the crowd around the merchant indicated that, indeed, we had all found our own stomachs in similar circumstances at some time in our lives.

"So it was," the elder Sinbad continued, "that I decided I would need to answer nature's call, and I must further confess to a certain modesty, for, although I was surrounded by nothing but figs, still were they intelligent figs, and I found a certain hesitancy about revealing my most intimate functions before even creatures as strange as these."

Again, the merchant was greeted by a murmur of assent. At this moment I had to admit that my rotund benefactor was indeed a master storyteller, to keep his audience captivated with even such a subject matter as this!

"Thus it happened," the merchant persevered," that I found a place between the rows of trees, a mound of sorts that seemed to be composed of bits of rotting fruit and leaves, and, perhaps from the telltale odor that I detected, the occasional leavings of some forest animal. It seemed the most natural place to leave some offering of my own, and so it was that I set about my business."

The merchant paused again for ever so slight a moment, in that way which I now realized meant that the next part of his story would contain a major revelation. "However," he continued once the dramatic silence had properly passed, "I had not yet truly begun before a new voice called out to me from somewhere nearby.

" 'I would appreciate it greatly,' this new voice spoke, 'if you might find some other place to perform your natural functions.' "

The merchant raised both of his hands in the air, as if he were as surprised at this moment as he was when he first heard this phantom speaker. "It was then," he recommenced, "that I realized that this new voice came not from anywhere around me, nor indeed from the fig trees or anywhere else above me, but from immediately below my form, in that very spot where I had intended to deposit my offering to the soil.

"You can truly imagine my astonishment at this new discovery. So great was my surprise, in fact, that I completely forgot the disquiet in my stomach. And my amazement increased tenfold when I took a step away from that pile, and looked back to see a pair of deep brown eyes gazing upon me amidst the leaves and offal."

At this revelation, the Scar completely stopped in his sawing to stare at the merchant, and was only encouraged to recommence with repeated kicks from his knife-wielding partner.

"Pray continue," Dirk said to the merchant tale spinner, "for you now have us more than awake."

Sinbad nodded happily, so enmeshed was he in his own story that he could perceive of no other course of events but to see this tale to its conclusion. "I immediately hailed this unfortunate creature, and asked him if he had somehow become buried beneath the compost.

" 'Alas, if only that were so!' a mouth opened beneath the eyes to announce. 'I fear that there is none of me to be buried, for I have myself become the compost!'

" 'What sort of magical creature have I stumbled upon?' I cried in reply.

" 'I have no magic except for that magic which I have found in this accursed valley,' the mound replied. 'For I was once as human as you, before I began to eat the figs.' "

The adventurous Sinbad hesitated an instant to hold his stomach before he continued.

" 'The figs?' I replied as that queasy feeling in my stomach was again renewed.

" 'Yes,' said the voice as it proceeded to confirm my greatest fears, 'many, many figs, for once you have eaten one, you feel you must eat them all.' And with that, the lowly voice rose in despair. 'Indeed, you now see where my consumption has led!'

" 'You ate a great number of figs?' I asked, hoping in my heart that a 'great number' would not be defined as the number seven.

" 'Indeed,' the voice within the pile answered me, 'at first I ate only a few. But there is naught else to eat in this baneful place.' The unfortunate creature paused an instant to moan softly. 'And alas, it was also my great misfortune to discover that a diet of nothing but figs causes the digestion to react at an invigorated pace.'

"I nodded my head at the creature's observation, for I could feel that pace quickening within me as well.

" 'And soon,' the voice proceeded, 'I found myself eating more and more to replace that which had been lost, and that lost ever faster, and then faster still, so that the figs sped through my form faster than I might eat them. And, at the same time, I detected a certain softening of my form, and a lassitude within my muscles. And the more I ate, the softer I became!' Words failed the voice at that point as it was overcome by great, racking sobs. At last, it took a ragged breath and was able to continue: 'I realized then, when it was already too late, that I was being transformed by that steady diet of figs, until I would become nothing more than the products of my own digestion.'

" 'It is truly a terrible fate,' I said in a true spirit of commiseration.

" 'Once I was a proud warrior,' the mournful voice agreed all too readily. 'Now I am little more than an odiferous mound.' "

And with this the merchant Sinbad stopped again, and I could tell that, with this occurrence, the pause was not for a dramatic effect, but because he was reliving the sheer horror of this other man's fate.

"It would truly be a terrible way to die," I mused in order to break the silence.

"But very regular," Achmed added helpfully.

Our urgings seemed to bring the elder back to his story, for he coughed and again began to talk. "Here, too, was my future if I remained in this valley. It was only now that I realized the ramifications of my own actions. For it was through this discussion with this mound that had been a man that I discovered that these figs spoke not so much that they might themselves be destroyed, but so that they might perpetuate their own kind. For this thing that was once human had eaten profusely of the figs, and had in turn been transformed into a rich and fertile mound which the fig trees might feed upon in turn."

"Mysterious are the ways of Destiny," Jafar interjected.

"Yes," his master agreed, "but it was a destiny I quickly decided would not be my own. So did I ask the mound before me if there was anything it might desire before I quickly left this place.

" 'You know,' the mound replied after a moment of thought, 'I wouldn't mind another fig or two. They really are quite tasty.'

"So it was that I quickly picked what figs I could manage, doing my best to shut my ears to the fruits' continuous implorations. Thus did I leave a half dozen figs touching upon the lips of the mound, and quickly bade him goodbye."

Sinbad shuddered as he continued. "But the figs would not let me leave so easily. 'Figs are the perfect energy food!' they called. And 'Figs are so portable! Easily carried in turban, robe, or pouch!' And even 'Have you had your figs today?' And all I could think of was their juicy sweetness, and how satisfying the pulp felt as it traveled from my mouth to my stomach." Even now, as he told the tale, the merchant swallowed in remembrance.

"It was indeed fortunate that I had trained myself to deny the cravings of my stomach in my time among the cannibals, and that lesson was all that bolstered my resolve at this time so that I might escape. But still did my mouth water profusely as I ran."

And with that did the merchant seek out one of our water sacks, and then pause to drink profusely.

"That is truly an amazing story," I commented enthusiastically, "as marvelous as anything you have told before."

"Ah," my elder namesake replied at a pause between swallows, "but it is not yet done."

"And what happens next," Achmed confided, "is even more horrible than what has gone before."

At this point, both Dirk and the Scar paused to stare.

"Now, that is something," the more talkative of the two said, "that even I find hard to believe."

Jafar cleared his throat. "I feel that what happens immediately thereafter is not of the utmost importance."

"What?" Sinbad remarked with indignity. "But what happens next—"

"Shows how you once again went from being penniless to becoming even richer than you were before," Jafar interjected without much enthusiasm. "I fear that no parts of your tales that work to your advantage will figure into the plans of whoever it is that is causing these adventures to repeat. So we can skim over the bits about you introducing the saddle to a kingdom in which all men had ridden bareback, and that had made you famous and a great favorite with the king, so that he arranged a marriage for you with a beautiful bride, and that woman and you lived harmoniously for some months."

"But I love relating that to my honored guests!" Sinbad protested. "That is one of my favorite parts of the tale!"

"Indeed it is," Jafar bluntly acknowledged. "It is also the portion that your honored guests usually sleep through. Now get on to the true conflict."

"Very well," the merchant replied with a sigh.

But another voice interrupted before the merchant could begin.

"The true conflict is here!" the deep voice said. But the night was without a moon, and the sky had become so dark beyond the confines of our prison that we could not see who owned that voice.

The Scar rushed over to the cooking fire, and grabbed a log that was burning on one end. He returned to the edge of the cage and pushed the burning wood through the bars. The fire illuminated the space immediately beyond our prison, and showed the cyclops standing but a few feet away, with both heads smiling.

But it was too soon for the monster's return! He should have been asleep. We had not yet finalized our plans!

"I find myself rather hungrier than I might have imagined," the left head said pleasantly.

"Yes," the right head rejoined. "But it is just the time for a late-night snack."

"First, of course," the left head added, "you will be entertained."

Chapter the Twenty-second,
in which we face terror, step by step.

We were about to be entertained, and I saw no sign of the magician. I could hear Achmed's urgent voice behind us. "Wake up! Oh, please, wake up!"

"What?" came the wizard's slurred tones. "Oh, pardon of pardons, but I seem to have dozed off for a moment. The last I remembered, they had reached a part of the story in which the elder Sinbad was showing bareback people how to make saddles—"

"It seldom fails," Jafar interjected. "But we require your attention. The cyclops is about to eat another one of us at any moment!"

I glanced about to see Achmed helping the wizard to his feet. "I'm waking up as fast as I can. An old man needs his rest, you know."

Either Dirk or the Scar screamed as the cyclops lifted up one end of the cage.

"The cyclops, did you say?" asked Malabala, suddenly alert. "Why didn't someone tell me about this?"

"Come, now, little men," the left head chided as all the others joined Malabala and Achmed at the very rear of the cage. "Who among you wants to spend the last few moments of his pitiful life being entertained?"

None stepped forward to volunteer, but Malabala shouted out a quick spell.

"My, one of you is quite noisy, isn't he?" the cyclops murmured as he quickly reached forward and plucked the magician from our midst.

Well, I reflected with a certain degree of controlled terror, at least the monster had taken the one among us best able to defend himself. That is, if the cyclops didn't immediately swallow Malabala whole, as it had with what we had thought was Achmed.

"Perfect," the wizard said from where he still stood by our side. I looked again at the magician that the cyclops held, and realized that other Malabala must be another one of the mage's sorcerous constructs.

"This gives us some time to plan," the real magician explained quietly to the rest of us. "Would that I had enough strength in me to make simulacra of us all, so that we would be able to escape at our leisure while the monster played with our likenesses."

The cyclops smiled at the thing that looked like Malabala. "But I have a story to tell you, and another question to ask." He placed the magical construct on top of a large rock before him. "Of course, I urge you—any of you—not to try to escape, for then I will have to eat you immediately. But on with my tale."

"The monster takes unfair advantage of his audience," Sinbad remarked grimly.

"Plying his spectators with terror, rather than with food?" Achmed queried.

But I motioned both of them to silence. I determined that we should listen to at least the very beginning of the cyclops's tale, to see if there might be anything therein that would aid us in our escape. Beyond that, I felt that Malabala should take the lead, which he seemed to do much more efficiently when he didn't have the distraction of sorcerously delayed conversation holding him back.

"Now shall I tell you the story of how I was so cruelly abused by what you call—civilization! For once I had a love, a female of my kind. But she left me for another, a mortal man who came from"—he hesitated, as if the next word were very hard to say—"Baghdad!"

The creature took a ragged breath before it could continue. "Even now, the name of that city makes my blood boil. Yet I could not convince my beloved that she was making a mistake, and that I would be lost without her. But I knew I must stop him! And so, on that day that they were to set out for that city whose very name sends me into a fury, I determined that I must act. But where did this man come from?"

He had asked the construct. But it appeared that the one shortcoming of these magical apparitions was that they could not speak on their own. Therefore, to see where the story was going, I shouted from amidst the crowd:

"Baghdad?"

"Exactly!" the cyclops cried with a shudder. "That most cursed of cities! But I could not let him leave! So slowly I turned, and approached him ever so carefully"—the monster lurched forward toward the false Malabala—"step by step, inch by inch, until my hands could reach around his scrawny human neck!"

The cyclops's hands reached around the construct's neck in demonstration. "I could feel his warm flesh collapse beneath my fingers"—the false Malabala's tongue protruded as its neck collapsed beneath the strong hands of the monster—"and I squeezed and I squeezed and I squeezed"—the false head bobbed about in such a way that it looked as if it might fall off—"and I shook and I shook and I shook"—the monster did just that, and the false Malabala's limbs bobbed up and down like a puppet's; a puppet with no life left in it at all—"and my mouth opened wider and wider and wider"—the right head did precisely that as the left head continued the tale—"and I devoured him without another moment's thought!" And as he spoke, he stuffed the thing into his mouth, chewing noisily before he swallowed.

The cyclops paused and frowned. "My stomach feels almost as empty as it did before. Somehow, none of you seem to provide the sustenance I require." He surveyed the huddled crowd at the back of the cage. "Perhaps we shall have to proceed further with the entertainment."

Malabala quickly shouted another spell as the cyclops appeared to pluck Jafar from our midst.

"Quickly, now," the wizard addressed the rest of us, the actual Jafar included, in quiet tones, "we must coordinate our actions, if we are to survive. Perhaps I can conjure some distraction of sufficient size to capture the monster's attention long enough for the real party to escape. But escape to where? And how do we prevent the cyclops from following us?"

"Why don'ts ya kill 'im?" the Scar demanded.

"The cyclops does go on about his entertainment," Malabala replied with a wry grin. It was true that the magician had raised many valid points, and even more dangerous reservations. But how, I wondered, could we coordinate our actions when we couldn't even coordinate this conversation?

"How was I to deal with my grief?" the cyclops wailed melodramatically. He appeared to be enjoying himself immensely. "But then another human chanced upon me in my distraught state."

"What?" Malabala answered in genuine shock. "Oh, no, I'm not the sort of magician that kills anything outright. It is totally against my code. Now, of course, if we could urge the cyclops to, say, fall to his death through the use of his own actions, that would be totally acceptable."

So, in other words, there was no simple way out of this mess. I asked a question of my own. "Is there someplace upon this island that the cyclops cannot reach us? Some cave, perhaps, that he is too large to follow us within?"

Meanwhile, beyond the confines of the cage, the cyclops continued his tale:

" 'Oh, what ails you?' the human called to me in commendable concern. So it was that I told how offended I had become with one of his own kind. Still did the human commiserate with me, and wonder how even another human could be so cruel. Then did I tell this new man that the human I killed had told me that he came from the greatest city upon the face of the earth, and surely that is where he got his cruelty. 'But I came from that great city, too!' the new man cried in surprise. And what city could that have been?"

"There is nothing that I saw upon my earlier visit to this island," Sinbad the merchant replied with a tone of great misery. "Not a single place that is safe from the cyclops."

"But might there be?" Dirk insisted as he continued to watch the drama between the cyclops and the false Jafar.

The merchant grudgingly agreed that there might be some place that they had missed.

"What if we could distract the monster for enough time to send the boy out to look for hiding places?" Dirk asked urgently.

"And where is that great city?" The cyclops turned away in frustration from the false Jafar. "Will no one answer me?"

"We must send Achmed," the real Jafar whispered. "That is the only way we will get back to Baghdad."

"Baghdad!" the cyclops screamed. "Slowly I turned, and crept over so carefully toward the vile human being, step by step, inch by inch—" The rest of the monster's speech, and his accompanying actions, were all too predictable, as he picked up the thing that looked like Jafar and proceeded to strangle it and shake it into total submission before he again stuffed the construct into his rightmost mouth.

"So you wish to send Achmed?" Malabala replied with a frown. "Let me see what spells will be required—"

"I am still hungry!" the monster screamed, his voice a mix of rage and frustration. And, with a quickness amazing in one so large, he plucked me from the crowd before Malabala even realized there was a need to utter another spell!

I could feel the monster's hot breath as he pulled me close to his dual mouths. "Where did the man that caused me grief come from?" he demanded. Apparently, his hunger was now so great that the cyclops was dispensing with any further bits of the story.

What could I say? Visions of strangled and shaken corpses danced in my head.

"Answer," the monster demanded, "or I will eat you now!"

Answer? I knew what would happen next if I told him the word he wished to hear. But my mind was numb with fright. What safe answer could there be?

The cyclops pulled me toward his open mouth.

"Anyplace but Baghdad!" I screamed.

"Very good," the cyclops remarked calmly as he placed me down upon that same rock where had stood the magical likenesses of Achmed and Jafar. Perhaps, I thought, I had given the correct answer. The cyclops took a deep breath.

"Baghdad!" the monster yelled with both his voices. "Slowly I turned—"

I knew then that I was surely doomed.

Chapter the Twenty-third,
in which we discover that the seriousness of a problem does not necessarily depend upon its size.

"Step by step," the cyclops intoned.

I looked wildly about for a place to hide, but saw nothing save the child Achmed, stealing away from camp.

"Inch by inch," the monster remarked as he extended his hands to grab me.

I found Malabala among the others, but he appeared to be his usual self, distracted and confused. How long, I wondered, would it be before he realized that the cyclops had taken me and not another one of the beings created by his spells? And would I still be alive when that realization occurred?

For want of something better to do, I screamed.

"Sinbad," a voice intoned.

"That is my name!" came unbidden to my lips.

The cyclops paused mid-grab. "Who dares to bother me in the middle of dinner?"

"My name is Ozzie," the other voice remarked. "And those I seek rarely call me a bother—at least to my face."

"Ozzie?" both of the cyclops's voices said together as they looked aloft to see a glowing green head hanging in the air. "What's an Ozzie?"

"You would be better off not knowing," the djinni replied with his best glower. "Those who become too curious are not among the most fortunate of beings."

The cyclops paused and frowned.

"Where do you hail from, O glowing head in the sky?" he asked with remarkable politeness. If he was not cowed by the djinni's threat, as least the cyclops had decided to approach the situation with a certain caution.

Ozzie smiled at that. He obviously savored getting this very sort of question. "Indeed, where do djinn originate? From everywhere, and nowhere. From the brightest heart of the sun and the darkest cloud on a moonless night. From within your deepest dream and beyond your wildest imagination. From—"

"So you are a djinni?" interrupted the cyclops, perhaps not quite as cowed as I had first imagined. Perchance the cyclops, due to his habit of eating travelers who had washed up upon his island from every corner of the world, had become more worldly than the rest of us.

But the djinni simply nodded. "I've been looking for my naughty Sinbads."

"That is my name!" both the merchant and I cried at the top of our voices.

"Sinbad?" the cyclops roared, as if the name enraged him almost as much as the mention of Baghdad. "That was the name of the merchant who sold me this suit of clothes, so many years ago!"

Both heads glanced over me in curt dismissal before seeking out the others in the cage. "But the young one is too skinny," the cyclops mused, his anger tempered by a certain confusion, "and the fat one is too old. Unless—" Two very, very widely set eyes squinted simultaneously at the merchant and myself. "Cyclops do not age in human terms, you know. Could this old scalawag be the same thief who tricked me all this time ago?"

Both heads turned to the merchant, who was pressing himself against the furthest corner of the cage in a patently futile attempt to make himself somehow less noticeable.

"That suit?" the merchant managed after it became apparent the cyclops would not look away. "Well, my, I could have sold it to you. There have been so many transactions, don't you know? It is difficult to recall exactly—"

The cyclops turned away from me and took a step toward my namesake.

"Of course, everything I sell comes with a full guarantee," the merchant added quickly.

The cyclops took another step.

Sinbad's speed of speech seemed to increase with the monster's proximity. "And if you tell me that I sold you these rags, who am I to doubt a cyclops of your integrity? So let me tell you that I am hereby authorized to replace your garments in full, without any further cost to you—"

"No cost?" The cyclops hesitated as Sinbad quickly concluded: "—except, of course, for some very modest shipping and handling charges, which we will gladly deduct from your hoard of gold and jewels."

"All monsters inevitably have a hidden hoard of gold and jewels." I heard Achmed's hushed tone from somewhere in the nearby bushes.

The cyclops only muttered something about salesmen, and took another step forward. Those huddled in the back of the cage shrieked with some alarm.

"Marvel of marvels," Ozzie interjected. But when I looked up at the glowing green head, the djinni was staring past the cyclops at the mass of humans still huddled in the cage. "If you fellows weren't always no noisy," Ozzie chided the lot of us, "I never would have found you. I've been looking everywhere!"

"Ozzie!" Malabala called from his side of the cage. He stood as tall as his aging body allowed; his demeanor one of brittle command. As a younger wizard, he must have been truly formidable. "It is time we had our moment of reckoning!"

The djinni appeared to take no notice of the magician's words. "I have good news for both of the Sinbads," he said instead. The merchant and myself made the usual reply. "Well, it's good news for me, even if it is certain doom for them. There will be no more debate who is the genuine item here." The apparition's evil smile returned in all its malevolent force. "My employer, whose true nature I am still not at liberty to divulge, has authorized me to seize both of the Sinbads—indeed, anyone named Sinbad is mine!"

Dirk and the Scar seemed to be having a hurried discussion by the side of the palanquin. They flung the compartment's door open. Both jumped within, and the palanquin door slammed shut.

I once again found it disquieting that, at the first sign of danger, these strong and vicious-looking individuals did their best to disappear. And what exactly, I could not help but wonder, were they planning to do in such an enclosed space, especially since that space also contained my beautiful Fatima?

"Ozzie!" Malabala yelled. "Prepare to meet the full fury of a magician's outrage!"

The djinni chuckled in his usual bullying manner. "Still, though I am a creature of virtually unmitigated evil, I am not without compassion. Therefore, I will allow a moment for both Sinbads"—we gave the usual response—"to bid a farewell to their fellows before they go to face their eternal damnation."

It soon became apparent to me that I might find another fact even more upsetting than the manner in which the two villains had chosen to hide: more specifically that, even after a full minute with the three of them in such a confined space as the palanquin, there had not been a single scream or other sound emanating from within.

I could do nothing but face the unpleasant truth. Might the beautiful Fatima possibly prefer the company of flashy ruffians to that of a poor but honest porter?

"I no longer desire a new set of garments!" the cyclops announced as he approached Jafar, Malabala, and Sinbad. "I desire a stomach full of raw, human meat!"

"You can desire all you want," the djinni once again addressed the cyclops, "but these humans belong to me."

With that, the monster turned to stare up at the glowing head. "I beg to differ," the cyclops replied with a certain degree of menace, "but anything that lands upon this island belongs in my stomachs."

"Ozzie!" Malabala called in a futile attempt to draw the djinni's attention. "Prepare for the consummate duel of your unnatural life!"

"Aha!" yelled a voice from among my fellows at the back of the cage. I realized, from the direction in which all the others had turned, that the cry had originated from within the palanquin.

"Very well, Sinbads," Ozzie began. We both called back, to the djinni's eternal amusement. "The time has come for us to go!"

"I beg to differ!" Dirk shouted as he leapt from the palanquin, a golden bottle in his hand. "The only certainty here is that it is time for the djinni to disappear"—he waved the bottle meaningfully—"one way or another!"

Ozzie squinted at the bottle, which seemed to glow even in this darkness. "What is that you're waving about in your hand? You humans are so pitifully small!" He paused, his illuminated eyebrows raised in surprise. But when the djinni spoke again, his tone of contempt had changed to one of respect, and perhaps even fear.

"That isn't what I *think* it is?"

"Your employer has forced our hand," was Dirk's reply. "You cannot have the Sinbads, for they are destined for that place which employs the two of us!"

"I had been warned about this very sort of thing," the djinni replied with a certain resignation. "You remember how I avoided you before?" The great head sighed with the force of a wind before an approaching storm. "But now I grew careless, with victory so close to my grasp." His voice rose in exasperation. "Oh, causing murder, plague, disaster—give me the simple pleasures. Abduction can be so complicated!"

The Scar roared at that response. "Gives 'im the bottle!"

"You wouldn't *really* use that?" the djinni asked softly.

"Well, perhaps there will be no need," Dirk considered as he continued to hold the bottle up for all to see, "if you were to use your magic to send us directly where we require."

"*Send* you?" Ozzie turned a much paler shade of green. "But what would my master—"

"You are a djinni," Dirk replied smoothly. "What need have you to fear?"

"Ozzie!" Malabala screamed. When he again received no reply, he began in earnest to chant mystic words and perform complicated gestures.

"But my master—" Ozzie muttered.

"I've had enough of this!" the cyclops declared. "I'm going to eat all of you!"

Dirk moved his free hand to the top of the bottle. "You leave me no choice but to pull the cork."

"Not the *cork*!" Ozzie wailed. "Anything but the *cork*!"

"I wonder how djinni head will taste?" the cyclops mused. "It certainly sounds appetizing."

The magician continued to chant and gesture, his actions and words becoming faster and wilder.

"Fulfill our wishes," Dirk demanded, "or it's the cork for sure!"

"But if He-Who-Must—" the djinni sputtered. "No! Even I do not dare speak his name!"

"But first," the cyclops declared, "I think I will swallow a rather portly and annoying merchant!"

The monster reached for my namesake, but, before he could grab the older man, the merchant displayed a remarkable burst of speed for one of his age and condition, running into the midst of the crowd.

"The bottle!" Dirk demanded as he pulled the cork.

"But the vengeance of He—" Ozzie still resisted.

"Shamaba Noofaba!" Malabala declaimed.

"Are you sure you still wouldn't like a brand-new set of garments?" Sinbad offered on the run.

"Stand still and get eaten like a man!" the cyclops insisted.

And then the cork was free. A great wind sprang up, rushing

toward the bottle's open mouth, as if the space within the bottle were much larger than the space without, and the emptiness within needed to be filled with air.

But whatever force might control the bottle appeared to desire more than air, for I could see the great head of the djinni being drawn inexorably toward the bottle's dark entryway.

"No! No!" Ozzie screamed as he was dragged through the air. "Help me! Help me!"

"Send us where we need to go!" Dirk demanded.

Sinbad the merchant continued to run, darting to one side so that Dirk and the Scar were between him and the cyclops.

"We have recently introduced a whole new line of designer colors!" he called back helpfully.

"Eat!" the cyclops replied in exasperation. "Now!"

"Zoobooba!" the magician exclaimed in triumph as a great ball of blue light grew around his hands.

"Decide!" Dirk demanded as he held the cork just beyond the opening of the bottle.

"Help me!" screamed Ozzie. His whole glowing head seemed both longer and somehow less substantial than it had before, as if his essence were indeed being sucked into the flask in Dirk's hand. "Help me! I'm melting!"

"Last chance!" Dirk declared, moving neither bottle nor cork.

"Very well!" the rapidly discorporating djinni agreed. "Forgive me, master, but I must give them a travel spell!"

The Scar laughed again and slapped his partner on the back. "We wins!"

But Dirk looked at his now empty hand in horror. "You fool! You've made me drop the cork!"

"Noopoobah!" Malabala announced as the blue light rushed from his hands and into the sky.

Dirk fell to his hands and knees, searching the ground for that thing which would stop the tremendous wind. The great Ozzie's head was also drawn earthward as the supernatural wind grew in force. The blue light leapt forward, barely missing the scurrying merchant as it raced for the djinni.

It was then that the light met the wind.

There was a blinding flash that caused me to fall to my knees and raise both my arms before my eyes. Then all was quiet.

After a moment, I lowered my arms. Not only was the wind gone, but the blue light as well.

"That was as close as I ever want to get to the bottle again," the great voice of Ozzie boomed behind me.

As I looked about the clearing, I saw that the wooden poles of the cage had been torn apart, the sawed and weakened rope no match for the supernatural forces that had swept through the clearing. The others sat or lay about the open space; Jafar, Dirk, and the Scar all huddled beside the palanquin, which had fallen over on its side but appeared otherwise intact. Even the cyclops was downed. And Malabala appeared to have lost consciousness entirely, the serenity of his prostrate form only disturbed by a slow and gentle breathing.

"But I am still here," Ozzie continued. "Excuse me while I rescind my travel spell. I have a pair of Sinbads to abduct."

"Da djinni is still widdout!" the Scar remarked in despair.

"With no help from you," Dirk complained. The Scar scowled at him. "Wait a moment!" Dirk stared at the bottle, which sat upon the ground next to him. The bottle jerked and jumped. "Even though the djinni has escaped our trap, the bottle seems to have caught someone else!"

"Someone else?" I turned to see the great head of Ozzie resting, chin upon the ground. And that great head was frowning. "But who could that insidious bottle have captured?"

I turned to look quickly about the rest of the clearing. It was only then that I realized that Sinbad the merchant was nowhere to be seen.

And then there was another wind, and another blaze of pure, white light.

"Oh, no!" Ozzie wailed. "It is the travel spell!"

"Then, djinni," Dirk called back in triumph, "You have kept your part of the bargain."

"Perhaps so!" was the djinni's reply. "But I have no idea where I am sending you."

✦

Chapter the Twenty-fourth,
in which we learn that both travel and storytelling
may sometimes leave you in the dark.

"I want Sinbad!" the djinni exclaimed.

"That is my name!" I called. Could there have been a second, smaller voice that said the same thing from within the confines of that enchanted bottle?

Apparently, Ozzie could detect sounds in a way that a mere human could not, for his great head began to roll toward the bottle.

"I will have Sinbad!" the djinni declared.

"That is my name!" I called again, and I, too, sensed, rather than heard, the response of that second voice.

"No, you will not!" came the high child cry of Achmed as the boy rushed from the bushes and lifted the golden bottle in his hands.

The head continued to roll, even faster, now chasing the fleeing Achmed.

The djinni called: "I will destroy anything that gets in the way of Sinbad!"

"That is my name!" I again parroted helplessly.

"And I think the Sinbads should be together!" Achmed cried over the ever-growing wind and the great, deep roll of the pursuing head. "Catch!"

With that, the boy tossed the bottle into the air, so that it was pushed upward by the next great wind gust, and flew in a great arc above the djinni's head to land within my waiting hands.

I closed my fingers over the bottle, which was pleasantly warm to the touch. The wind screamed in my ears. It seemed to have doubled in intensity the minute I grasped the bottle, and now swirled all about us, as though we were at the center of some great dust devil.

There was a second flash of light so bright we might have stepped inside the sun.

With that, the wind was gone, and all was darkness.

* * *

Only Allah knows how long I lay there in that deepest of nights, oblivious to all the world. But I was woken at last by a faint, yet familiar voice.

"Is anyone there?"

"Sinbad?" I asked as I realized I yet held the still-warm bottle in my hand.

"That is indeed my name," the voice replied. "Who am I speaking to?"

Could he not also recognize the sound of my voice? Still, perhaps being trapped in a bottle might alter one's perceptions. "I am the other Sinbad," I answered patiently.

There was no immediate reply.

"Sinbad the Porter," I further clarified.

"My good friend!" The merchant's voice now responded with enthusiasm. "You will have to forgive my momentary lapse. I have such trouble with names and faces. Not that I can see your face. It is exceedingly dark, wherever I am."

Dark? From the size and direction of his voice, I knew that Sinbad must still reside in the bottle, which I yet cradled in my hand. But I had to admit that it was exceedingly dark whether one was in the bottle or without.

"O great merchant and famed adventurer," I answered gently. "There seems to be no light at all in this world, as if we were deposited in a land of endless night, with clouds that covered the moon and stars."

" 'Tis a worthy explanation," the merchant's tiny voice replied, "save that it does nothing to explain the closeness I feel at the moment. I swear, good porter, that I can scarcely move!"

It only occurred to me then to imagine how Sinbad the merchant would have fit into this enchanted bottle. No doubt that widest part of him, his stomach, had become lodged in that narrowest portion of the bottle's neck. I could think of no better explanation than that sort of blockage for the cessation of the supernatural wind. In his way, then, Sinbad had become a human cork. Truly, the world was full of marvels!

But what might happen now? I remembered, all too well, Jafar's caution concerning the legacy of Sinbad's voyages, and how they had returned to haunt us. What if we were not merely beneath a cloudless sky, but in some other horrible place that the merchant had visited in one of his later adventures? For that reason alone, my quest for knowledge was again an utmost necessity. I quickly asked the merchant if he had ever had occasion to spend time on his voyages in places of exceptional darkness.

"Well," Sinbad in the bottle admitted, "there is one possibility. It would take too long to explain, but you could kick about with your feet a little bit and see if there are any corpses."

Corpses? My quest for knowledge might also become extremely unpleasant. No matter how long it took, I felt it most prudent to familiarize myself with the remaining voyages. "Tell me the rest of your tales now, O merchant," I said with a force prompted by fear. "As Jafar said, the knowledge we gain from these events might save our lives." My thoughts of the elder servant led me to add a final condition: "And please make them as brief as possible."

"Yes," Sinbad replied with more enthusiasm than regret. "I suppose you are correct. Poor Jafar. I wonder where the cursed djinni's spell deposited him? But where was I last within my tale?"

"You had been making saddles," I prompted, feeling my eyes grow heavy at the very thought.

"Ah, yes, the corpses came immediately thereafter."

This did nothing to calm my nerves. If the voyages were indeed following each other in some sort of order—

I forced the thought from my head, and, to reassure myself, I gently pushed my foot out before me. I felt something with my toes. Truly, though, it would prove to be nothing more than an exposed root.

Unless it was someone's skeletal remains.

I quickly withdrew my foot, deeming it more expedient, at this precise moment, to listen to the merchant's chronicle.

"Well, as you no doubt recall," the merchant began, comfortably resuming his tale, "I had gained great fortune in this new kingdom by introducing such unknown inventions as the saddle for a horse, and so was well regarded, and given a fine house and married to one of the most beautiful women in the realm.

"This, I thought, was true happiness, almost the equal of the best of times in my beloved Baghdad. But my joy was short-lived, for one day tragedy struck my neighbor—a tragedy that revealed the horrible truth about this land I now called home."

The merchant paused. "Excuse me. I have a bit of a cramp." He grunted substantially. "Ah. Much better."

I blinked. For an instant, I could have sworn I saw the bottle glow. Were my eyes playing tricks upon me in this never-ending darkness?

"My neighbor's wife had met with an accident, and had died," the tiny tale spinner continued. "At first, I thought my neighbor's anguished wails were merely grief over the loss of his beloved spouse, but soon he calmed enough to tell me the true horror of local custom, which was that, whoever should die first within a married couple, be it husband or wife, the other spouse would then be buried alive with his or her deceased mate!"

" 'This custom is truly barbaric!' I cried. 'But it is the law of the land,' was my neighbor's reply, and, indeed, at dawn the next morning, a detachment of the king's guard led my neighbor away to prepare him for his fate."

The merchant paused again, and I could feel the bottle move in my hand, as if the elder Sinbad were shifting about within. "Where are we, anyway? There is absolutely no room for my limbs." And, as the miniature merchant tried to find some more comfortable position in his bottle prison, I again felt the bottle warm in my hand, and saw a definite glow emanate from the golden metal flask.

I thrust the bottle forward, toward the spot where my foot had met the unknown obstacle. But the light was gone. The illumination appeared to originate whenever the merchant shifted about in his magic prison. Yet I was reticent to discuss this matter with my elder namesake, for fear that it might interfere with his story. As selfish as my motives might have been, I reasoned that the discovery that one has been supernaturally shrunk and stuck within a magic bottle is not among most persons' immediate lists of causes for celebration.

"I assume that your wife soon died as well?" I asked instead, to speed the merchant on with his tale.

"How could you tell?" The very small Sinbad's chuckle seemed to hold a hint of admiration. "For a porter, you have a great knowledge of storytelling."

But I would not let him distract me so easily. "And you were then buried alive along with your dead wife?"

"Precisely. The two of us were left in a large, lightless cavern, which was again the custom among these people. Luckily I was also buried with some quantities of food, to keep me alive for a week or more.

"But the great boulder was barely rolled to cover the mouth of the cavern before I realized I was not alone among the living in this cave. Indeed, there were other unfortunate victims of this custom, who had survived by killing unsuspecting newcomers and devouring their foodstuffs, and, when that failed them, dining upon human flesh."

This darkness Sinbad described seemed to grow more unpleasant with every passing word. It was so unpleasant, in point of fact, that I felt it prudent to further explore our surroundings.

"Pardon me for interrupting," I suggested, "but are you quite comfortable?"

"Now that you mention it, I am not." The merchant grunted and the bottle glowed.

I thrust it forward again, and discovered the object of my fear was nothing more than a gnarled root. So we were not in that fearful cavern. But where, then, had the djinni transported us? Rather than reassuring me, I realized that I almost might have rather discovered that cavern around me, for then at least I would know my danger. But now we were in some new place, perhaps awaiting some awesome peril as yet undescribed by the merchant. I decided to again hurry the merchant's tale.

"But you overcame these flesh eaters?" I asked.

"Why, yes," the merchant replied, "for I managed to grab a sturdy thighbone and fight—"

"And then you escaped from the cave?"

"Indeed," Sinbad hurriedly responded, "by following a wild beast who had entered the cave to feed—"

But I was relentless in my interruptions. "And no doubt you somehow amassed a great fortune?"

"Oh," the increasingly flustered merchant added, "of course, for there were a great many jewels and other valuables among the funeral offerings of—"

"And thus you returned to Baghdad, even richer than before?" I finished for him.

"You are interrupting the best parts of my story!" the merchant answered petulantly. "How am I supposed to enjoy my talk when I am being constantly interrupted?"

Alas, my terror of imagined death had perhaps temporarily overcome my sense of place. "Forgive me, O wise merchant, if I try to speed the information," I said in tones more suited to my station, "but I fear that some other man or creature from your tales will appear and interrupt us forever."

"I appreciate your concern," a much subdued Sinbad replied after a moment's thought. "Which story may I tell you now?"

What could I tell him? Only that I, myself, already knew of our surroundings. "Do you have any stories that prominently feature exposed roots?"

"Most of my stories take place upon the wild, uncharted islands at the very edge of the known world," was the merchant's reply. "Exposed roots are everywhere."

I therefore told him to proceed with his next story.

"Very well—" he began.

"But omit all those parts about leaving Baghdad," I added.

"Perhaps that is best," he agreed. "So we were many days at sea—"

"In the interests of time," I further amended, "it would probably also be wise to omit any lengthy mention of this particular shipwreck."

"Then I am to go immediately to the good parts?" Sinbad asked in none too happy a tone.

"For the sake of our lives," I urged.

"Thank Allah the audiences in Baghdad are not so demanding! But you are correct. Let me proceed immediately to the first danger, which again was a Rukh. No, not one Rukh, but two."

"This was the place where you partook of the Rukh's egg?" I asked.

"To my current sorrow," Sinbad admitted. "For the Rukhs destroyed our ship, and were only scared away by a great beast that even the Rukh fears—"

"Would this beast attack humans?" I asked.

"He is so great he makes the Rukh appear to be no larger than a sparrow. Man is so small as to be beneath his notice, no more bother than a flea upon the hide of the elephant." Somehow, even the merchant's simplest answers had a tendency to turn back into his story.

"Very well," I said, increasingly anxious to propel the tale onward. "We may come back to that part of the story when there is time. What happened when you reached the island?"

"Ah, it was a place that looked at first, with its profusion of fruit trees and game animals, like Paradise upon this earth."

"But it wasn't."

A deep sigh came from within the bottle. "No, for I soon spied an elderly man, whom I took to be another shipwrecked sailor. At first glance, his legs appeared to be gnarled and feeble, and he asked me ever so pleasantly to place him upon my shoulders so that we might ford a nearby stream and reach some fruit trees upon the other side.

"Here was my chance to do a good deed, so I took this stranger upon my shoulders and crossed the stream. But when I bade him to dismount upon the other side, he instead increased his grip upon my shoulders and neck. I looked more closely at his legs, and realized they were covered with dark fur, and this creature was not human, but some kind of demon. His grip upon my shoulders was so firm that I could not dislodge him, and, should I try for any length of time to disobey him, he would squeeze my neck with such force that I would pass from consciousness. Thus I became this demon's beast of burden."

"And how did you escape?" I asked, drawn into the story despite myself.

"By producing wine, and making the creature inebriated," the merchant admitted. "You see, if you squeeze grapes and leave the juice in an enclosed gourd in the sun—"

"No doubt," I quickly interrupted as soon as my curiosity was satisfied. "And then you once again reached civilization. How did you make your fortune this time?"

"Through the collection of coconuts and pearl fishing. But the true interest rests in how I accomplished these—"

"I have no uncertainty on that account," I agreed. "Then you returned to Baghdad, richer than ever before?"

"It is the best way to end a story," Sinbad admitted. "Shall I go on to the next tale?"

"Wait a moment," I instructed as I saw the sky slowly shift above me from black to gray with the first light of dawn. "I think it will soon be morning, and we will be able to determine our whereabouts."

"It is? Then why can I not see anything?"

Apparently, Sinbad had been sucked into the bottle headfirst. Perhaps it was time to take pity on the merchant and tell him of his predicament.

But then the gray light turned to gold upon the horizon, and I saw that we were on the lip of a great valley, and that the valley beneath us was filled with fruit-bearing trees.

"Hey there," I heard a voice from the tree nearest to where I stood. "Want a fig?"

♦

Chapter the Twenty-fifth,
in which we discover that all things come to him who travels, but some of those things don't stay very long.

"I didn't hear that!" the Sinbad within the bottle wailed.

But I could not lie to my elder about something as serious as this. "Alas, it is all too true. There are fig trees everywhere."

"Not the figs!" the smaller Sinbad cried. "Anything but the figs!"

"Do we hear someone admiring the figs?" a nearby fruit inquired.

"No doubt," a second vegetative voice chimed in. "For we are the most admirable fruits imaginable."

"At least I can't see them," the merchant added with a shudder. "But *why* can't I see them?"

Perhaps, I thought, it was time to tell my elder namesake about his bottle prison.

"We are plump and succulent," a fig added near my ear, "and ready for the plucking."

"Imagine your teeth breaking our delicate skin," a second fig added, "the sweetest of pulps rolling across your tongue, the ambrosia of our juices dribbling languidly down your chin."

To my horror, I discovered that my mouth was watering.

"I have gone blind!" the elder Sinbad moaned. "I will be forced to spend my few remaining hours sightless, eating nothing but enchanted figs!"

"And we are enchanted!" another fig agreed merrily. "Not only are we tasty, we are entertaining!"

"No, you are not blind, O merchant!" I called reassuringly to my elder. "To the best of my knowledge, the manner in which to describe your condition most appropriately is *stuck*."

"You're never stuck when there are figs around," yet another fruit added. "Figs make things move!"

"Brothers and sisters!" the enchanted fig called to its brethren. "Let us bring peace to these travelers with one of our songs!"

And with that, the whole orchard seemed to join in a great chorus.

> *"Oh, I heard it through the fig vine,*
> *Not much longer would you be mine—"*

I stared at them, rows on rows of perfectly formed oblong globes, all swaying gently together, back and forth, back and forth. They looked so round in the golden morning light, so juicy beneath their brownish-green skin, so—so—*edible*.

"So I'm stuck with them singing?" the Sinbad in the bottle remarked in an even-more-dismal tone than before.

I blinked, and ignored my heartily growling stomach. Those figs had almost lured me into their trap. If not for the whining of the merchant in the bottle, I would have plucked one of those figs, and placed it in my mouth, and bit through the skin with my teeth, and closed my eyes as the first sweet tastes hit against my tongue, and—

"I am indeed fortunate"—the merchant's voice once again broke the spell—"that I cannot see these figs as well as hear them, for I am certain that the combination would be more than a man could bare. But, pray tell, even more succinctly than your last explanation, why am I so fortunate?"

I swallowed. Never in my life had my mouth produced so much saliva. But I had to protect myself from the fruit's seductive spell. I bit my lips and thought of rotting produce, crawling with maggots; flies rising en masse from fetid swamps; anything to turn my stomach against the song of the figs!

"You are trapped," I managed to tell the small Sinbad from between clenched teeth.

"All men are trapped when they enter the valley of the figs," the merchant replied with a certain resignation.

"No, no," I further explained, and found there were many words that were difficult to say when your teeth were unmoving, "you are trapped in the magic bottle."

"Bottle?" the merchant replied in incomprehension. "I know of no bottle large enough to contain—"

"Indeed there is not, were you to have maintained your original magnificent size," I continued my clarification as gently as possible. "But you have not. You have changed, much as the djinni Ozzie must shrink to fit within that very same enchanted vessel."

"I am trapped in Ozzie's bottle?" the elder Sinbad cried out in disbelief. "I have shrunk so far?"

"It is the truth," was my most sympathetic reply. "Only perhaps not far enough."

"It *is* a little tight around my stomach," Sinbad admitted.

"Figs are the perfect solution for those who want to trim those waistlines," a nearby fruit suggested in the most helpful of tones.

"Never!" the merchant called in desperation. His shout seemed to echo slightly in the confines of the bottle. "I would rather be stuck for all eternity!"

"Figs offer an eternity of pleasure!" rhapsodized another limb-hanger.

"If eating these figs doesn't kill us," a young voice piped up from between the trees, "their chatter certainly will."

"Who's that?" the merchant in the bottle demanded.

"Could it be?" I asked aloud. And indeed it was, for as the sun rose fully over the valley's edge to bathe the trees in its golden light, Achmed stepped into view.

"I trust that my entrance is properly dramatic," he commented lightly.

"It is Achmed," I cried with delight. "The travel spell must have caught more than the two Sinbads!"

"Achmed?" the merchant called in some confusion.

"Your young servant, whom you have brought along upon this peril-fraught voyage," Achmed explained with practiced ease.

"Ah!" the merchant's voice echoed enthusiastically. "*That* Achmed! It is such a common name, you know."

"Figs are anything but common," said one of the nearby fruits.

"There are so many of us," commented another, "but each of us is unique." Apparently, this latest drama had left the figs feeling overlooked.

"Try a few," a third fig joined in. "Every fig is a taste sensation!"

"It is my misfortune, but they are all too correct!" came the mournful sound of the bottled voice. "I can remember their succulence even now!"

Here was a man who could not retain the names of his traveling companions, yet he seemed to recall every nuance of these figs. The mystic power of this fruit must be truly awesome. I remarked upon this wonder to Achmed.

"Alas," was the boy's reply, "you forget that the memory of my master's stomach is far more generous than that of his head."

But the figs were calling out at this very moment, elsewhere in the grove. And yet another voice was calling back.

"We are so close!" the many voices called. And "We are so available!" And further, "Reach out for a fig today!"

"I cannot!" cracked an aged voice, heavy with concern. "I must not, even though, for one of my advanced age, the action of the fruit might prove beneficial!"

I would recognize that quavering voice anywhere.

"Jafar!" I called.

"Your elderly majordomo, whom you have also brought along on this peril-filled journey," Achmed explained before his master even had a chance to ask.

"Most certainly—Jafar!" the merchant roared. "Excellent. We are reunited by the djinni's spell."

"Certainly this seems most fortuitous—" I began.

"Figs are the most fortuitous of fruits!" called a voice from the trees. Apparently, the fruit grew increasingly tired of being ignored.

"Figs are the most serendipitous of snacks!" other fruit in the vicinity took up the chant. "Figs are the most enchanting of edibles!" and "the most delirious of diets!" and even "the most vivacious of victuals!" On and on, the many fruits proclaimed their good fortune.

"What can *one* hurt?" a gruff voice broke through the vegetative chorus. It appeared to come from the grove behind me.

"One will never hurt!" the local figs agreed enthusiastically. "And a dozen will hurt even less!"

"Quiet!" another voice demanded. "I thought I heard humans speaking up ahead."

"Who needs human voices," the fruit interjected sweetly, "when you can listen to the music of the figs?"

And with that, the figs behind us began to hum.

There came a great crashing sound, as though vast quantities of branches and leaves were being ripped asunder.

"Back! Back!" the second voice yelled with more than a trace of panic. "Dirk will never be defeated by a bunch of fruit!"

As if in answer, the fruit began to sing:

"There is nothing like a fig, nothing in the world—"

"Scar eats soon!" the first gruff voice interjected. "Scar needs strength!"

But the fruit were relentless: "There is nothing you can dig," they sang, "that is anything like a—"

"There they are!" Dirk shrieked with a tone of total desperation. "Forget the figs! We have found the Sinbads!"

I spun about to see the two muscled ruffians burst forth from that side of the grove, the conveyance that they still carried now rather scarred from recent abuse. Apparently, from the evidence of the dents and scrapes in that once-glorious box, they had traversed the densely forested hillside by brute force, pulling their palanquin through no matter what trees or other obstacles stood in their way.

"But we needs to keep our strength!" the Scar argued loudly. "We needs to get the Sinbads back to—"

"Figs will not solve our problem!" Dirk replied urgently. "Don't you remember the merchant's story?"

But the gruffer muscleman seemed to only have eyes for the fruit. "Scar is stronger dan any fig!" he insisted.

"Figs are the perfect energy food!" the surrounding fruit urged now that their song was done.

"Feeling lethargic?" one fruit asked.

"Run-down?" the next added.

"Your pep all pooped?" came from the next.

"It's time for figs," all three said in chorus. "The better way to a cleaner, healthier you."

"If you don't stop your chatter," a new voice cried in exasperation, "I shall cause all of you to immediately rot upon your branches!"

The fruit appeared momentarily stunned into silence as Malabala stumbled against me, almost knocking the bottle from my hand.

"Forgive me," said the wizard. "This cacophony of figs has me temporarily undone." He took a deep breath, then whistled softly. "I am continually impressed by the subtlety of the djinni's spell. To cause even the speech of the figs to speed ahead—such magical thoroughness is uncanny!"

"Who are all these people?" the voice cried from the bottle. "And why did the earth shift so?"

"We have all returned," I explained briefly. "All of us together upon that island. Apparently, the djinni cast his spell upon the entire group of us. And as to that shift, I am afraid it was not the earth, but only the bottle around you which moved."

"The earth has shifted?" Malabala asked doubtfully. "Will this spell prevent me from experiencing the world around me as well?"

"The djinni has taken us all?" Jafar wailed as he realized the full implication of my statement. "But that would mean—"

"There you are!" the cyclops bellowed. I saw him wave to us from where he towered above the figs trees. "Have you tried these figs? They're absolutely delicious." He smacked his lips as he ambled forward. "I tell you, a constant diet of human flesh leaves something to be desired. After I ate that stew, I realized that I needed a serious change in my choice of cuisine. And then I got no enjoyment at all out of eating your fellows. I realized I could no longer savor the experience. It was almost as if, in gobbling those insignificant humans down, I was eating nothing at all!"

The appearance of this cyclops seemed to dampen what was already an uncertain mood among my fellows. In point of fact, besides Malabala, who was muttering something about "Bottle? What bottle?," I noticed many of my companions already beginning to cringe and whimper. I, however, felt that perhaps there might be some simple way to eliminate this complication.

I therefore asked: "Then the figs satisfy your need for variety?"

"Indeed they do," the cyclops agreed affably.

"Well, then," I quickly added, "it has been very nice making your acquaintance, and we trust we will see each other again, perhaps in the extremely distant future. Gentlemen," I said to the others about me, "I believe it is time we were moving on?"

But the cyclops stepped forward to block our collective retreat. "The figs supply my immediate dietary needs, that is true." He paused to allow his mouth to twist upward into an all-too-familiar grin. "But I still need you humans to provide that which is even more important—the entertainment."

And yet with that, his triumphant grin fell as quickly as it had arrived. "Oh, dear," he added in a somewhat more uncertain tone. "Excuse me. I have to answer nature's call."

The figs, then, had already begun their hellish work! It occurred to me that, if the cyclops continued his current dietary course, we would have to do nothing but wait and he would eliminate himself. That is, of course, if he did not decide to add the occasional human to his diet for that much-needed variety.

"Shouldn't we escape somewhere?" Jafar mentioned with a certain urgency. "While he's momentarily preoccupied?"

"But we barely even know where we are," Achmed reasoned, "and that knowledge has come from Sinbad's story. We need the merchant to show us the way."

"Exactly," Jafar said with more enthusiasm, confident that they had found a solution to our current dilemma. "And then we will escape with alacrity. Where precisely is our master?"

I held up the bottle. "He resides herein."

"He is trapped in a bottle?" Jafar asked with all enthusiasm fled. "How can he direct us when he is so imprisoned? Soon, all of us will end up as the cyclops, victims of the figs."

But I would not listen to the majordomo's defeatism. It was time, rather, to once again exercise my porter-trained wiles.

"Is this place not called the valley of the figs?" I therefore asked.

"It most certainly is," Achmed replied after it appeared that Jafar had become too busy being fretful and miserable.

"And none of you have ever heard of the hilltops of the figs?" I further inquired.

This latest query caused even Jafar to look up from where he was attempting to stare through his outer garments at his umbilicus.

"No, I have not," he said with the slightest bit of surprise.

"I suggest, then, that we climb," was my answer.

"Oh, then it is not I who is trapped in a bottle," Malabala remarked with a certain brightening of tone. "I was beginning to doubt myself. One must be careful. When a wizard loses confidence, the results can be disastrous. I must ponder this latest course of events as I follow you—wherever it is you are bound."

"And where do you think you are going?" asked the cyclops, who had reappeared in our midst with the greatest suddenness. He paused to pick a handful of figs. The fruit obligingly giggled in delight as he opened his mouth and gulped them down.

"Scar want food!" the disfigured muscleman shouted at the sight of another eating. "Scar needs figs!"

"And the figs need you as well," the fruit of a nearby tree said soothingly. "What would it hurt you to pick but a single one of our number?"

"The first one is free," a fellow fruit cajoled.

"In fact," a third added brightly, "all the figs are free."

Every fruit upon the tree laughed at that. I was afraid I would never be dispassionate enough to comprehend fig humor.

"Not that I need you anymore," the cyclops continued jovially, "for, while I was momentarily occupied, I passed the time talking to the trees. So it was that I found myself instructing the figs in my entertainment needs. Tell me, figs. Where do you come from?"

"Baghdad!" the treeful of figs exclaimed obligingly.

"Slowly I turned," the cyclops intoned gleefully. "And step by step, inch by inch—" He jumped upon the tree and began to ingest figs indiscriminately.

"He has found the perfect entertainment," Achmed remarked in an uncharacteristically sober tone. "All of his life is now contained in a singular bodily process."

"Oh, dear," the cyclops said as he stopped suddenly. "We'll have to continue this in a moment." All of us shuddered as the monster once again excused himself to answer nature's call. So dramatic was this behavior that it appeared to convince even the doubter among us.

"That come from eating figs?" said a somewhat abashed and very flawed ruffian. "Maybe Scar waits for dinner, after all."

"We climb," I instructed the others, and turned to proceed back up the hill that I had previously descended when I first entered into this cursed place.

"We walk?" Malabala mused, seeing our movement before he could hear any instruction. "I suppose I can ponder the situation every bit as well while walking. But I must be careful to ponder, and not to doubt."

But we had not proceeded a dozen paces upon the path between the trees when I spotted a diminutive man of such great age that he made even Jafar appear to be a youngster.

"If I may beg your pardon?" the elderly gentleman remarked as we approached.

And indeed, there was no way he could not beg my pardon, since he sat squarely blocking our path of escape.

"I am an elderly fellow," the wrinkled man spoke as he looked up into my face, "and I do not move with the same agility I once had when I was younger. I was wondering if you might do me a small favor."

I stated that we were in a hurry to be elsewhere, but, as fate may smile upon the generous, a small favor might be possible.

"Ah," he responded graciously, "if you could then carry me over to that copse of nearby trees? The figs appear so full and juicy over there."

Well, that did not seem to be an unduly arduous request, except, of course, that it might be my duty to first describe the awesome power of these enchanted figs that the elder chose to sample. So it was that I began: "I would be honored to perform such a service, O venerable elder, if you still desire it after I inform you—"

"I do not need to be informed!" the elder yelped. "Oh, forgive me. I sometimes become the slightest bit snappish when I am hungry. It is a problem of my aged but infirm form. But it is a problem quickly solved if I might be carried quickly to that tantalizing fruit!"

I had been told, in no uncertain terms, then, that this elder did not wish my counsel. And indeed, with someone in such a state of aged disrepair, a final meeting with the figs might be perceived in some circles as an act of kindness.

But there was a peculiar note to this old man's complaints. If he was so famished, why did he not simply reach up and pluck one of the nearer figs that appeared to grow upon every sun-drenched inch of this peculiar valley. Now that I had paused to think upon it, I realized there was something disturbingly familiar about this whole scenario. Where had I heard in the not-too-distant past of an elderly man needing to be carried to his goal?

"Who's that, now?" Sinbad demanded from within his bottle.

"It is an elderly man who bears a remarkable resemblance to a demonic character from one of your later voyages," was Achmed's quick response.

This was the demon, then, that attached himself to the merchant's shoulders? But, from my understanding, he was not supposed to appear until a later voyage. Shouldn't he therefore reside upon an entirely different island?

"I am often told I look like others," the man who might have been a demon continued. "But if I am to be carried to those other figs, I shall show you a gratitude unlike any you have ever known."

"Don't listen to him!" came the urgent cry from within the bottle. "Kick him out of the way!"

"Don't do anything of the sort!" announced the thing that held the guise of an elderly man. "I suppose even someone as decrepit as myself may be able to bring himself to move a little."

So saying, he rose from his squat to reveal that his legs were indeed rather long, so long that they appeared more suited to the proportions of a wild hare than a man. The legs also showed none of the age that appeared on his face, but were instead at the very least as well muscled as the arms of Dirk and the Scar, and were further covered with the coarsest of deep brown hair. He hopped, the slightest of movement for the muscles above his feet, which, when you looked at them carefully, bore more than a passing resemblance to a pair of cloven hooves. But when he landed again, it was at the distance of some twenty feet.

"I do not like what this suggests," Jafar said in his usual dour manner.

"And what is that?" Achmed asked for a clarification. "You do not appreciate creatures who appear to be old and infirm but actually can jump unusual distances?"

"Our master met this creature upon a later voyage than the adventure that included the talking figs," Jafar replied even more soberly than before. "I fear that, thanks perhaps to the djinni's spell, we are no longer precisely following the dangerous route that our master took in his younger years."

"But is that not good news?" Dirk asked.

"It would be," Jafar agreed, "save for the manner in which I suspect that the spell has been turned about. From this most recent evidence"—he nodded at the hopping creature, who had once again folded his legs beneath him so that he might resume looking aged and pitiful—"I suspect that, rather than being fated to retrace the dangers of Sinbad's earlier voyages, we will now be fated to have those dangers visit us."

"As much as I dislike to confirm your suspicions," Achmed said as he pointed into the distance, "that is a terribly familiar speck flying toward us from the horizon."

"If what you say is true," Malabala piped up as he finally heard Jafar's conjecture, "that is a truly diabolical spell. But, from my personal experience with the dread Ozzie, I know he is far more magically adept than one's first impressions might indicate. Still I, as a wizard, must not begin to doubt myself, must I?"

I stared at the indicated horizon, and thought that perhaps I could see that speck Achmed had mentioned.

"My pardon," Achmed amended. "There are two specks."

"It is the sixth voyage!" Jafar gasped. "And it is approaching us directly!"

What might be the true meaning of Jafar's newest panic? I realized I had never heard the details of the sixth voyage. And it seemed that the merchant did not wish to even begin to talk about the true nature of the seventh voyage.

"Baghdad!" the figs again shouted behind us.

"Slowly I—oh, dear, you'll have to excuse me again," was the cyclops's response.

I decided then that, no matter what dangers awaited us, it would do us no harm to put some distance between ourselves and this accursed valley.

No matter what unknowns still awaited me within the retelling of the merchant's last two voyages, I could not see how our present situation could become any the worse.

Never, of course, have I been more incorrect.

♦

Chapter the Twenty-sixth,
in which our heroes must face some truly
grave concerns.

"It is, of course, the Rukh," said Jafar with his familiar fatalism as we resumed our climb.

"But Achmed said there were two specks up there," I said, for, in all frankness, I was tired of being ill informed. "Are they two Rukhs?"

"Would that were the case," Jafar replied with an elaborate shiver.

I pointed up at the second speck. "Then what is that?" I queried, feeling a further need to speed communication.

"Exactly," Jafar agreed miserably.

"Pardon?" I further questioned.

"They is that," Achmed agreed smugly. Or at least that was what he seemed to say. I had a sudden feeling of déjà vu, as if I were once again trapped in one of the cyclops's entertainments.

"Oh, dear," Sinbad the merchant's voice moaned from the bottle. "Yes, yes, it occurred well into the sixth voyage. I had meant to tell you about that peril as well. Where *does* the time go?"

"The creature that even the Rukh fears," Achmed further explained.

"Oh," I repeated, trying to make some sense out of all this. "They—is—that."

Jafar nodded impatiently. "The Izzat."

"The creature that even the Rukh fears," I added, comprehending at last. "But when I said 'What is that?'—"

"No need to explain further," the majordomo interrupted with authority. "The confusion is natural, for that is where the phrase originated."

"Oh," I replied. And a moment later, I added, "Pardon?"

"The Izzat is such a massive creature that it makes the Rukh appear to be as small as a hatchling chick in comparison," Jafar

explained without discernible enthusiasm. "But you asked about
the origin of the phrase."

I had? Well, perhaps I had, although I had thought we were
escaping from the valley of the figs. I knew that, unless we might
find a cave or other likely place to hide, there was no escaping
from the Rukh. And this other thing—the creature that even the
Rukh feared—was, from Jafar's description, a hundred times
larger? Why did we bother to attempt escape at all?

"The Izzat?" Malabala muttered, half to himself, and it was an
uncertain mutter at best. "Even a wizard who had no doubts about
himself might have trouble with such a being."

"Now, as to the nature of the Izzat," Jafar continued as if
escape were the furthest thing from his mind, "the great bird's
discovery goes back to ancient history; to that time before time,
when men were first upon the earth and were but newly come to
the naming of things. 'This looks like a rock!' they called out at
a round thing near them upon the earth. And 'Look overhead! That
certainly must be the sky.' "

"The Izzat?" another voice called from up ahead. I looked, and
saw that the same demon, in the guise of an aged man, had
somehow gotten before us again. "Oh, surely, I will need some
assistance to escape such a fearsome thing as that."

"So it was," Jafar continued in the best ignore-all-outside-
distractions manner of his master, "that in the naming of things,
they spied this largest of large creatures, for it really is so huge
that you cannot help but notice it."

"They wanted a name that said the creature was massive
beyond imagining, and swifter than human thought. And the name
our wise forefathers chose was *Izzat*."

"To hear the name makes my aged bones shiver!" the demon
cried in the most pitifully palsied of tones. "I must be carried
away from such a danger!"

"Yes," Achmed added to help the human elder along, "and
because the creature was so large, everyone was constantly
noticing it, and so they had the opportunity to use the phrase
repeatedly."

Jafar nodded as if such a conclusion were obvious. "Everyone
asked 'What Izzat?' so often that the phrase became part of the
common tongue."

"Perhaps I do not need to be carried!" the demon called to me
as I started down a side path that would circle around him. "I'm

sure I could make my way if you simply reached out and took my hand."

I continued up the alternate path.

"But—" I thought to object to Jafar's line of reasoning.

"Every phrase must originate somewhere," the human elder lectured. "'What Izzat' has, of course, become debased in common usage, and now is used to describe almost any old thing. But once—"

"Rawn," the Rukh called to interrupt Jafar's philosophic discourse.

"All right," the aged demon called quickly as I began to pass him by. "Let us not be hasty here. Although my bones are aged, I imagine I am not so infirm that I need to be constantly led. But I could still use some assistance. What if you were to give me a hearty push?"

"Rawn," the smaller of the gigantic birds called again, and I used the occasion to look up into the sky. There indeed was the Rukh, still so distant that it appeared only so large as one of Fatima's dainty fingernails. And traveling behind that bird was another flying thing, far more distant still, which thus appeared only so large as Fatima's palanquin.

"The Izzat," I said in wonder.

"The creature that even the Rukh fears," the demon of elderly appearance agreed. "So a hearty push is out of the question as well?" His voice seemed to grow more frantic as the last of the party passed him by. "What if I were to simply ask for directions?"

"Is that a Rukh I hear?" Malabala demanded as he wrinkled his nose. "Disgusting creatures. I think that even a wizard with self-doubts could handle a Rukh."

"Before you disappear forever," the demon called after us, "the least you can do is give me a farewell handshake!"

"Rawn," the Rukh called. "Rawn rawn rawn. *Squawk!*"

I looked again to the sky, and saw but one very, very large bird, who had now grown to the size of a small palace.

"The creature that even the Rukh fears," Achmed said to confirm my suspicions.

"So the Rukh is no more," said I. "But what of the Izzat?"

"We should have nothing to fear from the Izzat," Jafar replied in the dourest of tones.

I could not comprehend the majordomo's lack of concern.

"Considering the difference in size, shouldn't we fear the Izzat one hundred times as much?"

"No," the elder reasoned, "for we are so insignificant to such a gigantic thing that we are totally beneath its notice."

"Unless it decides to land," Achmed added helpfully, "at which point it will surely crush us all, and whatever landmass we happen to be occupying at the time."

I looked again to the sky. Contrary to Jafar's reassurances, the extremely large bird-thing appeared to be headed directly toward the path upon which we stood.

"How bigs is that?" the Scar asked from his position at the rear of the palanquin.

"Some philosophers have hypothesized," Jafar answered, "that the earth is not really a solid mass at all, but is but an egg, and when that egg hatches, it will produce an Izzat."

The Scar used some inappropriate language to convey his astonishment.

"Of course," Achmed amended, "the egg would hatch naught but an infant Izzat. It is a full-grown bird that approaches us now."

"The impossible has occurred," Jafar said with a mix of wonder and anguish. "The Izzat has noticed us, and is indeed approaching. Perhaps now is the best time to give way to total despair."

"No!" Dirk called from where he led the palanquin. "We have had enough of all this. In the brief time we have traveled with you, we have learned that the legends are true. The name of Sinbad seems to bring with it constant danger, but it is also a danger always avoided." He pointed past me up the hill. "We are nearing my homeland now. If you recall your master's stories, you know what kingdom borders the valley of the talking figs."

"Oh, no!" the merchant called from within his tiny prison. "Not that again!"

Not which again? Too many things had happened upon too many voyages for me to instantaneously remember which of the merchant's many adventures the ruffian could be referring to. Perhaps, I thought, someone should write down all these voyages somewhere, so that one might refer to them in this sort of confusing situation.

"It is time we finished that which we were sent do to," Dirk concluded. "You are coming with us." I noticed that both he and the Scar had drawn knives to help make their point. "We must insist that you return with us"—he flicked his knife toward the top of the hill—"to your grave."

Oh, of course, it was *that* adventure. All at once, many of these miscreants' actions appeared to make a renewed sense. I therefore asked: "So you seek to return the merchant to that burial cave from which he escaped?"

"It is but the first of our duties," Dirk clarified as he jumped forward. "The holy graves were blasphemed, so a price must be paid."

Somehow, although he and the Scar still carried the palanquin between them, Dirk's blade was pressed against the fabric that covered my chest. "To appease our local customs, we must bury all the rest of you as well."

From the sudden closeness of the villain's knife, I realized that the promised burial did not necessarily need to be made while I was still among the living.

Chapter the Twenty-seventh,
in which the past and the present appear to become one, and the future does not portend to be all that promising, either.

"The Rukh is gone?" Malabala asked rather after the fact.

"The Izzat," Jafar explained briefly.

"And something else flies toward us through the sky," Malabala further remarked with that same tone of wonder and terror that occurred to all who set eyes upon the more gigantic than gigantic bird.

"Surely a great magician such as yourself," Jafar asked with a pitiful shred of hope, "would have a spell to stop such a thing?"

"The creature that even the Rukh fears," Malabala agreed.

"But you are a mage who can change the very weather!" Jafar blurted, in either panic or frustration that it took the wizard so long to respond.

"A magician who did not doubt himself perhaps could manage something," Malabala agreed. "But one who was confronted by a djinni's spell of such subtlety that he found himself hopelessly lost in endless self-examination"—the wizard paused to sigh—"well, he would be lucky to conjure something that might even ruffle the Izzat's feathers."

"The Izzat has feathers?" I found myself asking. Somehow, the very notion of a feather seemed far too delicate for a being so large.

"Once," Jafar all too readily related, "the story goes, the great bird shed but a single feather. It fell upon a city fully half the size of Baghdad, yet that one feather totally crushed the city walls and suffocated every person therein."

"And dat ding's coming for us?" the Scar asked with more respect in his voice than I had ever previously heard.

"Who can fathom the thoughts of a being so large and strange?" Jafar mused hopelessly. "Unfortunately," he added a second later, "that appears to be the case."

"Surely we are all doomed," another voice called from slightly up ahead. "What does it matter if you were to carry an elderly creature like me for the last few moments of your miserable existence?" The apparently elderly demon had once again gotten in front of us, and now sat upon the very top of the hill.

"Eh, what's that?" he added a moment later, even though no one in my party had replied to him in any way. He frowned and looked behind him. "Oh, dear. You'll have to excuse me. I simply don't care for crowds."

And with that, he leapt straight up into the air, higher and then higher still, until he was nothing but a speck in the great blue sky, and then was lost behind the clouds.

"What could cause a demon to act in that way?" Achmed wondered in a voice decidedly less cheerful than was his usual.

"It makes no difference," I replied with conviction, and the sure knowledge that Dirk's knife was very close indeed. "For, no matter what lies before us, it has to be better than a rapid death in the valley of the figs."

"That is the correct answer," Dirk said with the most unpleasant of smiles. "Now let us travel before that huge creature above grows any closer." And with that, he let me take the lead up the hill. He, of course, followed directly, his drawn knife mere inches from my back.

"There must be something I could do about that very large bird," Malabala mused somewhere at my rear. "If only I could follow this conversation more precisely."

"It is a shame that you have to be buried alive so soon," Dirk considered as we climbed. "The habit the Sinbads have, wherein they find themselves in dire danger and then somehow survive despite overwhelming odds, is quite diverting. The Scar and I will genuinely miss these adventures." He patted me in a comradely fashion upon my back with a blunt instrument that I imagined was the hilt of the knife. "Were your life to continue, I'm sure it would be most interesting. It is unfortunate, in its way, that my partner and I are being paid such an enormous fortune to ensure your demise."

Knife or no, I stopped abruptly when I saw what rushed toward us over the hilltop.

"Ook!" the leader of the invading force claimed. "Ook ook ook!"

And then the apes descended upon us, a hundred strong.

"It is all coming back at once!" Jafar bemoaned. "All to haunt us!"

"What's going on now?" the merchant demanded from his bottle prison. "Is that apes that I hear?"

It was apes indeed, and not simply any band of wildly marauding beasts, for these apes were dressed as sailors, and were no doubt the same creature crew we had met upon the ship before. But if the crew rushed toward us now, could their queen be far behind?

"Ah," a deep voice cried down from the heavens. "There you are!"

I quickly looked aloft, wondering if the Izzat could speak as well. But the great bird, who now took up fully half the sky, was still some distance away. The enchanted voice belonged to the great green head of Ozzie.

"I knew I had to find you before you got away!" the djinni cried triumphantly. "And this time there will be no escaping. I have brought reinforcements!"

But I had no true interest in the djinni's words at that moment, for who should arrive, carried aloft by four of her kind, but the queen, still wearing her full bridal regalia.

She spotted me before I could do any more than think of hiding.

"Scree!" she announced. "Scree scree ook scree!"

Even though I could not catch her meaning, it did not sound good.

"Quiver in fear, O pitiful mortals," Ozzie chortled above us, "for I have brought the enchanted saxophones!" He yelped suddenly. "What was that?"

The elder demon had once again dropped into our midst. "My, my fellows. The sky up there is becoming so crowded, there's nowhere for a self-respecting demon to escape!"

I looked beyond the djinni, and saw the truth in the demon's words. Almost everywhere I looked, where once there was sky, there was now Izzat.

The thing was dark, darker than the deepest storm cloud. Its never-ending bulk blotted out the light of the sun above, so that we upon the hill were plunged into the deepest twilight, where all around was drained of color and became indistinct shapes of gray. It was as if the sky above and the world below were being consumed by a shadow that went on for all eternity.

"Something is falling!" Malabala called to all those around. Apparently, his mystic senses could detect things that the rest of us could not, especially things dropped from an eternally dark Izzat. I had an image of the world's most monstrous feather.

There came a sharp banging upon the rocks above us, as if we were in the midst of a hailstorm.

"Jewels!" Achmed called to the rest of us. "The monster is dropping jewels!"

"So even Sinbad's fortune follows him," Jafar marveled.

"Jewels?" Dirk wondered. "Perhaps we could rethink our position concerning burial."

"Beware!" Malabala called out again. "The creature has dropped some more!"

I looked aloft, and swore, in that weird half-light, that I could see a weirdly glittering mass directly above us, growing at tremendous speed. The jewels had been dropped directly upon us! There must be perhaps a thousand gems above us, harder than hard, plummeting in such a way that they would cover our entire party.

"It will be a most expensive death," Jafar said in a resigned tone.

I closed my eyes and waited for the end. But instead of a crushing weight upon my head, I felt my feet leave the earth.

Once again, I was flying.

Chapter the Twenty-eighth, in which we discover that, while birds might always return to the nest, a human's instincts will generally fall elsewhere.

"You may thank me now," a voice spoke in my ear, "or you may thank me later."

I knew, without looking behind or above me where I was held, that I was once again within the care of the bird woman. I also realized that I no longer held the bottle. I must have dropped it in my surprise, and thus had left Sinbad to face the cascading jewels. Perhaps the magic bottle would protect him. It was unfortunate there was no larger bottle for the rest of my companions.

But I had not seen them die. Perhaps the good luck of the Sinbads would burnish their destinies as well, and they would survive. And I was flying.

"Then I am destined to live?" I asked in a mixture of wonder and amazement, for I could not believe my good fortune. If it indeed was good fortune that smiled upon me now, for I had no knowledge of the true purpose of the bird woman's actions. Nor could I truly bring myself to ask about the fate of those my savior had left behind, even though they were still truly on my mind. At any moment, I fully expected to hear their final cries of anguish as they were buried beneath that priceless avalanche of gems.

Instead, all I heard was the passing wind and the warbling voice of my feathered guardian.

"You are destined to do far more than that," she said to me, "for I am going to take you to my home."

"Home?" I asked, and realized I had even less control over my destiny than I had before. Apparently, I would never see my companions again, even if they were not smashed horribly beyond recognition.

For the first time since perhaps I had entered the valley of the figs, I thought wistfully about my Fatima. If only she hadn't screamed when I at last thought to approach her. That sort of thing was certainly an aspect of our relationship which we would have to work upon.

Or would have worked upon, if this hadn't happened. But Fatima, and most likely every other strictly human woman, was beyond me now, and might be beyond me forever.

What precisely did this beautiful creature, who now carried me in her claws, intend to do with me? I found myself reticent to inquire as I remembered the way her hard beak had glinted in the sun. Instead, I asked about her home.

"Is it far?"

This caused the woman to laugh, a sound like a nightingale's call on a warm summer evening. "If it were any closer, I never would have been able to leave. We fly directly beneath it at this very moment."

Beneath it? I stared up at that moving shadow that seemed to swallow all the sky. Did she mean that she made her home upon the Izzat? I considered to ask her to further explain herself, but was silenced by the immense darkness that we now rose toward; so immense, and so omnipresent, that any speech, indeed, anything that the human mind might conceive, was dwarfed into insignificance.

So we flew, ever upward, angling toward the great thing until I saw a long line of blue beyond it that showed the space between the Izzat and the earth. And the band of sky grew larger as we flew.

"My people live upon the left wing," my savior explained as we were propelled at last beyond the great shadow of this thing that appeared as large as the moon itself. The sky that now surrounded us was such a sudden, brilliant blue that it hurt my eyes, and I had to blink repeatedly to adjust my vision to the light. We flew upward as another great dark shape slashed down to fill half the sky. In the sunlight, I could see that this new thing was covered with dark feathers, not black, but rather a midnight blue, so that they shone faintly with a violet radiance, the color of the evening sky at the moment when dusk flees the horizon. This great moving thing, I realized, must be the Izzat's wing.

We spiraled down to join it as the wing reached the lowest part of its great arc. We seemed for an instant then to hang motionless in the air, and then the wing, so large that it looked like a great island unto itself, rushed up to meet us.

We were so close now that I could not see the entirety of a

single feather, and instead became fascinated by the intricacy of those parts of which the feather was composed, like a great pattern emanating from either side of a shaft wider than even the river below Basrah at that point where it meets the sea. From this great, central rod there spread lesser, pointed poles, and from those poles there emanated even finer shafts, and from those there grew even more delicate wands, from which there emerged still thinner filaments, and so on and on, although none of the great parts appeared in the least frail, for the whole of a single feather would indeed compare to the size of a city.

Still did we plunge downward, or perhaps did the wing rush upward, and I saw that even the finest of the parts of the wing were so widely separated that we could easily pass between those filaments without harm, and so we did, weaving between the parts of that feather and those feathers that grew beneath it until we reached what must have been the skin of this creature so great that I would never be able to get a true picture of its whole.

Oddly enough, though, as we flew deeper and deeper within the feathered coat of this greater than great thing, my fear again left me, and I found out I was once more concerned with establishing my own significance. We are all assigned our tasks upon this earth, and mine was, in its way, every bit as unique as that of the Izzat. Or, to put it in simpler language: We might be about to land upon the most tremendous creature in all of creation, but I had no doubt that, if it were to attempt to be a porter, the Izzat would show it was little more than a big bird.

So it was that I truly found my voice again.

"What happens to me now?" I asked the bird woman as we alighted.

"Now," she replied, "I take you to meet my family."

With that, she used her feathered wings to shoo me forward, through a place that looked like a great jungle of dark ferns, the feathers above filtering the sunlight so that it might never get brighter here than dusk.

I walked between the great shafts, and saw a structure loom before us, a two-storied affair, composed of branches and bits of straw, that somehow seemed to suggest both an elaborate grass hut and an avian nest.

"Mother! Father!" the bird woman called out as we approached. "I've brought that young man whom I told you so much about."

I heard a pair of warbled greetings as two more bird people strode forward upon their webbed feet from the darkened recesses of their home. Both were squatter and more stolid than the woman behind me, but they shared the hard, beak-dominated faces and brilliant feathered coats of their daughter.

"Yes, dear," chirped the high voice of one of the pair. Could this, I surmised, be the mother? "And he does seem very nice indeed, for a human." From the tone of her speech, I gathered that, in their society, the race of men was slightly better regarded, but only slightly, than such things as worms and mealybugs.

"So you are called Sinbad?" the other, deeper voice called with all the menace of a crow.

I thought it only polite to nod, as the father bird continued curtly: "And how, exactly, do you plan to provide for our daughter in the future?"

"Oh, Daddy!" The bird woman behind me spoke as if that were the most foolish question in the world. "He can't help but provide! Don't you know that he's *fated*?"

"Now, dear," the mother bird replied consolingly. "Don't raise your voice so to your father. It's decidedly unladylike. Besides, that talk of fate is but a rumor—"

Their daughter snorted, a sound that seemed not only unladylike but unbirdlike as well. "Some rumor! He's obviously been chosen as the toy of Destiny. Why, he's simply been faced by djinn and Rukhs and demons and monsters every single minute since I first heard about him!"

"Well, perhaps, dear," her mother replied in an all-too-reasonable tone. "But is that truly Destiny, or is he simply having a bad day?"

It was, frankly, a question I had pondered myself.

"And would Destiny even bother with somebody like that?" the father remarked with a dismissive shake of his feathered head. "He looks a little puny, even for a human."

The young bird woman covered my shoulder with a protective wing. "You can argue all you want, but you can't dispute the facts. Have you not noticed the recent changes in climate of our home? The Izzat has gone far out of its way in order to kill him!"

"Really?" her mother said as she cocked her head to one side. "Yes, now that you mention it, I had noticed a certain increased warmth beneath the feathers." For a change, she chirped pleasantly in my direction. "The Izzat generally dwells in those cold and forbidden places far beyond civilization, don't you know?"

I smiled at the older bird woman. If I was going to spend time among these creatures, I might as well make it as pleasant as possible. Still, her mate did nothing but scowl.

After a moment, though, even he added, in the most grudging of tones, "That is impressive. Our home is attempting to destroy this insignificant mortal?"

"The Izzat doesn't do that for simply *anybody*," their daughter insisted.

"In fact," her mother mentioned, "I never remember the Izzat doing anything like that for anybody, at least, not since that other human named Sinbad."

"Can't you see?" their daughter chirped, her voice even higher and more excited than before. "That's what I'm talking about! No matter what terrible danger threatened, the other Sinbad walked through it as you or I might stroll on a day in springtime. And this boy is named Sinbad, too! And he is obviously fated to carry on that charmed life."

"He is?" The father bird emitted a low whistle, then paused a minute to stare at me again. "The ways of Destiny are very strange indeed."

"And our little girl picked him out from all those humans?" the mother bird interjected, her feathered breast swelling with pride. "Perhaps she holds talents that we do not realize."

"Then I can keep him?" asked the younger bird woman.

Keep him? I was taken aback by that precise use of language. I knew, when the bird woman took me, that I might be carried far from my kind, but those two words made this sound so permanent. Was I now to have no further say in my future—ever?

"I'm not sure," her father replied doubtfully. "Humans can be such a problem around the nest."

But their daughter would not be denied. "I could always peck him a little bit to keep him in his place!"

Her mother glanced briefly at her mate. "Yes, males do seem to respond well to that sort of thing."

Her father shifted from foot to foot, but then admitted, "Perhaps it will teach her the meaning of responsibility."

"The heavens know we haven't been able to," her mother agreed. She turned back to the younger woman. "Oh, very well, if you promise to keep him cleaned and groomed."

"I knew you'd let me!" Their daughter flapped her wings with glee. "So, welcome, Sinbad, to your new home."

I was to be kept, then. Apparently, I would never have a say in anything again.

"Where are your manners!" her mother chided. "Perhaps you should offer your guest some refreshment. Tell me—Sinbad, that is your name—would you care for some grubs? I assure you, they're very fresh."

I attempted to look upon the bright side. Perhaps I would starve here, and my stay would not be very long at all.

"He isn't very communicative," her father said doubtfully. "Are you absolutely *sure* he is fated?"

"Oh, Daddy," the daughter answered dismissively, "a girl just knows that sort of thing! Besides, Wisha wanted him!"

"Oh!" her father replied as if somehow this fact explained everything that had happened. "So it's your *cousin's* doing!"

"We should have known, Father," his mate added in the same knowing tone. "Those sea harpies can be so precocious!"

"Aha," the father agreed with a wry chuckle. "You know how it is with young harpies. When one decides she wants a human male, the others just can't keep their hands off him."

They both had a good laugh over that one.

"Mommy? Daddy?" their daughter chirped in disbelief. "What are you talking about? Parents never understand *anything*!" Feathers ruffled, she stormed inside the hut.

"Well, that's your daughter for you," the male bird remarked as he puffed out the plumes upon his chest.

"My daughter?" the female screeched. "When she acts like this, why is she always my daughter?"

The two of them seemed to have forgotten about me for the moment. Now that the bird woman was gone, what was to happen to me? Perhaps, while these two were otherwise involved, I should try to disappear among this forest of giant feathers.

"And where are you going?" the male demanded as I took my first quiet steps away. "Our darling Kawda would never forgive us if we lost you."

"That is," the female added reasonably, "if we decide to keep him at all."

"What should we do with him, then?" Father asked. "Maybe it would be better to dispose of him right now."

Mother took a moment to shake out her wings before replying:

"It would certainly be easier for Kawda to forget him if she didn't have a chance to become attached."

The male turned his head to one side to regard me more closely. "He *is* sort of soft and pudgy. Reminds me a little bit of a worm in that way, doesn't he?" He glanced speculatively at his mate. "I suppose we could eat him."

I despaired. Did everything in the world want to eat me?

But, fortunately for my continued existence, the female disagreed. "More problem than it's worth," she cawed. "That sort of meat never keeps. Besides, look at him. There's nothing on those bones but gristle. And then there's our daughter. You know that Kawda might object."

Father bobbed his head. "Youngsters can be so sentimental about the strangest things."

"Give me a big batch of grubs any day," the female enthused.

"My, dear, you certainly know the way to a bird's heart," Father agreed heartily. He looked at me again. "So, shall I remove him from the nest?"

"I think that would be best," the mother said as she turned away to reenter her nest, no doubt to tend to her daughter.

"Very well, off we go." He flapped his wings and took flight, swooping among the giant feathers until he was behind me. I felt a pair of large claws dig into my shoulders, nowhere near as gently as had the claws of this bird man's daughter.

But I was once again aloft, and it appeared that this bird would remove me from the Izzat, so that I might once again have a chance to walk through the world of men and attempt to lead a normal life. As strange as my recent experiences had been, perhaps what happened now actually would be for the best.

The father bird soared, his strong wings carrying me even more swiftly than the earlier trip I had taken with his daughter, and we were soon flying high above the surface of the great Izzat.

"I am taking you to the edge," the father informed me. And indeed, I could see the blue sky beyond the tremendous bird's wing.

"After that," he continued, "you will have to fend for yourself." He paused for an instant to consider something. "Oh, that's correct, you can't fly, can you? Humans do seem so limited, don't they? Well, I'm dropping you off up ahead, one way or another, and, after that, I'm washing my wings of you."

We had at last reached the edge of the Izzat, and I could see the clouds spread out far beneath us.

"If you are fated," the bird said most conversationally, "as my dear daughter believes, you will certainly survive. And if you don't, it will serve you right for lying to our sweet child. Happy landings."

And with that, he dropped me.

♦

Chapter the Twenty-ninth,
in which our hero discovers that sometimes
even water will not put out the fire.

I fell.

I looked down and saw the ocean. I realized then that the Izzat was so large, he must have covered the entire landmass where my companions and I had been stranded. Therefore, when I was dropped from the wing, I was already far out at sea. And I further discerned that my surmise could only be correct if the Izzat still somehow flew over that same landmass. Which, considering the size of the Izzat, and the speed with which the Izzat flew, was doubtful in the extreme. But then I imagined that all these things were possible, since everything about the Izzat appeared doubtful in the extreme.

I had time for all these thoughts and more, so far did I have to fall. The father bird had wondered if I was fated. I only knew, in those still-too-brief moments, that I was fated to be dead, for I was falling with such force from the heavens that even a giving substance such as water would cause my every bone to break.

Still, in this brief time I had spent with Sinbad the Sailor—it had yet to be three full days!—I had faced adventures and visited realms that most men would not dream of in a dozen existences. My body had spent long years working as a porter, but my mind had spent these last few hours communing with the spirits and wonders of this great world.

I thought of that song I had sung, at the gate of Sinbad's estate, and how those simple rhymes had gained me entrance to this world of marvels, the same world which is surely around all of us every day, if only we might look beyond the burdens that we carry upon our heads. I was inspired then to compose another song, so that I might leave this new life in much the same way I had been ushered into it; a song that would praise the great diversity of this world, and how all men must realize what a privilege it is to dwell therein.

227

I thought then about how I might begin. Perhaps a rhyme that spoke of adventure, "dare" being coupled with "falling from up there." Or, as my romantic nature might dictate, "love" being coupled with "falling from up above."

My conjectures were abruptly forced to ride the back hump of the camel as I saw the ocean rushing toward me. I had taken too long on my rhymes. If there was to be a final song, it would have to be sung in the next life.

And yet, before I could close my eyes to prepare myself for my imminent demise, I witnessed yet another wonder, no less magnificent than all that had gone before. The ocean was no longer a flat surface beneath me, but had parted to accept me, as though it were my lover and waited for me with open arms.

Still I fell, but no longer through the open air, for I was now surrounded by a great circular wall of water. And there was water more directly around me as well, at first only a fine mist caressing my skin, but growing in density as I dropped into it, so that it soon felt as though a rain shower were falling somehow upon me from down below. This magic shower grew in intensity as well, first to a steady storm and then on to a hurricane, and the water walls about me grew closer, so that I saw I was not in a passageway so much as a funnel that came together beneath me. I further realized that, as the force of the water increased, so did the speed of my descent decrease, so that, an instant later when I found my body passing through those water walls, I discovered myself placed beneath the water with the same gentleness that a mother might place an infant to wash him in a stream.

It surprised me not in the least that I could breathe even though the waters had closed above me, for I had been to this place before. Neither did it startle me in the slightest that, as my eyes grew used to the dimmer light below the ocean's surface, I saw a naked green maiden swimming toward me through the deep.

"So you have come back to me at last?" she said as she approached. She stopped, and the whole ocean about her was lit by her smile. She was a truly beautiful creature, and her nakedness and perfection of form enticed me in such a way that I could feel the whole of my physical form fill with desire.

But I was made of more than simply the physical. The events of the past few days had opened my eyes to all the glories given us by Allah, and my fall from the sky, when I was sure that I was close to death, had opened my mind to me as well. I had discovered new parts of me, new attitudes and new strengths, and I realized they were all parts of this voyage that I now traveled.

I knew now that this was the same voyage that my namesake had spent his entire life pursuing, and, even though he had broken that expedition down into seven different adventures, it was really but one long journey, as all of us travel from the day of our birth until that day we die. Sinbad the Sailor was gifted with the ability to witness the fantastic, and yet return home safe and whole. And it was a gift that he cherished, no matter what he might say. It occurred to me that he might even plan in some way (perhaps not even with his waking mind!) to bankrupt himself over and over again, so he would have an excuse to resume that voyage and experience that gift again.

It was a gift that I would cherish as well. And one that had brought me into the arms of the sea maiden.

"You have returned to me for a third time," she said as she swam closer still. "That means that you may stay forever."

And end my voyage, I thought. As much as I desired this woman of the sea, I wanted the voyage more.

"You breathe the water through my magic, but you are not yet truly a part of the sea. Come." She leaned forward then, as if she might kiss my face. "Open your mouth," she said instead, "and let the ocean in." She touched me then upon the cheek, and her fingers felt as cold as the ocean's depths.

I did my best not to shiver. This woman was now asking me to drown. Yet what else could I do, for I was as much a prisoner here under the sea as I was upon the wing of the Izzat, with no way to ever join the rest of humankind. It was a decision I was not prepared to make.

"Are you known as Wisha?" I asked instead.

She laughed, sending a delightful cluster of bubbles soaring toward the surface far above. I again found my loins longing for her. If only she would not force me to make such a choice!

"How did you know this?" she asked.

"I have spoken to your cousin," I began. I explained then to her about my rescue from the rain of gems by Kawda, and the unfortunate conversation we had had with Kawda's parents.

"Kawda is such a child," she said as she laughed again. "My parents will never know anything of you. Our love will be our eternal secret."

I did not care for that word, *eternal*. Better, I decided, a short life of roving adventure then forever spent drowned in the deep.

Still was this sea creature so close to me, her firm, round, and scaled breasts so inviting in the half-light of the ocean floor. If only I could sample the wonders of this woman before I fled back to the surface.

Perhaps that is why I asked the next question.

"Why did you choose me in the first place?"

She again stroked my cheek, and this time her touch did not feel so cold as before. "Because you smell of the world above, of sunlight and dirt. And because your name is Sinbad."

"Then it was my name that drew us together?" I asked.

"And your fate," Wisha admitted.

"Then I am to survive all the dangers that I face, as has my elder namesake?"

"All," she agreed, "save perhaps one."

"And what is that?" I asked, fully expecting her to answer that it was my present situation.

"It is best that I do not explain," she said instead, "or I might bring that doom down upon you from which you have been rescued."

"Rescued?" I asked in incomprehension.

"I do not think you will be followed to the ocean deep," she explained, "although, in dealing with one of such power, one can never be sure."

"One of such power?" I further asked.

"You do not know?" Wisha asked in astonishment. "Your merchant has not told you of his seventh voyage?"

"No," I admitted, "I have only barely learned of the Izzat upon his sixth adventure."

"I am not surprised. It is dangerous to even allude to this being in too frequent a fashion. Perhaps it is for the best that you never know."

Now that I thought upon it, I recalled on more than one occasion that the merchant had seemed overwhelmingly afraid of something that had happened upon his seventh journey. Was this the same danger that the sea woman would not speak about? And what could be that much worse than the horrible dangers Sinbad had already discussed, or that we had all braved upon our current voyage?

I felt, more than ever before, as though I were some character in a storyteller's fantastic tale, and further, that I was not only unaware of the tale's ending, but the teller had neglected to relate the beginning as well.

"You should be especially thankful to me, then," the maiden said coquettishly. She now swam so close that her scales rubbed against my water-soaked robe. "By taking you now, I have surely saved you from a horrible fate."

But her newest story had strengthened my resolve in a manner which the sea maiden did not anticipate. I shook my head firmly. "I cannot stay here with you. From what you tell me, my companions are in deadly peril. If the merchant and the others must face danger, I must be there with them."

The sea maiden looked at me sadly then. "I am sorry, my Sinbad, to deny you this thing. You may have the desire to join your friends, but you do not have the means." She attempted a smile, and tossed her head gaily, so that her sea hair spread outward upon the gentle currents. "But, come! This world is not so bad as it may seem. We will take two sea horses and explore the ocean floor. And we will find quiet places among the weeds, where we might dally for hours. You must stay with me."

I found myself becoming angry at the way this woman sought to control me. "So I must stay, even though, if I do as you bid and let water into my lungs, I will surely drown!"

"That is one way you may think of it," she said more soberly, to my surprise agreeing rather than arguing. "And if you do not do as I request, I will withdraw my magic. You will not only drown, but you will die."

I had no answer of my own but my anger. If that was the only choice offered to me, then I would never breathe again.

But the sea woman had other weapons than her words. Her hands had somehow made it through the folds of my robes, and she touched my naked flesh beneath.

All my breath left me in a rush, and I felt water run into my mouth and lungs.

"I am sorry it has to be like this," she said with a mixture of sadness and anticipation, "but I promise it will not be unpleasant." She leaned forward, and gently nibbled my ear as a fish might chew at a bit of seaweed. "Soon," she whispered, "you may learn to love it."

It appeared that I had no choice. There was no breath left in me, and no way to gain anything in my lungs save water. This was the end, then, of my life as a mortal man. I expected to be consumed by total darkness.

Instead, I heard a great blare of noise, and my world was filled with blinding light.

◆

Chapter the Thirtieth,
in which we truly learn why ignorance is bliss.

I coughed water and breathed air, and realized that the bright light I saw was nothing beyond the bold brilliance of the noonday sun. And, as my ears cleared, I heard the strangest music, bright and bouncy and oddly propulsive.

"You did not think you could get away from us that easily, did you?" I heard the extremely annoying voice of Ozzie purr as the music faded.

"But I was about to die by drowning—" I attempted to explain as I looked aloft.

"No one dies without my permission," Ozzie replied smugly. "Don't worry. I intend to give my permission very shortly." He chuckled, a sound like rocks tumbling down a desert mountainside. "I can do whatever I want, now that I have brought my brethren."

And indeed, I saw that the head of Ozzie was not alone in the sky, but was flanked by half a dozen other djinn, except that these further creatures sported torsos and arms, and in their arms they carried strangely shaped instruments of beaten gold.

"Yes, lady and gentlemen," said Ozzie, his voice welling with pride, "let me introduce you to Sam Ifrit and his All-Genie Band!"

As if in greeting, the other djinn raised their instruments to their lips and blared forth a single, raucous note.

"No one can withstand the music of the enchanted saxophone!" Ozzie was clearly enjoying himself. "I realized, with that certain, indefinable power that was Sinbad's—"

"That is my name!" I shouted. And it was to my great relief that I heard a smaller voice call out as well from a bottle nearby. So I had dropped the bottle, as I suspected, and it had been rescued by another in our party. I risked a quick glance away from the enchanted creatures in the sky.

There were piles of gems everywhere. But all of those whom I had left upon the hill seemed none the worse for wear; even Fatima's palanquin looked no more scratched and battered than before. Achmed held the magic bottle. No doubt he had caught it in his quick hands as I had been hauled aloft.

"Malabala's magic saved us," the lad explained at my questioning glance. "It appears that he is an excellent magician, so long as he does not have to rely upon the spoken word."

I recalled now how the wizard had also stopped the great storm. But my conjecture was halted when I glanced up to the top of the hill, and there saw perhaps a hundred apes, and before them all, their queen!

"*As I was saying,*" Ozzie continued loudly, "I had to reckon with the peculiar luck of Sinbad—"

"That is my name!" tore again from my throat.

"Much better," Ozzie quickly added, allowing for no further interruptions. "And when I saw that luck carried not only for the merchant but for this young porter as well, I knew that even one as powerful as myself might experience some difficulty. And then I encountered all those other individuals, human and otherwise, whom the two Sinbads"—he waited until we had shouted again—"had discovered in their travels." He waved at the All-Genie Band to either side of him. "It was obvious that a djinni, even one of my immense gifts, might need some outside help. And what a help they are! For our first number, they brought the porter back from wherever he had gotten to, proving there is truly no escape from Ozzie's wrath! Now, if you will excuse me for a second, it is time to plan your final fate."

He turned to the other djinn, and became temporarily lost in conversation.

The Scar nodded pleasantly in my direction. "He's fulla hot air. Two ta one he can'ts pull it off."

It was true that, the more I came to know Ozzie, the more the word "inept" sprang to mind. Still, he had brought an additional, unknown force with him. Perhaps they would actually cause him to succeed.

"Well," Dirk said casually, "I hope he again fails miserably as soon as possible, so that we may get on with business of our own."

It appeared to me that these two were still being unnecessarily obfuscatory about their plans for the rest of us; an occupational hazard, I imagined, of being a ruffian. Still, I could not help but glance about at the piles of glittering wealth and wonder what they could possibly want with us now.

And yet, there had been far too many uncertainties in my life of late. Ruffians or no, I decided it was time to bring this problem to a quick and satisfying conclusion.

"But what of us?" I therefore asked. "You have more jewels hereabout than you can ever use. Obviously, we should be free to leave."

"We have thought about your situation," Dirk replied with his usual gracious but evil smile, "and have devised a two-tiered plan. First, we will load the palanquin with as many jewels as we can carry, and will live the rest of our lives as rich as sultans. But for the second part—"

He waved to his partner, who gleefully continued:

"We's gonna give you to our sultan, anyway! He pays us even more! We lives even better than sultans!"

"The Scar devised that plan all by himself," Dirk mentioned proudly. "And it is a very thoughtful solution. Our sultan does not like to be fooled. That is why he originally hired us to hunt down Sinbad, and if we deserted him, he would only hire more to find us." He paused to gesture grandly at the palanquin. "Besides, we must deliver Fatima, for she is a gift from the Caliph of Baghdad, and destined to be the latest of our ruler's hundred wives."

So that was their sinister purpose all along! But that meant, once she was delivered to her new husband, that Fatima would come under the sway of that barbaric custom whereby my elder namesake had been buried alive! I could not lose that delicate hand, or that beautiful laugh, to such cruelty. I knew then that I must renew my resolve to rescue her, even though she might scream at me a thousand times.

But then it occurred to me that perhaps the custom was not the same for the sultan as it was for others in that city.

"Your sultan has a hundred wives," I therefore asked, "and every one of them is healthy?"

"Well," Dirk replied most reasonably, "from what we understand, not all of them are currently in the harem. There may be as many as a couple dozen who are off visiting their mothers and suchlike."

"Somes has been visiting dere mudders for years," the Scar added conspiratorially.

"It is some relief," Achmed commented softly, "to know that politicians are the same the world over."

So the sultan was not only a barbarian but without honor besides! And it did not matter to these vile characters that Fatima would be used so horribly. She was indeed lucky that I was here to save her from such a fate!

"And you expect Ozzie to simply let you do this thing?" Achmed asked bluntly.

"So perhaps we will have to defeat the djinni before we can take you to our city," Dirk admitted. "And it is true that we have temporarily lost our foremost weapon."

"You mean the bottle that contains the merchant?" I asked.

"Most perceptive," Dirk agreed. "We need to get Sinbad out of the bottle so that we can get the djinni in."

"I says shakes 'im out!" the Scar demanded.

"Crude," Dirk replied, "and perhaps not effective. We must deliver the merchant in one piece to our sultan so that he can once again be buried alive." He smiled to the rest of us. "And you, of course, will be buried alongside him. We would not be so cruel as to break up a set."

The Scar, whose face had fallen at his partner's reproach, once again brightened. "I says wakes up Malabala!"

At that, Jafar spoke for the first time since we had returned. "The wizard needs his rest."

So Malabala was asleep? I looked about, and realized he must be that pile of robes I saw gathered against one of the mounds of gems. I recalled now how he had slept, for quite some period of time, after he turned back the storm.

"It is true," Dirk remarked in a far more sober tone of voice. "Remember the insects."

The Scar buzzed deep in his throat, deeply troubled.

"Still, we must revive the magician, if we are to have any hope of success." Dirk looked to his partner. "We will do it together. Gently."

So it was that the ruffians moved quickly to the sleeping mage, and I was left alone with Achmed, Jafar, and the bottle containing the merchant.

"We have to prepare him somewhat," Jafar shouted urgently into the bottle. "It would be too cruel otherwise."

"What?" the bottle asked back. "Prepare who?"

"The other Sinbad," Jafar explained.

"The other who?" the bottle asked.

"The porter," Achmed quickly explained, "who, after arriving at our gate and singing a song—"

"Oh, that Sinbad!" the voice in the bottle exclaimed. "It is also a common name, after all. I can think of at least two of them."

"But we must prepare him," Jafar continued to insist in a low but urgent tone.

"Prepare him for what?" was the bottle's reply.

"The seventh voyage!" Jafar exclaimed.

"Oh, yes, we never did get around to that, did we?" The merchant cleared his throat. "So it was that I again found myself in Baghdad."

"We have no time for that!" Jafar insisted. "Begin with the actual voyage!"

"I have to leave out all the information about being a messenger for the caliph?" the merchant asked, disappointment obvious in his voice. "And all the fantastic gifts that I had to take with me upon my—"

"Get to the city!" Jafar demanded with growing impatience.

"So that I cannot talk about the sea monsters, and how our ship was destroyed—" the merchant despaired.

"I would go beyond the city," Achmed urged, "and proceed directly to the discovery of the men with wings."

"I therefore have to pass over that informative part where I received good counsel from another merchant and was able to again increase my fortune tenfold—" the elder Sinbad protested.

"Forget all that folderol!" Jafar demanded. "Tell him about what is important!"

"What?" the merchant replied in the most confused of tones. "What is important, after all?"

"You know," Achmed said, and his voice again fell to a whisper. "What happened at the end."

"The end of what?"

"Who you met!" Jafar insisted.

"Who?" the merchant replied again.

"It is impossible!" even the formerly patient Achmed replied. Jafar took a deep breath. "Oh, very well. It must be up to me to speak the dreaded name. But listen carefully, for it is of the utmost importance that I only say it once."

He paused and I nodded.

"He-Who-Must-Be-Ignored," were the next words from his mouth.

"He-Who-Must—" I began.

"Do not repeat it!" Jafar cried urgently. "For, should his name be repeated three times by three different voices, this primal force will appear in our midst, and we will be surely doomed."

"What part of the story do you wish me to tell?" came the merchant's peeved tones from within the bottle.

But Jafar ignored his master and continued the tale himself. "On the seventh voyage, my master came to a city where all men could fly, but they worshipped a false deity. Perhaps this creature was a great demon, or perhaps he was a god of the ancients. It did not do to look too closely, for the peril of the creature was truly revealed by its name, which I shall not speak again, for, if you do not ignore this being entirely, you will be forever under his spell."

I gasped. This latest being sounded a hundred times as dangerous as the pleading demon. No wonder Sinbad and his servants all hesitated to speak of it.

"Now who are you talking about?" came the voice from the bottle.

It was Achmed's turn to relate the tale. "This being, it seems, gains its control from the total mastery of his subject's emotion and thought; indeed, he commands their very complete and thorough attention—forever. My master, with his short attention span and inability to retain names, could not remember him, and so broke the spell."

"Oh!" the Sinbad within the bottle called out. "Of course! I remember now! He-Who-Must-Be-Ignored!"

And with that the djinni laughed, loud and long.

"I knew, if I but waited a sufficient time, that you would speak my master's name. Once it came from the lips of the elder servant, and again from the merchant within the bottle. Now I shall speak it a third time, and my master will arrive, and wreak the vengeance upon you that you so richly deserve!"

"Who?" the elder Sinbad asked. "What? Did I say something wrong?"

"Sam?" Ozzie asked. "If you would play something bright and bouncy?"

The other djinn complied, all wailing upon their magic saxophones.

"Lady and gentlemen," Ozzie intoned, "I present, for your ultimate subjugation, He-Who-Must-Be-Ignored!"

"Would someone please tell me what is going on?" the merchant in the bottle demanded.

I decided that he was better off not knowing.

✦

Chapter the Thirty-first,
which is far too confusing to summarize
at the present time.

"What's going on here?"

I looked about to see an impatient Malabala. Dirk and the Scar stood behind him. Apparently, they had been able to successfully wake him without being turned into insects. But how could I quickly explain, especially to the wizard, what now transpired?

"Excuse me, O wise and powerful mage," I began cautiously.

"Yes, yes," Malabala replied impatiently. "Do get on with it!"

"What is this?" I cried in astonishment. "You no longer suffer the speech delay—"

Malabala nodded abruptly. "You mean that the djinni's spell is not causing me to hear people before they speak, but never mind. I have once again been freed of the magic in Ozzie's presence. The djinni becomes too sure of himself. What now transpires?"

"We are about to be visited by an awesome deity," Achmed explained, "one who must be—um—excluded."

"Oh!" the wizard said in sudden comprehension. "You mean He-Who-Must—" He stopped himself. "No. I will not say his name entirely. It does no good to encourage that sort of thing. Oh, dear. This comes as quite a challenge for one who has doubted his magic."

"But you saved my companions from that deadly downpour!" I objected. "Surely you must still have that magic within you."

The mage considered this for a moment as the saxophone music built behind us. "It *did* feel bracing to deflect that rain of gems. Perhaps there is still some substantial wizardry left within me. But to take on an ancient deity; I am not at all certain."

"What is happening?" Sinbad called from his bottle home.

"A change is in the air!" Dirk called as he looked about. The very atmosphere appeared to vibrate, pulsing with the enchanted music. And indeed, when I looked aloft, I saw that the sky above us had turned from blue to shimmering gold.

"Excuse me, fellows," the demon called from within our midst. "I seem to recall an appointment upon an entirely different island. You can all do me that favor some other time." And with that, he jumped in a low arc out over the nearby hill, and soon disappeared as he met the horizon.

I believe we all realized how truly minor that jumping demon was in the scheme of Destiny by what next occurred.

Dirk and the Scar cried out. Jafar and Achmed opened their mouths in astonishment. Even the apes appeared upset.

"Ook scree ook!" the queen called down from the hill.

"What does she say?" I asked the mage.

"There is danger nearby," the wizard replied curtly.

"Scree ook scree!" she added insistently.

"She also wants you to know she's happy her banana boy is back," Malabala continued.

Banana boy? This, I thought, was perhaps even too much for me to cope with. Perhaps I should rather fall immediately under the spell of this ancient deity—who seemed to be taking a great deal of time in arriving—and forget all about my worldly cares.

And then I heard even Fatima's voice call out from the palanquin!

"Dirk?" she asked in a musical tone that put even the enchanted saxophones to shame. "Scar? Isn't it time we left?"

What a beautiful voice. What perfect tones! And she had spoken at the perfect time, as if she knew that I needed a sign to pull me back from the black abyss of doubt. But I had heard her voice, and my life was changed again. I had to survive this latest threat, if only for my Fatima!

But I had no further time for thought, for the music swelled to an ear-shattering intensity. And there, upon the golden horizon, there shimmered a darker shape, at first only the consistency of mist, then on to the density of morning fog and thence to the thickness of a great storm cloud. But this storm cloud had the shape of a man, save that the man was a hundred feet tall.

The cloud grew darker still, so that it took on the color of granite, and the man shape became even more defined, so that I could see he was not only toweringly tall but rather overweight as well, as if his very essence sought to consume all. And upon the rounded top of that shape, there grew features nearly lost in great folds of fat, and enormous jowls that made those upon the merchant Sinbad appear to be but the wrinkles of a man cursed with anemia.

"Undoubtedly," Achmed murmured in my ear, "this is the sort of deity who prefers a dramatic entrance."

"Do anything but pay attention to him!" Jafar cried as the being opened his mouth. I followed the elder's example and quickly looked away.

"I AM HE!" the giant creature bellowed.

"Can you believe this weather?" Jafar mentioned all too casually to the rest of us.

"Nice day if we don't have a dust storm," I agreed as I saw the majordomo's purpose.

At that moment, Achmed began to casually whistle with a vengeance.

"I WILL SHOW YOU, SINBAD, WHAT HAPPENS TO THOSE WHO TURN UPON ME." The saxophones honked ominously. "OF COURSE, ONE GOOD TURN DESERVES ANOTHER. HAHAHA." The saxophones blared for emphasis.

"You won'ts take dis guy anywheres!" the Scar announced. "We takes 'im back to our city and buries 'im!"

"YOU'RE A PRETTY GRAVE FELLOW. HAHAHA." The saxophones whooped again. "BUT I CAN DIG THAT. WHAT'S A SIX-FOOT HOLE IN THE GROUND BETWEEN FRIENDS? HAHAHA!" The enchanted instruments were going positively wild.

"He?" the Scar muttered. And then there occurred something even stranger than the speech patterns with accompanying saxophones of He-Who-Must-Be-Ignored, for, on every occasion that the large and exceedingly gross deity began to laugh, the Scar began to laugh as well.

"It would be an especially nice day to take a voyage," Jafar mentioned between gritted teeth.

Achmed began to purposefully whistle sea songs.

"It wouldn't be a bad day at all to start back to Baghdad," I agreed as easily as possible while having to listen to that huge thing's never-ending prattle.

"Baghdad!" a familiar voice cried from somewhere down the hill beneath us. "Slowly I turn—"

I looked down to where I heard the sound, but at first thought that I could see no manifestation of the cyclops. However, I then noted a slight rise halfway up the path, a rise that was visited often by flies and other insects, as if the way were just there blocked by a mound of odiferous feculence. Had our two-headed adversary, then, come to this?

"BUT I HEAR ANOTHER FUNNY MAN OUT THERE IN THE AUDIENCE. WANT TO JOIN ME HERE ON STAGE? OF COURSE, I DON'T WANT TO MAKE A PRODUCTION OF IT. HAHAHA."

There came but a single word from the brown pile upon the hill: "He." And now there were two laughing at He, the Scar and the formerly monstrous mound of dung.

"Scar!" Dirk called. "Where are you going?"

"HE'S JOINING ME. WE'RE ALL ONE BIG HAPPY FAMILY. AND ANY FAMILY WITH ME IN IT WOULD HAVE TO BE BIG. HAHAHA!"

"No!" Dirk announced. "Not with—He." And then the second ruffian was silent as well.

"SO I GOTTA TELL YA. I WAS SITTING AROUND WITH THIS SULTAN THE OTHER DAY, AND I BURPED. HE SAYS TO ME, 'IS THAT HOW YOU TREAT ROYALTY?' SO I CROWNED HIM! HAHAHA!"

And now I heard three laughs besides the chuckle of the obnoxious deity.

But this was terrible. He-Who-Must-Be-Ignored was capturing us, one by one. I looked down the hill, and saw that the fly-covered mound seemed to be flowing upward. I imagined, if I dared to risk a look, I would see both Dirk and the Scar walking as well.

"BUT I SEE WE HAVE SOME APES IN OUR AUDIENCE. AND THERE'S THE GORILLA MY DREAMS. OOK OOK SCREE GROWL OOK! HAHAHA!"

Fully half the company of apes muttered, "Ook!" together, and began to laugh. And then they, too, began to march toward the towering He, urged on by the bouncy saxophones.

"BUT I GOTTA TELL YOU—I SEE SOME OLDSTERS IN OUR AUDIENCE. HEY, IT MAKES NO DIFFERENCE TO ME."

"Heard any good stories—" Jafar began. But then his mouth fell open upon He's next utterance.

"YOUNG, OLD, I'M AN EQUAL OPPORTUNITY ENTITY. HAHAHA!"

"He," Jafar whispered, his eyes suddenly losing all focus. He stumbled forward, toward the corpulent demonic presence.

"I must act now, or it will be too late!" Malabala screamed, rapidly beginning a complicated conjure.

"AND A WIZARD, TOO? COME UP HERE AND SIT A

SPELL! TAKE MY ENCHANTMENTS—PLEASE! HA-HAHA."

But instead of the usual string of arcane and impossible words issuing forth from the magician's mouth, there came but a single syllable.

"He."

And then the mage, too, began his walk forward, laughing all the way. So even Malabala was not immune to that awful power. But if a wizard could not stand against such as He, what hope was there for a poor porter?

There had to be some method of halting this demon's spell, for the merchant was still among us. I turned to Achmed. "We are surely doomed unless we do something quickly. How did Sinbad defeat this creature before?"

Achmed nodded and lifted the enchanted bottle before him. "Only our master could stand against him, because he could not—"

But even Achmed paused when he heard the next line from the immense jokester.

"BUT I SEE THERE'S A CHILD IN THE AUDIENCE. YOU KNOW, I ALWAYS WAS A GREAT KIDDER. HAHAHA!"

"He," the lad muttered, and, although his face was graced with an expression of great pain, Achmed laughed as well. I snatched the bottle from his hand before he had a chance to move away. But what had Achmed been attempting to tell me?

"SINBAD," He-Who-Must-Be-Ignored intoned. He had apparently saved us for last. "WELL, HELLO, SAILOR!"

"Who's that?" the elder Sinbad demanded.

"AN OLD ACQUAINTANCE, WHO'S LONGING TO BE-COME MUCH CLOSER," remarked the demon with evil intent.

"Could you make yourself a little clearer?" the merchant in the bottle asked in not the most patient of tones.

"I AM HE."

"Is that supposed to mean something to me?" the merchant demanded. "I'm a busy man. I know a lot of he's. Known a couple of she's in my day as well."

There was a change then in the demon's voice. "THIS CAN-NOT BE HAPPENING AGAIN!"

Of course! This was how my elder namesake had survived before. He-Who-Must-Be-Ignored thrived on recognition. But Sinbad the merchant couldn't remember anybody!

Even the saxophone music seemed to be faltering.

"I WILL NOT BE DEFEATED. I'VE GOT A MILLION OF THEM!"

"Whoever you are," Sinbad muttered, "you certainly are annoying." I almost laughed for a completely different reason. With the merchant's obfuscatory powers, even a demon was truly doomed. It was a great good fortune that I rescued the bottle from the hand of Achmed. Perhaps what everyone conjectured was true, and Destiny was indeed on the side of the Sinbads.

"Uh, boss?" another voice interjected. Even without looking, I could recognize the overweening tones of Ozzie.

"WHAT IS IT? CAN'T YOU SEE I'M DYING OUT HERE?"

"There is more than one Sinbad," the djinni mentioned.

What, I wondered, could he mean by that?

"There is?" the Sinbad in the bottle retorted. "Oh, yes, there is. But that still doesn't tell me who *he* is!" Whatever Ozzie's dire plan, the merchant appeared to still be immune.

"OF COURSE!" resumed the demonic deity's voice, once again brimming with confidence. "I'VE BEEN NEGLECTING THE PORTERS IN OUR AUDIENCE. BUT I GOT TO TELL YOU, WHY DON'T YOU JUST CARRY ON? I GUESS YOU'VE GOT A HEAD FOR PACKAGES. IF YOU GO THE OTHER WAY, DO YOU BECOME A STARBOARDER? WHATEVER HAPPENS, I'M SURE YOU'RE SHIPSHAPE."

With that, I heard this elder deity with a surprising clarity. And, now that I paid attention, I admired how he could take the oldest jokes in all the world and make them new again.

"He," I said in admiration. But why was I standing so far away? I had to get closer to this wondrous event, and closer to He.

"Who?" the Sinbad in the bottle called again. Poor merchant, who couldn't relate to the simple but hilarious mirth that this great demonic presence was dispensing. Then again, I wasn't supposed to be listening, either, was I? I looked forward at the fascinating fellow, and saw a whole line of humans and apes marching before me. The Scar was first, and reached out to touch the great He's foot.

But in that instant the Scar made actual contact, the ruffian changed, his skin shifting from a robust tan to the same ashen gray as the gigantic demon. Then did the man's very form seem to alter as well, for his skin sagged and collapsed as if he were a water bag from which all the fluid was poured; and then the shell of what was once the Scar fell down from before the great being and blew away like so much paper. But the rest of the Scar now seemed to reside within the demon's skin, and crawled up within the leg to join the great mounds of fat above.

Why was I walking toward this thing? This was horrifying.

"AH, A TASTY MORSEL. BUT DON'T ANY OF YOU WORRY. I NEVER EAT AND RUN. WHEN YOU'RE MY SIZE, YOU NEVER RUN ANYWHERE. HAHAHA."

Yes, he was horribly funny. I was having the time of my life.

"What is going on here?" my namesake in the bottle demanded. "Who is carrying me, anyway?"

The merchant's voice brought me again to my senses. "It is I, Sinbad." And, as I looked forward, I saw Dirk touch the leg of the creature, and, an instant later, there was naught left of the second ruffian but skin, and his essence flowed also upward within the great mass of the demon. This was the less-than-pleasant fellow that I was walking toward. And, even worse, this was the doom toward which I carried our only hope of salvation. I had to drop the bottle this very instant, before the creature joked again.

The great being winked in my direction. "LET ME SAY THAT THIS HAS BEEN A REALLY MOVING EXPERIENCE. OH, BUT CAN I BEAR TO GO ON! HAHAHA!"

I had to admit it. The jokes were even funnier when they concerned porters.

"There's something wrong here," came the voice from the bottle. "I recognize that kind of speech. I believe it occurred on one of my voyages."

What was the merchant talking about, anyway? I decided that he could probably only appreciate the demon's humor when we got very close. Then he would be able to hear everything clearly, even if he was in that foolish bottle.

The first of the apes reached the demon. A moment later, there was nothing but an apeskin rug. It was really quite fascinating. I couldn't wait to move closer for a better view.

The jolly demon laughed. "NOW I HAVE YOU ALL! I THINK I'M GOING TO GAIN A FEW POUNDS. YOU KNOW WHAT? I CAN'T WEIGHT!"

I saw the disembodied head of Ozzie lean close to the comic genius. "Uh, boss? There's one more." A hand materialized and pointed over my shoulder.

"IN THE PALANQUIN? OF COURSE!"

He was talking about Fatima!

The next burst of laughter calmed my breathing. Odd that I should feel a moment of panic. I was sure Fatima would find this thoroughly amusing. And, after all that she meant to me, I wouldn't want to experience this—or anything else!—without her. I clutched the bottle tighter in my hand. It wouldn't do to misplace it now. I was sure this demon was working his way to an hilarious conclusion.

"OH, YOU IN THE PALANQUIN!" the demon called. "COME OUT, COME OUT, WHEREVER YOU ARE!"

"Are you talking to me?" Fatima demanded.

"NOW, DON'T GET CARRIED AWAY! HAHAHA!"

"That's the whole problem," Fatima admitted. "I'm not getting carried anywhere."

"WHAT'S THE MATTER? HAHAHA. LEAVE YOUR SENSE OF HUMOR IN YOUR OTHER PALANQUIN?"

But Fatima wasn't to be mocked. "You'd be in a bad mood, too, if you had to spend your entire life in a palanquin, let me tell you!"

Oddly enough, now that she mentioned it, I didn't find the demon all that funny anymore, either.

"OZZIE!" the demon called in a panicked tone. "SHE'S DESTROYING MY ACT!"

"Is that what you call it?" Fatima asked ungraciously.

He-Who-Must-Be-Ignored began to quake, an awesome sight with all that fat. I decided that, for the moment, I didn't want to get any closer.

"PLEASE!" the demon moaned. "I AM A TALENTED PERFORMER!"

"From where I sit," was Fatima's reply, "it looks like the only performing you ever do is at the dinner table!"

"AUUUUGGGGGGGGGHHHHHHHHH!" the demon screamed.

Enchanted saxophones blared as the world exploded around us.

✦

Chapter the Last,
where all is set right again,
more or less.

The sky was blue again.

I saw it immediately, because I was lying upon my back on the hillside. As I lifted my head to look around, I thereupon saw Achmed, Jafar, Malabala, a number of apes, and—surprise of surprises—Sinbad the merchant, restored to his full, magnificent size! As the apes awoke, they cried in fear and scattered. The explosion had been too great for them, and many of them had already disappeared, including, to my great relief, their queen. It appeared that the apes would trouble us no more.

Then, to my further astonishment, the bottle I still held in my hand spoke to me!

"Let me out," the voice said, "and I will show you the most amazing trick." Small as it was, I recognized that voice. Ozzie had returned to his bottle home.

"Sorry," I replied. "But I believe the djinni is back where he belongs."

"Have mercy!" the djinni cried. "It is far too crowded in here with all these saxophones!"

"And loud as well, I would imagine?" Achmed remarked as he rose to join me.

"But what of"—I hesitated, careful not to speak his name—"the other being?"

It was Jafar's turn to respond, as he sat up and dusted off his frail form. "He has, no doubt, returned to whatever hellish realm he came from, to sulk. I understand that is what comes to pass whenever one of his performances goes wrong."

"Who was that?" Sinbad the merchant asked. "Where am I?" Apparently, the elder had returned not only to his normal size but also to his usual level of concentration.

"I am still hearing you as you speak!" Malabala called with

246

great excitement. "The clever spell has been lifted from every one of you!"

"Apparently, the demon's anguish has greatly adjusted the magics hereabouts," Jafar commented.

"And it was all Fatima's doing!" I called. "The demon could not fathom the woman's sense of humor!" But I would, I swore, as soon as we became properly acquainted. And speaking of my beloved, what had happened to her? I turned and saw the palanquin, resting upon its side at the bottom of the hill. I hoped that the woman of my dreams had not been injured!

"I will go to the top of the hill and determine our whereabouts," Achmed announced as he sprinted away.

"And I will quickly conjure some assistance," Malabala added. "How wonderful and new the world seems, now that the curse has left all of you."

"Dirk and the Scar have been consumed by the demon," Jafar recounted, "and so are no more." He frowned. "There is still one being unaccounted for. What of the odiferous mound?"

I paused to smell my clothing, and it was my turn to frown. Apparently, the mound could not maintain its shape during the cataclysm, and with the explosion flew into the air to dissipate upon us all. I sighed. It would soon be time to take another bath. I hesitated. Perhaps I should wait to make a better impression upon my beloved.

"Look at all these jewels!" the merchant called out in delight.

"Yes," I replied, "there must be five hundred on this hill around us, another two hundred on that hill over there, and perhaps twelve hundred and fifty in the valley below."

"It sounds like a more-than-fair estimation," the elder Sinbad remarked with respect. "How do you come by such a gift?"

"I am very good with valuables," I responded. "It comes from having so few of them." I reminded him then of how I had found gold in a treasury that they were sure had been bare.

"Ah, yes, when we could not find the hundred dinars." He waved at the jewel-strewn hillside. "I think everyone here shall be able to take a hundred times a hundred dinars. And perhaps, after we return to Baghdad, my namesake can keep the treasury, so that Jafar will never have to worry about such things again."

I could not believe my poor ears. The great Sinbad the Sailor was offering me a position. My future would be secure, and I would never have to port again.

"Perhaps he can even dabble in that new scheme of numbers," Sinbad called jovially. "What is it called? Accountancy!"

"Pfaw!" Jafar remarked dismissively. "Some even call it a true science, like astrology." The old man guffawed at the very comparison.

But I smiled for other reasons. After what had happened to me in these last few days, accountancy sounded like all the adventure I would ever need. And this news was truly more wonderful than everything that had gone before. Manure or no, I had to share my good fortune with the woman of my dreams.

"I am sending for help," the wizard announced as he began to conjure.

"The ocean is beyond this hill!" Achmed called when he had reached the summit. "And there is a ship!"

Malabala looked at his hands in his astonishment. "Even I did not know I was that fast. Why did I ever doubt myself?"

"Remarkably," Achmed further remarked, "it appears to be the same ship from which we were captured by the apes. Although, after you have worked for my master as long as I have, you realize there is nothing at all remarkable about it."

The good news was everywhere. My spirits rose with every step I took. My Fatima! I would go and embrace her at last.

Something thumped within the palanquin, as if a great weight were shifting therein. Fatima could not be too badly injured, then. My hopes soared further still. I noticed, as I neared, that a bit of her dress hung out beyond the closed door of the conveyance. It was a fine piece of cloth, the sort only used in wedding gowns. So she, too, was dressed to be wed. How thoughtful; for, as soon as I had convinced her of my virtue, we would be married at once.

But I could delay this moment no longer. I reached forward and firmly grasped the handle. On this occasion, I would make certain that my beloved Fatima did not cry out. I pulled open the door with the manliest effort I could muster.

"Fatima!" I called.

"Ook, ook," came the sound from within.

I only had time for a single scream before a hairy arm dragged me within.

But that is enough story for one day.
Do you wish more?
Then witness
A Bad Day for Ali Baba,
a further Arabian night,
forthcoming presently.